The Payout

Bryan Cassiday

Bryan Cassiday

Bryan Cassiday
Los Angeles

ISBN 978-0983498995
Printed in the United States of America
First edition: October 2018

BOOKS BY BRYAN CASSIDAY

Force of Impact (Ethan Carr Thriller 4)
Wipeout (Ethan Carr Thriller 3)
Dying to Breathe (Ethan Carr Thriller 2)
Countdown to Death (Ethan Carr Thriller 1)
The Bus Stops Here—and Other Zombie Tales
Two Moons Rising
Alien Assault
Comes a Chopper
Zombie Apocalypse: The Chad Halverson Series
Helter Skelter
The Anaconda Complex
The Kill Option
Blood Moon: Thrillers and Tales of Terror
Fete of Death

Chapter 1

July 27, 2017.

That was the day he killed himself.

It was the day he staged his death in a boating accident off the west coast of Oahu so his wife could collect on his life insurance policy with Lion Life.

But today was today—almost a year later. And matters had changed.

He wasn't killing himself this time. It was his wife he was killing.

He was dragging her body wrapped in a powder blue blanket down a wooden dock in Malibu in the dark, a lunula of moon in the sky. He could smell the briny ocean and hear the waves' slurping against the dock's piles as the combers rolled in toward the beach.

She seemed a lot heavier than he had expected, as he hunched down and, sweating, hauled her body over the weather-beaten floorboards toward the end of the pier, where he had moored to a bollard a compact Boston Whaler fitted with a 25-horsepower Mercury outboard motor. His back was bothering him. He had to pause. In his forties he couldn't call himself young.

He stood up, straightening out in order to stretch the aching muscles in his back. As he worked the kinks out of his back, he discerned a dark bulk at the end of the pier. He became alert.

It looked like somebody was sitting there facing the sleek gloom of the ocean. Or were his eyes deceiving him? Nobody had been sitting there when he had secured the boat's painter to the bollard. But that was over a half hour ago.

Somebody could have visited the pier while he was retrieving his wife from his car parked on the side of the road

4

and dragging her across the beach. Was the newcomer fishing? he wondered. Wasn't it kind of late to be fishing?

The dark figure was sitting motionlessly and did nothing to indicate it was aware of Catton's presence on the pier.

The figure presented Catton with a dilemma. He wondered what he should do. He wanted to get his wife's body off the pier, into the boat, and into the ocean as soon as possible. The longer it took him, the longer it exposed him to being discovered.

Christ, he thought. What kind of an idiot would sit on the end of a pier in the middle of the night?

Catton didn't see a fishing rod extending from the figure into the ocean. Then what was the numskull doing there? Catton was in no mood to drag his wife's corpse back to his car and try reloading it into the boat after the figure had departed. His back was hurting him enough already.

No, it was now or never.

He decided to continue hauling her to the motorboat. After all, the blanket covered her body. The figure would just see him loading a ruglike object into the boat. Nothing to rouse the guy's suspicion.

Catton bent over, glommed onto the blanket with two hands, and pulled it after him as he backed toward the end of the dock, feeling the muscles in his back burning.

The figure, who must have heard the scraping of the blanket's sand-dusted nap across the floorboards, turned around to determine the source of the sound.

When Catton craned around to see where he was going, he realized it was a woman sitting near his boat with her face turned toward him watching him with curiosity. Her thirtyish, hollow-eyed face was livid and haggard. Her lifeless doe eyes followed him without blinking.

He continued dragging the body to the end of the pier, stood up, and, regaining his composure, looked at her without surprise, as if she belonged there.

5

"Hi," he said.

She didn't say anything, just looked at him as if in a funk, her unkempt dark hair framing her oval face. Maybe she would have been pretty if her face wasn't so drawn.

He didn't like the idea that she had seen him. On the other hand, why did it matter? he decided. What had she seen? Just a man dragging a rolled-up blanket to his boat. There was no crime in that.

He didn't understand why she was sitting on the end of a deserted pier in the dead of night. Her face was etched with misery. Could it be she was considering drowning herself? Maybe he should just ignore her and get on with his business.

That was when he heard somebody moaning. The sound was enough to make his skin crawl.

But it wasn't the girl on the end of the pier doing the moaning. She had heard the sound too, and was now gazing at the rolled-up blanket Catton had deposited beside her. Then she saw with consternation a hand emerge from the end of the blanket.

Christ, thought Catton. His wife was still alive. He thought he had killed her. Or was it a reflex motion of the corpse?

The girl's grey eyes became pools of terror.

Now she was a problem, decided Catton, because now she was a witness to the disposal of a murder victim.

The girl was paralyzed with fear. She didn't know what to do.

Catton had to think fast.

He realized she was younger than he had first thought. Now that her face had brightened as a result of adrenaline coursing through her body, she looked like she was in her twenties. Her haggard expression must have made her seem older when he had first laid eyes on her. No matter how old she was, she was plenty scared.

His wife Rachel moaned again in the rug.

6

Shut up, he thought, clenching his teeth.

Not a reflex motion, he decided with alarm. Rachel was still alive. He had no idea how she could be. He had stabbed her enough times to draw a river of blood.

Catton didn't want to have to kill the girl, but he had to finish off Rachel and he couldn't have a witness. It would defeat his purpose to leave Rachel alive. With her alive, he couldn't get his hands on her money, which she wouldn't have in the first place if it wasn't for his staging his own death so she could collect on his life insurance policy.

"I don't want to have to kill you," Catton told the girl.

She riveted her eyes on his face, gawping in fear.

Stop looking at me like that, he thought. He needed to get her on his team. Maybe explaining his side of the story to her would help.

"I had to kill my wife to get my money back from her," he said. "She stole it from me."

The girl kept staring at him like he was a cobra fixing to strike her throat. She said nothing.

He needed to engage her in conversation to get her to lighten up.

"Why are you sitting here in the middle of the night?" he said.

She heaved a sigh. "I was depressed."

At least she was talking to him now, he decided. A step in the right direction.

She turned her head and gazed into the undulating ocean of ink.

"You were thinking about drowning yourself?" he said.

She didn't answer, but kept staring into the ocean as if it was beckoning her.

"Financial problems?" he coaxed.

She didn't answer, but he detected an expression of agreement on her wan face. He saw an opening.

"If you help me kill my wife, I can help you," he said. "I'll have plenty of money with her out of the way."

She unlocked her gaze from the ocean and whipped her head toward him.

"I'm not a killer," she said, eyes still huge.

"Nobody is until they have to be."

"That's crazy talk."

He had her attention, he decided.

"Actually, it's true," he said. "Underneath, we're all hardwired to kill. We're all capable of committing any crime. Scratch anyone's skin and you'll reveal a monster ready to strike. It's a survival mechanism. The human race is still alive because humans are willing to kill to go on living. Kill, kill, kill, and kill again."

"I never killed anyone."

"Not yet."

"And I don't want to kill anyone."

"Why not? If you kill, you'll be rewarded handsomely."

"I don't want to."

"It's easy." Catton withdrew a hunting knife out of the rear waistband of his jeans and proffered it to her. Its blade had traces of his wife's blood on it. "Just stab her until she stops moaning. You don't even have to look at her. The blanket's covering her. All you need to do is stab her through the blanket in the chest area. I'll point it out to you."

Overwrought, the girl clutched her face. "That's sickening."

"What's your name? Mine's Gage Catton," said Catton, changing his grip on the knife so he was now grasping the blade with the haft pointed toward her like a peace offering.

"Mina."

"Mina. That's a nice name. I don't know any Minas."

Mina was still clutching her face with both hands, refusing to eye the knife.

Rachel groaned inside the blanket.

"Make her stop," said Mina, squirming, kicking her feet that were lolling out over the ocean at the end of the pier.

"*You* can make her stop by stabbing her. You have the power."

"I don't want to stab her. Get away from me."

"Are you afraid of the power you have?"

"I don't know what you're talking about."

"A lot of people don't realize how powerful they really are. All you have to do is use your power. If you don't use it, you don't know it's there."

"I don't want to kill anyone."

"You make it sound difficult. It's not."

"I'll get caught and go to jail."

"There's no way that's gonna happen."

"I don't even know her. Why should I want to kill her?"

"That's the beauty of it. That's why nobody will suspect you. You have the perfect alibi—you don't even know her. You're not going to jail for anything. Because *you* have the power."

"I don't have any power. I'm a nobody," said Mina, and hung her head in her hands.

"Only because you *think* you're a nobody. Think about all the power you possess and use it."

"I don't know what you're talking about." Dropping her hands from her face, she stared out over the ocean in a trance. "My mother always told me I wasn't any good at anything. My sister was a goddess in her eyes, but I couldn't do anything right. I can't even bake a decent cake, according to her. She called me an accident."

"She kept putting you down in order to control you. That's how she convinced you you're a nobody. It's not true. You have great power. But you'll never know unless you use it."

She faced him. "I ran away from home. I couldn't stand it anymore."

9

"The best thing you could do. But you still don't realize how powerful you are."

Rachel groaned inside the blanket again, this time louder than the preceding times.

"Make her stop," said Mina, shaking her head and clutching her ears so she wouldn't have to listen to Rachel.

He couldn't blame her. The sound was getting to him too.

"You're the one that can make her stop. Take the knife and finish her off," he said, pushing the knife's haft toward her.

"No."

"You don't want to be free of your financial problems?" said Catton. "Everybody needs money."

Chapter 2

"I don't want to think about money," she said.

"Nobody *wants* to," said Catton. "Why should you? Money has no intrinsic value. But everybody *has* to think about it—or they starve."

"I'm not a killer."

"Just because you haven't killed before doesn't mean you can't kill. It'll feel like you're stabbing a rolled-up blanket with a side of beef in it because you won't see her face. What's the big deal? It's nothing to be afraid of."

Rachel moaned.

"I can't stand listening to her," said Mina, grimacing and latching onto the knife in Catton's hand.

Catton squatted on his haunches next to the blanket and felt along the top of the blanket, trying to determine the location of Rachel's chest by feeling the contours of her body underneath the wool. It wasn't that difficult. All he had to do was follow her arm, which was exposed, down to her shoulder and then down to her chest. After he located it, he pointed out the area to Mina.

"Stab there into her heart," he told her.

Knife in hand, Mina twisted around in her seat and craned her neck around to see where he was pointing.

"This is awful," she said.

"Stab her and get it over with. I'll pay you well."

Catton didn't want to have to kill Mina. He already had one murder on his hands, though it was taking Rachel much longer than he had expected to die. He'd rather enlist Mina as a confederate than kill her. He could see she was balking. He needed more leverage.

"This is wrong," she said.

"It's only wrong if you think it's wrong. It's all in the head."

11

"I don't want to kill her," she said in an outburst of frustration.

He felt like he was losing her. "If you don't kill her, I'll tell the cops you're the one that killed her."

"What!" she said, eyes popping out of her face in disbelief.

"I'll have to, so they won't suspect me."

"They'll never believe you."

"I'll say I caught you in the act. Then they'll have to believe me."

"You're insane."

"I'm not insane, but I want my money. And I'll do anything to get it."

"If you tell the cops I did it, I'll tell them *you* killed her."

Catton chuckled. "They'll never believe you."

"Why not? You're her husband. You have motive."

Catton cracked a smile. "Because I have the perfect alibi—I'm dead. You see, ratting me out won't do you any good at all."

"You're not dead."

"Everybody *thinks* I'm dead. Perception, not reality, is what matters. Dead men can't go around killing people."

"I'll tell them I saw you alive."

"They'll never believe you. The only thing you'll accomplish is implicating yourself in Rachel's murder."

"How do you figure?"

"They'll suspect you when you rat me out and they'll ask you how you know about her murder in the first place." He paused. "You have nothing to gain by going to the cops and everything to lose."

"No, I don't believe it," she said, shutting her eyes.

"I'm invisible. Nobody can touch you when you're invisible."

"This is horrible," she said, shaking her head. "Why are you doing this to me?"

"Because I need your help."

She made a guttural sound as if she was drowning.

"Remember," he said. "It's only wrong if you think it's wrong."

Rachel groaned and wriggled in the blanket.

"I can't stand that sound," said Mina, throwing up her hands in anguish, cocking up her head and eying the moon as if beseeching it for energy.

Knife in hand, she crawled closer to the body and knelt over it. Gnashing her teeth she fell to thrusting the knife into the blanket over and over in the area designated by Catton.

A ghastly rattle issuing from her throat, Rachel grasped the air, opening and closing her fist in agony.

Her moans became even more dreadful to listen to, which infuriated Mina and prompted her to stab deeper and more often, drawing blood that oozed out of the blanket in a crimson smear.

"Shut up, shut up," Mina hissed.

"Good work," said Catton. "I knew you could do it."

Rachel's moans died out, and her hand lay limp now on the dock, devoid of motion, like a dead fish.

Seeing the bloodstained knife in her hand, horrified by what she had done, Mina flung the weapon into the ocean, where the rippling ink swallowed it.

"I wouldn't have thrown it there," said Catton with concern. "I would have taken it out to deeper water." His eyes lingered on the spot where the knife had splashed and submerged.

He debated whether to dive into the ocean and attempt to retrieve the knife. But how could he see it in the murk?

"I couldn't help it," said Mina, shivering.

"It could pose a problem. Both of our fingerprints are on it."

"But it's at the bottom of the ocean."

"Except the waves might wash it onto the beach since it's so close to the shoreline," he said, surveying the nearby shore.

"Oh," said Mina, not paying attention, her head down.

The more he thought about it, the less he worried.

"I doubt we need to worry though," he said. "The salt water will take care of our prints before the knife washes ashore. And it might not even wash ashore."

"I want to get out of here."

"First, we have to dispose of the body."

Chapter 3

"I don't want to do this anymore," said Mina, getting to her feet on the dock.

"You can't undo what you did," he said, standing near her.

"I don't want to talk to you. You're making me go nuts."

"I'm you're only friend now. You need to listen to me."

She stood on the pier, confused. She said nothing.

"You need to help me load the body into my boat," he said.

"I don't know what to do," she said, biting her lip.

"Grab the other end of the blanket, and I'll take the front end so we can haul her into the boat."

"I don't want to do this."

"We need to finish it. We can't leave her here. The cops'll find her. We need to drop the body deep in the ocean where no one will ever find it."

Fetching a sigh, Mina gave a hopeless shrug. "Let's get it over with."

She leaned over and picked up the end of the blanket nearest her.

Catton climbed into the pitching boat, from which he latched onto the front end of the blanket and hauled it off the dock toward him. Mina helped him load the corpse onto the boat's deck then stood on the pier and stared at Catton as he bobbed in the boat in front of her on the water.

"Now climb aboard," said Catton, "and we'll push off."

"Why do I have to go?"

"You're part of the team."

"I've never been on a boat before," she said, eying the watercraft charily.

"There's nothing to be afraid of. This won't take long. We're teammates. Let's work together."

15

"I dunno."

"I need your help. Now climb aboard," he said, extending his hand to help her onto the boat.

She took his hand and boarded, stumbling but regaining her footing as she acclimated herself to the rocking of the boat on the incoming waves.

Catton untied the painter secured to the bollard, and the boat drifted away from the dock, parting the water like slicing through black silk. He started the outboard, grabbed the wheel, and guided the craft out to the dark ocean, spewing up a rooster tail of sea spray behind him.

"Tie the anchor on the deck to the blanket," he said above the chugging Mercury motor. "We need to weight the body or it'll float to the surface and drift ashore."

Mina sat down on the thwart beside the corpse and fumbled with the rope attached to the anchor, trying to find the end of it so she could wrap it around the blanket.

"When do I get the money?" she said.

"As soon as I do. I have her bank's ATM card and I know her PIN. I got it from her before I stabbed her. All I have to do is go to a bank after we're done."

"I don't know how I got into this," she said, fiddling with the rope, spindrift misting her face.

"What matters is, we did it. This is better than being depressed, isn't it?"

She didn't answer.

He craned his neck around to look at her. She was intent on fiddling with the rope as she sat near the stern. He faced fore again, hands on the wheel.

"I don't feel good," she said.

"Are you seasick?"

"This isn't right."

"Why not? We have more right to my money than she did. What makes her better than us?"

"Why do you hate her so much?" said Mina, pausing from fidgeting with the rope and looking up at him.

He was looking out to sea steering the boat, which was chopping through the ocean, the engine churning the dark water into white froth.

"She stole my money," he said.

"How could she steal it if it was hers?"

"I faked my death so she could collect on my life insurance policy. Then she double-crossed me, fled with the money, and deposited it in a new bank account in her name only."

Mina nodded. "Tricky."

"So you agree I had the right to take my money back and do away with her?"

"I don't know about killing her. But you had the right to take your money back."

"Then you're in this with me?"

"I don't like killing people," she said, and returned to sorting out the rope.

"But you had no problem killing Rachel. You did it like a pro. That was great," he said, turning around to look at her, one hand on the wheel, looking like he was posing for an aftershave ad.

"I don't know what got into me."

"You took control of your life for the first time. You asserted your power."

"I couldn't stand listening to her moaning," she said, gazing at the rope in her hands like it was a puzzle impossible to solve.

"We'll dump her in the ocean soon, and then we can forget any of it ever happened. And we won't have to worry about the cops coming after us."

17

Chapter 4

Murder, murder, murder, Mina was thinking. The words tumbled through her mind.

She was trying to understand what had happened, and the word *murder* kept interrupting her thoughts.

How could she have let this stranger talk her into killing someone? It felt all wrong. He had weird eyes, almost like they were electric. They looked more purple than blue. Like amethyst. She had never seen purple eyes on anyone before. There was something magnetic about them. They had all the charm of a snake's eyes.

Her life had been coming to a dead end, slowly but surely. Then he walked into it, and it was like she was diving off a cliff now, precipitating her demise as she hurtled toward the ground, the dead end about to smash her in the face any second.

Thinking about the corpse near her she felt like retching.

It did give her a sense of power, though, no matter how much she refused to admit it. She had exerted her power over another person, she, Mina, who had no power, and had won. But it was stomach churning. How could a sense of empowerment be a good thing if it made her sick to her stomach? Killing someone to feel empowered—it didn't feel right.

This was what she got for taking advice from a madman.

Still, she didn't feel depressed now. She felt too alive to feel depressed. Fear of being caught made her feel more alive. The problem was, instead of feeling depressed she felt miserable—alive but miserable. With chagrin she wondered which was better—feeling like you didn't want to go on living, or feeling sick about being alive?

She wondered if she could get out of this predicament. As long as they were on the boat, she couldn't. She didn't know how to swim, so she couldn't jump overboard and make a swim for it. She wondered if Catton might decide to kill her.

Figuring she better do as he said, she started wrapping coils of rope around the rolled-up blanket. If she disobeyed him, he might turn on her. Now that she wasn't depressed, she was fighting for her life. She had to be careful with him. After all, she was all alone with him in the middle of the ocean.

She was scared he might be playing a sinister game with her, like a cat playing with a mouse before it tears the mouse's head off and devours it. She better play along with him for now.

He seemed to need her in some inexplicable way. Or why hadn't he just killed her along with his wife and dumped both of them in the ocean? Why go to the trouble of enlisting her aid in his crime?

She would try to play on his need, if she felt he was about to do away with her. She needed to reinforce his feeling that he needed her. The problem was, she didn't understand why he did need her—unless it was a power thing and he liked controlling her. That was the only angle she could figure. Or did he want her as his girlfriend? She couldn't tell. The idea of being his girlfriend rattled her.

Right now it was best for her to play along, which would give her time to figure out the solution later.

He cut the engine.

The boat bobbed to a halt.

"Here's as good a place as any," he said.

Chapter 5

Dropping his hands from the wheel he got up from his seat and faced her. She had a weird look on her face as she was staring at him. He didn't know what it meant.

"Did you tie the anchor to her?" he said.

"Yes," she said.

"Then let's throw her over," he said, and stepped toward the corpse swaddled in a blanket. "First, we'll toss over the anchor."

He leaned over, picked up the anchor from the deck, and cast it overboard.

The rope uncoiled, whipping out into the ocean till it ran out of slack and pulled up tight.

"All right, let's get her over," he said, sliding the corpse toward the hull's side.

He lifted the corpse to the gunwale and let the arm and head dangle over the ocean tipping the boat to port, while he gathered his strength and a second wind. Dead weight wasn't the easiest thing to lift, he decided.

"Now I need your help," he said.

Mina didn't move.

"I'm not returning to shore till we dump her," he said. "Grab the other end of the blanket."

She saw no point in arguing with him.

She grasped the bottom end of the blanket, while he did the same with the top end, and they lifted the corpse to toss it over the side.

As she walked forward, the boat took a sharp dip to port. She lost her footing and her balance and somersaulted into the water with the corpse. Gulping water she flailed one arm helplessly in the ocean, terrified, as she continued to grip the blanket.

"I can't swim," she cried.

"Let go of the corpse. It has an anchor on it," said Catton, watching her as he balanced himself on the rocking boat, trying to prevent it from capsizing.

Realizing she was still clutching the blanket she released it and now flailed both arms.

"Help me," she cried, gasping for breath, struggling to keep her head above water.

He kept watching her from the boat.

"I can't swim," she said, her face drenched, spitting out water as her head bobbed up from below the surface.

"I'm your only friend," he said.

"Hurry," she screamed.

"Are you on my side?"

"Yes, yes," she said, gagging on the water. "Help."

Her head went under a second time. She came up coughing water, gasping for breath.

He retrieved the life preserver from the boat's stern and flung it to her. She hugged it for dear life. He pulled on the rope that was attached to it and towed her toward the gunwale, where he helped her climb onboard, making sure to distribute his weight so the boat wouldn't founder.

Shivering, she hunkered over the thwart.

"Lucky it's a mild night," he said. "You'll be OK."

"Let's get out of here," she muttered, her teeth chattering.

He scoped out the ocean making sure Rachel's body wasn't floating to the surface anywhere. He saw no sign of the blanket breaking the surface in the moonlight.

He fired up the engine, took hold of the wheel, swung the boat around, which spewed up white sheets of seawater, and returned to shore.

"I had to do it," she said.

"What?" he said.

"I had to kill her or you would have told the cops I did it."

"You did the right thing."

"Even if I didn't kill her, you would've told them I did."

21

Catton nodded. "Like you said, you had to do it. Don't worry about it. We're all killers under the skin."

"You forced me to do it."

"Not really. In the end, you did it with your own hands. I wasn't holding a gun to your head."

Chapter 6

She felt terrible listening to him. If making her miserable
was what he was trying to do to her, he was succeeding.
Would she always feel like this? Or would it go away? she
wondered. Why couldn't she have refused to obey him when
he told her to kill his wife? *Murder, murder, murder . . .* the
word kept racing through her mind, as though it had been
unlocked from her subconscious and was running amok like a
gremlin plaguing her.

"Maybe I should confess to the cops," she said.

"Not a good idea," he said.

"Why not? You'd be home free if I take the blame."

"Not if you tell them about me," he said, spotting the pier
jutting into the ocean bathed in moonlight in the distance. "It
would prompt them to reopen my case. Then they might find
out I'm still alive."

"I want to confess."

"No, you don't. You want to forget it ever happened and
get on with your life."

"What if I can't?"

"Don't think about it."

"I can't help it. When I confess to the cops, I won't
mention you," she said, struggling with qualms of guilt.

"Then your story won't hold water. They'll figure out
you're holding something back and you'll implicate me."

"I'll say I killed her then dumped her in the ocean. Why
doesn't that make sense?"

"They'll ask you why you killed her."

Mina thought about it, but couldn't come up with an
answer. "What difference does it make?"

"The cops'll want a motive. If you don't have a credible
motive, they won't believe you. They'll keep grilling you till
you rat me out."

"Don't you get it? If I confess, they won't come after you. You'll have nothing to worry about. You should want me to confess. I'll say I did it all by myself."

"There's another reason I can't let you confess you killed her," he said, eying her. "If the authorities think she's dead, they'll freeze her bank account, and I won't be able to withdraw money from it."

"They'll do that anyway."

"Not unless someone reports her as dead. And that's not gonna happen as long as we're the only two that know what really happened to her."

The motorboat approached the dock. Mina smelled gasoline fumes from the outboard.

"I have something to tell you," she said.

"What?"

"I didn't tie a knot in the rope I wrapped around the blanket."

"You what?" he said, tensing.

"You heard me."

He eased up on the throttle.

She wondered what he was thinking. Probably, he was debating whether he should return to where he had dumped Rachel. But then what? Wait there till her stomach filled with gases, the current swept her free of the anchor, and she floated back to the surface? That could take days, weeks, or even years.

In any case, she knew he couldn't go back because he could never be sure of the exact location where they had thrown her overboard. No, there was nothing he could do about it now.

She waited apprehensively for him to burst into a rage at her.

"There's no guarantee she'll break loose from the rope and resurface," he said at length.

"A current could free her."

"If they find the body, they'll know she was murdered and they'll look for the killer," he said, thinking it through, stroking his chin. "Then again, the body might never float to the surface."

"We can't count on that."

"We can't do anything about the body now. I'll have to withdraw all her money from her checking account before the DA gets an injunction to freeze it. And that's not gonna happen till someone finds the corpse."

"Are you sure?"

"There's no proof she's dead," he said, slowing the boat as he nosed it closer to the pier, preparing to dock, the motor humming.

"Her friends will become suspicious when they never see her anymore."

"That's gonna take a while, and they still won't have any proof she's dead. She could have decided to move without telling anyone."

He killed the engine and fastened the painter to the bollard on the pier as the boat pitched in the water. He clambered onto the pier and helped her after him. They walked along the pier's weathered grey floorboards to the beach, the waves crashing beside them like cymbals, her gait uncertain.

"We'll make a great team together. You and me," he said.

She felt herself shiver, and she doubted it was from the cold.

Chapter 7

Catton felt uncomfortable with the arrangement. He hadn't expected to meet anyone sitting on the pier when he returned with Rachel's body to his boat. He didn't want to have an accomplice, but now he had one.

It was pure chance Mina had decided to sit on that particular pier at that particular time. That was all. Things rarely happened the way you planned them, he knew from experience.

Now he had to make sure she wouldn't rat him out. By convincing her to take part in the murder, he had made her his accomplice, thus making her as guilty of homicide as he was in the eyes of the law.

They trudged through the dark cool sand back to his car, which was parked on the shoulder of the Coast Highway.

With her killing of Rachel fresh in Mina's mind, he figured he had established leverage over her. He wasn't sure if it would hold up over time, but for now he figured she wouldn't rat him out to the cops lest they jail the both of them.

He didn't want to exert too much control over her, though, or he felt she might crack and decide to rebel against him by going to the cops. He had to cut her a lot of slack, but not too much. He had to let her know he had leverage on her without making her feel intimidated. In the end, his goal was to get her to side with him of her own volition. Such an alliance would be stronger than one forged by threats.

Right now he didn't trust her, and he wanted to keep her under surveillance to make sure she didn't go to the authorities.

"Are you hungry?" he said, as they crossed the beach.

"Not really. I could use a drink, though."

"Good. We'll go to a restaurant and unwind."

He would return to the pier tomorrow morning and sail his boat back to Marina del Rey, where he had a slip.

He was playing this by ear because he had no plan beyond doing away with Rachel so he could get his money back. The fewer people that knew about the murder the better, as far as he was concerned. The fact that he wasn't the one that had actually killed Rachel didn't absolve him. He had taken an active part in her murder. Hell, it was his idea in the first place and he had knifed her to the verge of death. The murder never would have happened if he hadn't initiated it.

Mina was twirling the ends of her hair with her fingers as she plodded across the beach with him.

With discomfort he realized his track shoes were filling with sand. He should have taken them off and carried them in his hands while he was on the beach. He could forgive himself. He had more important matters to tend to. Like how was he going to move all of his money at once out of Rachel's bank account to his account?

Up until now he had been withdrawing cash from her bank's ATM, but there was a thousand-dollar limit per withdrawal per day. At that rate, it would take him years to transfer all of it. And during that time, the authorities might freeze her account if they thought she was dead. The sooner he transferred the entire amount into his account, the better.

The trouble was, he didn't have the password to her online bank account. He wondered if he could find it in her condo. If he could access her online account, he could transfer the money electronically to his account all at once, no questions asked. But he had no idea where she kept her password. She might even have committed it to memory, in which case he would never find it.

He wondered if Mina could help him somehow to transfer the money. Right now he didn't see how, but he figured there must be a way to utilize her.

27

"Where's your car?" she said, as they arrived at the parking lot.

"Wait a second," he said.

He sought out a cement bench and sat on it. A fine layer of sand mantling the cool cement crackled underneath the seat of his jeans as he sat down.

"Are you tired out, too?" she said, following him.

"There's sand in my shoes."

Leaning over he untied his track shoes, removed them one at a time, and, turning them over, shook out the sand that had accumulated inside them. He also brushed off his socks, which had grains of sand lodged between the cotton strands, careful to keep his feet from touching the asphalt, which had sand scattered over it.

Satisfied he had removed most of the sand from inside his shoes, he put them back on and tied the laces.

Mina followed his example, taking a seat beside him. She sounded like sandpaper scuffing the bench as she sat down in her jeans.

He wondered if he could trust her to keep their secret. He didn't really have a choice in the matter. He needed to keep her on his side.

"Are you sure nobody'll suspect she's dead?" said Mina.

"I don't see why they would."

"Maybe she told somebody about your being still alive."

"Why would she confess to anyone that she filed a fraudulent claim on my life insurance policy?"

"I don't know the law very well. Is that a crime?"

"It's fraud."

"Still, she might've had an accomplice."

Catton had never thought of that. Of course, he had never thought Rachel was going to double-cross him either. Was she seeing someone else? he wondered. He didn't think so. But maybe he was wrong about that, too. If someone else was involved with Rachel, that person might be able to access her online bank account—and drain it.

"I don't think so," he said, becoming concerned.

"You don't sound sure."

"I have no reason to believe she was seeing anyone else."

"But you're not ruling it out."

Catton shrugged. "Maybe I didn't know her very well."

"Why did she decide to double-cross you and take all the money for herself?"

"Greed. What else?"

"Or somebody was advising her."

Catton gave her a look. "You're jumping to conclusions."

"Just saying."

Chapter 8

Catton didn't like showing up around Rachel's condo because one of her friends in the neighborhood might recognize him. But if he wanted to search her place for her password to her online bank account, he would have to return to her condo. He did have her key, so he wouldn't have to break in.

He would have to disguise himself when he went back there.

He felt hungry. The adrenaline charge of stabbing Rachel and dumping her at sea, as well as enlisting Mina to his cause, must have stimulated his appetite.

His shoes back on, he stood up.

"Let's go eat," he said. "I could eat a horse."

They returned to his car that was parked along PCH. He was driving a six-year-old six-speed eight-cylinder Mustang 5.0 with a stick shift.

He unlocked the door with his remote fob, and they got in.

He didn't have far to drive. There was a seafood restaurant nearby. It was the better part of a mile away. He parked in the lot.

As they got out of the car, a jeans-clad swarthy guy in his forties standing in the parking lot watching them hawked and spat onto the asphalt.

After Catton locked his car with the remote, he and Mina headed to the restaurant that had a turquoise neon sign saying Seafood on top of its low-slung roof. A couple of Harleys were parked near the entrance.

Catton and Mina entered the restaurant and stood in front of the hostess, who was standing behind a black wooden desk. They asked for a table for two on the deck outside under the moonlight.

A waitress appeared a few minutes later and showed them to a table that overlooked the ocean, not far from a large table of boisterous surgical staff in scrubs, predominantly women, who were having a good time.

Smiling, the waitress offered menus to Catton and Mina, as they sat down. "Care for a drink?"

Catton looked at Mina.

Mina studied the menu in her hand, scanning the Drinks section. "I'll have a Corona."

"I'll have a Coors," said Catton.

The waitress departed.

"I can't believe how hungry I am," said Catton. "How about you?"

"I'm more thirsty than hungry," said Mina, sitting opposite him.

Maybe she didn't have an appetite for murder, decided Catton. He, on the other hand, was ravenous. What did that mean? he wondered. He felt no remorse for having stabbed Rachel within an inch of her life. After all, she had deserved it. She had cheated him out of his money.

Catton felt his smartphone vibrating in his trouser pocket. He fished out the phone. It wasn't his, it was Rachel's, which he had commandeered from her before throwing her overboard.

He didn't know if he should answer it.

"What?" said Mina, watching him with interest.

"This is Rachel's phone." He lowered his voice, but he doubted anyone could overhear him on account of the racket the surgical staff was making at their nearby table. "I don't know if I should answer it."

"Who is it?"

Catton checked the phone's caller ID, which said Private. "Don't know."

31

He didn't think he should answer. On the other hand, if she *was* seeing someone, it would be a good idea to know who it was.

"Let it go to voice mail," said Mina.

"She might not have voice mail, and whoever it is might not leave a message."

He swiped the phone with his finger and took the call. But he didn't say anything. Instead, he listened.

The person at the other end of the line said nothing.

All Catton could hear was the rambunctious surgical staff chattering and laughing. He figured they were making so much noise the caller could hear them, too. Catton waited, holding the cell phone pressed to his ear.

The caller said nothing.

The silence on the airwaves lasted a full minute.

Catton was tempted to say hello, but checked himself.

Without identifying himself, the stranger terminated the call.

"What was that all about?" said Mina, watching Catton put away the phone.

"I dunno."

"What did he say?"

"Nothing."

"Maybe the background voices scared him off."

"Why should they?"

Catton couldn't think of a reason.

"He must've been suspicious when you didn't speak," said Mina.

"Maybe."

"What other explanation could there be? Why wouldn't he say something?"

"Maybe he thought it was voice mail because it took me so long to pick up."

"But there was no recording. Why would he think it was voice mail if there was no recording?"

"Good question," said Catton, puzzled. "Maybe he thought the voices in the background were the recording. They confused him, so he said nothing."

"You want to know what I think?"

"What?"

"Rachel has a secret friend who doesn't want to talk over the phone unless he's sure he's talking to her."

Catton thought about it. "I hope you're wrong. Somebody like that might have a key to her condo."

A grizzled, middle-aged member of the surgical team wearing scrubs and wire-rimmed glasses walked over to their table babbling into her cell phone and parked herself in front of them.

Catton gave her a look.

What was she doing over here? he wondered. He had as much interest in her phone conversation as did the other members of her retinue. Why did she decide to come over here to blat into her phone?

Mina was looking at her, too.

They must have been thinking the same thing, decided Catton, exchanging glances with Mina.

The waitress returned with their beers.

Preoccupied, Catton had forgotten to check out the menu.

"Are you ready to order?" she said.

"Almost," said Catton over the nearby surgical member's prating voice. He scanned the menu. "I'll have the filet mignon."

"How do you want it?"

"Medium well."

Mina changed her mind about not being hungry and decided to order an entrée. She seemed to have perked up after Catton received the phone call, though Catton couldn't figure out what prompted the change in spirits.

"I'll have the sockeye salmon," she told the waitress. "And broccoli with that."

33

"Very good," said the waitress, gathered up the menus, and left.

"You got your appetite back," Catton told Mina with a smile.

"The aroma of cooking food made me hungry. I like seafood."

Catton was beginning to like Mina, even though he hadn't liked the circumstances under which they had met. He hadn't wanted to run into somebody while he was disposing of Rachel's body. He didn't like the fact Mina had incriminating evidence against him. But Mina had shown up, whether he liked it or not.

He hoped he wouldn't have to kill her.

He was still somewhat surprised she had agreed to finish off Rachel with the knife. He hadn't been sure he would be able to talk her into killing for him. He was cynical enough to believe that everybody was corrupt at heart and would commit murder if it served their interests, but still . . . He wondered about her.

How long would she stay loyal to him? She knew enough about him to put him away for a long time. And he could do the same to her, as well. In many ways they were now joined at the hip.

He wished the RN or whatever she was would stop yakking on her cell phone directly behind his back. He had no desire to listen to her family problems. Her voice was grating on his nerves.

He turned around and glared at her.

"It's goddamn hot in here," he said, loud enough so her caller could hear him.

The woman appeared lost in her urgent conversation, but she must have got the message because she started backing away from his table—out of earshot, he hoped—though she didn't acknowledge his presence, continuing to stare into the distance, her mobile glued to her ear.

Catton's filet mignon arrived, and he dug in.

Mina attacked her salmon with relish.

Finished with her phone call, the RN returned to her table.

Catton wondered if she was glowering at him behind his back. He hoped she was.

Chapter 9

He drove Mina to the motel he was staying at and found a space in its parking lot under a scrawny palm tree that had seen better days.

"Do you want me to drive you home?" he said.

She looked at him in bewilderment.

"I was staying at a friend's," she said at last.

"Do you want to stay here with me?"

"Can you get me a room?"

"Sure."

He checked her into a room at the front desk, where the bespectacled middle-aged manager was sitting wearing red suspenders over his white button-down shirt. His green-eyed black cat with drooping white whiskers was perched on the front desk like a sentinel and showed no sign of moving.

Mina walked over to the cat, which let her pet its head and purred, holding its head up.

"I need another room," Catton told the manager, smiling.

"What's wrong with the one you got?" said the manager.

"It's not for me. It's for my friend."

The manager stood up and shuffled to the desk, his left hand trembling like he had Parkinson's.

"Are you paying with a credit card?" he said.

After he was confirmed dead by the insurance company, Catton had to stop using credit cards. He wasn't convinced the company wouldn't send someone to investigate his death, since his corpse had never been found. The use of credit cards was traceable, he knew. The only way he could return to using a credit card was if he got one in another name. To stay off the grid he had to make cash transactions only.

"No," said Catton. "Cash like last time."

"I don't like having a lot of cash lying around the office," the manager grumped, but Catton knew he'd take it.

36

Catton said nothing.

"Where's your luggage?" said the manager, looking at Mina, who had no bags with her.

"We'll pick them up after we're checked in," said Catton.

"Whatever," muttered the manager, shrugging as though he'd seen it all.

Finished checking in, Catton accompanied Mina to her room, which was six-odd rooms away from his.

As soon as she entered the room, she darted over to the TV set and turned it on with the remote.

"What are you watching?" he said.

"I want to see the news."

"Good idea. We need to know as soon as possible if Rachel's body surfaces."

"Yes," she said, her eyes glued to the news program.

"Tomorrow I want to go to Rachel's condo to see if I can find her password for her online bank account."

Catton stood in the room watching the news with Mina for a while. When he didn't hear anything about Rachel, he decided he should return to his room.

However, he was reluctant to leave Mina, concerned she would report him to the cops as soon as he left. But what could he do about it? He had already warned her that their lives were mutually entwined now, since she had murdered Rachel for him. How many more times did he have to tell her?

The only other alternative was to have her stay in his room with him. But she wanted her own room. He didn't want to force her to stay in his room. He didn't want her as a prisoner. He wanted her as somebody he could trust.

"Will you be all right here?" he said, smiling.

"Why wouldn't I be?" she said, turning away from the TV to face him.

"Do you feel OK now? You were feeling sick before."

"You don't have to worry about me."

"I just want to make sure you know how things stand," he said, shutting the door so nobody could hear them from the hall.

"What do you mean?"

"You're in this up to your neck with me. We're best friends now," he said, still smiling.

"You make it sound ominous."

"I'll make it simple. If you rat me out to the cops, I'll tell them you killed my wife."

"Why would I kill your wife?"

"You killed her out of jealousy."

"You have a good imagination," she said with a trace of a smile.

"This is the real deal," he said, face stony now.

"Why do you keep harping on this? It's getting old."

"There's a lot riding on our relationship. We're bound together."

"You make it sound like we're married."

"Our bond is stronger than marriage. We're tied together by a secret that nobody else can ever know."

She turned away from him. "I don't want to talk about it."

"As long as you know how things stand."

"I know," she muttered, her back toward him.

"Nothing can be the same for us after tonight. We're walking on a tightrope together. If I fall, you fall."

Catton made for the door and departed.

Returning to his room he wondered if she had got the message. With a sigh he didn't think he would ever stop wondering. He would always entertain a shadow of a doubt about her. She was the one that could do him the most harm, and vice versa. He wondered how long this rocky relationship could last before it foundered. He didn't want to have to kill her.

He used his key card to let himself into his room.

Outside his window, out of view, a couple of drunks in a pickup drove by, screaming unintelligible words out their open windows.

Chapter 10

The next morning, Catton and Mina went for breakfast to the nearby Denny's, which was jammed with patrons.

They were sitting at a table near the window overlooking the parking lot, a plate of buttermilk pancakes and three strips of crispy bacon in front of Catton, and scrambled eggs with sausage in front of Mina.

"It's better if you go to Rachel's instead of me," he said.

"How do you figure?" she said.

"Somebody might recognize me if they see me hanging around her condo."

"Why do you want me to go there?"

"To look for her online bank account's password."

"Great. Where am I supposed to find that?"

"I dunno. Try searching her bureaus in her bedroom. Search any desk you see."

"Like finding a needle in a haystack," said Mina, and took a pull on her orange juice.

"I need to be able to move that money out of her account."

He chewed a mouthful of maple syrup–drenched pancakes.

"But you have no idea where her password is?" said Mina.

"None. I can only guess. I can't even be sure she wrote it down anywhere."

"I don't like my chances of finding it."

"Any chance is better than none."

"That's not saying much."

"I need to get my money out of her account ASAP."

"Where will you be when I'm searching the condo?"

"I'll sit outside in the car till you come back."

They finished eating and drove to Rachel's condo in Brentwood. It didn't take long, since it was less than ten miles from the restaurant.

Catton parked the Mustang on the side of the street, a view of a grassy median strip lined with coral trees through his windshield. Beyond the median strip was a schoolyard skirted by a chain-link fence and numerous trees that restricted the view of the asphalt playground.

He killed the engine and handed the condo's key to Mina, who was riding shotgun. For the umpteenth time he wondered if he could trust her.

She accepted the key.

"If you don't trust me, you can come with me," she said, as if reading his mind.

"I can't come with you. I told you, one of Rachel's neighborhood friends might recognize me. I don't want anybody to see me going into Rachel's condo. They could get suspicious of me and report me to the cops."

"Maybe they'll get suspicious of me going into her room, too."

"It doesn't matter if they report *you* to the cops. You aren't supposed to be dead like me."

"It matters to me. I don't want to be reported to the cops."

"They're not gonna report you to the cops. Just don't let anyone see you enter Rachel's room, if you can help it. I can't even be seen in this neighborhood."

Mina opened the car door. "Whatever. I'll see what I can turn up. Which building is it?"

"The lime-colored three-story one in the middle of the block."

Mina scoped out the block. "The Spanish-styled stucco one?"

"Yeah. Room 205."

"Does the building have a security door?"

Catton nodded. "The code is 721."

"How do you know all this?"

"I visited her here once. That's why I can't be seen here after her death. The neighbors could become suspicious."

Mina got out of the car, closed the door, and walked down the block.

Catton watched her. What was to prevent her from finding the password and not telling him about it? Then she could try to loot Rachel's bank account herself. But she wouldn't succeed, he realized, because Rachel had two-factor authentication on her bank account, which meant the password alone wasn't enough. After the password was entered, the two-factor code would be sent to Rachel's e-mail address, which Catton could access through her smartphone but Mina could not.

Still, Catton had doubts about letting Mina into Rachel's condo by herself. She might find something there she could use to access Rachel's bank account. For instance, Rachel might have another ATM card, which Mina might find and then withdraw funds from Rachel's bank.

Catton couldn't risk being seen by neighbors, though. He had to stay away from Rachel's apartment. He had to let Mina conduct the search by herself. It was his safest option.

Maybe he was paranoid thinking Mina might double-cross him, he decided. On the other hand, he hadn't expected Rachel to double-cross him and she had. You could never be sure of anyone where money was involved.

She was still walking toward the condo, he could see in his rearview mirror. He had a sudden urge to jump out of the car and accompany her, but he suppressed it. If anyone should recognize him here, all bets were off. After all, he was supposed to be dead.

Chapter 11

Mina punched in the security code at the front door to the building and entered the atrium, which had rows of mailboxes lining opposite walls and a six-foot-high gurgling fountain in the middle of it. The fountain had a two-foot-high round cement basin encircling its pool. A few scattered pennies lay on the basin's bottom glittering in the sunlight.

Mina checked the mailbox for room 205 and saw Rachel's name on it.

She noticed a middle-aged man in Bermuda shorts and a bright blue flower-print aloha shirt standing in the shade beside a garden of agaves and ficus in the atrium. A cell phone in one hand, he was watching her through grey-tinted sunglasses. She didn't let on that she was aware of his presence as she strode to the elevator and took it to the second floor.

She exited the elevator and studied the arrows on the wall that indicated which rooms were at which end of the hall. Noticing that 205 was to her right, she headed in that direction and located the room.

She inserted the key into the door's dead bolt, unlocked it, and undid the lock in the doorknob, using the same key, which worked for both locks. She nudged open the door, and out of the corner of her eye saw that the man who had been in the lobby was standing at the elevator watching her.

"Hello," he said, smiling and waving at her, and bustled down the hall toward her.

Her heart thumping like mad, she stared at him with a vacant expression as he neared.

"I'm looking for Rachel Catton," he said, coming to a halt beside her.

"Do I know you?"

"Am I speaking to Rachel Catton?"

For a brief moment Mina considered impersonating Rachel, thinking it would explain away why she was entering Rachel's room. But she nixed the idea.

"No, you're not," she said.

"I'm Randall Dunleavy, an insurance investigator," he said, fishing his wallet out of a pocket in his Bermudas and displaying his card to her.

She glanced at it without paying much attention. "I'm sorry. I can't help you."

"But this is her apartment, isn't it?"

"Uh, yes," said Mina, wondering how she could get rid of this guy.

"And you've got the key to it."

Thinking fast, Mina tried to come up with an answer. "I'm her friend. She wanted me to water her flowers while she was gone."

"Gone?"

"Yes."

"Hmm. The police got a missing person's report about her from one of her neighbors. Nobody seems to know where she is. Do you know?"

"No. She didn't tell me where she was going."

Mina could feel her face getting hot from apprehension. She wondered if she was sweating.

"She didn't tell you where she was going?" said Dunleavy.

"No."

"But she asked you to water her plants for her while she was gone."

"That's correct."

"Then why did a neighbor file a missing person's report about her?"

"I dunno," said Mina, still holding the door open.

"Did you know her husband disappeared a year ago?"

"No. I don't know her very well," said Mina, twisting the doorknob back and forth in her hand nervously.

"The authorities came to the conclusion he died, but they never found his body."

"How sad."

"And now she has disappeared, it seems. It's ironic, don't you think?"

"Is it?"

"Well, the husband disappears without leaving a trace, and then a year later the wife disappears mysteriously. Don't you think that's odd?"

"Why are you asking me? I never met her husband."

"Oh. But you *are* her friend?"

"Yes. I haven't known her that long, though."

Mina wished this guy would leave. He was disconcerting her, and he was preventing her from scoping out Rachel's room.

"She didn't even tell you where she went?" said Dunleavy.

"No."

Dunleavy cocked an eyebrow. "Did she say when she's gonna return?"

"Nope."

"I'd really like to speak to her about her husband's disappearance. She also needs to contact the police to let her know she's not a missing person. Could you tell her that?"

"I have no way of contacting her."

He twisted his mouth. "The cops are gonna keep looking for her as long as she doesn't report to them she's OK."

"I can't help you with that. I'm sort of in a rush, if you know what I mean," she said, hoping he would take the hint to bug off.

"There are inconsistencies with her husband's disappearance."

"Inconsistencies?"

"Like, if he's really dead, what happened to his body?"

"I don't know anything about it."

She was hoping the guy would leave before a neighbor spotted her entering Rachel's apartment. She didn't want to have to do any more explaining about what she was doing entering Rachel's place. She was supposed to be in and out of the apartment in fifteen minutes. She was spending the better part of that time talking to Dunleavy.

She wondered what Catton would think when she didn't return to the car in the agreed-upon time limit.

Dunleavy searched her face. "I find it odd."

"What?"

"That you know her well enough that she gives you her key, but she won't even tell you where she's going or when she'll be back."

Mina shrugged at a loss. "I dunno. Maybe she did tell me and I forgot."

"Did she send you a postcard or anything from where she's staying?"

"No."

Dunleavy grunted. "So odd. This case is getting odder by the second."

Mina said nothing, hoping Dunleavy would finally get the message and leave.

But, to her dismay and aggravation, he persisted, his face intent.

"Originally, the insurance company, my employer, thought her husband was dead so they allowed payment on his life insurance policy. But now they're not so sure—especially since his wife has gone missing without explanation."

"I'm sure there's a simple explanation. She's probably on vacation."

Dunleavy relaxed his expression and moved two steps back from her. "Yeah, yeah. I wouldn't doubt it. But you know me. I'm an investigator. I'm always looking for the bad in people. Always suspecting the worst when it comes to them."

"You have a bad perspective on people because of your job."

"Yeah, yeah," said Dunleavy, scratching his temple, shutting his eyes, and smiling. "I hope I haven't been too much of a bother."

"No. You just caught me at a bad time," said Mina, smiling as if all was forgiven.

Dunleavy paused, looking like he was preparing to leave. Then he said, "So you have no idea where Rachel is?"

"None."

"Is she still in this country, do you know?"

"I couldn't say."

"The reason I ask is because maybe she fled the country with all the money she got from her husband's insurance policy. Close to a million bucks ain't chickenfeed."

"A million bucks?" said Mina, eyes widening.

"Yeah. A lot of dough. She might've fled the country with the money so she wouldn't have to pay taxes on it."

Mina shook her head, eyes blank.

Dunleavy retrieved his wallet from his shorts again, dug out one of his business cards, and handed it to her.

"Be sure to give me a call if she contacts you and tells you where she is," he said.

"I will," said Mina, pocketing the card in her jeans.

Was this guy ever going to leave? she wondered.

"By the way, I'm from San Francisco. That's where I grew up."

Now what? she wondered. Was he trying to pick her up?

"That's nice," she said, face expressionless.

"Do you ever get up that way?"

"No."

He turned his back to her, and she thought he was going to leave. Then he turned around and faced her again.

"Do you know if your friend Rachel has been spending a lot of money lately?" he said.

"I wouldn't know that."

"Of course not. I just thought I'd ask. I try to be thorough."

"Yes," she said, trying to cut the conversation short with curt answers.

"Do you know if she's seeing someone?"

"Someone?"

"Another man. Has she been seeing another man since her husband died?"

"I dunno. How should I know that?"

"I don't mean to pry. I'm just conducting my investigation. You know what they say, 'It's nothing personal.'" He smiled at her. "I mean, how would you know something like that? How would you know who your friends are seeing? That's not something girlfriends would talk about now, is it?"

His smile could have double meanings, she decided. It could be construed as an apology, or as amusement at her dissembling. She couldn't tell which.

She glanced at her wristwatch. "I really have to water the plants and get going."

"Women don't share personal matters like that with each other, do they?" he said, smiling again.

"I don't know who she's seeing—if anyone. She was very broken up by her husband's death," Mina added for good measure, having no idea whether it was true or not.

Dunleavy bowed his head. "Of course." He paused, almost like he was expecting her to elaborate on her answer. When she didn't go on, he said, "Well, I'll let you go. Thanks for your help . . . What did you say your name was?"

"Mina."

She probably shouldn't tell him that, she decided, but she didn't see what harm it could do. Anyway, she couldn't remember if she had already given him her name or not.

He made his way down the corridor to the elevator. Midway, he turned around to smile at her.

Now what? she wondered.

"I hope I'll be seeing more of you," he said, waved, and resumed his walk to the elevator.

Mina shook her head and hurriedly closed the door behind her before he turned around again. She was already late and didn't want to talk any more with him. She wondered how Catton was handling her tardiness.

Bryan Cassiday

Chapter 12

Was this a double-cross? wondered Catton, sitting in his car, fit to be tied that Mina was taking so long. She was supposed to take only fifteen minutes. He didn't want her over there long enough for any of the neighbors to see her entering or leaving Rachel's apartment. If the neighbors saw a stranger in Rachel's apartment, they would become suspicious and might contact the cops.

A half hour had passed, and still no Mina.

He was getting antsy, sitting in the car, which was becoming warm under the rising sun. He inserted the key in the ignition, turned on the battery, and powered down both windows, letting the air in. He should have parked under some trees to make use of their cooling shade, but he hadn't expected to stay here this long.

What if she had split? he wondered. Maybe she had gone out the back entrance and booked. He hadn't thought she would try to leave him. He thought they were inextricably bound thanks to their murder of Rachel. But you could never count on anything, he knew. Things had a way of not working out the way you planned.

He couldn't understand why she would split, unless—

Could she have found the password to Rachel's bank account and decided to loot the account by herself?

He felt the blood rush from his face. Would Mina dare do something like that, knowing he could report her to the cops for murdering Rachel?

Why else would Mina be taking so long? he wondered. Had a neighbor been in the hallway to Rachel's room, which would prevent Mina from entering? That was a possibility. He had told Mina not to let herself be seen entering Rachel's place.

Yes, that could be it, he decided, not fully convinced, but relieved after a fashion. He sat back in his leather car seat and looked through the windshield at the tree-screened playground past the median strip and rested his eyes for a moment.

Then he glanced in the rearview mirror searching for Mina on the sidewalk. He didn't see her.

If Mina had taken a powder, was she going to the cops or was she going on the lam to try and fend for herself? Catton didn't want to speculate.

For all he knew, she might still be searching Rachel's condo. But what was taking her so long? He didn't want to hang around in this neighborhood much longer. If he stayed here too long, he might arouse suspicion among the neighbors. He didn't want anybody to pay attention to him. He wanted to glide in and out of here like a ghost.

Mina was screwing up his plans. He consulted his wristwatch again. Forty-five minutes had passed since she had left.

He massaged his furrowed brow, wondering what to do. The only way he could know for sure what had happened to her was by entering the condo and seeing if Mina was still in Rachel's apartment. If he entered the building, he ran the risk of being seen by a tenant. If the cops ever found Rachel's corpse, they would, as a matter of course, ask neighbors if they had seen any strangers in the building. He didn't want to be included on that list.

His only other option was to wait for Mina to return to the car, probably the safest option. But the waiting was driving him up the wall. A feeling of helplessness overwhelmed him as he waited. He felt like he was waiting to be discovered and arrested.

He wished he had some way of contacting Mina. Why hadn't he gotten her cell phone number before she had left? he asked himself. Because he didn't expect her to take this long, he answered.

51

He chewed himself out for not being better prepared for their excursion to the condo. He hadn't expected to be working with a partner, and now he was paying for it with his lax preparation.

What he should have done was gotten Rachel's online bank password before he killed her. But he had let his emotions overwhelm his intellect when he had started stabbing her in a blinding rage, bent on getting back at her for double-crossing him and stealing all his money.

Again he checked out the rearview mirror.

Where the hell was she?

Maybe he should drive out of the neighborhood so nobody would see him, and return later. But what if she returned from the condo after he left and couldn't find him? It would freak her out. There was no telling what she might do.

He figured it was a better bet to stay put, even though he increased his risk of being spotted by the neighbors the longer he remained here. Stay put and wait.

And wait.

Watching the rearview mirror he saw the condo building's front door open. At last, he decided. She would be here in the car soon—

It wasn't her, he realized with a sigh. It was a middle-aged man in Bermuda shorts.

Chapter 13

Mina was having no luck finding the password to Rachel's bank account. She was rooting around everywhere for any notebooks she could find. She couldn't think of any place where you would keep a password. Then she thought maybe it was in Rachel's cell phone. These days, people kept everything in their cell phones. She wondered if Catton had checked out her cell.

She picked up on an electric clock on the bedroom bureau and realized she was taking way too long in here. Catton's deadline had long since passed.

She started when Rachel's bedroom phone rang next to the clock.

She knew she shouldn't answer it. But she had her doubts about whether Catton was telling her the whole truth about him and Rachel.

Mina was tempted to answer the phone. Maybe answering it would be a way of finding out whether he was on the level with her.

After all, she didn't have to say anything into the phone. If she said nothing, nobody would know it was a stranger in Rachel's room. But her not speaking on the phone would make the caller suspicious.

Maybe it was the same person that had called Rachel's cell phone in the restaurant, decided Mina. She shrugged it off. She wasn't going to pick up.

She resumed her search for the password, entering the bedroom closet and casting around for a notebook secreted on one of the upper shelves above the clothes hangers. She dragged down a pasteboard box and tossed it on the made bed.

She opened the box and sorted through it. There were hundreds of photos of Rachel and Catton in it, some of them by themselves, some of them of the two together. They were on a boat together in their bathing suits in several of the pictures. She flicked through them. They looked happy together in most of the photos. She wondered what had happened to turn them against each other. Was it just the money?

You could never underestimate the power of money, she decided.

She flinched when she heard a car honk outside. She wondered if it was a signal from Catton.

She closed the box and replaced it on the shelf.

She shut the closet and pelted toward the front door. Passing through the living room she noticed Rachel's laptop open on a desk. She came to a halt and, standing beside the laptop, roused it out of Sleep mode. She was hoping the screen would open without requesting a password.

The screen lit up and demanded a password.

Oh well, it had been worth a try, she decided, then sprang to the front door and pressed her ear to it, listening for the sound of voices or footfalls in the corridor. She didn't hear any.

Satisfied nobody was outside, she cracked the door and peeked into the hall. No sign of anyone. She was relieved the nosy Dunleavy had left. She half expected to see him lurking in the hall waiting for her to reappear so he could badger her with another flurry of questions.

She needed to slip away without making any noise that would alert the neighbors.

Sneaking into the corridor she eased the door shut behind her, twisting the doorknob to hold the latch open as she closed the door so the latch wouldn't snick when it struck home against the metal strike plate. The door shut, she eased the latch home, locking the door. She locked the dead bolt with the key.

Light on her feet, she hastened to the elevator but didn't break into a run, hoping the floor wouldn't creak. In case any of the neighbors opened their doors she didn't want them to see her running, which would draw their unwanted attention.

She made it to the elevator, relieved she hadn't met anyone. In her high-strung condition, the last thing she needed was to run into a neighbor.

Chapter 14

In the driver's seat Catton thought about honking his horn to warn Mina to leave Rachel's condo. But he didn't want to be noticed. Neighbors would be curious about a car honking several times. And, anyway, how would Mina know he was the one doing the honking?

That was when he caught sight of movement in the rearview mirror and spotted Mina exiting the condo building's entrance.

He blew out his cheeks with relief. He didn't even realize he had been holding his breath.

Mina strode to the car like a businesswoman in a confident stride but not running as she went about her job.

She was holding up well so far, decided Catton, watching her in the passenger's side-view mirror. Maybe she had discovered the password.

She opened the car door and climbed in.

"What took so long?" said Catton.

"Some guy started talking to me when I was entering Rachel's room," said Mina, and took a deep breath, trying to relax.

"A neighbor?" said Catton with concern.

She paused like she was lost in thought.

"I guess," she said.

"What did he want?"

"He wondered where Rachel was."

"And *that* took forty-five minutes?"

"He kept asking me questions about what I was doing."

"What did you say?"

"I said I was watering her plants for her."

"That it?"

"He wanted to know where she was. I said I didn't know."

"Did he look like he believed you?"

"I think so."

"I don't like it," said Catton. He looked away from her and out the windshield. "We need to get out of here."

He figured they had overstayed their welcome a half hour ago.

Scoping out the neighborhood making sure nobody was watching him, he fired the engine, put the Mustang into gear, and peeled away from the curb.

He almost forgot why they had gone to Rachel's condo in the first place.

"Did you get the password?" he said, as they rounded the corner in the Mustang.

"I couldn't find it."

"I'm not surprised."

"I didn't know where to look. Where does someone hide a password?"

Catton didn't answer her question. "It's all about taking risks."

"What?"

"Getting out of this mess. That's the only way we're gonna get out of it. We had to try. We need that money in her account. Taking out a thousand bucks every day from her ATM is too slow, and it might attract attention from her bank."

Chapter 15

Mina was thinking about something else. She wished she had never stabbed Rachel. The way things were going Mina would find herself in jail soon. What had possessed her to kill a complete stranger? she wondered.

There was no point in thinking about it, she knew. There was nothing she could do about it now.

She had been thinking about telling Catton about her meeting with the insurance investigator Dunleavy, but decided not to at the last moment. She might be able to use Dunleavy against Catton in some way, in case he tried to hang her out to dry.

At this point she didn't see how she could use Dunleavy and the information he had given her. Still, knowledge was power, and she had knowledge that Catton didn't. She knew the life insurance company was investigating his disappearance, suspecting fraud. This knowledge gave her leverage over him, she figured, if she knew how to use it.

Her problem was, she didn't know what she wanted. Did she want to get away from Catton, or did she want to stay with him as his partner? Her life was going nowhere before she met him at the pier. Now she was on the run from the cops. Not good. But if she left Catton, he might decide to tell the cops she killed his wife.

If she *did* leave Catton, what would she do? Her life had no direction before she met him. Left to her own devices again, she might go back to contemplating suicide. The idea of suicide didn't enter her mind when she was with Catton. With Catton she was concerned solely with dodging the cops so they wouldn't bust her for murder.

He had a weird hold over her that she couldn't explain. Maybe it was the same hold a rattlesnake had over a rabbit before it attacked. Or maybe it was a case of the Stockholm syndrome. She didn't know what it was. It was fascinating, but she realized it could also be deadly.

Which was why she needed leverage she could use against him if necessary—like Dunleavy's investigation of him. She wondered what Catton would do if he knew the life insurance company was investigating his death. It might even turn him against her, which was another reason she held back the info from him. Though, she didn't see how he could blame Dunleavy's presence on her. She didn't even know Catton when he faked his death. She had nothing to do with it.

The more she thought about it, the more undecided she became.

Maybe she should just tell him about Dunleavy and get it over with. If Catton wasn't aware of the insurance company's investigation of him, he might not take enough precautions against discovery and allow himself to get caught by them.

They were driving along the beach, a sea breeze whipping by their open windows sounding like a bandage being ripped off flesh.

She realized they depended on each other now, whether she liked it or not. She decided to tell Catton about Dunleavy.

"An insurance investigator questioned me at Rachel's," she said.

"What?" said Catton, turning his head to stare at her.

"The life insurance company thinks you might still be alive."

"Why would they think that?"

"I dunno."

Mulling over her info, Catton looked back out the windshield at the road ahead. "It could be just a routine investigation they go through whenever one of their clients files a claim."

"I guess."

"Did he say why they suspected I was still alive?"

"No."

59

She didn't tell him everything. She didn't tell him she had Dunleavy's phone number.

"It's lucky he didn't see me sitting in the car," said Catton.

"Yeah."

"What did he look like?"

"He was wearing Bermuda shorts."

Catton squinted in thought. "I think I remember a guy in shorts leaving the condo."

"Did he see you?"

"I doubt it. I was looking in the rearview mirror when I saw him."

"What are we gonna do?"

"It means I gotta get all that money out of Rachel's account before the insurance company decides to get the DA to freeze the account. Did the guy say what his name was?"

"Dunleavy. Randall Dunleavy, I think."

"Hmm. If you see him again, let me know."

"OK."

"I'll have to wear a disguise, for sure now. Maybe a beard would help," he said, glancing in the rearview mirror and stroking his cheek. "Shades and a beard."

"Can you grow a beard quickly?"

"Not a thick one. I'll need a thick one for it to be a good disguise. I'll have to visit a costume shop and buy a fake beard."

"Is that gonna fool a lot of people?"

"As long as it fools this Dunleavy character you're talking about, I don't care about passers-by. Joe Six-Pack in the street isn't gonna know me from Adam. Dunleavy's the one that can put me behind bars for fraud."

"I doubt he's going away any time soon."

He turned toward her. "Why do you say that? Did he say he has evidence against me?"

"No. He seems to like sniffing around, though."

60

He turned back to the road ahead. "That's his job."

"Maybe we would be safer if we skipped town."

"I'm not through with Rachel's condo. Maybe you didn't look in the right places."

"Does that mean you're going back there?"

"Maybe."

There was silence between them.

"Are you religious?" she said.

"Religion is for cowards."

"What do you mean?"

"Religious types can't accept that their lives are meaningless, so they take refuge in religion."

"You don't believe in karma?"

"No."

"I don't think we're gonna get away with this. Maybe we should pray."

"I need to get my hands on that money. Then we'll be home free."

"Where are we going now?"

"I need a haircut."

Chapter 16

Dunleavy didn't like the idea of somebody getting something for nothing. That was why he had become an investigator. Anybody that didn't work for their money annoyed him. He wanted to see them punished. All his life he had to work for his money, even if, at times, it was a job he detested, his current occupation excluded.

He was sitting now at a table on the sidewalk in a waffle joint nursing a coffee near the beach, a plate of residual maple syrup left by the waffle he had consumed in front of him, maple aroma filling his nostrils.

Tourists were roaming around the sidewalks, chattering. None of them spoke English. As a result, he couldn't understand what they were saying so he didn't listen to them. He concentrated on his thoughts.

For insurance claims he was naturally suspicious when the corpse didn't show up, as in Catton's case. Catton was presumed dead by drowning after he had disappeared while boating on a summer vacation in Oahu, Hawaii.

Eyewitnesses on a catamaran said they had seen someone in the ocean floating near a drifting boat, which turned out to be Catton's, in the ocean. When they sailed over to help him, he had disappeared.

Catton went off the grid afterwards.

He never returned to his hotel room to pick up his luggage. Hotel personnel notified the Honolulu PD, as did the eyewitnesses who claimed they had seen him drown, though they couldn't ID him since they were too far away to discern his face. They conceded what they saw might even have been a reflection on the water, a trick of the light.

Not much to go on, decided Dunleavy. And now Catton's wife, who had collected on his life insurance policy, had disappeared. All these disappearances made Dunleavy suspicious.

It was harder to go off the grid these days in the surveillance state the country had become. Closed-circuit security cameras were mounted everywhere videotaping customers at banks, stores, restaurants, you name it, Dunleavy knew. Even your cell phone took a picture of your face every time you used it, if you had face ID on it. No matter where you went, a camera was filming you, it seemed.

So how could Catton still be alive without ever being photographed? wondered the life insurance company executives who dragged their feet, but in the end authorized payment on his policy to fend off a lawsuit from Mrs. Catton. The answer, they decided, was, nobody was looking for him, since the cops had declared him dead, and therefore nobody was inspecting possible videos of Catton.

Still, without the presence of a corpse, the suits at the insurance company suspected fraud, and that was where Dunleavy came in. The suits thought Catton was dead, but they wanted to make sure. Dunleavy's job was to make sure.

Of course, Catton might have had plastic surgery done, which would make him harder to find, Dunleavy knew. But Catton would only have done so if he was worried about being ID'd and busted.

Dunleavy had no idea how worried Catton was about being busted. Frankly, Dunleavy didn't even know if Catton was alive. The guy might indeed have drowned, and the ocean currents had swept his corpse out to sea never to be seen again. As yet, Dunleavy had uncovered no evidence to the contrary.

He was in the act of investigating Catton's disappearance when he had discovered Catton's wife Rachel had disappeared recently. It made Dunleavy wonder. Had they skipped the country to meet somewhere and spend their ill-gotten gains in anonymous bliss?

Dunleavy ordered another waffle. He knew he was putting on weight, but so what? It wasn't like he looked like Brad Pitt, so why worry about putting on a few pounds? Life was short. He might as well enjoy what he could of it.

He didn't have many likes, but he liked food. He had a middle-aged paunch, he knew, glancing down at his belly, but he didn't consider himself fat. *Fat* was a guy that couldn't fit in a plane seat. And Dunleavy could still do that, though the seats did seem to be getting snugger every time he boarded a plane.

He wasn't going to worry about his weight with all the other worries he had to plague him. It was a waste of time.

During the course of his investigation he had discovered that Rachel Catton had paid the life insurance company with two checks for miscellaneous charges from different bank accounts. He learned that she had closed her joint bank account with her husband and opened a new checking account in her own name. He wondered why she didn't just have her allegedly deceased husband's name removed from their joint account? Why go to all of the trouble of opening a new account?

He could think of only one reason.

She didn't want her husband to be able to access the bank account. He wouldn't be able to access a brand-new account in Rachel's name, whereas he could still access the joint account—*if* he was alive. And that was a big if.

But why else would she open a new bank account in her own name? She would have to have new checks printed up with the new account number on it. It was a big hassle for something that wasn't necessary, Dunleavy decided.

Still, maybe she didn't want to be constantly reminded of him whenever she made out a check and saw his name as the joint owner. Maybe she thought seeing her husband's name there all the time would depress her.

Dunleavy admitted to himself he was speculating, but a lot of what he did in his business was speculation. He had to train himself to think like a crook and then speculate what a crook would do under certain circumstances.

Was Catton really dead, or was he scamming the life insurance company? Were he and his wife both in on the scam, or was Catton acting on his own? If Rachel was in on the scam, why did she open a new bank account that froze Catton out? If she *was* in on the scam, why would Catton want her to open a new bank account in her name only?

Maybe the guy really was dead, decided Dunleavy. Maybe investigating him was a waste of time.

There were many questions that needed to be answered, decided Dunleavy and smiled as the waitress deposited a fresh Belgian waffle in front of him. He didn't want to think anymore. He wanted to eat.

He poured maple syrup on the waffle topped with whipped cream, watching the amber liquid pool around the plate.

He remembered watching Mina get into someone's car at Rachel's condo. He wondered who the driver was. Her boyfriend? Girlfriend? Dunleavy wasn't standing close enough to the car to be able to make out the gender of the driver. He had been tempted to follow them, but he hadn't been standing near his Challenger, which he had parked a block away, and by the time he reached it, they would have been well out of sight.

Dunleavy took a bite of the waffle and savored it. Nothing else mattered now but the succulent taste of the waffle.

Chapter 17

Catton had to sail his Boston Whaler back to Marina del Rey where he had a slip. He wanted Mina to drive down there to meet him so his car would be waiting for him.

These days when he drove, he had to be extra careful about obeying the speed limit. He didn't want cops pulling him over and inspecting his driver's license—the license of a dead man.

Mina didn't have to worry about a cop inspecting her license. At least, he didn't think she did, unless she had a criminal record. But she didn't look like a hardened convict to him. No tattoos. No attitude. No track marks on her arms.

The problem with letting her take his car was, she might take it for good. He didn't think she was a convict, but he didn't trust her, either.

They were sitting in a parking lot along the Coast Highway overlooking the Pacific near Malibu.

"Can you drive a stick?" he said from the driver's seat.

"Yeah," said Mina.

"That's a surprise. A lot of younger people don't know how to drive stick shifts."

"My mother had one on her Taurus. I learned on it for my driver's test."

"My car's more powerful than a Taurus. Do you think you can handle it?"

"Why not?"

"Good. Drive down to the Marina and wait for me at the Blue Dolphin Café on the dock. I'll meet you there after I dock my boat."

He still had doubts about whether he could trust her, let alone trust her with his car. He punched in the restaurant's address on the Mustang's dashboard-mounted GPS.

"OK," she said.

He prepared to get out of the car. "You're not gonna run off on me, are you?"

"Where would I go?"

"And if you take off, you won't get any of the money when I get it out of Rachel's bank account."

She said nothing.

He knew he had leverage on her because he had witnessed her stabbing Rachel to death, and yet he didn't trust her completely. What if she didn't care if he reported her as a murderer to the cops? After all, she was on the verge of committing suicide when he had met her sitting on the dock. But that was then.

He didn't think she felt suicidal anymore, not with oodles of money within her grasp. Acquiring a bundle of dough could change your aspect on life, making it a whole lot rosier.

Still, it was hard for Catton to trust anyone all the way when it came to money, especially after his own wife had scammed him.

If he didn't trust Mina, his only alternative for sailing the boat to Marina del Rey was for both of them to take the boat. But then he and Mina would have to take Uber back to Malibu to collect his car, which would saddle him with another witness to his movements. He had more than enough witnesses with Mina.

It wasn't that he distrusted her, it was that he didn't trust her completely. How could he? She was a total stranger. He had only met her last night. Trust took a while to be earned, was his experience. And even then you could never be sure.

If he sailed with her back to Marina del Rey, she might draw the conclusion that he felt he didn't have leverage on her since he was apprehensive of her trying to jack his car if he let her drive it, which might give her ideas about taking a powder.

Since he *did* have leverage on her he needed to exercise it to make her aware of her precarious arrangement with him, or there was no point in even having the leverage. In other words, he had to use it or lose it. He had to make it obvious to her that he would use the leverage if she absconded with his car.

"Don't even think about jacking my car," he said. "You know I have you by the short and curlies."

"What would I do with a jacked car? What's the point of having a car when I have no place to go?"

He thought she was telling the truth.

"Drive carefully," he said. "I don't want a cop pulling you over and checking the car registration."

"Of course," she said, somewhat annoyed at him for feeling he had to point out the obvious.

"Depress the clutch when you start up or it won't start."

He got out of the car. To show his leverage, he would let her drive his car and he would meet her at the marina after he docked his boat.

He walked toward the beach to retrieve his boat. He heard her fire the Mustang's ignition behind him and the harmonious rumble of the eight cylinders kicking in under the hood. Keeping his pace steady he didn't look back at her.

By not looking back he was showing her he had no doubt she would do as he had told her because he was in absolute control of her—or so he hoped.

Chapter 18

Shirtless and wearing jeans, he sailed south on the calm sea hugging the coast down to Marina del Rey and docked at his slip in the harbor without incident.

Now it was a matter of meeting Mina. He didn't know how long it would take her to get to the Blue Dolphin. She had to deal with traffic. On the other hand, he hadn't gone very fast in his motorboat. He was lucky to get it up to 30 mph tops.

He put on a polo shirt and strolled along the dock past wheezing wooden boats bobbing on the water as they sat moored in disuse. Gulls wheeled overhead, crying out to each other as they swooped.

The Blue Dolphin was in walking distance, and he struck out for it, his legs getting used to terra firma during his trek.

He felt better about having his boat docked. Now he didn't have to worry about a stranger finding it in Malibu and reporting it. It was all about tying up loose ends. He was convinced he didn't have to worry about getting discovered if he tied up loose ends and covered his tracks. You couldn't find someone who left no trail, especially if that person had been declared dead.

Then all it was was a matter of striking a pose, like it was for everything.

He entered the Blue Dolphin Café, stood on the sawdust-covered floor, and cast around for Mina. He didn't see her. Maybe she had got caught in traffic, he decided. LA was famous for its traffic, or more like infamous. He didn't see how she could have got lost since she had the GPS device in the car.

He wished he had some way of contacting her. They needed to get burner phones that were untraceable.

The news was on the high-definition TV set mounted behind the bar. He stood and watched it for a while.

Nothing about the surfacing of Rachel's body. It was the only news he cared about.

He sat at a table where he could watch the door and see who entered.

The Blue Dolphin was a small seafood restaurant with a pelagic décor. In the corner of the room where he sat, a fisherman's net hung like a cobweb. There was a stuffed swordfish hanging on top of the picture window that gave onto the dock. In the corner opposite him a harpoon stood clamped to the wall. He ordered a Corona longneck.

The young waitress brought it with a wedge of lime stuck in the neck.

Maybe Mina couldn't find a place to park, he decided, gazing out the window and seeing no sign of her. He took a slug of beer.

He would have to continue to live his life in the shadows now that he knew the insurance company had hired a detective to investigate him. Maybe he should leave the country. The problem was, he couldn't do anything without the money. Before he could do anything else, he had to get his hands on his money in Rachel's bank account.

Until that time, and even after it, he would have to keep to the shadows and make only cash purchases, which left no trace. He could still withdraw cash from her bank's ATMs, but not more than a thousand dollars a day from her near-million-dollar account. It was like knowing you had a hundred gallons of water, but you could drink only one drop at a time. It would drive you nuts, if you thought about it long enough.

He finished his beer, and Mina still hadn't arrived. He ordered another.

There was nothing else he could do except wait for her to show up. What if she had been in an accident? he wondered. There was nothing he could do about it.

Then he wondered why the insurance company had hired a detective to investigate him after they had already awarded the money to his wife. Something must have happened afterward that aroused their suspicions. Could somebody have reported spotting him to the company?

The sight of Mina entering the café and looking around for him released him from his thoughts. He waved at her. She came over to his table.

"Any problems?" he said.

"I couldn't find anywhere to park," she said, sitting opposite him. "Have you been waiting long?"

"As long as you're here, that's what counts."

He felt relieved she had shown up. It confirmed his power over her. He trusted her more now than before, trusted she wouldn't run out on him. Was it really relief he was feeling, or was he feeling happy to see her? Maybe his feelings were becoming too involved in this relationship. He would have to watch out for that.

He had to make sure she understood her dependence on him, and that it wasn't the other way around. He didn't want her to get the crazy idea that she was in charge. After all, he was the one with the money. She didn't have anything. Not that he had the money yet, either, but he would have it soon. It was his money, and he was going to get it or die trying.

Chapter 19

Mina had thought about taking off on her own while she was driving Catton's Mustang.

She had thought about a lot of things, including the insurance investigator Dunleavy. It was when she was thinking about him that she had pulled into a parking space on the side of PCH facing the beach and, reading his number on his business card, called him on her cell.

She wasn't going to call him while she was driving because it was illegal and she didn't want a cop to see her and pull her over. She hardly ever saw cops busting drivers for talking on their cells while driving, but, on the lam in a car that didn't belong to her, she didn't want to risk it.

He answered on the fourth ring.

She told him who she was.

"What happens if you don't find Rachel Catton?" she said.

"Why wouldn't I find her?" he said.

"I dunno. Maybe she doesn't want to be found."

"Why would she be trying to hide?"

"Maybe she just wants to forget about her prior life and live a new life."

"If she doesn't want to be found, I would be very suspicious."

"Why?"

"Because I would suspect she took off to meet her 'dead' husband and enjoy their ill-gotten gains."

"Oh."

"Are you trying to tell me you think she's in hiding?" said Dunleavy, an edge to his voice.

"I have no idea where she is," said Mina hurriedly. "I'm just wondering what you would do."

"Why do you care what I would do?"

"Maybe there's a little reward for helping you find her . . ."

Dunleavy hung fire. "I'm not convinced she really is missing at this point. She just got reported missing. She may still show up. Are you saying you know how I can find her?"

"Suppose I did know?"

"I don't deal with hypotheticals. I deal with facts. Do you know where your friend Rachel is?"

"No," said Mina, and terminated the call.

After she had called him, she wondered what she had expected him to say. She was trying to get out of this predicament she was in, but she didn't know how. She thought maybe he might be able to help her in some way that she couldn't foresee.

Thinking about it now, she figured her call was ill advised. It just served to rouse his suspicions of the whole Catton affair, which wasn't going to do her any good that she could see. She was up to her neck in it without even wanting to be involved in the first place.

She had called Dunleavy hoping he might have a way out for her. But she had no idea what that way was. And now, it seemed, he had none.

She needed to figure out specifically how he could help her before calling him again.

She could just drive off into the sunset and forget she had ever met Catton and his wife. She doubted that would work. In the end, it would catch up with her. Catton would come looking for her because she had the goods on him (and he on her).

Yet it was a big world out there, she decided. Couldn't she disappear in it? But then what would she do? She still had the feeling she was at loose ends, her life unraveling.

Murder, murder, murder . . . And there was the voice again echoing through her mind. Closing her eyes in frustration she wished she knew how she could make it stop.

She better go back to Catton, she decided. She didn't want to have to worry for the rest of her life about him tracking her down seeking to shut her up permanently so she couldn't rat him out about his faked death and about their subsequent murder of his wife.

It was best to keep him close, letting him think he could control her at will—for the time being, anyway, until she could come up with a better option.

She fired the ignition, reversed out of the parking space, threw the car into first gear, and peeled off for the marina to meet him, the sea breeze blowing through the open windows into her hair, carrying the briny tang of the ocean.

Chapter 20

Dunleavy was lying on a chaise longue on a motel patio that overlooked the ocean. It wasn't a cheap motel by any means. He had always admired the rich and powerful. They had the good life, he decided.

He couldn't afford renting this place on what he made, but he was going to charge the expense to the insurance company that hired him. They wouldn't complain about the charge if he was able to find out that Catton was still alive and had faked his death. They would be glad to pay him whatever he asked, since they would be able to recover their money from Catton's fraudulent claim.

Wearing Wayfarers he was lying on his back in sandals, shorts, and an unbuttoned fluorescent green aloha shirt, nursing a cabernet and wondering why Mina had called him.

It wound up that she didn't reveal much of anything, only hinting that she might know something that had to do with his investigation. But that was all it was—insinuations, from which he could draw no conclusions. Then why had she bothered to phone him? he wondered. Was she sounding him out for some reason?

Her conversation befuddled him. If she didn't know anything that could help him, why make the call?

He got the impression she *did* know something about Catton's disappearance, but she wasn't ready to talk about it just yet. His responses to her questions must not have encouraged her to open up to him.

He didn't know what kind of answers from him would have stimulated her to talk. She had asked for a reward in return for her information about Rachel's whereabouts. But there wasn't any reward that Dunleavy knew about—not yet, anyway. Rachel hadn't been missing long enough for a reward to be posted.

Mina must have had some reason for making that call that revealed nothing to him. He doubted she just wanted to hear the sound of his voice. Was it really just a reward that she wanted? he wondered.

He decided to call his employer the insurance company to ask for a clarification. He set his drink on the cement patio floor at his side, punched their number into his cell, and put the cell to his ear, listening to it ring.

Knowing it was him from the caller ID on their phone, they answered on the second ring.

"Are you offering a reward for information leading to the whereabouts and capture of Gage Catton?"

"Did you find somebody who knows where he is?" said a male voice with precise diction.

"I dunno. If she does know, she isn't talking right now. A reward might loosen her lips."

"Do you think Catton's still alive?"

"This case is getting more complicated. I can't locate his wife. Somebody filed a missing person's report on her to the cops. Makes me wonder."

There was a pause on the other end of the line, and Dunleavy could hear unintelligible whispering between two individuals in the background.

"We'll offer a ten-thousand-dollar reward for information leading to Catton's arrest," came the reply. "A small price to pay, if we find he chiseled us out of close to a million dollars."

The man hung up.

Scratching his chin Dunleavy pocketed his cell. Now he had something he could trade for information, he decided, which should speed up getting results from his investigation.

He sighed and took hold of his wine glass. Maybe he was spinning his wheels. Life in this business was like that a lot.

He had no proof Gage Catton was still alive. On the other hand, he had no proof the guy was dead either. Until he had proof one way or the other, his investigation would proceed.

He thought Catton's wife should know better than anybody whether Catton was alive. It was an axiom in his business to follow the money, and the insurance payout all went to Rachel Catton. But where the hell was Rachel Catton?

Chapter 21

"We need to get burner phones," Catton told Mina, sitting across from her at the Blue Dolphin.

Mina looked puzzled.

"They're cheap prepaid phones that can't be traced," said Catton. "We can get some at Radio Shack."

"I already have a cell phone."

"So do I. But I don't want anyone to know of a connection between us. Our current cells can both be traced when used, so I don't want us to use them to contact each other. We need a way to contact each other in secret."

"Why do we need to contact each other?"

"I didn't know what happened to you at Rachel's, why you were taking so long. What if you had been in an accident or something? I had no way of knowing."

Mina nodded. "How's the food here?"

"Not bad." He read from the menu. "Wild-caught salmon with the hook still in its mouth."

Mina froze, her face pale.

"You don't have to get anything if you don't want to," said Catton, amused by her reaction.

Then he realized she was staring over his shoulder. Craning his neck around he saw the TV behind the bar playing a news report. He managed to read the chyron at the bottom of the screen: Body found in ocean.

Now he realized why the blood was draining from her face.

He bolted out of his seat and bellied up to the bar so he could hear the news report. A fisherman had found the corpse floating in the ocean while he was fishing in his boat. The cops hadn't ID'd the body yet.

It must have been Rachel, decided Catton. Why would there be another body floating around in the ocean at this time? He had stripped her of any ID, so the cops would have to use another way of ID'ing her. It wouldn't take them long to find out who she was. They could check their missing persons' reports and see if she matched any descriptions in them, and then they could check her fingerprints to make sure.

The cops already knew they had a murder victim on their hands thanks to the multiple stab wounds in her body. Mina was right when she had told him she hadn't knotted the anchor's rope around the blanket Rachel was rolled in. There was nothing he could do about it now.

The TV screen showed EMTs on a dock's weathered floorboards trundling a gurney loaded with a corpse under a sheet to an ambulance with its emergency lights flashing and its back door open.

Feeling ill Catton returned to his table, where Mina still sat, her eyes wide and riveted on the TV screen.

"They don't know who she is, but they will soon enough," he said.

"Are you sure it's her?"

"How many other dead bodies can there be floating around in the ocean?"

The waitress wandered over to them, concern etched on her face as she eyed Mina. "Would you like an aspirin, dear? You don't look well."

"Just a glass of water, thank you," said Mina.

The waitress disappeared.

Mina turned to Catton. "What do we do now?"

Catton kept his voice low, even though there weren't any other customers sitting within earshot of his table. "There's nothing that can tie us to her murder."

"Then why do you look sick?"

"I'm not the only one."

The waitress returned with a glass of water for Mina and, smiling with compassion, left a small package of two Tylenols on the tabletop in front of Mina, then left.

79

Mina gave her a grateful look.

"It's gonna make my job of getting my money back more complicated," said Catton.

Mina ripped open the foil pack of extra strength Tylenols and gulped the two tablets down with a swig of water.

"Why?" she said.

"The authorities are gonna be suspicious of any withdrawals made from her bank account now that they know she's dead."

"So what can they do about it?"

"They could stake out the ATMs I've been using and see who's withdrawing the money. Or . . ."

"Or what?"

"They could try to get the DA to freeze her account. I don't know how long it would take them to get a court order. Probably not long."

"Maybe we should turn ourselves in."

Catton ignored her. "If I could just get that money into an offshore asset-protected account, then they couldn't freeze it."

"How can you do that?"

Racking his brains Catton ran his fingers through his hair. "I dunno. It depends on how long it takes the courts to freeze her account—which they might not even do in the first place."

"You don't sound optimistic."

"The bottom line is, we have to act quickly. We can't depend on their inaction."

"Then we're in a worse situation than ever."

"It *would* be even worse if they knew we're the ones that killed her."

"How comforting."

"The problem is, now they know she *was* murdered. Before, they thought she was just missing. Her murder could lead to their reopening their investigation of my death."

"Maybe they won't."

"I can't take that chance. I need a disguise. I'm gonna have to go to a costume shop."

Chapter 22

Dunleavy was watching the TV news in his motel room with interest. The newscast said a fisherman had found a murder victim's corpse floating in the ocean. The cops had ID'd the corpse as that of Rachel Catton, who was the victim of multiple stab wounds.

Dunleavy's search was over. He had come to LA to find her, and now he had found her. However, his investigation was just beginning. Rachel's murder threw a dark cloud over the Catton case, suggesting a possible swindle of the insurance company. Since murder was involved, money could be the motive. But who benefited from Rachel's death? That was a problem, since her husband was also dead.

Dunleavy wondered if Rachel had written a will that listed a beneficiary to her estate. And then there was Gage Catton, whose corpse had never been found. Was he going to reappear out of the blue and claim Rachel's estate?

Dunleavy didn't see how Catton could pull it off. If it was discovered Catton wasn't really dead, the insurance company could put him behind bars for fraud if he tried to claim the deceased's money. And if Catton *was* alive, he might have had something to do with Rachel's murder.

A lot of ifs, decided Dunleavy. He didn't have much to go on other than speculation. But why would somebody want Rachel dead, if it wasn't for her money? Unless she had had a lover's quarrel with a new boyfriend. The boyfriend angle. That was something worth looking into, Dunleavy decided.

And what were the chances that both Rachel and her husband had died separately under mysterious circumstances? Rachel had been murdered, but nobody knew what had caused Gage's death—be it accident or foul play.

Using his cell he put in a call to the insurance company.

"I don't know if you've heard, but Rachel Catton was murdered," he said. "It's on the local news here."

There was a pause.

It was Traska, the insurance guy that had hired Dunleavy, that answered. "They're sure she was murdered?"

"Positive. She had multiple stab wounds."

Traska was a middle-aged guy with a world-weary face and a prominent nose. Dunleavy had never seen him without a black suit on. He was the type of guy you gave wide berth to, because you didn't want him to get too close to you lest he discover some dark secret you were trying to hide. Traska figured everybody was guilty of something. It was just a matter of finding out what.

"Do they have any suspects?" said Traska.

"Not that I know of. They just found the corpse floating in the ocean."

"Meaning the murderer tried to cover it up."

"Looks that way. Why else would you dump a body in the ocean?"

"Isn't it strange how as soon as she gets all our money, she gets herself murdered?"

Dunleavy nodded. "Money may be at the bottom of it."

"It's at the bottom of everything. I'm still suspicious of Gage Catton's supposed death."

"Maybe the same person killed him and his wife."

"Could be. Or he may've faked his death so his wife could lay claim to his life insurance policy and then he murdered his wife."

"But I don't see how he gets his hands on her money without revealing himself. If he reveals himself, he'll go to prison for faking his death with intent to defraud the insurance company."

"I dunno."

"I haven't found any proof that he's still alive. Nobody's using his credit cards. He's not leaving any trail of expenses. Nobody has sighted him, as far as I know."

"Look harder," said Traska, and hung up.

You're guilty until proven innocent, was Traska's motto, Dunleavy knew. The problem was, the law said just the opposite. In other words, Dunleavy needed to find proof of Gage Catton's guilt and to do that he first needed to prove Catton was still alive.

Dunleavy's cell phone vibrated. He answered it.

"I think my life may be in danger," said Mina.

"Is this Mina?" said Dunleavy.

"Yes."

Dunleavy's best lead so far was Mina, Rachel Catton's friend he had bumped into. She might know something about Rachel's relationship with her husband. She might even be able to suggest a suspect in Rachel's murder.

"Why do you think your life's in danger?" said Dunleavy.

"I just found out somebody murdered my friend Rachel. Maybe he'll come after me next."

"Do you know who the murderer is?"

"No."

"Then why do you think the killer will come after you?"

"Because I was Rachel's friend."

"That doesn't necessarily mean he'll come after you— unless he thinks you know who he is."

"I don't know who the killer is."

"Maybe you saw him with her once. It could be that simple. You just didn't know he was the killer."

"If that happened and he saw me, I'm definitely in danger. Now I'm even more worried."

"What do you want me to do?"

"You're a detective. Maybe you can help me."

"Let's meet."

Chapter 23

Mina didn't trust Catton. She needed to get out of their twisted relationship. That was why she had called Dunleavy. She thought maybe he could help her. At this point, she didn't see how, but she wanted to leave her options open by keeping in touch with him.

The problem was, she didn't feel safe with Dunleavy either. He could have her thrown in jail if he found out she had helped murder Catton's wife. He was a professional detective. He was trained to find criminals. In her position it made sense to keep him at arm's length.

On the other hand, Mina needed somebody she could play off Catton, and Dunleavy was her best bet.

She didn't know how much she could risk telling Dunleavy about her knowledge of Rachel's murder. She wasn't going to up and tell him Catton had done it, because she knew Catton wouldn't hesitate to implicate her if she ratted him out.

She was sitting alone now in the Blue Dolphin, peering out the window at the marina where sailboats bobbed, their sails furled, their masts jabbing at the sky like spears. Catton had left, saying he needed to buy burner phones and some other stuff. He had told her to meet him in two hours at a saloon called the Oyster, which was within walking distance.

In the meantime she had decided to contact Dunleavy.

Twenty minutes later, Dunleavy ambled into the restaurant wearing madras shorts, a Tommy Bahama white silk shirt, and espadrilles. Pushing his sunglasses onto his forehead, where he left them, he scoped out the restaurant, spotted her, and approached her table.

"What did you want to see me about?" he said, taking a seat opposite her.

"I want you to protect me," said Mina.

85

"From what?"

"Like we said over the phone."

"Like a bodyguard?"

"I dunno. My life's in danger. I think you can help me."

Dunleavy leaned back in his seat. "I already have a job. Maybe if you identified who is trying to harm you, I could help you."

Mina wasn't about to tell him it was Catton. She didn't want Dunleavy to know Catton was alive, because if Dunleavy knew that much it could jeopardize Catton's getting ahold of Rachel's money. Mina didn't want to lose out on the money that Catton promised to give her.

She wanted to be able to get in touch with Dunleavy if she felt Catton was going to harm her. She suspected that Catton could turn on her on a dime, like he did on his wife. She wanted Dunleavy to help her in case that nightmare transpired. But she knew Catton wouldn't want him around—unless she could concoct some story why Dunleavy needed to be with them.

"Rachel's murderer might come after me next," she said.

"You already told me that. But what's his name?"

She fixed her hair at her temple. "I dunno."

"We're going around in circles," said Dunleavy, shoulders slumping in disappointment. "I came all the way here to see you for nothing."

"I want you to come to my aid in case I call you about being attacked."

"I wish you could give me more on this killer. It might help me in my insurance investigation as well."

"I can't help you with that."

Dunleavy searched her face.

"I wish I could believe you," he said, stroking his chin.

"Why would I lie?"

Dunleavy grinned. "Why does anybody lie?"

Mina leaned forward over the tabletop toward Dunleavy. "What if I did know who killed Rachel? What then?"

"I would track the guy down and have a talk with him about Gage Catton."

"And then you would report the killer to the cops?"

Dunleavy thought about it, wondering what her angle was, wondering if she was protecting someone. "Maybe not. It depends. I'm not a cop, you know. My job is to find Gage Catton, if he's still alive. It's not to capture murderers."

Mina leaned back in her seat. "Interesting. You're not a cop, but you investigate crimes."

"Not all crimes. Only defrauding insurance companies."

"Not murder?"

"I told you, I'm not a homicide cop. But if Rachel's murder had something to do with defrauding my employer, yeah I'd be interested and I'd report it to them." Dunleavy paused. "Why all these questions?"

"I'm trying to decide whose side your on."

"I'm on my side, but I also have a job to do. I'm on my employer's side."

"I see."

"Do all these questions mean you know who killed Rachel?" said Dunleavy, leveling a steady gaze at her face.

"Um . . . I was speculating. I'm trying to find out if you're the right person to help me."

Disenchanted, Dunleavy got to his feet. "I can't help you unless you give me something for my trouble, namely information."

Mina said nothing. She was debating whether to tell him about Catton's involvement in Rachel's murder. She didn't know if she wanted to open up to him, revealing too much about herself that he could use against her. However, she still wanted to enlist somebody she could use against Catton if he became too belligerent toward her and caused her to fear for her life.

"I may be able to help you," she said, trying to get him to stay.

"Then out with it."

Mina said nothing, unsure of how to proceed.

"And I may be able to help you," said Dunleavy. "Lion Life is offering a ten-thousand-dollar reward for information leading to Catton's whereabouts."

Ten thousand versus close to a million in Rachel's checking account, decided Mina. No contest.

She said nothing.

Waving his hand in dismissal he turned to leave. "You're jerking my chain. You don't have anything."

He retreated toward the exit.

Of two minds, she didn't call him back. She didn't want to put herself in the precarious position where both Catton and Dunleavy had leverage on her. She wasn't signing off on Dunleavy, she was temporizing. She still had his phone number, and she would wait for a better opportunity to present itself.

Chapter 24

Catton drove to a costume shop on Wilshire. He parked along the curb, got out of his car, fed quarters into the meter, and strode into the shop that had mannequins in costumes standing in the display window with the cardboard cutout of a grey stone wall as a backdrop behind them.

Catton figured a beard would be enough of a disguise. He already wore a pair of Persol wraparound sunglasses that obscured most of his face. He didn't think he would require plastic surgery to remain incognito, and, to boot, surgery was expensive and he would need to use a credit card to pay for it—which was out of the question.

He suspected Lion Life Insurance was still monitoring his credit-card activity, especially now that the cops had discovered Rachel's murdered corpse. If the company had closed his case, they would be reopening it posthaste, as his wife's murder cast suspicion on his already-mysterious disappearance.

He found a section in the store for phony beards, which were packaged in cellophane bags that hung from metal hooks that projected from a pegboard. He didn't want a beard that hung down to his navel. He just wanted a bushy one that would cover most of his face and alter its shape.

He wondered how realistic they were. He didn't want something that looked obviously fake. On the other hand, when he thought about it, most beards he saw looked fake. They could easily have been pasted on with no one the wiser.

He ended up buying a dark full beard. It didn't matter if the color didn't match his hair exactly, as his hair could have been dyed. The color was close enough. He also bought a tube of spirit gum for attaching the beard to his face. It wasn't some cheap beard you could hang from your ears with plastic hooks that wouldn't fool a soul.

A middle-aged woman with sneering, withered lips took his money at the cash register.

He said nothing to her, since he didn't want her to remember him. The fewer persons that remembered him, the safer he felt from discovery.

Eager to try on his beard, he drove his Mustang back to his motel room, unpacked the beard, entered his bathroom, applied spirit gum to his face, and attached the beard, which gave him the appearance of a Hasidic rabbi, he noted as he peered at his face in the mirror over the sink. All he needed was one of those black fedoras they wore.

The beard covered his cheeks and reached his sternum.

He didn't think he looked recognizable.

Feeling more at ease now that he didn't have to worry about being ID'd, he drove to the nearest Radio Shack to buy burner phones for him and Mina. He decided to buy four, in case he had to dump any to avoid being traced. To start, he would give only one to Mina and hold onto the other three.

He bought the burner phones from a thirtyish cashier, who had a midsized black mutt on a leash sitting beside her behind the counter. He paid for the burners in cash.

Panting, its moist tongue dangling out of its mouth, the dog watched the transaction in earnest with its brown eyes. The cashier tossed the burners into a white plastic bag and handed it to Catton.

Accepting the bag with one hand, Catton scratched his cheek with the other.

The only problem with the beard was that it itched and made his face feel hot. He would just have to get used to it. Now that the insurance company would step up its investigation of his death thanks to the cops' discovery of his wife's murdered corpse, he had to be more vigilant than ever about being recognized.

It would also be wise for him to stay away from his wife's condo. However, he didn't know if he would be able to do so.

In order to get his hands on his money that she had transferred to her personal bank account he needed to know the password to access her account via the Internet. That password might be secreted somewhere inside her condo.

If he ventured to go near her condo again, he would wear the beard. He might in fact wear the beard all the time—just to play it safe, especially in light of what Mina had told him about the nosy insurance investigator Dunleavy who had pestered her about Rachel.

Bag in hand, Catton made a beeline for the exit. Dunleavy spelled trouble, Catton knew. He needed to get the guy off his trail.

"I rock-climb on the weekends," said the cashier.

Catton looked back at her over his shoulder. "I thought so."

Which wasn't true. She didn't look like a rock climber. If anything, she looked out of shape.

He walked out of the shop.

Chapter 25

Mina was sitting alone in the Blue Dolphin café sipping iced tea through a plastic straw when she saw the news on the TV set mounted behind the bar.

She pricked up her ears when she heard the blow-dried newscaster announce that police had discovered evidence that Rachel had been tortured before she died. He didn't go into the details.

Tortured? wondered Mina. What was he talking about?

She left the café to find out more details about the murder in the local newspaper, which she bought at a vending machine on the sidewalk at the street corner. Paper in hand, she returned to her table at the café. Newspapers always had more details than the TV news, she knew.

Spreading out the newspaper on the tabletop before her, she found the article on Rachel's murder and read it.

According to the article, police had found cigarette burn marks on Rachel's corpse and abrasions on her wrists as though she had been handcuffed or manacled.

Mina found the information disturbing. Did Catton have anything to do with the torture?

Looking up she set the paper aside. Yet another reason for her to be wary of him. Then again, maybe he had nothing to do with it. Rachel could have been burned with cigarettes by anyone. As for the abrasions on Rachel's wrists, maybe Catton had bound Rachel's hands when he stabbed her, which was possible. All Mina knew for sure was that Rachel's hands weren't bound when she was wrapped in the blanket—which by itself proved nothing. But, come to think of it, she remembered seeing scratches on Rachel's wrist as it popped out from the blanket on the dock and scared the bejesus out of her.

It wasn't like there was much she could do about it, she decided. She had to stay with Catton because he saw her stab his wife to death. He could report her as a murderer to the cops. She could say Catton forced her into it, but she doubted the cops would believe her.

No, she better stay with Catton, she decided, even though she was feeling more and more uneasy about him.

Glancing at her wristwatch she realized it was time for her to meet Catton at the Oyster several blocks away.

Chapter 26

Mina walked into the Oyster saloon and claimed a table near the window. A stuffed seahorse hung on the wall behind her. She figured a seahorse was more interesting than having a stuffed oyster up there.

She sat on the banquette facing the door so she could see Catton and signal to him when he entered. The aroma of fish cooking in the kitchen whetted her appetite.

Five minutes later, a bearded guy sporting sunglasses and clutching a plastic bag entered the saloon and gazed at her. Though she couldn't make out his eyes behind his tinted lenses, his steady gaze disconcerted her.

Was the guy going to hit on her? she wondered, not encouraging him by looking away from him and out the window at the wharf.

When she looked back toward the entrance, the guy was still standing there, looking like he was trying to figure out whether to approach her or not.

She wondered how to discourage him. She picked her nose. Maybe that would turn him off, she decided.

She looked out the window again for the better part of a minute then looked back toward the entrance. He was still standing there eying her.

Was he working up the courage to mack on her? she wondered with irritation. Beards didn't do anything for her. Didn't he get the message? She wasn't interested in him.

She grimaced at him to get him to go away.

To her dismay, he walked toward her.

Crap, she thought, tensing.

He veered toward the bar.

Good, she decided, glad to see him go elsewhere and slumped back in her seat at ease.

Out of the corner of her eye, she watched him order a mug of beer from the bartender. But he wasn't sitting down at the bar.

Beer mug in one hand, the plastic bag in the other, he headed back toward her table.

Was he bringing her a beer? she wondered with a combination of apprehension and disgust. He just didn't get the message.

Placing the mug on her tabletop, he sat across from her on the banquette.

"I'm waiting for someone," she told him. "That's his seat you're taking."

"Who are you waiting for?"

"That's none of your business."

"I think it is."

She was about to snap at him when she realized his voice sounded familiar.

"If you're waiting for somebody else, I'm not gonna be happy," said the guy. "Is that why you didn't signal to me at the entrance when you first saw me?"

Now she was convinced it must be him. "I didn't know it was you with that beard on."

He nodded. "That means it's a good disguise. Are you really waiting for somebody else?"

"I didn't know it was you," said Mina, flustered. "I thought you were a stranger trying to hit on me. That's why I said that. I don't like guys in beards."

"I figured. If you're really waiting for somebody else, we got problems."

"I was waiting for you."

He took a pull on his beer, opened the plastic bag, fished out a burner phone, and handed it toward her. "This one's for you."

"Are you really gonna walk around like that?" she said.

"I don't have any choice. With Rachel dead, they're gonna start looking for me again. I know how they think." He gestured with the burner. "Now take this. This is your phone from now on. Only use this, nothing else."

Mina accepted the cell phone, unimpressed. "What's so hot about it?"

"It can't be traced to you. After you've used up the prepaid minutes in it, throw it out."

She laid it on the tabletop in front of her. "Are you that worried they're onto you?"

"We can't take any chances. I have to stay off the grid at all costs. From now on, we communicate with these phones," he said, dredging out another burner from the bag and showing it to her.

"Whatever."

"I'm serious."

"OK, OK. Don't have a cow."

"Unless you want to be busted for murder," he said, stiffening.

"I said OK."

"What's wrong?"

"I don't like your disguise," she said evasively. "You look like an old geezer that sits in the park and has pigeons crawling all over him. Like you've got pigeon turds splattered all over your clothes. Yucky."

Catton chuckled. "Good. If even you can't recognize me, nobody else can." He searched her face. "But there's more to it than that, isn't there?"

She debated whether she should tell him. The news report was nagging at her. She decided to go ahead.

Chapter 27

"The paper said Rachel had cigarette burn marks on her body and had been tortured," she said, wondering how he'd react.

"Ah. I can see how that would bum you out."

"What happened to her?"

"I dunno. It's news to me. I wonder what the hell's going on."

"You don't know anything about it?" she said, mystified.

"No. Maybe she's got a new boyfriend who's into S and M."

"It's sick."

"He could mean trouble if we ever meet up with him."

"You never saw burn marks on her body?"

"Nope."

Catton gulped his beer.

She didn't like that beard he was wearing. It prevented her from seeing his mouth and concealed his facial expressions. It made him more difficult to read.

"What about the torture the papers are talking about?" she said.

"They're speculating that it was torture. Maybe she got burned in a fire. How can they know for sure she was tortured?"

"Why would they speculate?"

"Maybe they're trying to draw the killer out by spreading fake news to incite him. Speculation is fake news."

"To incite him?" she said, not understanding.

"To get him to reveal himself."

Mina had her doubts about his explanation. "I've been meaning to ask you, how did you get Rachel to give you her ATM PIN?"

"I asked her for it."

"And she gave it to you just like that?"

"Yep. Why wouldn't she? I'm her husband." He wiped beer foam from his mouth and beard with the back of his hand. "Husbands and wives do that sort of thing. I guess you've never been married."

Mina held her head down in contemplation. "No."

"Why are you asking me all these questions?"

Mina raised her face and confronted him. "The cops think we tortured her before killing her. That'll be bad for us when they catch us."

"They're not gonna catch us."

"I'm worried. It feels like they're closing in on us. What if we left evidence on her body?"

"We didn't. I made sure of it. As long as you do as a I say, they're not gonna catch us."

Mina drummed a tattoo with her fingers on the tabletop. "What if the cops know more than they're saying? All the technology they have nowadays, they could already know we did it."

"You watch too many cop shows on TV. *CSI* whatever. They got nothing. How are they gonna find the murder weapon when it's at the bottom of the ocean? Without that they got bupkis."

"What if we left our DNA on the body without knowing it?"

"Even if we did, the seawater rinsed it off. Don't forget she was at the bottom of the ocean engulfed by constantly moving water. It's like a giant washing machine down there. You worry too much."

"A tiny hair from your arm left on her body could give us away."

"Or from your arm."

"Exactly."

"I'm telling you, the ocean washed her clean. The cops got zilch. Now let it die."

Mina wasn't convinced. She wished she could work up the nerve to walk out on him. But their complicity in murder bound them together like handcuffs.

"We need to be careful, is all I'm saying," she said.

"Granted. That's why I bought these burner phones for us."

She felt his gaze probing her face.

"Have you been talking to anyone?" he said.

Palms clammy, she felt her heartbeat ramping up. How could he know she had met with Dunleavy? she wondered. There was no way he could know. Had he been watching them without her being aware of it? That would be the only way he could know. She hadn't been paying attention to anybody in a beard as she had been talking to Dunleavy at the Blue Dolphin. Had Catton seen her and Dunleavy together there?

"No," she said.

"Keep it that way. The fewer people you see, the better. The same goes for me. For our own good, we can't let anybody get close to us."

"I don't know if I can live like that."

"It's just until we can get my money out of her checking account. Then we can split, and nobody'll ever find us."

Mina heaved a sigh. "I guess we don't have a choice."

"We need to go back to her condo and find her bank account password."

"We already tried that."

"It's not an option. We have to go back. We need that password."

"What if the cops are staking the condo out?"

"It won't matter. They won't recognize you."

"There must be another way."

"Everything's gonna work out fine. You'll see."

He knocked back his beer, feeling smug.

99

She peered out the window at the wharf and the bobbing boats thrusting their masts at the cloudless blue sky and wished she had never met him that fateful night. If she could only go back in time and choose a different path . . .

But she couldn't. This was her life, and she had to live it.

Not only did she have to worry about the cops, she had to figure out how to keep this wife killer from turning on her.

"We must be in love," he said, eying her with a smile.

"What?" she said in astonishment.

"Two people inextricably twined. Two people whose lives depend on each other. Two people who can't live without each other. Isn't that love? It's not that silly stuff they sing about in love songs. That's got nothing to do with it. This is it. This is love."

Everything was becoming worse by the second, decided Mina, not knowing what to say. She didn't want to encourage him. On the other hand, she didn't want to defy him, since she knew he was capable of violence. His wife's groaning in extremis as she lay in the blanket was etched into Mina's memory.

Murder, murder, murder . . . There was that word again, pelting her mind.

Mina twisted in her seat, feeling hot and uncomfortable.

Chapter 28

Catton stood up to leave.

"I need to get gas," he said. "I'll be right back."

He still didn't trust Mina, he decided, striding out of the saloon onto the sidewalk under the blazing sun that poured down on him. He didn't know what she was up to, but he had the feeling she was up to something. He needed to exert more control over her so she wouldn't try to double-cross him.

Thanks to all she knew about him she was his Achilles heel. And yet he needed her to act for him, since he had to remain off the grid or risk exposure.

He located his Mustang parked in front of a meter and climbed into the driver's seat. Firing the ignition, putting the car in gear, and pulling away from the curb, he checked the rearview mirror and picked up on a car behind him pulling out at the same time.

Maybe it was a coincidence, but, concerned he was being tailed, he wanted to make sure.

He drove around the block, periodically glancing at the rearview mirror to check on the other car, a Dodge Challenger.

The car was still following him, he noticed with discomfiture. He found it unlikely that the other car would be circling the block like him—unless it was following him.

Flooring the gas pedal he veered around the next corner, tires screeching and smoking. He had to ease up on the gas since the speed limit was 30 mph in this neighborhood.

He made for Main Street where he could go faster.

Out of the corner of his eye he consulted the rearview mirror. Sure enough, farther back, the car was still headed in his direction.

Whoever it was must be following him, decided Catton. He couldn't discern the driver's face because the guy had his windshield's sun visor flipped down in front of him.

A plainclothes cop? wondered Catton.

But how could the cops have tumbled to him? There was no reason for them to suspect he was in the area. He was officially dead, as far as they were concerned.

Then who was it?

Catton checked out his speedometer. The last thing he wanted was to get busted for speeding.

He slowed down. The guy in the mirror was still following him and was closing ground, unconcerned about breaking the speed limit, his eight-cylinder engine churning. Of course, if the guy was a cop, he could break the speed limit any time he wanted. But as a plainclothes cop he was driving an unmarked car—which would draw the attention of uniformed cops if he was speeding.

Catton had no idea if the guy was a cop. He just wanted him off his tail. There was no way the cops could know he was here, he decided.

Somebody else . . .

Catton hung a hard right onto Lincoln Boulevard, sped up. He could go faster here, but so could the other guy.

Catton had to lose him. He decided he wasn't going to lose him by staying on the same road. The situation called for evasive maneuvering. He would need to keep turning corners until he ditched the Challenger.

He hugged another right, tires screeching, drawing attention from pedestrians. Another right. Then another. Until he was back on Lincoln and headed toward LAX in Inglewood.

A deafening garbage truck was emptying a Dumpster into its cargo area on his right.

Catton powered up his passenger window to help drown out the ruckus. He turned on the car radio.

There was no way the cops could know he was here, he decided. He refused to believe it was them. Had Mina involved somebody else in their arrangement? Was she siccing some guy on him? She wouldn't dare. He had too much leverage on her. She would be crazy to involve somebody else. Did she have a boyfriend? he wondered.

Catton checked the rearview mirror. He didn't want to drive all the way down to the airport. But he had to shake the tail. He didn't see the Challenger in the rearview mirror.

Catton pulled into a Ralph's supermarket parking lot and slotted his car.

He fished his burner out of his trouser pocket and rang Mina, all the while watching Lincoln for any sign of the tail.

A street sweeper thundered by, its whirling brushes spewing up clouds of dirt onto the sidewalk, drove around an illegally parked SUV and then back to the curb, where it kicked up more dirt.

Mina answered on the third ring.

"Get out of there," he said. "Make sure nobody's following you."

"What's the matter?" she said.

"Somebody may be watching that saloon."

He terminated the call.

He needed gas.

Chapter 29

Mina woke up the next morning naked on her back in her motel bed, spread-eagled, her arms manacled to the headboard, her ankles bound to the bed legs. The drapes were drawn in the dim-lit room.

She tried to pull her hands out of the manacles, without success. She kicked her legs and tried to free them, with the same result.

Terrified, she wondered what was happening.

She didn't see anybody in the room.

She was tempted to scream for help, but she didn't want to draw the attention of the cops. She had too much to hide to want to talk to them.

Catton walked out of the bathroom and into her sight. Dressed in only his briefs, he was smoking a cigarette and was carrying something in his hand.

"I don't want you to scream," he said, approaching her.

"I won't," she gasped through a dry throat. "What—"

Catton stuffed a pair of balled-up black cotton socks, the object he had been holding in his hand, into her mouth to gag her.

"Just a precaution," he said. "This is gonna hurt. I can't afford to have you scream."

Mina squirmed in fear. What was he going to do to her? she wondered, panic-stricken. It was bad enough being manacled to the bed buck naked.

She didn't have to wait long to find out.

Her worst suspicions about him were coming true, she realized in horror.

Catton withdrew the smoking cigarette from his lips and moved the burning tip toward her belly just above the navel.

"I don't want you talking to anyone," he said. "Do you understand?"

She nodded her head, frantically.

"I don't think you do," he said, lowering the burning cigarette toward her flesh.

The cigarette was so close to her stomach she could feel the warmth of its burning tip. She shivered with fear, her eyes bugging out.

She nodded so hard this time it hurt her neck, trying to convince him she understood.

He didn't care. He kept lowering the cigarette toward her flesh.

No, she wanted to scream at him.

She felt agonizing pain as the glowing orange cigarette tip seared her skin. She smelled the nauseating reek of burning flesh and wanted to retch. The gag cut off the scream in her throat. Feeling like she was suffocating she shut her eyes, willing it all to go away.

She saw him pull down his briefs and start to masturbate with his other hand, an intense gleam in his eyes.

She didn't know how much longer she could stand the pain of the cigarette burning through her flesh.

In agony, she heard herself make animal moans in her throat, which would have turned into screams had they been able to leave her mouth.

"I don't want to come now," he said, yanking up his briefs. "I have work to do."

The pain in her stomach eased as he pulled the cigarette away from her burned flesh.

"I mean business," he said, standing over her. "Don't talk to anyone, not even your friends."

Friends, she thought. *What friends?*

Eyes watering, she nodded. She felt so helpless she would agree to anything. Could he possibly know she had contacted Dunleavy? she wondered. She didn't see how, unless Dunleavy had contacted him. But how would Dunleavy know where to find him? Maybe Dunleavy had stood outside and watched the restaurant after he left her after their talk and spotted Catton.

Mina didn't know. All she knew was Catton was psychotic and capable of anything, including torture. Horrified, she wondered if he was going to rape her. Maybe he already had. He must have used something to dope her, or how else could she have ended up handcuffed to her bed like this? She had no memory of what had happened last night or how she had gotten here in her room.

"Do you understand?" he said, looming above her, smoking cigarette in hand.

How many times did she have to nod? she wondered. If he wanted her to talk, why didn't he take the gag out of her mouth?

"I can do anything I want to you," he said. *"Do you understand? We can't live without each other. We are in love."*

I can do anything I want to you, she thought. That was the sickest description of love she had ever heard, wishing he would let her go. What more did he want?

"I need you," he said. "I can't have you betraying me."

She lay there on the bed, limp, knowing that struggling to free herself was futile.

He walked over to the bureau and stubbed out his cigarette in the round cut-glass ashtray on top of it.

He returned to the bed and pulled the gag out of her mouth.

She felt like she could breathe now. She gasped for breath.

"Somebody was following me," he said by way of explanation, the saliva-soaked balled-up socks in his hand.

"I don't know anything about it," she managed to say, still apprehensive, the taste of the cotton socks lingering in her mouth.

"You didn't tell anyone about me?"

"No."

"Then who would be following me?"

"Maybe they weren't following you."

"You don't know anything about it?"

"No."

"We make a good couple, you know?" he said, ogling her supine body.

She didn't know how to answer that. She didn't want to encourage him, but she didn't want to provoke him into torturing her again either.

Consternated, she said nothing, waiting for what he would do next, hoping it couldn't be any worse.

"I put something in your drink last night, in case you're wondering," he said. "A roofie."

She didn't answer. She just looked at him.

"Can I trust you now?" he said.

"Yes."

He disappeared into the bathroom.

When he reappeared he was fully clothed.

Key in hand, he unlocked her handcuffs then untied the ropes that bound her ankles.

Sitting up in bed, Mina massaged her chafed wrists. She inspected the burn mark on her stomach, which was still smarting.

"You can put ice on that," he said, and left.

Chapter 30

An empty wine glass in his hand, Dunleavy was standing in his shorts on his motel balcony overlooking the ocean, which stretched to the sky on the horizon in invincible majesty. A few drinks in him, Dunleavy felt invincible, too.

He was starting to suspect an insurance swindle after he found out that Rachel Catton had been murdered. There were too many coincidences for him to believe everything was on the up and up with Gage Catton.

Consider the facts. Catton mysteriously disappeared at sea, his corpse never discovered. His wife collected on his life insurance policy. Then his wife was murdered. How could Dunleavy not believe that the two deaths were related somehow? Even though he had no direct proof of an insurance scam, the circumstantial evidence was too glaring to ignore.

And who was that guy hanging around with Mina, who said she was Rachel's friend and wanted to talk to Dunleavy about something but was afraid to for some reason?

Dunleavy had driven his Challenger in pursuit of Mina's friend but lost him after the guy made him. The guy obviously didn't want to be followed. But why not, unless he had something to hide?

Gage Catton's case had *hinky* written all over it.

Dunleavy didn't want to go to the cops with his suspicions, though. He had no evidence to back him up.

He paced around the balcony, which was big enough to be a patio. He figured there was a better way to handle this than going to the cops.

In any case, he believed he was a couple steps ahead of them, and he believed he was getting closer to Mina. He even believed she would open up to him, once he earned her confidence. He had been almost there the last time he met her, he decided. One more meet with her might be enough to do the trick.

He was convinced Mina knew more about Rachel's murder than she had told him so far. Maybe when she felt the cops closing in on her, she might reach out to him.

He didn't want to come on too hard with her or she might take a powder. He had to let her come to him lest he lose her. It was like playing a fish. You had to give it enough slack before you reeled it in, or it would break free.

On the other hand, he didn't want to take too long reeling her in because he wanted to beat the cops to the punch.

He spat over the balcony parapet into the street below, not caring if the spittle hit a passing vehicle.

For him it was a waiting game now, and waiting was the hardest part in this racket. He would just have to wait for her to call him.

And she *would* call him again, he was sure of it.

Meanwhile, he would help himself to another drink of cabernet.

Chapter 31

Mina was terrified of Catton. After their recent torture session, she didn't know what he might try next. Murdering her was a distinct possibility. Torture was but one remove from murder, as she saw it.

In her motel room she tried to figure out what to do, as she sat on her bed cross-legged in her bra and panties and applied a swab of alcohol to the burn mark on her belly. It was an ugly-looking wound, and she didn't want it to become infected.

She needed some way to defend herself from him without having to resort to going to the cops. Her frantic thoughts lit on Dunleavy again. She had backed out of telling him too much during their last meet because she was scared he might tell the cops, who would bust her and Catton.

But could she trust Dunleavy any more than she could the cops? she wondered. She thought maybe she could. She sensed he was attracted to her, which could work in her favor.

She didn't see that she had much choice. Catton was an off-the-wall sadistic maniac. There was no way she could trust him. As she saw it, she stood a better chance with Dunleavy, even though she hardly knew him. For that matter, she hardly knew either of them.

Her only other option was to enlist the aid of somebody else. But nobody she knew could get her out of this kind of a jam. Dunleavy was used to dealing with criminals like Catton. She opted to go with Dunleavy. He would know what to do.

She had the goods on Catton. She just didn't know how best to employ them. A guy like Dunleavy should know, she reasoned.

She approached the door to the hall and peeked out the peephole to make sure Catton was gone. She didn't see anyone.

She retrieved her personal cell phone and Dunleavy's business card from her clutch and, satisfied that Catton wasn't in earshot, punched out Dunleavy's number.

Listening to the phone ring she angled across the room to the curtains and parted them in the middle with her hand to peer out the window to see if Catton was anywhere in sight in the parking lot below. Not seeing him she withdrew her hand from the curtains and let them draw shut.

Dunleavy answered on the fourth ring.

"I want to talk to you," she said, cell to her ear. She held her voice down, afraid lest Catton might appear at her door and listen in.

"Is this Mina?" said Dunleavy.

"Yeah."

"What do you have?"

"There's something I didn't tell you."

"Shoot."

"I'd rather not say it over the phone."

"Then where?"

"At a British pub called the Guy Fawkes."

She knew it was within walking distance of her motel. She wouldn't have to drive Catton's Mustang or take Uber to get there. She could walk the six blocks. The exercise would do her good.

"Is your intel gonna help my investigation?" he said.

"It will."

"OK. I'll meet you when?"

"Can you get there in an hour?"

Dunleavy paused. "No sweat."

"See you then."

Mina terminated the call.

She decided to leave her room now. She didn't want Catton coming over here and preventing her from going out. It wouldn't take her an hour to get to the Guy Fawkes, but in the meantime she could sit on a park bench, soak up the sun for a while, then head over there.

She stole toward her door, willing the floor under the carpet not to creak, and reached the peephole, which she peered through again into the corridor in search of Catton, who was nowhere in sight.

She opened the door, locked it behind her, let it swing shut, and, heart beating up a storm, edged into the hall, on the alert for Catton's presence. No sign of him. Deciding not to take the elevator to avoid running into Catton, who might be coming up from the lobby, she struck out for the stairwell at the end of the hall.

In order to reach the stairwell she had to pass Catton's motel room door. There was no other way she could get there.

Creeping toward his door she wished she could silence her thumping heart, which was kicking up a frenzy. Its rataplan sounded so loud she thought Catton might hear it as she passed in front of his closed door.

As she walked directly in front of his door, it burst open, and Catton stalked into the hallway.

"Where are you going?" he demanded.

She had to think fast.

"I need to go out," she said, hoping her vagueness would be of no interest to him.

He wasn't having any of it. "Out for what?"

Her mind turned over multiple possibilities in split seconds.

"For Neosporin for my burn," she said, grimacing. "I think it might be infected."

"I doubt it."

"How can you be so sure?"

"Ever hear of cauterization? That's what I did to you with the burning cigarette. Cauterization prevents infection. They used to cauterize wounds back in the Middle Ages."

"I don't know anything about that. All I know is it hurts. I want to put antibiotic on it."

Catton shrugged. "You worry too much. It's not infected."

She decided to bluff her way past him.

"Then why's it hurt so much?" she said, walking by him, trying to conceal her fear, which was raging through her body like a California brush fire on a parched day. "You're the one that worries too much."

"What do you mean?" he said, scowling.

"What can I do to you? We've got a secret. I can't hurt you without hurting myself."

His smile didn't reach his eyes, which remained dark. "I'm glad you remembered."

"I have to go now."

"Then why are you going the wrong way? The elevator's the other way."

She hadn't expected to meet him here. She had to come up with an explanation. Adrenaline surging through her, her mind kicked into action.

"I need the exercise, so I'm taking the stairs," she said. "I'm getting too fat."

Catton snickered.

She had to keep going, she told herself as she edged past him. She couldn't let him bully her into submitting to his will. Feeling his eyes on her she tried not to cringe. She didn't want to appear intimidated. Displaying her fear would stoke his sadism, she knew.

If she could just keep going without passing out—

"You'll need an ocean of Neosporin if I find out you're bitching me," he said.

It looked to her like he was thinking about accompanying her as he watched her pass, in which case she'd have to call off her meet with Dunleavy. If she did that, Dunleavy might bail, and she wouldn't have anyone left to ask for help.

113

Palms sweaty, she kept walking, wondering if he could see her sweating. She held her palms out of his line of sight.

She was almost at the stairwell. She didn't hear him say anything. More important, she didn't hear him walking after her, either.

She shoved the crash bar on the metal fire door and entered the stairwell, without looking back at him, trying to appear nonchalant.

When the door swung to behind her, she breathed a pent-up sigh of relief and hastened down the staircase.

Chapter 32

The Guy Fawkes British pub had an interesting décor with fagots for bonfires suspended from the dark blue walls, Mina decided as she entered the bat-cave dimness of the lobby, wondering if she had gotten here ahead of Dunleavy.

When she had left the park she had been sitting in, she had fitfully checked to see if Catton wasn't lurking behind her, even doubling back a few times to make sure. As best she could determine, he wasn't, unless he was some kind of Jack Griffin, the Invisible Man.

After she left the brilliant sunshine to enter the pub, her eyes had to adjust to the indigo gloom.

She scanned the interior, casting around for Dunleavy. She didn't spot his pink face at the bar or at any of the tables or banquettes.

She selected a sequestered booth to sit at, ordered a beer, and waited for him.

Ten-odd minutes later, he materialized in the doorway, his body highlighted by the blinding sunlight behind him. She didn't know if it was him at first because she couldn't make out his features, but he had the right build, according to her recollection.

When the door closed and her eyes adjusted to the dimness, she got a better look at his face. His complexion appeared ruddier than usual, she decided, perhaps because he had recently spent time out in the sun. He was wearing khaki Bermudas with his espadrilles on this occasion.

She flicked a brief wave to him.

He came over and sat across from her.

He signaled to the waitress, a big-boned thirtyish woman with white hair piled on her head, and she approached, humming a pop tune that Mina didn't recognize.

"A Stella," said Dunleavy.

The waitress retreated.

"What have you got?" Dunleavy asked Mina.

Now that he was sitting across from her eye to eye, she felt a lump in her throat. She had reservations about telling him. After all, the information could land her in prison.

She extended her leg under the table and, locating his foot, kicked it.

He shifted in his seat.

"Oh," she said, a coy smile on her lips.

The waitress returned with Dunleavy's Stella, set the mug before him, and left.

"OK," he said. "Let me have it."

"I need your help," said Mina.

"I don't understand."

"If I give you this information, I'm gonna need your help."

"I still don't get it," he said, hoisted his beer to his lips, and took a pull. "I don't see how I can help you."

"I'm in a situation." She kicked his foot again under the table and moistened her lips.

He looked thoughtful. "Yeah, OK. I'll help you. Let's hear it."

"I know where Catton is."

Beer mug half raised in his hand, he stared at her. "His body, you mean?"

"Yeah, his body."

"Wait a minute. As in 'dead' body?"

"No. As in 'living' body."

Dunleavy set his beer mug down on the tabletop, eyes intent. "He's alive?"

"Alive and well."

Dunleavy thought about it. "How can you be sure it's him? Do you know what he looks like? He's supposed to be dead."

"He told me."

116

Dunleavy fished his wallet out of his shorts, pulled a photo out of it, and flashed the photo in front of her eyes. "That the man you saw?"

Mina cast a glance at the photo. "Yep."

Dunleavy replaced the photo in his wallet and pocketed the wallet.

"You realize what you're saying?" he said.

"I do."

"If he's alive, it means he's guilty of defrauding his life insurance company. He faked his death to collect on it. The cops'll wanna hear about this."

"This is between you and me."

"Come again?"

Mina struggled to figure out a way to say this. "Catton and me have a relationship."

"A romantic relationship?" he said, confused.

"No." She didn't want to explain about their collusion in Rachel's murder. That would be telling him too much. "Isn't there a better way to handle this than to go to the cops?"

He shook his head. "Call me stupid. I don't get your drift."

Mina marshaled her thoughts. She decided to take the risk and plunge ahead, calling a spade a spade.

"You can make money out of this," she said.

Dunleavy sat back on the banquette, letting her words sink in.

Bryan Cassiday

Chapter 33

"Are you saying what I think you're saying?" Dunleavy said at length.

Mina kept her voice low, even though she didn't see any customers sitting near them. "With the insurance payout in our hands we could pay you a lot more money than the insurance agency's paying you."

"You *do* know that what you're suggesting is illegal?"

"Look, it would take you twenty years or more in your line of work to make what we're offering you. We can give you that money now, and you can invest it in the stock market and live off the interest."

"Is Catton in on this offer you're making me?"

She looked down at the tabletop. "Not yet."

"What makes you think he'll go along with this deal?"

"He'll have to, now that you know he's alive."

Nodding, Dunleavy hiked his eyebrows. "You got a point."

She kicked his foot under the table again and unleashed another coy smile his way.

"It's in his best interest to go along with us," she said.

"He's not gonna like this, though. I can guarantee you that. There's no way he's gonna want to split his take three ways."

"What do you mean?"

"We're all gonna get equal parts of the pie. How can he like that?"

Mina took his words in with concern. "I didn't say we're all getting the same cut."

"You really think I'm gonna settle for less?"

"I was gonna offer you 20 percent of the total."

Dunleavy snickered. "I can give you an answer right away, then. No."

118

"All right, all right. We'll all get equal slices of the pie."

"And you know Catton will go along with this how?"

"He won't have a choice. He knows you'll snitch to the cops about his being alive if there's no deal between the three of us."

He idly spun his mug around on the tabletop. "I don't know what gives you the idea I'm a criminal wannabe."

"What crime are you committing? You're just not telling the cops that you know Catton's alive. What's illegal about that?"

"Withholding evidence of a crime isn't illegal?"

"How will they ever find out that you know about Catton's fraud? You're sure not gonna tell them. And I'm not."

"*You* might if you could save your own neck by ratting me out."

"Ratting you out would implicate me in Catton's fraud."

He mulled over her offer some more. "Knowingly accepting stolen money is a crime in California."

"You could say you didn't know it was stolen."

Dunleavy knocked back his beer. Watching her he sat speechlessly.

"You said you weren't a cop," she said.

"I'm not."

"What about an ex-cop?"

"Nope."

"Then what's the problem? Why don't you want in on this deal?"

He hung fire, turning over his response. "I'm not convinced Catton's gonna go along with enlisting me in his gang."

"I'll talk him into it."

"It's not gonna be that simple. He has a lot of dough to lose if I'm in."

"The alternate option for him is worse."

119

"That I go to the cops and tell them he's alive?"

She nodded.

"He isn't gonna like you for telling me about his faked death," he said.

Dunleavy was right on that score, Mina knew. Which was why she wasn't going to tell Catton she was the one that had ratted him out to Dunleavy.

"There's nothing he can do about it now," she said.

Dunleavy stared at her a long time.

She squirmed in discomfort, breaking into a sweat under the intensity of his gaze.

"What?" she said.

"Did he kill Rachel?"

"No."

She had to lie. She didn't want to go into Rachel's murder at this time. She saw no percentage in telling Dunleavy the murderer's identity, not yet anyway. After all, she was complicit in the murder. It was a can of worms better left unopened. If opened, it would give too much leverage to Dunleavy. He would be able to hold a murder charge over her and Catton's heads.

"He has a lot to gain with her out of the way," he said. "He wouldn't have to split the insurance payout with her."

"Maybe she had a lover's quarrel with her boyfriend who decided to get back at her."

"You mean, she was seeing someone else, even though she was married?"

"Her husband was officially considered dead. Why wouldn't she be seeing another guy?"

"Then she didn't know he was still alive? Is that what you're saying?"

"How do I know what she knew?"

"It's hard to believe she wasn't in on the fraud scheme from the get-go. After all, she was the beneficiary of all the insurance money after her husband's fake death."

"What difference does it make if she was in on it?"

"If she *was* in on it, her husband wouldn't want her fooling around with another guy. And if he caught her doing that, it could spell murder, as in *her* murder."

"Catton didn't tell me Rachel was fooling around."

"Why would he want to tell you something personal like that?"

"I told you, we have a relationship. A close relationship." Too close, she decided. Shackled together by murder. *Murder, murder—shut up.* "That doesn't mean she wasn't fooling around. It just means, he didn't know about it."

"Anything's possible, I guess," he said, but he didn't look like he believed it.

"Does that mean you're in," she said, sliding her fingers up and down the side of her beer mug.

He stood up. "I need to think this over."

She looked up at him. "Why? You're not doing anything illegal by joining us."

He leaned forward, putting the knuckles of his fists on the tabletop. "I'd be scamming the insurance company as an accomplice of you guys."

"Nobody could ever prove it."

"That's what you say," he said, straightening up.

"Whatever you do, don't tell Catton about this meeting we had."

Mina was scared to death what Catton would do if he found out about her effort to enlist Dunleavy in their scam. She knew with a hundred percent certainty that Catton wouldn't want to split the insurance payout with Dunleavy. She also knew Catton was violent, and he wouldn't like it at all if he cottoned to her trying to suborn Dunleavy.

Dunleavy said nothing.

He retreated toward the door.

Mina couldn't tell if he was in on the deal or not. She needed him to say yes. If he wasn't in, he might rat Catton out to the cops. And then Catton would rat her out to those same cops, implicating her in Rachel's murder.

Why couldn't the idiot just say yes? she wondered. Didn't he want to lay his hands on all that cash? She didn't see him as the self-righteous type that believed money was the root of all evil. Couldn't he see he was passing up the opportunity of a lifetime if he didn't agree to join the scam? What if she had made a mistake sizing him up? What if he *was* the self-righteous type that wouldn't take a bribe no matter how large and attractive it was?

She fretted.

She heard her stomach gurgle thanks to her worrying. Apprehension always had that effect on her digestion. The trouble was, now she had made herself vulnerable on two fronts, from an attack by Catton on one front and by Dunleavy on the other.

Still, she didn't regret her decision to enlist Dunleavy's aid. She needed someone to help her fight off the psychopath Catton. She didn't know a better choice than Dunleavy.

Why couldn't anything ever be easy? she wondered. Why didn't the idiot Dunleavy join them right off the bat? He should be chafing at the bit at her offer of easy money.

What if he ratted her out to Catton? she wondered. But why would he? What possible good did it do Dunleavy to snitch to Catton about her offer to him?

All this thinking was bumming her out.

She slumped back in her seat. She would just have to wait for Dunleavy to make his next move. Either he would join them or go to the cops and rat out Catton.

She hoped she didn't have to wait long. Her nerves were already frayed. And now she had to go back to Catton, who might become suspicious if she overextended her stay away from him.

It wasn't too late for her to take off on her own, she knew, but now that Dunleavy knew about Catton's scam, she had to worry about him as well as Catton coming after her. She doubted that striking out on her own was a viable option anymore—if it had ever been in the first place.

But if Catton tried to kill her, she *would* bug out on her own, no matter how many people came after her.

Chapter 34

Mina went to the nearest CVS drugstore to buy
Neosporin. She got a package of Advil as well for her
headache.

When she returned to the motel, Catton was all smiles and
politeness. It was like he was a different person, she decided.
The sadistic maniac with a smoking cigarette and a gag in his
hands had vanished. In his place was the guy she could trust.
The smooth-talking guy that had convinced her to stab his
wife to death.

He had seen her enter the lobby where he had been sitting
on a sofa next to a small table that held a planter containing a
spider plant with helter-skelter leaves.

With misgivings she wondered if he had been sitting there
waiting for her return, which might indicate he didn't trust her.

In any case, he seemed pleased to see her, so she felt more
relaxed in his presence this time.

Was it all an act with him here in the lobby? she
wondered. But which personality was the act? Which was the
real Catton?

Mina didn't want to think about it.

"Did you find some aspirin?" he said, standing up to greet
her with a smile.

"Neosporin," she said. "Yes."

"Good."

She wished he'd ditch the beard. It looked like he had
walked out of a Matthew Brady Civil War daguerreotype.
Bearded guys turned her off. They reminded her of guys that
belonged to a different era or of lice-infested vagrants.

The better part of a minute later, she was shocked to see
Dunleavy enter the lobby. He must have followed her without
her noticing, she decided.

Did it mean he was going to join them or was he going to confront Catton? she wondered, disconcerted. Or worse, was he going to bust Catton? She wished Dunleavy had told her in advance he was coming with her. The fact he hadn't unsettled her. She didn't like surprises, especially if they turned out to be nasty. And this one could turn out to be a doozy.

He whisked past her without acknowledging her and approached Catton.

Catton looked bewildered as Dunleavy stood in front of him and greeted him.

"I believe you're the man I'm looking for," said Dunleavy.

Mina was grateful Dunleavy had ignored her. She didn't want Catton to suspect she had told Dunleavy where to find him. She had already told Catton about meeting Dunleavy at Rachel's condo, but not that she had told Dunleavy where to find him.

"I doubt it," said Catton, not recognizing Dunleavy.

"Yeah, it's you," said Dunleavy, searching Catton's face. "Even with the beard I recognize you."

"I have no idea who you are."

"We got a problem, though."

"The problem is you. I don't know you, and you don't know me."

What game was Dunleavy playing? wondered Mina. If he came here to bust Catton, where were the cops? The fact that he had come alone encouraged her. Maybe he wanted to cut a deal. But then why didn't he tell her he was coming?

She didn't trust him.

"That's not the problem," said Dunleavy. "The problem is, you're supposed to be dead."

If Catton was surprised or worried he had been discovered, he didn't let on.

"Which just proves you got the wrong guy," he said. "As you can see, I'm not dead."

125

"I think we should continue this conversation in private. What do you say?"

"I don't see why. You're obviously mistaken about me."

"Does that mean no?"

Catton didn't answer right away. He wanted to know what Dunleavy's angle was, but he didn't want to make a scene in the motel lobby and draw the attention of guests.

"We've never met each other," he said. "I don't understand what we need to talk about in private."

Dunleavy leaned closer to Catton and lowered his voice. "Maybe I should tell the cops you're here."

"Look, I don't know who you are or who you think I am, but maybe we can clear this up in my room."

"Good idea."

Mina was glad Catton hadn't called Dunleavy's bluff about calling the cops. She didn't think Dunleavy really wanted the cops here or he would have brought them with him. She was starting to believe Dunleavy wanted to cut a deal.

"Follow me," said Catton.

He took them to the bank of elevators. The three of them took the next elevator to Catton's room.

"Do you know Mina?" said Catton, ushering them down the corridor to his room.

"I believe we've met," said Dunleavy.

"Really?"

Catton exchanged glances with Mina, who had a blank expression on her face.

"I wonder why she didn't tell me about it," said Catton.

"Maybe she did," said Dunleavy, bud didn't elaborate.

Catton thought about it, trying to figure out what was going on.

He used his key card to unlock the door, and they entered his room.

He turned on Dunleavy. "You got sixty seconds to tell me what the hell you're doing here before I kick you out."

"I don't think you want to do that, Catton," said Dunleavy.

"I don't know any Catton. My name's John Hogeboom."

Smiling, Dunleavy shook his head. "You can stop with the act."

"You've mistaken me for somebody else."

"Then throw me out." Dunleavy paused. "And then I'll get the cops."

"What's your name, and what do you want?" demanded Catton, nettled.

"I'm Randall Dunleavy."

Recognizing the name Catton cut his eyes toward Mina to verify his suspicion.

Mina nodded.

"What's your angle?" Catton asked Dunleavy.

"I'm not gonna beat around the bush. I'm an insurance investigator, and I'm investigating your alleged death."

"I don't know what you're talking about."

Dunleavy smiled knowingly. "You can drop the pretenses now, Catton."

"So you believe I'm somebody I'm not. So what's next?"

"That's up to you."

"Get on with it."

"Do you want me to report you to the cops?"

"It would be a waste of their time."

"I can call them right now," said Dunleavy, withdrawing his mobile from his trouser pocket.

Catton shook his head. "Get to the point. Why are you here?"

Gloating, Dunleavy put away his mobile. "I believe we can come to an arrangement."

"About what?"

127

"About the insurance money. We divide it between us three."

"What insurance money?"

Dunleavy sighed on account of Catton's stalling. "The money from your life insurance policy your wife received."

Chapter 35

Catton stalked to the window and gazed outside. Half a minute later he slewed around and faced Dunleavy.

"Let's suppose for sake of argument that I know what you're talking about," said Catton.

"I'm getting tired of playing games. Maybe it's time to go to the cops," said Dunleavy, turning to leave.

"How much do you want?"

Dunleavy turned back to face Catton. "Now we're talking. Even Steven. We divide it equally between the three of us."

"Out of the question. I was the one that took all of the risks. Why should you two be equal partners?"

"Because you need us to succeed."

"Succeed at what?"

"At getting the insurance money in Rachel's bank account."

"You know about Rachel?"

"I know about everything. I was investigating your case for Lion Life Insurance."

"I still don't understand what you have to offer me."

"That's simple. I won't report you to the cops or to Lion Life, if we split the money."

"I'm paying you all that money for you to keep your mouth shut?" said Catton, eyes widening.

"You don't seem to understand your situation. I can have you put behind bars for most of your life."

"You're blackmailing me."

"The word *blackmail* has such negative connotations. I prefer to call it 'cutting a deal.'"

"*That which we call a rose—*"

"Call it whatever you want, then. Are you cutting me in or not?"

Catton crossed the carpet to Dunleavy. "There's something you should know, namely that I don't have the money."

"Meaning you don't have the money *yet*."

"It's not looking good for my getting my hands on it."

"I don't understand."

"I can't put an honest claim on the money, because I'm officially listed as dead. If I reveal myself when I go to collect the cash, they'll bust me for faking my death and committing fraud."

"Then how do we do it?"

"I have to get into Rachel's bank account somehow and drain it."

"Then do it."

"I can't. I don't know the password to her online bank account."

"Well, get it."

"I'm working on it. But nobody gets any dough until that little problem gets solved."

"Then we're partners, I take it," said Dunleavy, extending his hand and smiling.

His expression unreadable, Catton stood there looking at Dunleavy for a few moments.

Mina didn't know what Catton was going to do. Hopefully, he would realize he had no choice and would agree to the deal. Otherwise, she didn't know what *she* would do. He might blame Dunleavy's presence on her and take it out on her. She dreaded the thought.

"OK," said Catton, but he didn't shake Dunleavy's hand.

Unsmiling, Dunleavy looked at his hand then dropped it. "You won't regret it."

"I better not, or you will."

"What's that supposed to mean?" said Dunleavy, taking umbrage.

"Figure it out."

"It sounded like a threat. You're not in any position to make threats against me."

"Don't get any ideas."

"I wouldn't advise leaving town unless you tell me where you're going," said Dunleavy.

He retreated to the door.

"Nobody's leaving town," said Catton, watching Dunleavy exit with an impassive face.

Chapter 36

As soon as the door shut behind Dunleavy, Catton turned to Mina to train a glare at her.

Mina was relieved Dunleavy hadn't told Catton about her offer to Dunleavy to join the scam. It made it look like Dunleavy had dreamed up the angle on his own and it left Mina in the clear—at least as far as that matter was concerned. She still had to deal with Catton, the homicidal maniac and torture-happy sadist.

"Is that the guy you ran into at Rachel's?" he said.

"Yes."

"Did you tell him about me?"

"No. Of course not," she said, feeling uncomfortably hot.

"How the hell did he know where to find us?"

"He must've followed me here."

"Why was he even tailing you in the first place?"

"I dunno."

He stared a hole in the floor. "We have to get rid of him. He can scuttle our plans."

"How do we get rid of him? He knows too much."

"I don't understand how he recognized me. He recognized me as soon as he walked into the motel lounge. How did he see through the beard so quickly?" said Catton, stroking his beard.

Mina wished he would drop the subject. She didn't want him thinking about it too long or he might dope out that she was the one that had told Dunleavy about him, which was why Dunleavy ID'd him on the spot.

"We have to cut him in or he'll go to the cops and snitch on you," said Mina.

"I know, but I don't trust that guy farther than my arm."

"If you do anything to him, he can have you put in jail."

"Not if we kill him."

Mina stared at him in stunned silence.

"That's a bad idea," she said, after she had collected her thoughts.

"It may be our only solution. He's gonna be a thorn in our side as long as he knows my true identity, even after he has his cut."

"He won't bother us after he has his cut. There'd be no reason."

"He might decide he wants more money from us. What's to stop him from blackmailing us forever?"

"He won't do that," said Mina, though she wouldn't bet on it.

As a matter of fact, she wanted Dunleavy to be a threat to Catton for as long as possible, which would take the onus off her of being the only one that knew about Catton's scam and therefore the only one that could hurt him. Now Dunleavy could hurt him just as much, meaning Catton had to worry not only about Mina but about Dunleavy as well. Both Mina and Dunleavy could put Catton in the joint.

Hopefully, that meant she could relax a bit in Catton's presence. Maybe he wouldn't try another torture session on her. On the other hand, the maniac was capable of anything, as far as she was concerned.

The more protection she had against him, the better.

Catton poured himself a drink from a bottle of scotch at the minibar. He took a pull and smacked his lips.

"Do you think he was drunk?" he said.

"No."

"I smelled booze on his breath. He must've needed Dutch courage to confront me."

"So he's a lush. What are we gonna do?"

"We could report him to the insurance company he's working for," he said, shot glass in hand.

"Report him for what?"

"For double-crossing them."

133

"But then they would know you're still alive."

"Yeah . . . We'd have to report him for something else. Nah, it won't work. Whatever we do, he still has dirt on us and can put us away. We don't have any choice. We have to take him out."

"We can let him join us. If he's in with us, he's not gonna snitch on us."

"He might when it suits his purpose."

"But then we could snitch on him as being part of our scam."

Catton slammed down his shot glass on the bar's Formica counter with a resounding smack.

"We're gonna have to deal with him sooner or later," he said.

"We can't go around leaving dead bodies all over the place," said Mina, stalking around the room, worked up.

His answer pulled her up short and chilled her to the bone.

"Why not?" he said.

Chapter 37

He didn't look at all fazed by his answer, Mina realized. He dug out Rachel's cell phone from his trouser pocket.

"I've been thinking," he said. "Maybe we've been looking in the wrong place for Rachel's bank account password."

"What do you mean?" said Mina.

Punching out Rachel's smartphone's four-number password, he accessed her smartphone and studied the screen, determining where to search for her checking account's password. "Maybe it's a matter of hide in plain sight."

"How did you get her cell phone password, anyway?"

"It happens to be the same as her ATM PIN."

"Then maybe it's the same for her checking account."

"I already tried. It doesn't work," he said, examining the smartphone screen.

"What are you doing?"

"The password to her Internet bank account may be stored here on her phone somewhere, if I can find it."

"Why would she put it there?"

"In case she forgot it, and she carried her cell phone wherever she went—even took it to bed with her. This would be a perfect place to hide the password."

"Or she could have memorized it."

"How many passwords can you memorize, especially when everybody has hundreds of them these days?"

"She could have used the same password for everything."

"The tech experts advise against doing that. Anyway, like I said, I already tried it on her bank account, and it didn't work."

"So who listens to these so-called experts?"

"Rachel must have."

135

Catton searched various sections of Rachel's phone for her bank account password.

Starting, he almost dropped the cell phone as it came alive chiming and vibrating in his hand.

The caller ID said Private.

"Don't answer it," said Mina.

"I bet this is the same person that called at the restaurant before," said Catton. "I want to know who it is."

"One of Rachel's friends probably."

"Then why's the caller ID blocked? A friend wouldn't block their ID."

"Who knows?"

"I'm gonna answer it."

"No, don't."

But it was too late, she realized, seeing him raise the cell phone to his lips.

"Hello," he said.

There was a pause on the airwaves.

"Hello?" said the caller on speaker. "Who is this?"

"Who is *this*?"

"I'm a friend of Rachel's. What are you doing with her phone?"

"What kind of friend?"

Mina didn't know what Catton was doing. Why was he even talking to this guy in the first place? He shouldn't have answered the phone. She feared Catton was losing it. He was becoming more and more unstable.

"What kind of a question is that?" said the caller. "Why do you have her phone?"

"Friend like in *boyfriend*?"

"If you don't tell me who you are this minute, I'm going to report you to the cops."

"For what?"

"Rachel was murdered, and you have her phone. Two and two make four."

"Do you want the phone?"

Flabbergasted, Mina couldn't get her head around Catton's actions. What was he trying to do?

"Yes, I do," said the caller. "It should be turned over to the police. There might be evidence in it ID'ing the killer."

"All right. I'll give it to you. Where do you want to meet?"

Mina signaled frantically for Catton to hang up.

He turned away from her, concentrating on the phone in his hand.

"At the Pacific Dining Car on Wilshire," said the caller.

"A steak house. Great. See you in an hour."

Catton terminated the call.

"What are you doing?" said Mina, at her wit's end.

"Rachel was fooling around," said Catton heatedly. "She was two-timing me while I'm risking my neck to get the insurance money for us. The bitch."

"Are you sure?"

"Rachel was a thirty-five-year-old hottie that just got her grubby little hands on beaucoup bucks. Who wouldn't want to jump into bed with her?"

"Didn't she think you'd find out?"

"Didn't she think I'd find out she swindled me? She must've thought I'd never find her." Making a sweeping gesture with his arms Catton shook his head with a cynical grin. "Not only was she greedy, she was stupid. She had me pegged all wrong. There's no way I'm gonna let her get away scot-free with all my money."

"Think what you're doing. What if this guy brings the cops with him?"

"He won't. Not at first, anyway. He's trying to figure out who I am. Maybe he even wants a cut of the take, like Dunleavy."

"Do you think she told him you're still alive?"

"If he's her boyfriend, she might've told him. She must've told him about all the money she's got, in any case. I'm sure she told him that much. About the scam, I'm not so sure. I don't think she'd want to implicate herself in the scam."

"Then he might not know you're still alive."

"It depends on how close they were. And I'm getting the impression they were real close—like lovers. That's why his phone number's ID says Private. He didn't want anybody to know he was fooling around with her, in case somebody was watching her answer her phone."

"How will you recognize him at the restaurant?"

"I'll call him on Rachel's cell phone when I'm there and tell him where I am."

"Then he'll recognize you before you recognize him. And that'll give him an advantage."

"Not gonna happen. I'll know it's him before he knows it's me. I guarantee it."

Proud of himself, Catton stalked to the minibar and poured himself another scotch.

Mina heaved a sigh. Maybe it was for the best he was seeing the guy, she decided. The cops would bust Catton at the meet, and she'd be free of his sadistic hold on her. But then again, he'd also tell the cops she was the one that stabbed Rachel to death, and they'd come for her.

"Did you find Rachel's password on her iPhone?" she said.

"No, not yet. For all I know, she might've given her password to lover boy."

"Why would she give it to him?"

"Because he's her lover."

"But you were her husband, and she didn't even give it to you."

Catton mulled it over. "True."

"Why would she give him the password to her bank account? That would be stupid."

He took a pull on his scotch and made a face. "Just covering all the angles."

"If he has her password, he could've drained all the money out of her account by now."

"Yeah. I doubt he's got it. She had a lot of air between her ears, but not that much."

"Then why even meet with him?"

"He's gonna be a problem we're gonna have to deal with down the road. It might as well be now. I want to know how much he knows about me."

"I don't see how he's a problem."

"He may know I'm alive."

"If he does, what can you do about it?"

He ignored her question. "He might have a key to her condo, and he might be looking for her bank password just like we are. What if he finds it before us?"

"He's looking for who killed Rachel. That's what he's doing. And you're leading him right to you."

"He has to be dealt with," he said, his final word on the subject. "Anyway, you're the one that killed Rachel, not me."

Mina wanted to scream. She wished Catton was dead.

Chapter 38

Ed Bendix, a car insurance salesman who spent most of his time behind a desk, was devastated when he heard about his lover Rachel's death on the news.

He had never had much luck with women until he had met Rachel. It was like he had been looking for her all his life. He always ended up with the wrong woman, the one that was already married or the one that was a lesbian. There was always *something* getting in the way.

He was well-nigh fifty, a mere two months short of it, and it had looked like he would be a bachelor till the end of his life. And then Rachel had walked into his life. And things started working out fine.

She had told him she was recently widowed and wanted to settle down in this area away from her dead husband and her memories of him, to start a new life here. That was a month ago.

Things between her and him proceeded quickly from there. She had a joie de vivre that intoxicated him and made him want to see more of her. They had fun together. They went to the Santa Monica Pier one night and rode the Ferris wheel like they were kids again.

She also had a mysterious aura about her—like she knew something nobody else did.

And then the mystery deepened when she disappeared as abruptly as she had appeared. He couldn't find her anywhere. None of her friends knew what had happened to her.

It wasn't long before the cops found her corpse floating in the middle of the ocean, the victim of foul play.

Bendix couldn't believe it when he heard the news. Everything had seemed so perfect after he met her. Now she was gone already. It seemed so unfair. Not that he wasn't used to life being unfair at this point, but being used to it didn't inure him to it. He doubted he would ever become inured to the cruelty and unfairness of life.

So who killed her? he wondered. She never told him she had any enemies. Was it some sick psychopath that had robbed her of life for no reason at all? He read about these sickos in the papers all the time nowadays, mass murderers who killed for no reason at all, a sniper in Las Vegas who gunned down over five hundred people from his perch in a high-rise casino with an automatic rifle with a bump stock, a high-school student who machine-gunned fellow students like it was a homework assignment for some sick course on mass murder he was enrolled in . . .

Or had somebody killed Rachel for a reason? wondered Bendix. He figured that was the more likely answer. But for what reason? Did somebody hate her enough to want her dead? Or had she been mugged for a few bucks in her purse?

And who was that guy that answered her cell phone when he had called her number? Bendix wondered. Was that guy the killer? Had he murdered her and robbed her phone? But if he was the murderer, why did he agree to meet with Bendix? Wasn't the guy afraid Bendix might try to have him busted?

Maybe he was reading too much into it, decided Bendix. Maybe he was being paranoid. It could be that the guy that talked to him on the phone was a Good Samaritan that wanted to give him the phone just like he said. Or maybe the guy thought there was a reward being offered for its return.

Bendix wasn't big on Good Samaritans. How many Good Samaritans had he actually run into in his life? he wondered. Not a whole lot. Maybe one or two. But if the guy on the phone stole Rachel's mobile, why did he agree to meet with Bendix?

There was something hinky about all of this, Bendix decided, but he wasn't sure what. To play it safe, maybe he shouldn't show up at the steak house. But this guy might know something about her murder. The question was, how did he get her phone? Which wasn't the only question Bendix wanted to ask him.

This was the sole lead Bendix had uncovered so far. If he didn't follow it up, he had zilch. The cops had no leads. If they did have any, they weren't sharing them with him. He hadn't told them about his locating Rachel's phone, because he didn't think they were doing a very good job of investigating her murder. He figured he could do a better job himself.

The last time he went to the police station to see how their investigation was proceeding, they had told him they didn't have enough manpower so they had to go slow. In other words, they were getting nowhere. Either that or they didn't want to tell him anything. So why should *he* tell them anything?

He would follow this lead on his own hook.

He couldn't accept the fact that nobody cared enough about Rachel's murder to do anything about it.

While he was studying business at Berkeley, he had been too busy to think about women, and the few he did meet he didn't get along with for one reason or another. Now, he had a job, and he was still too busy. But somehow he had bumped into Rachel, and everything seemed to be going right for him.

And then, just like that, it wasn't.

He climbed into his used cream Mercedes at his apartment and headed for the Pacific Dining Car, which wasn't a long drive from here.

Chapter 39

Bendix handed his car keys over to the chain-smoking Korean valet at the restaurant and entered the leather and wood interior, which did indeed remind him of a dining car on an old train. The venerable restaurant had been around since the 1920s.

The décor was all green walls with brown wainscoting, imbuing the restaurant with a clubby ambiance that brought to mind clouds of cigar smoke lingering in the air as bald-headed middle-aged men in pricy suits chewed the fat. The banquettes along the walls were separated from the main interior by plush green drapes. The mahogany bar was polished to such brilliance that you could see your reflection in its mirrorlike surface.

So where was the guy? wondered Bendix, standing next to the bar. Was he in a booth, at a table, or at the bar? The restaurant was half-full at this hour of the day. He figured he should be looking for a man sitting alone somewhere. Everybody sitting at the bar was sitting alone with an empty stool between them, which didn't narrow down Bendix's choices in that area.

The tall, clean-cut, fortyish maître d' approached Bendix and asked him in a baritone voice where he wanted to sit. Bendix was still waiting for a sign from one of the customers indicating he was the guy that had Rachel's phone. Bendix didn't see anybody gesturing to him.

Bendix figured he must have arrived before the other guy.

"I'll sit at the bar," he told the maître d'.

"Very good, sir," said the maître d' and handed him a menu.

Bendix sat down on a leather stool. He noticed there was a large mirror on the wall behind the counter that he could check out to watch any newcomers arriving.

143

He had no idea what this guy looked like. The guy had sounded like an adult male, maybe in his thirties or forties, over the phone. Beyond that, Bendix couldn't say for any certainty. The guy may have been in his fifties or sixties, for all Bendix knew. How could you tell a guy's age from his voice alone?

How was the guy going to recognize him, for that matter? wondered Bendix. This seemed like a fool's errand. Could the call have been a practical joke? Maybe he should just leave and forget about it.

He decided to stick around a little while longer. If this was a good lead, he wanted to follow it to the end.

He surveyed the seated customers in the restaurant. Nobody was paying any attention to him. And why should they? The guy on the phone had no idea what Bendix looked like. The guy was as much in the dark on that score as was Bendix.

Well, this was the way the guy wanted to play it, decided Bendix. There was nothing Bendix could do about it but play along. Either that, or write it off as a bad idea, bug out of here this minute, and forget about it.

But Bendix wanted to know why this guy had Rachel's mobile and who he was. Bendix had the feeling he'd never find out the reason if he didn't meet with the guy right now as promised.

Bendix's cell phone vibrated in his trouser pocket. He dug out the phone and consulted it. The caller ID said Rachel.

Eager for news, he answered on the second ring.

"I'm in the bathroom," said the guy. "Walk into the men's room looking at your cell phone so I know it's you."

"Wait a second. How will I know it's you?"

The guy terminated the call before Bendix had a chance to finish his question.

Bendix wondered if he had seen the guy when he had entered and scoped out the restaurant, or was the guy already in the men's room when Bendix had entered?

Bendix would rather meet with the guy in the dining area, but he guessed the caller wanted to keep their meet secret.

Bendix cast around the dining area for the restrooms. He spotted the men's room in the back. Mobile in hand, he slid off his seat and made a beeline for it, feeling misgivings, yet eager to meet the guy and find out his name.

Bendix pushed open the wooden swinging door and entered the men's room, holding his cell phone in front of him pretending to read it.

The guy that was in the bathroom kicked a brown rubber wedge underneath the swinging door as it closed, jamming it shut then looped a piano wire around Bendix's neck from behind and commenced to garrote him. Bendix tried to insert his hand between the garrote and his neck, but it was too late. The guy was already strangling him, as Bendix's cell phone clattered to the floor, cracking its glass face.

Thrashing in the guy's grip, Bendix raised his feet and kicked the porcelain sinks beneath the mirror, thrusting the strangler back into a stall's metal door with a raucous crash. But the strangler didn't loosen the wire loop around Bendix's throat. Bendix felt warm blood streaming from his gashed neck down his throat.

He tried to scream for help, but his windpipe was being crushed, cutting off the scream in his throat. He jammed his elbows backward, trying to hit the strangler in the rib cage and dislodge the guy from his back. Bendix felt his elbows strike their target a couple of times, but they didn't do enough damage to deter the strangler, who wasn't loosening his grip. Instead, the garrote's collar grew tighter.

Struggling to breathe, Bendix felt he would pass out soon, when he heard somebody shoving against the restroom door then rapping on it three times.

145

"Five minutes," said the strangler.

"Some people," grumbled the visitor through the shut door.

"It smells bad in here."

It did indeed stink, decided Bendix, realizing he had voided his bowels.

He wanted to tell the visitor to stay, but he couldn't squeeze the words out of his injured throat. Meanwhile, he heard the newcomer's footfalls retreating into the dining area.

"Did Rachel tell you about me?" said the strangler.

"What?" Bendix managed to gasp, his face a rictus of pain.

"Did she tell you her husband was still alive?"

Rachel said her husband was dead, decided Bendix. Then who the hell was this guy trying to kill him?

Bendix didn't say anything.

"Just tell me if she did before you die," said the strangler.

Bendix couldn't think clearly. His mind was going. He felt like his head was going to burst. A balloon swelling not with air, but with blood. His blood. His head would burst any minute and spew blood all over the linoleum floor.

Seconds later, Bendix blacked out.

Chapter 40

Wearing latex surgical gloves Catton lugged Bendix's corpse into a stall and propped it in a sedentary position on the toilet. He stuffed the bloody piano wire into his trouser pocket, noticing the wire had sliced through one of his gloves and cut his palm drawing a bead of blood that nevertheless hadn't leaked out of the glove.

He felt relieved none of the blood had escaped from the glove. He didn't want to leave any of his DNA behind at the scene of the crime. The cut wasn't bleeding anymore. There was just the one bead. He shifted the glove on his hand so the tiny hole in the latex wasn't near his scratch. He couldn't afford to let any of the blood leak out of the glove.

Rachel's cell phone he wiped clean of his prints with a handkerchief and inserted into Bendix's trouser pocket. Deciding to make the killing look like a robbery, he withdrew Bendix's wallet from the same pocket and stuffed it into his own.

He knew the cops could trace her cell phone when they found out she had one, and he didn't want to be the one carrying it when they did. He had already deleted all of the information from the cell phone in case there was anything there that incriminated him.

He took one last look at the twisted corpse sitting on the toilet and smiled. Strangled while taking a crap. What a joke. He wondered if the cops would appreciate it.

He left the stall and closed its door behind him, the smile lingering on his face like a hangover.

Leaning over he removed the rubber wedge from under the restroom's swinging door and cracked the door, checking to see if anyone was standing in the hall as adrenaline coursed through his system. Nobody, he realized. The visitor had left.

Hyperalert, Catton stole into the hall, struck out for the back entrance, and exited the restaurant into an alley without anybody seeing him.

He removed his surgical gloves in the alley, thought about dumping them in the green Dumpster, and was in the process of raising the Dumpster lid with his elbow to flick the gloves into the bin, when he remembered his blood in the slit glove. He took the gloves off and stuffed them in his trouser pocket. He would get rid of them later when he was farther away from the scene of the crime.

Then he donned his sunglasses.

He had foregone the valet and had parked his car on a side street at a parking meter to avoid giving the valet an opportunity to recognize him and report him to the cops when they arrived.

Not that anybody would be able to give a good description of him since he was wearing the beard and sunglasses. Nevertheless, he didn't want the valet to know he had ever been there.

He strolled down the sidewalk like any other pedestrian. He realized with a grin that he didn't even exist. He was already dead, as far as everybody else was concerned. Gage Catton had officially died a while back. Nobody knew otherwise, except Rachel, and now she was dead. And Mina . . . he couldn't forget her. She knew he wasn't dead.

But to everybody else he was already dead. He didn't exist. He was walking through life as an invisible man. It made him feel powerful in a way, like he knew something that nobody else knew.

He had cheated death by faking it.

But then there was the downside. He was a nobody. He didn't exist because he was written off as dead. He had no life.

He liked being anonymous, though. It meant he could glide through the indifferent world without any strings attached. Like he had been reborn. He was a baby in this world, a new man. And since nobody knew about him, it meant he could do things nobody else could. The cops would never suspect a dead man of murder. He was free.

He wanted to laugh. There was something silly about it all. A dead guy was free to do whatever he wanted. It was absurd. A dead guy that was still alive. When you were dead, you could do whatever you wanted. It didn't get any more absurd than that.

A middle-aged woman bumped into him as he rounded the corner. The little white dog on the end of her leash yapped at him. She glared at him and kept walking past him, tugging her dog after her. The dog kept yapping and started fighting its leash, doing backflips, all but hanging itself on its leash trying to turn around to keep barking at him.

Not quite dead, he decided, and not invisible. He was still alive, and he had to watch his step. He was only pretending to be dead.

He reached his car and, despite his sunglasses, needed to shield his eyes from the blinding sunlight to inspect the parking meter, which he saw still had three minutes left. He didn't have to worry about getting a parking ticket at this location at this time of the day, a ticket that would have announced to the cops his presence at the murder scene.

As far as he knew, there was no tangible proof he had been here during the murder that had just taken place in the Pacific Dining Car. How could there be any tangible proof left by Gage Catton? After all, Gage Catton had shuffled off this mortal coil.

Who was that guy he had just killed, anyway? Catton wondered as he slid into his Mustang's driver's seat. He fished the guy's wallet out of his trouser pocket and flipped through it. Some guy named Ed Bendix. Catton had never heard of him. Bendix had picked the wrong guy's wife to fool around with. The son of a bitch had got what he deserved.

149

Bryan Cassiday

Catton didn't have time to think about it. He wanted to get out of here before the cops arrived to investigate the murder.

He fired his engine, put the car into first gear, and swung into traffic.

Chapter 41

Mina heard knocking on her motel-room door.

She opened it.

Smiling, Catton walked in.

"Did you talk to the caller?" she said.

"Yeah."

Mina wanted a longer answer from him. "Well, what did he say?"

"He said he didn't know Rachel was married."

Expectant, Mina waited for him to elaborate.

Catton went to the minibar and poured himself a scotch, clinking the bottle against the glass's lip.

"That's all he said?" she said.

"He didn't say a lot."

"Why did he call you on Rachel's phone?"

"He wanted to know who I was. I told him the truth, that I was Rachel's husband."

"But then he knows you're still alive," said Mina, alarmed.

"Yeah," said Catton, unconcerned. He smacked his lips after gulping his drink.

"What makes you think he won't go to the cops with what you told him?"

"I'm positive he won't."

"He might even try to blackmail you."

"He wouldn't dare. Anyway, he can't."

Mina bit her lower lip, trying to understand his answer. "I don't think you should have told him anything."

"Why not?"

"You could become a prime suspect in her murder, if the cops know you're alive."

"Bendix isn't gonna talk."

"Who's Bendix?"

151

Bryan Cassiday

"The guy I ki—, talked to. The guy with the phone."

"How can you be so sure he won't talk?"

"We cut a deal. I won't tell the cops he was fooling around with my wife, if he doesn't tell them I'm alive."

Mina was skeptical. She didn't understand why Catton looked so calm about the whole thing. If Bendix thought Catton had killed Rachel, why wouldn't he report Catton to the cops, deal or no deal? Committing adultery with someone's wife wasn't anywhere near as bad as murdering someone.

"How can you trust him to keep up his end of the deal?" she said.

Catton withdrew Bendix's wallet from his trouser pocket and flipped it onto the sofa near Mina.

"There's his wallet," he said. "We'll need to get rid of it."

Mina screwed up her face. "Why would he give you his wallet?"

"He dropped it. I found it in the alley after he left."

Mina was finding Catton's story increasingly hard to believe. What were the chances Bendix would lose his wallet in the alley right after meeting with Catton? Her pulse was ratcheting up. She was getting scared.

How could Catton be so sure Bendix wouldn't talk unless Catton had killed him? she wondered.

"Did you give him back Rachel's phone like you planned?" she said.

"I did, indeed. I deleted everything from it, though, in case he knows her password. And I removed the SIM card."

Mina still found Catton's story implausible, but she didn't want him to suspect it. If she said she didn't believe him, he might kill her. She figured he was going to kill her eventually, anyway, but she wanted him to put it off as long as possible—until she could find a way out.

And she had to find a way out. *She had to.*

She needed to get Dunleavy more involved. He was her only protection against Catton.

"Wanna drink?" said Catton, holding his half-full glass up toward her.

"No," said Mina.

"Suit yourself." He paused. "We still need to find Rachel's bank password."

"It wasn't on her cell phone?"

"I couldn't find it there."

"Where else can we look?"

"We're running out of options. We'll have to try her condo again."

"Aren't the cops gonna prevent people from entering it, since she got killed?"

"It's gonna be harder to get into it if the cops are there." He snapped his fingers. "That reminds me. I need to go to her bank to make a withdrawal. I bet they're gonna freeze Rachel's account any day now, as soon as the bank's notified she's dead."

"You shouldn't show your face at the bank. A teller might ID you to the cops."

"I never go inside. I only use the ATMs, and I keep going to different branches."

"A lot of ATMs have cameras installed on them."

Catton tugged the tip of his beard. "That's why I'm wearing this, and I'll have my shades on, of course."

Catton downed the rest of his scotch, put his empty glass on the minibar, spun on his heel, and booked out of the room.

As soon as the door closed behind him, Mina was punching out Dunleavy's number on her cell phone.

Chapter 42

"Hello?" said Dunleavy, picking up.

Mina had to get this off her chest. She didn't mince words. "I think Catton might've killed someone."

"Wait a minute. Why would he?"

"A guy called us up and said he wanted Rachel's cell phone back. He knew we had it because Catton took his call."

"You saw Catton kill the guy?"

"No."

"Did Catton tell you he killed him?"

"No."

"Then what makes you think Catton killed him?"

"Catton told me he gave the guy the phone, and the guy took off."

"Well, there you go."

Mina scowled. "His story doesn't add up."

"Why would he lie?"

"He doesn't want me to know he killed someone."

"Maybe you're too suspicious."

"If Catton really gave the guy Rachel's phone, like he said, the guy saw Catton's face and can ID him to the cops. No way is Catton gonna let that happen. Why would he risk that?"

"Could be Catton didn't give the guy his real identity."

"Why go to the trouble of giving Rachel's phone to the guy, though? It makes no sense. Why risk exposing himself to the guy?"

"Then why do you think he did it?"

"It was an excuse so he could find out who the guy is and then kill him."

There was a long pause on the line.

"OK," said Dunleavy. "Let's assume Catton *did* take out this guy. What do you want me to do about it? Do you want me to tell the cops?"

"No, no, no. That's not the way to handle this. That would screw up our plans."

"Exactly. Then we'll never get Rachel's money. So what do you want me to do?"

Mina didn't relish saying this, but it had to be said. It was the only option she could think of.

"You need to kill him," she said.

Another long pause.

Mind wondered if Dunleavy was still there. She couldn't hear a thing over the line. She didn't want him to hang up.

"Hello?" she said.

"I don't think I heard you right."

"We don't have any choice."

"I'm not a hired gun. I'm an insurance investigator."

"You're not seeing the problem."

"What problem?"

Mina tensed, clenching her cell phone till her knuckles turned white, as she heard footsteps approach her motel-room door. Holding her breath she said nothing, cell phone in hand. Was Catton coming back to her room so soon? she wondered.

"Hello?" said Dunleavy.

Mina waited till she heard the footsteps in the hallway pass her door before she resumed breathing. Whoever it was out there wasn't headed to her room, though that didn't rule out Catton, she realized. Had the passerby stopped to listen at her door? She couldn't tell. But Catton was supposed to be on his way to the bank. So he had said, anyway.

"What problem?" repeated Dunleavy, annoyed.

"What's to prevent Catton from killing you and me?" she said, convinced the footsteps weren't returning to her room.

"So he doesn't have to split his take with us, you mean?"

"Now you're getting it."

155

Pause.

"We shouldn't talk about this over the phone," he said.

"Why not?"

"Call me paranoid. Phones can be tapped. Believe me. I know. In my business, it's SOP."

"Is this your way of saying you agree with me?"

"It's not my way of saying anything other than what I just said."

Mina shook her head in frustration. She didn't think he would be so difficult to deal with. Their only recourse was obvious to her. Couldn't he see that Catton was a homicidal maniac? Sure, he had his affable side, a persuasive concerned side, a smooth-talking side, but it was all a mask she was finding out. Was she the only one that could see through his mask?

"Where can we meet, then?" she said.

"Somewhere that can't be bugged."

Mina blew out her cheeks. "I can't think of such a place."

"How about the beach?"

"All right. But don't tell Catton anything about our conversation."

Dunleavy laughed. "I'm sure I'm gonna tell him I'm gonna kill him."

Mina didn't appreciate his sense of humor. She terminated the call.

Chapter 43

Mina could walk to the beach from her motel room. She didn't want to take a bus, and she couldn't use Catton's car because he had taken it.

The beach was several blocks away. It was a long walk, but it was a beautiful day with a refreshing sea breeze blowing onshore, the sun rising in a cloudless sky so blue it hurt her eyes to look at it, and she needed the air.

She was becoming claustrophobic locked up in her small room all day, terrified of Catton and what he would do to her next. The walls were closing in on her, crushing her will to act.

Getting outside was the best thing for her, she realized. Walking in the clean air would do her a world of good.

Her walk wasn't without risk. She had to keep looking over her shoulder to make sure Catton wasn't following her. When she left the motel, she hadn't seen any sign of him.

Still, she felt compelled to keep glancing over her shoulder to make sure he wasn't sneaking up behind her.

Reaching the bluff that overlooked the beach, she descended the wide, rough-hewn wooden planks embedded in the side of the bluff that acted as steps that wound down to the sand and the slate-colored ocean. The planks snaked down the bluff and led to a chain-link fence–encased pedestrian bridge that spanned the Coast Highway, which was throbbing with motor-vehicle traffic. She crossed the bridge.

At the end of the bridge she descended cement steps that fed onto the sidewalk that skirted the beach. Speeding cars whooshed by her as she strode down the sidewalk past a solid row of beachside houses and condos skirting the freeway and entered the sand-mottled parking lot alongside PCH.

She angled across the half-empty parking lot to the beach. Since it was a weekday in autumn, the beach wasn't crowded.

157

Bryan Cassiday

She sat down on a sunbaked cement bench, took off her
shoes and socks, which she stuffed into her shoes, held the
shoes in one hand, stood up, and walked onto the sand, which
felt warm on the soles of her feet.

She scoped out the beach for any sign of Dunleavy.

A smattering of people roamed the shoreline. Holding his
head up, his eyes closed, face sweaty, a thirtyish man in red
beach trunks was jogging along the water's edge away from
her toward the bight to the north. He jogged past the empty
baby blue lifeguard tower.

Mina didn't see anybody swimming in the tenebrous
water whose waves crashed on the sand. She saw a man
standing by himself with his back toward her watching the
surf roll in, his arms crossed over his chest.

She decided it might be Dunleavy and trudged through
the sand toward him. All of the other people she saw looked
like vagrants either lying on the sand or shambling around in
drunken stupors.

The man with his arms crossed was wearing sunglasses,
Mina saw.

When she was ten feet away from him, he turned his head
from the sea and acknowledged her, as a gull wheeled and
caterwauled over them in the limitless blue sky.

"Have you decided how you're gonna kill him?" said
Mina, surprised at herself for being able to broach the subject
with no hesitation, like the word *kill* was a normal part of her
everyday conversation, like it was no big deal with her.

Murder, murder, murder . . . If only that damn voice
inside her head would shut up, she thought.

"I didn't sign up to whack anybody," said Dunleavy,
unfolding his arms.

"Then how are we gonna protect ourselves from him?"

"There may be a way."

"I'm listening."

"Insurance."

"Insurance?" she said, puzzled. "Like life insurance, you mean?"

"In a manner of speaking." He paused. "Have you ever heard of the Dark Web?"

"No."

"You can only access it using a special browser like Tor."

"What's the point?"

"There are things on the Dark Web that you can't find on the ordinary Web."

"Like what?"

"Like stuff that's illegal."

Flummoxed, Mina squinched her eyes shut then opened them. "I don't see how that relates to our problem."

"You can hire people on the Dark Web who do illegal things."

"What's your point?"

"Let me be blunt. You can hire a hit man."

Chapter 44

There was a lot she didn't know about the way the world really operated, Mina decided. Hiring a hit man on the Internet was something that had never crossed her mind. But then again, why would it? She didn't go around all day thinking about people she wanted to kill. Why would she do that? . . . Not until she met Catton. *Or . . . or what? Wait a minute. Murder, murder, murder . . . Not again.* And Catton was just one person, not a bunch of them. She didn't particularly want to kill him. She didn't want to kill anyone, for that matter. Not exactly true. Sometimes she did feel like killing. Killing people who made her life miserable. Yes.

In Catton's case, she felt like she *had* to kill him or he would kill her. With him around, she was convinced she was living on borrowed time.

"You think we should hire a hit man to take care of Catton?" she said.

Dunleavy nodded solemnly. He scanned their surroundings casting around for anybody that might be watching them.

"Do you think we'll be able to find a hit man?" said Mina.

"I do. It's all a matter of looking in the right place," said Dunleavy, craning his neck around so he could complete a 360-degree recce of the area. "Did anybody follow you here?"

Feeling apprehensive Mina hunched her shoulders like somebody was spying on her from behind.

"I didn't see anyone," she said. "I checked behind me a couple times on my way here."

"I don't see anybody within earshot. Nobody's near enough to us."

"Then what are you worried about?"

"Haven't you ever heard of directional mics or parabolic mics?"

160

"No. I don't have a degree in electronics," she said in a huff, feeling like Dunleavy was putting her down for being ignorant.

"A parabolic mic could pick up our voices from a half mile away, depending on ambient sound. So could a directional mic. Since we're standing pretty much alone on the beach, there's not much ambient noise to block our voices. Only the sound of the surf breaking. But the surf can be quite effective at drowning out our voices if we're close enough to it."

"How do you know all this?"

"I'm an insurance investigator. Investigators spy on people to find out the truth."

"Have you ever used one of these mics to spy on people?"

"Indeed, I have."

"I doubt Catton has a parabolic mic on him."

Dunleavy nodded. "They have a pretty conspicuous dish that's hard to conceal, especially here since there's nothing around us except flat sand."

"So nobody can hear us?"

Dunleavy shrugged, continuing to survey the beach, his gaze intense. "They could be using a directional mic, which is easier to conceal."

"The only one that would have any reason to follow us would be Catton. And I doubt he followed me." She paused. "Unless he followed you."

"I'm a pro. I made frequent checks for surveillance when I came here. I didn't see anyone tailing me."

He halted his recce when he picked up on a motorboat sailing about a half mile from shore.

"Somebody on that motorboat could be listening to us," he said.

Mina started.

"Catton does have a motorboat," she said, throat tight.

"Does that look like the one he owns?" he said, motioning with his head toward the vessel in question.

"I dunno," she said, studying it. "They all look the same to me. A boat with a motor on them." She shook her head. "I'm not a boat person."

"Outboard or inboard motor?"

Mina tried to remember. "He has an outboard on his boat, I think."

"So does that motorboat."

She narrowed her eyes gazing at the motorboat, trying to see if it looked familiar. She shook her head inconclusively.

"You can't tell, huh?" he said.

"I don't see how he could have gotten to his boat and sailed here in the time it took me to walk to the beach. How would he know I was headed to the beach? I didn't tell him."

Dunleavy relaxed a bit. "OK. Where were we?"

"You want to hire a hit man to take care of Catton."

"*You're* the one that wants to get rid of Catton."

"If you won't do it, we need to get somebody else to do it."

Mina still couldn't believe she was discussing hiring a hit man with Dunleavy. It was like a scene out of a Tarantino movie.

Her heart sank when Dunleavy commenced walking away from her. "I'm not hiring a contract killer. It's on you. All I'm giving you is advice. Take it or leave it."

"I'm telling you, he's gonna kill both of us. He has to kill me, and you as well, so he can get all of Rachel's money for himself. He's only using us till he can get his hands on her money. Then it's over for both of us."

Dunleavy stopped in his tracks, thinking without turning around to look at her. He resumed walking away.

"Your shoes are gonna fill with sand," she said after him, noticing he was wearing his shoes as he traipsed through the sand.

Maybe he didn't hear her, she decided, carrying her shoes in her hand.

"Idiot," she said under her breath. "You have no idea about Catton."

Maybe she should have told Dunleavy that Catton had tortured her, she decided. She had to find some way to get the guy to realize how much danger he and she were in.

What had Catton told her before? she wondered. That everybody was capable of committing evil? That it was part and parcel of human nature? That it was a survival mechanism? Something like that.

Then there had to be a way to get Dunleavy to hire a hit man, since he wouldn't kill Catton himself. She just had to figure out what it was.

Chapter 45

Mina returned to her motel, chewing over Dunleavy's suggestion of hiring a hit man on the Dark Web.

Maybe that was the best way to handle it, she decided. But where was she going to get the money to pay the guy? She was broke. She couldn't use the insurance money until Catton got it first. She would have to tell the contract killer she would pay him after he completed the job. Would a contract killer accept those terms from an unknown client? She doubted it in his line of work. But then again you never knew with these underworld types. Not that she knew any underworld types.

As she came in sight of her motel, she wondered if Catton was back and whether he had managed to get any money from the ATM.

Not eager to see him but knowing she had to keep dealing with him for the time being, she went to his room and knocked on his door. She never knew what to expect when meeting with him. Would he tie her up again and start torturing her or would he act decent? Heart pounding, she waited in front of his door.

When he answered it, he looked agitated.

She didn't think it was on account of her. Something else was stressing him out, she decided.

He had been watching the TV news, she realized as she entered the room and closed the door behind her.

"Did you get the money?" she said.

"Yeah," he muttered, watching the TV newscaster.

"Then what's wrong?"

"The news. They're saying Rachel's still alive."

"What?" Mina couldn't believe her ears.

"They say they made a misdiagnosis. She was originally diagnosed as deceased. Then they realized she was still alive."

"That's impossible. How could she be?"

"I know, I know," he said, pacing back and forth in front of the TV set. "If she didn't die from the stab wounds, she would have drowned. She was at the bottom of the ocean for Christ's sake."

"There must be a mistake."

"Unless—"

"Unless what?"

"We don't know how long she was underwater. You said you didn't tie knots in the ropes around her. She could've floated loose from the anchor and come to the surface soon after we threw her overboard, time enough for her to continue breathing."

"That's hard to believe."

"I know. Believe me, I know. But it *is* possible." He paced in silence for a moment. "But then why did they report her as dead in the first place?"

"Because they made a misdiagnosis, you said."

"Yeah, but how many times have they done that before?"

"This is the first time I ever heard of it happening."

"Exactly. That's the problem." He came to a halt in the middle of the room, his eyes lighting up. "It could be fake news. The cops are trying to see how we'll react if we think Rachel's still alive."

"Fake news?"

"There's fake news all over the place nowadays. It's everywhere. On the airwaves. On the Internet. These news broadcasters are bought and paid for. They say what they're told to say by their bosses. The fake news has nothing to do with the truth."

Mina wasn't convinced. "It's hard to believe they would take such elaborate measures to trick us."

"On the other hand, it makes sense. Don't you see?"

"No."

"That's why I'm still able to make withdrawals from Rachel's bank."

"I'm not following."

"The DA can't freeze her account because she's still alive."

"But that could be a trick, too."

Catton mulled it over. "Possible. It could all be an elaborate con."

"What are we gonna do?"

"We need to empty her bank account and get out of here ASAP."

"How?"

"We need to search her condo again and get the password to her bank account. We have to move the money online into my account. It's the only way to move all of it at once. It'll take way too long to withdraw it from ATMs."

"What if the cops have her condo staked out? If this is fake news about her being alive, they could be drawing us into a trap at her condo."

"If she really is still alive, the cops wouldn't be staking out her condo for a homicide investigation since there hasn't been a homicide."

Mina's head was spinning. If this, if that—none of it made any sense. Fake news, not fake news. She had no idea what the truth was. Was Rachel really dead or not? If not, that meant Mina wasn't a murderer. *Murder, murder, murder*—why was she always harping on murder? There couldn't be a murderer unless there was a murder. It was giving her a killer headache thinking about murder. She didn't want to think about murder anymore.

"I don't know what to believe," she said, massaging her throbbing temple.

"It's all the fault of this fake news. It's all over the place," said Catton, gazing at the talking head on the TV screen, a middle-aged man with a full head of hair and a perfect tan he got in a tanning salon.

The guy was explaining that it was possible, though rare, to make a misdiagnosis of death, even in this day and age of modern science and technology.

"I don't see how she could survive being stabbed and drowned," she said.

"I don't see it either." Catton paused in thought. "Which means this has to be fake news. I don't think we can believe it. The cops may think if they lie and say Rachel's still alive, the guy that attempted to kill her will turn himself in."

"Is it legal for the cops to spread lies on TV?"

"Everybody else does it. Why not the cops?"

"How are we supposed to tell what's fake and what's real?"

"We're not. That's the whole idea."

They fell silent, the newscaster jabbering in the background.

"If Rachel's alive, does that mean she told the cops we tried to kill her?" said Mina.

Catton took a pull on a Corona longneck that he scoffed up from the sideboard. "It's even harder to believe she's conscious than it is to believe she's still alive."

"Meaning?"

"Meaning if she's still alive, she must be in a coma. Which would explain why they misdiagnosed her as dead."

"Then she didn't tell them about us."

"She has to be in a coma. It's the only explanation that makes sense. If she's even alive in the first place."

Mina didn't want to talk about it anymore. She opened the door to return to her room.

"Where are you going?" said Catton.

"Back to my room."

He shook his head no. "We got work to do. We have to search Rachel's condo for her password."

"How many times do we have to do it?" said Mina, thinking another search would be fruitless.

"Until we find the password."

Mina had an idea. "What if we get Dunleavy to do it?"

"Why Dunleavy?"

"He's sort of a cop. Maybe they won't bother him if he searches her condo."

"The trouble is, I don't trust him. What if he finds the password and decides to keep it for himself?"

"But you can trust me?"

"You better believe it. I saw you stab my wife to death— or tried to if she's still alive—which means you've got a murder rap hanging over your head, or attempted murder at the very least."

Chapter 46

Dunleavy was lying on his back in his bare feet on a comfortable chaise longue on his motel-room patio thinking about pulling out of this deal he had struck with Catton after Mina had tried to drag him into a murder plot.

Nobody had told him anything about murder. For him it was an insurance scam, pure and simple. And, as anybody could tell you, insurance companies could afford getting swindled, what with the enormous profits they raked in on their premiums. In the end, most of their customers were paying for nothing except peace of mind. He had no regrets about taking an insurance company for a ride.

Murder was another matter. Even hiring a hit man to do it for you.

Dunleavy wasn't any saint, but he didn't go around killing people.

Still, if he had Catton killed and pleaded self-defense, maybe the court would buy it. However, he wasn't so sure he could convince a court of his justification. Hiring a hit man rarely qualified for a plea of self-defense.

What difference did it make what a court thought? Dunleavy wondered. What mattered was what he thought. It was all about survival. He had to do what he had to do to survive. Maybe Mina was right that Catton was a threat to his survival that needed to be removed. But murder was a whole different ballgame. It was the big kahuna. It was a fucking death sentence.

Sweating, Dunleavy was having second thoughts. Maybe he should back out of this deal with Catton and Mina, do his job as an insurance investigator, and report Catton to the authorities. That would be the safest option to take, but not the most profitable. He had learned in his life that the safest option was rarely the most profitable. It reminded him of

169

something Balzac had once said, that behind every great fortune was a crime.

In other words, play it safe and get nowhere in life, like he had been doing at his job.

He was tired of getting nowhere. He wanted a piece of the action. Beaucoup bucks. Along came Catton, and here was his chance for the big time.

The irony was that if Dunleavy went along with Catton's scheme, he would have to whack out Catton in order to stay alive, according to Mina. Dunleavy didn't know if he could trust Mina, but what she had told him made sense. If Catton did indeed take out the guy that wanted Rachel's cell phone, it meant Catton was a murderer and therefore might whack out Catton and Mina—to keep all the loot for himself.

After all, how could you trust a murderer? wondered Dunleavy. And likewise how could you trust a guy that was running a scam on the insurance company?

Yeah, it wasn't looking good for Dunleavy's life expectancy if he let Catton live.

Dunleavy wondered if Mina would hire a hit man on the Dark Web like he had suggested to her. For sure, either he or she would have to do it. He would rather have her do it, so he could keep his hands clean of the matter. But he didn't know if she had the balls to pull it off.

He had only just met her. How could he tell much of anything about her? He would have to go on first impressions, which meant he figured he would have to be the one that hired the hit man if he decided to go through with this scam. With her big innocent eyes she looked too young and naïve to hire a hit man.

Dunleavy heaved a long sigh, watching the westering sun without looking directly at it.

The problem with hiring a contract killer was that these guys didn't come cheap. The guy's fee would cut into Dunleavy's and Mina's split of the take. On the other hand, if

Catton was eliminated by the hit man, Dunleavy and Mina would get Catton's cut, supplementing each of theirs.

So maybe the hit man would be worth hiring, decided Dunleavy—as long as the guy didn't demand too steep a price.

Dunleavy decided to temporize.

He would wait and see what happened in the next few days before making up his mind about the hit man. As far as Dunleavy knew, the insurance scam wasn't going to pan out unless Catton could get his hands on the money in Rachel's bank account. Catton's attempts so far had been stymied.

If Catton couldn't get Rachel's bank account password, the scam would fall through—in which case nobody would get anything. If that happened, Dunleavy would be better off reneging on his deal with the scammers Catton and Mina, reporting them to the insurance company, and collecting his paycheck.

Dunleavy relaxed back in his chaise longue and reached for the glass of pinot noir he had set on the patio's cement floor in the cool shade of the chaise.

It was too early for him to see how this was all going to play out. Waiting was his best bet for now, until he got a clearer idea of the endgame. The money from Rachel's bank account had to be in play before he could plan his next move.

The vibrating of his cell phone in his trouser pocket disrupted Dunleavy's chain of thought.

He picked up.

"Hello," said the caller. "This is Lieutenant Philippe Duquesne, LAPD Robbery-Homicide Division."

Dunleavy jackknifed to attention in his chaise.

Chapter 47

Dunleavy didn't know what was going on. He had no idea why a cop would phone him. He figured it had to be bad news. And how did they get his number in the first place?

"Yeah," he said into his cell phone's transmitter.

"I want to speak to Randall Dunleavy," said Duquesne.

"Speaking."

"Do you mind if we have a conversation?"

"What's this about?"

"I would like to speak to you in person, if you don't mind."

"I don't understand why."

"This is about the attempted murder of Rachel Catton."

Attempted? thought Dunleavy. He thought she was dead.

"OK," he said. "But I don't see how I can help you. How did you get my number?"

"From Lion Life Insurance."

"Where do you want to meet?"

"Could we come to your place? I'd like this to be a private conversation."

"Sure. Why not?"

Dunleavy didn't want to give the cops a hard time, whatever this was about. He gave them his motel address over the phone.

"Could we talk in twenty minutes?" said Duquesne.

"I'll be waiting for you."

"Thank you, sir."

Agitated, Dunleavy terminated the call. Cops bending over backwards to be polite aggravated him. They were almost always excessively polite right before they slipped the handcuffs on you.

But what could they bust him for? he wondered. He hadn't done anything illegal. Not yet.

It didn't take them twenty minutes. They were there in less than fifteen.

They must have been nearby, decided Dunleavy. Lion Life had probably told them where he was staying. Then why did they bother calling him first? To see if he might bolt? Maybe they had even staked out the motel before calling him in order to follow him if he bugged out.

Dunleavy opened the door and let Duquesne and another guy in.

The two cops were dressed in plainclothes. Duquesne was wearing an off-the-rack grey blazer, his companion a navy blue one. They both wore shiny black oxfords.

"This is Detective Patrick," said Duquesne.

Dunleavy nodded.

"And are you the man I spoke to on the phone?" he asked Duquesne.

"I am Lt. Duquesne."

Duquesne was pushing forty. He was already starting a receding hairline. Five ten, he had a large head and an aquiline nose. For some reason, Dunleavy got the impression the guy should be smoking a pipe. Perhaps because Duquesne had a somewhat sophisticated air about him, despite his choice in haberdashers. In any case, he was obviously in charge.

Patrick, who was in his thirties and in inch shorter than Duquesne, looked like he wanted to fade into the woodwork. He stayed at least a step behind Duquesne, surveying the motel room with a detached air, as though he wasn't paying attention to the conversation. From his erect carriage, he looked like he worked out in the gym regularly.

Duquesne motioned to Patrick with his head, and Patrick closed the door behind them.

"What did you want to see me about?" said Dunleavy.

"We're investigating the murder attempt on Rachel Catton's life, sir," said Duquesne.

"The news reported her as dead," said Dunleavy, trying to sound them out.

"You haven't been listening to it lately. The ME made a misdiagnosis. Rachel Catton is still alive," said Duquesne, searching Dunleavy's face.

Dunleavy raised his eyebrows and nodded. He had never heard of a misdiagnosis by a trained police physician when it came to death, which made him suspicious. But he supposed it was possible.

"I see," he said without expression.

Dunleavy and Duquesne stood looking at each other, sizing each other up.

Dunleavy didn't want to offer the lieutenant a seat, because he wanted the guy to leave. Maybe if the guy stood long enough, his legs and feet would ache and he would leave sooner. That was what Dunleavy hoped, anyway.

This conversation was making Dunleavy nervous. He got the impression Duquesne knew something he wasn't telling him.

Chapter 48

"I understand Lion Life Insurance hired you to investigate George Catton's disappearance," said Duquesne.

"Gage Catton," said Dunleavy.

"Oh, that's right. Gage Catton. My bad."

Dunleavy felt like he was being set up. He said nothing.

"Well?" said Duquesne. "Is it true Lion Life hired you?"

"Yeah," said Dunleavy, not eager to elaborate.

"Have you found any information in that case?"

"Nothing helpful."

"Have you confirmed that Gage Catton is dead? I understand that's your assignment."

"It is. But I haven't found any evidence to suggest Catton's alive."

"Then you think he's dead."

"The police report said he drowned at sea."

"But they never found the corpse, as I understand it."

"That's what the report says."

"And you agree with it?"

"I haven't found anything to call it into question."

"Have you found any evidence that he is, in fact, dead?"

"No evidence. No corpus delicti. That's the only evidence that would serve as proof."

"But you have determined that Gage Catton is dead, in spite of a lack of evidence?"

Dunleavy didn't want to commit himself. He wanted to make sure he could claim plausible deniability as an exit route, in case the cops found out the truth about Gage Catton, that the guy was alive. Dunleavy wanted to make sure the cops couldn't charge him with anything regarding Catton. He wondered if Duquesne had any evidence that Catton was alive.

"I haven't come to a conclusion," said Dunleavy. "I'm still investigating."

"We think he might be alive."

"Oh? Is that what his wife said?"

"His wife is comatose. She can't speak," said Duquesne, turning away from Dunleavy and gazing out the window at the ocean. "You have a nice view."

"The insurance company's paying for it."

"The sea looks so beautiful, but it can be treacherous."

"What makes you think Gage Catton is alive?"

"Whenever anybody disappears without a trace, we always find it suspicious, especially when a life insurance policy is involved."

"Suspicious, but possible."

"We're not ruling out his death. We just think it needs further investigation in light of the murder attempt on his wife."

"I don't see the connection."

"It adds to the suspicion, don't you see? Isn't that why you're investigating Catton's disappearance, because you think he might be alive?"

"I'm not paid to think. Lion Life hired me to do a job. I'm doing it."

"So you have no opinion in the case?"

"That case was closed by the local cops that investigated it."

"But Lion Life wants to reopen it. Isn't that correct?"

Dunleavy shrugged. "They want to make absolutely sure Catton's dead, because they paid out a shitload of money to his wife."

"We understand. They're suspicious, like we are. Are you sure you haven't found any evidence that he's alive?"

Dunleavy pulled at his eyelid absently and inspected his fingers. "That's correct. Why do you think I know anything?"

"Because you've been investigating Catton's case longer than anyone else. You're the expert, so to speak."

Dunleavy unleashed a brief smile. "Flattery, Lieutenant?"

Duquesne returned the smile. "It's the truth."

"I haven't found anything," said Dunleavy, face impassive.

"You haven't found anything to prove he's alive?"

"That's what I just said," said Dunleavy with a trace of annoyance.

"But you didn't say it in those exact terms." Duquesne hung fire. "Let me rephrase. Have you found any evidence to indicate that Catton is alive?"

"None." Other than the fact that he had met Catton in person, Dunleavy decided.

"Then why are you still here investigating the case? I don't understand."

"I haven't finished my investigation."

"Oh, I see."

Dunleavy noticed Duquesne's gaze fall on the open bottle of wine on his sideboard.

"Would you care for a drink?" said Dunleavy.

Duquesne shook his head and smiled. "I'm on duty."

"Will that be all, then? I have things to do and places to go."

"Of course. Well, thank you for your help," said Duquesne, handing Dunleavy a business card.

Duquesne headed to the door to let himself out, the mute Patrick in tow.

Doorknob in hand, Duquesne turned around toward Dunleavy. "If you find any evidence Catton's alive, let us know ASAP. It would help with our investigation of the attack on his wife."

"Sure," said Dunleavy, relieved to see them go.

Could they possibly know he had found Catton? he wondered. If they did know, they were playing their cards close to their vests. Dunleavy shook the idea off. There was no way they could know. If they knew, they'd haul him down to the station and give him the third degree about Catton's whereabouts.

Dunleavy padded to the window and looked out at the gleaming ocean.

He still didn't see how Catton was going to collect the insurance money from Rachel's bank account—and without that money there was no deal between them. He glanced down at Duquesne's business card in his hand. Deciding he might in the end need to call this number, he pocketed the card.

He couldn't figure out how Mina fit into this. She was the one that had gotten him involved in the scam. But why? Why did she want a third person involved? It reduced the size of her slice of the pie. Was it because she was attracted to him? She *had* kept kicking his leg under the table at the restaurant during their talk, and it wasn't any accident. She must have known he was attracted to her. Her big, liquid grey eyes, her lithe figure. Insatiable in bed—

Did Mina dream up the insurance scam with Catton or did she come in later? Dunleavy wondered. He couldn't figure out what the relationship between the two of them was or how long it had been in effect. Were they lovers? Did that have something to do with the scam? Did she want him for a threesome?

He couldn't tell if they were lovers. He didn't think so. She must be terrified of Catton, or why else would she want a hit man to take him out? Maybe they had started out as lovers, and the affair soured.

Dunleavy couldn't figure it out.

He cut across the room to the patio and, stooping, collected his glass of pinot from the floor.

Chapter 49

Lieutenant Philippe Duqesne returned to his unmarked patrol car parked on the side of the street in front of Dunleavy's motel.

Duquesne was a French Canadian by birth. He had been born in Toronto, but moved to the United States in his late teens to attend college at St. John's University in New York. He married an American woman at college, was able to get a green card as a result, and became an American citizen three years later.

He had no trace of an accent and spoke English like a native American without a New York accent. Though his mother was French and could speak French, Duquesne could speak but a smattering of the language. He was fluent only in English. He even preferred the Americanized pronunciation of his Christian name Philip to the French pronunciation of Philippe, which his mother preferred.

Sick of the cold winters in Toronto and New York, he moved his family to sunny Los Angeles and joined the LAPD after graduating from St. John's University with a degree in criminal justice.

Outside Dunleavy's motel, Duquesne slid into the driver's seat of his black unmarked Charger. Patrick got in beside him.

"What do you think?" said Duquesne, sitting in the car without starting the engine.

"I dunno," said Patrick.

"You don't know if he can help us in our investigation, you mean?"

"He doesn't seem to know much about Gage Catton."

"Don't you think that odd?"

"Odd?"

"Here he's been investigating the guy for a while and has come up with nothing. You would think he would find something on the guy."

Patrick turned to face Duquesne. "You think he knows more than he's telling us?"

"He didn't seem eager to talk to us. How did he strike you?"

Patrick nodded yes. "That's about right. He didn't say much."

"Of course, maybe he really doesn't know anything."

"Yeah."

Duquesne knitted his brows. "But this whole Rachel Catton thing bothers me. Her husband disappears without a trace in the middle of the ocean and is declared dead. She collects on his life insurance policy. Then she ends up in the morgue. I suspect a connection between all of these things."

"But if Rachel Catton is dead, who gets the insurance money?"

"Her husband can't collect it. If he appears out of the blue and tries to collect it, the life insurance policy he took out is canceled since it was contingent on his death."

"Then who gets the money, if Catton can't get it?"

Duquesne fired the engine. "That's what we need to find out. The guy who collects is our probable murderer."

"Lion Life Insurance would get the money back."

"Only if Catton reappears and tries to collect it."

"Could the same person have killed both Catton and his wife?"

"What does that person have to gain from both murders?"

"Maybe he just hated them."

"Why?"

Patrick walled his eyes. "I dunno. I'm making this all up."

"You'd make a good lawyer."

Patrick grimaced at the insult. "How do we even know that Gage Catton was murdered? Maybe he drowned accidentally at sea as reported."

"All I know is that something's hinky here. Where there's a lot of money and murder involved, I figure there's a connection."

The police radio squawked.

Chapter 50

"Lieutenant, you know that murder in the Pacific Dining Car?" came the voice through the radio static.

It was Officer Carmody, the thirtysomething guy with a flattop and ears that curved out of his head like they were trying to hear better, Duquesne realized. They looked like they belonged on a cartoon character.

"That guy named Bendix?" said Duquesne.

"Yeah. We found two cell phones on the corpse. One of them was erased. The other one was his."

"What about it, Carmody?"

"His cell phone had an interesting phone number on it. You'll never guess whose."

"I hope this is leading somewhere," said Duquesne, tapping his fingers on the steering wheel impatiently, the Charger's motor running.

"Do you want to know the last number he called?"

"Is this the high point of your day? Just give it to me for Christ's sake."

"Rachel Catton's."

Duquesne jerked to attention, fingers clenching the steering wheel. "When was the call placed?"

"An hour or so before he died, according to the ME."

"She's in no condition to talk. Did somebody take the call?"

"Yep."

Frowning, Duquesne chewed it over. "Somebody else has her phone."

"What was Bendix doing calling Rachel Catton?" said Patrick, listening to the conversation.

"They must know each other. This is what we have to look into."

"Did the same murderer go after both of them?"

"It looks that way, Counselor. Since Rachel and Bendix knew each other, I'd say we could be dealing with the same perp."

Patrick winced at the term *counselor*. "Maybe Bendix was just mugged. The perp did take his wallet."

"It could've been staged to look like a mugging. There are too many coincidences here. Rachel and Bendix know each other and they both get attacked only a few days apart. What are the chances? There must be a connection. We have to look into their relationship."

"There's something puzzling me," said Patrick. "Why was Bendix carrying two cell phones?"

"Yet something else that doesn't add up." Duquesne spoke into the radio. "What about the other cell phone on Bendix, Carmody?"

"What about it?" said Carmody, yawning.

"Am I keeping you awake?"

"No. I—"

Duquesne cut him off. "Were there any calls to Rachel on it?"

"There was nothing on it."

"What?"

"Everything was deleted."

Duquesne exchanged looks with Patrick.

"Is there any way forensics or our IT guy can find out what used to be on the phone?" Duquesne asked Carmody.

"No," said Carmody. "It's an Apple iPhone. Its memory was wiped clean, and the SIM card was removed."

Duquesne turned to Patrick. "Why would Bendix be carrying around a cell phone with nothing on it?"

"Maybe he just bought it," said Patrick.

"Why did he buy it if he already had a cell phone?"

Patrick shrugged. "Maybe he bought it as a gift for someone."

Duquesne pulled a face. "Possible." He paused. "Carmody, see if you can get any prints off the blank cell phone other than Bendix's."

"We're way ahead of you, Lieutenant."

"And?"

"We couldn't even get Bendix's prints off the blank phone, let alone anybody else's."

"Say again."

"We need to upgrade our radio," Carmody said in annoyance. "The blank cell phone had no fingerprints on it," he said, raising his voice. "Nada, as in nix."

Scowling, Duquesne turned to Patrick. "Was Bendix wearing gloves?"

"I don't think so. Why would he be wearing gloves in the head? Unless he's got a hang-up about touching his dong," said Patrick with a grin.

Duquesne gave him a world-weary look. "I want more information on that blank phone. Find out whatever you can about it," Duquesne told Carmody.

"Like what?" said Carmody.

"Like where Bendix bought it. Get its serial number. Trace it to where he bought it. Whatever you can get."

"Roger, Lieutenant."

"Over and out." Duquesne turned to Patrick. "How did Bendix put the phone in his pocket without touching it?"

Patrick thought about it.

"Come on, Counselor," said Duquesne. "We're in Double Jeopardy now. Alex Trebek is waiting. He's a fellow Canadian by the way."

"Will you cut it out with the 'counselor' stuff."

"I'm busting your balls," said Duquesne with part of a smile.

Patrick thought it over. "Bendix used a Kleenex to put the phone in his pocket?"

"Why? Why would he?"

Patrick shook his head, unable to come up with an answer.

His mind spinning with questions, Duquesne pulled away from the curb in the Charger, kicking up gravel on the street with his rear wheels.

Chapter 51

Mina felt like the walls were closing in. She thought it might be time to take a powder. After all, how could Catton find her? It was a big world out there.

And yet it always seemed like he knew what was going on in her head. Like he could figure out where she would flee and find her. But how could he? her rational mind said. How could anyone know where you were going to go? Even she didn't know where she would go yet.

The guy terrified her. Of that there was no question. She had every reason to fear him. Who in their right mind wouldn't fear a sociopathic murderer? He had nearly killed his wife, and Mina was convinced he *had* killed Bendix. And Catton had tortured her. Torture and murder went hand in hand, Mina knew.

The way she figured it, the only reason Catton hadn't killed her was because he needed her to find the password to Rachel's bank account. If he wasn't afraid to search Rachel's condo himself, Mina would be dead by now. She had no illusions about it. She was his cat's-paw. Nothing else.

She paced around her motel room like a caged animal, thinking she was losing her mind. She couldn't decide what to do.

If she did everything he told her, he would kill her as soon as he got his hands on the money in Rachel's bank account. If she ran, he would track her down and kill her.

If she did as he said, she would be safe until he glommed onto Rachel's money. Then her days would be numbered. Which meant if she found the bank account's password and gave it to him, it was her death sentence. In her mind there was no escaping that conclusion.

She hadn't even thought of that before. She stopped in her tracks, reassessing her situation.

It meant she had to do everything she could to prevent him from finding that password. Earlier, she had been acting on the assumption she needed to find the password to save her life. But that was back when she trusted Catton more or less. Now she was convinced he was a serial murderer.

Her situation was fast becoming untenable.

Catton had this air of all-powerful menace about him. It seemed like he could control her, like he had some weird power over her that she could neither understand nor resist. Perhaps if she could understand it, she could figure out how to resist it.

She had to calm down and think rationally. But how could she do either when her life was at stake?

Maybe her best bet was to hire a hit man on the Dark Web, as Dunleavy had suggested. Except she couldn't afford a hit man. She didn't even own a credit card, let alone cash— that was, if she could *find* a hit man who took credit cards, and she probably couldn't. After all, credit cards were traceable, and the last thing a hit man wanted was to be traced.

She was working herself up into a tizzy, thinking about her predicament and how she was going to extricate herself from it. She concluded she was left with three choices: keep helping Catton and stay alive a little longer, kill him herself and be done with him, or bug out for parts unknown and vanish from his crosshairs.

She couldn't afford a hit man, and she couldn't work up the courage to flee Catton. She wished she had been able to convince Dunleavy to take out Catton, but Dunleavy seemed intent on limiting his involvement with her and Catton so he could claim plausible deniability if the cops came for him.

She got the impression Dunleavy might back out of the scam any minute, thereby exposing her to additional risk, because then she wouldn't be able to play him off against Catton. Enlisting Dunleavy's aid in the scam was the one thing she had going for her at the moment.

For the time being she decided she better keep playing along with Catton, doing his bidding, as much as she hated it. *Yes, homicidal maniac, I will do whatever you say because I know you'll kill again, and I don't want to be your next victim.*

If she could ever break his Rasputin-like spell over her, she would cut and run. Then she realized he could still hurt her even if he couldn't track her down. He could go to the cops and tell them she murdered Rachel. The only thing that might prevent him from ratting her out was his fear of being identified and caught by the cops. Of course, he could always send an anonymous tip to them, keeping his ID covert.

There were too many ways he could get to her, she decided, wringing her hands and grimacing.

Of course, if Rachel wasn't really dead, like it said on the news, then Mina wasn't facing a murder charge. Though she could still be charged with assault with a deadly weapon.

But she didn't know if she could believe the news. She could have sworn Rachel was dead when they threw her overboard. She had stopped both groaning and moving. Mina had decided Rachel must be dead, but she must have been wrong. Which was a good thing for her. It meant she hadn't committed murder. *Murder, murder, murder.*

It was all so confusing, she decided, gritting her teeth and yanking out a clump of her hair. Wincing at the pain in her scalp, she eyed the hair in her hand in dismay. If Catton wasn't mutilating her, she was mutilating herself.

She had to pull herself together, she told herself. She couldn't keep pushing herself this hard without its taking a toll on her health.

Taking deep breaths she slowed down her pacing. Who needed enemies when she could stress herself out like this without half trying? She was her own worst enemy. She was better at torturing herself than Catton was, and she didn't need a burning cigarette to do it.

188

Why did she have to go to that pier when Catton was murdering his wife?

There was nothing she could do about it now, she decided. She had been in the wrong place at the wrong time. It was better not to kick herself thinking about it. The die was cast. Next problem, please.

Which brought her back here to this motel room at this moment in time at the mercy of the psychopath Catton.

Again, she heard the word *murder* repeated over and over in her head. Was that her only escape? The only answer to her misery? Murder? Did everything come down to murder? *Murder, murder, murder.*

Why was the word pounding over and over again inside her head? Maybe her only escape was through insanity.

She clutched her ears wishing she couldn't hear the word anymore.

She wanted to scream.

She started when she heard a knock on her door.

Chapter 52

When Mina answered the door, Catton was standing there.

He bulled his way into the room.

"I hope you're not thinking about running away," he said, taking command of the center of the room, standing there with his beard like he was Karl Marx.

"Why would I do that?" she said, closing the door, wondering how he could have read her mind. Or was it obvious that she didn't want to be around him?

"If you *do* make a run for it, I'll find you. And when I do, it won't be pretty. There's no way you can escape me. How many times do I have to tell you that?"

"If I take off, I won't get any of the money. Why would I want to leave?"

"No matter where you run off to, I'll find you. Your only chance to go on living is if you stay with me."

"I'm not leaving."

"You better not. Your life is hanging by a thread."

She was sick of his trying to intimidate her, though she dissimulated her feelings, trying to make herself appear harmless so he wouldn't suspect her of defying him. She didn't want anything to do with this guy. As soon as she could figure a way out, she was gone.

"Why do you keep harping on this?" she said.

"Don't even think about leaving me."

"I have nowhere to go."

"That's right. I'm your lifeline, and don't forget it."

What if she hired the hit man *after* she got ahold of the money? she wondered. Then, unlike now, she would have the wherewithal to pay him for his services. But that would be playing it close to the edge. She doubted Catton would let her live much longer after he latched onto the money. He would have no need of her. That would leave her only a small window of opportunity in which she would be able to recruit a hit man and have Catton eliminated.

There was a knock on the door, followed by two more.

Mina froze. She exchanged looks with Catton.

"Have you been talking to anyone?" he said under his breath, eyes glowering.

"No."

"Then who's at the door?"

"I dunno." She was as puzzled as Catton was about the identity of the stranger.

Another round of rapping on the door.

"Should I answer it?" whispered Mina.

Catton said nothing, watching the door.

"It's me," said a male voice in the hallway.

"It sounds like Dunleavy," Mina told Catton.

"Let him in," said Catton, not eager to see Dunleavy.

Mina followed Catton's instructions.

Entering, Dunleavy was surprised to see Catton.

"The gang's all here," said Dunleavy.

"What's this about?" said Catton.

"I got bad news."

"Spit it out."

"The cops may be onto you."

"Impossible," said Catton, face grim. "They reported me as dead a year ago. Nothing's changed since then."

Dunleavy cocked an eyebrow. "Nevertheless, they just paid me a visit at my motel room."

"What?" said Catton, incredulous.

"They were asking about you."

"Asking what?"

"They wanted to know if I had found any evidence you're still alive."

"They must suspect you had something to do with Rachel's murder," Mina told Catton.

"I don't like cops snooping around," said Catton, turned away from Mina and Dunleavy, and approached the window. "But there's no way they know I'm alive. I've been too careful about staying off the grid."

Inadvertently, his gaze fell on a squad car that happened to be cruising down the street below.

"Then why did they ask me about you?" said Dunleavy.

"It must be about Rachel's murder," said Mina.

"That's another thing they brought up. They told me Rachel's not dead."

"We heard that on the news."

"What did you tell them about me?" said Catton, still looking out the window.

"I said I didn't find any evidence you were alive," said Dunleavy.

"They must know you're an investigator working for Lion Life."

"It wouldn't be hard for them to find that out. I've been asking around about you, and I haven't made any secret of it."

"That doesn't necessarily mean they know you've hooked up with me."

"I don't see how they could know that."

Catton wheeled around to face Dunleavy. "They may've hung a tail on you."

Dunleavy shook his head no. "I thought of that. I checked it out. I didn't see anybody tailing me when I drove here."

"We need to limit our meets if you're on their radar."

"They have no reason to suspect me of anything illegal. I'm just doing my job for the insurance company."

"Maybe they think you had something to do with Rachel's murder," put in Mina.

Dunleavy pulled a face. "That makes no sense. What motive could I possibly have to take her out?"

"We gotta wind up this operation and get out of here chop-chop," said Catton.

"I think they're gonna catch us," said Mina. "Maybe we should forget the whole thing and leave town now."

"They're not gonna catch us," said Catton. "I'm smarter than them. I'll always have a step or two on them."

"I dunno," said Dunleavy, having second thoughts.

"You want out?"

Dunleavy said nothing.

"It's too late for you to get out," said Catton. "You know too much."

"What's that supposed to mean? It sounds like a threat."

"There's nothing to worry about. I'm smart. I went to Princeton."

"They taught you how to become a swindler?"

Catton didn't see the humor in Dunleavy's remark. "I studied business there."

"Pretty much the same thing, huh?"

Catton didn't laugh. "And I know how to stay invisible. I've had practice."

"If you stay invisible, how are you gonna collect Rachel's money?"

"All I need is a computer, and then I can transfer all of *my* money, not her money, out of her account into an account I set up under a phony ID. That money's mine. She stole it from me and thought she could get away with it because as a corpse I wouldn't be able to do anything about it."

"So do it already."

"I need her password."

Dunleavy pondered it.

Mina wondered if Catton had really gone to Princeton. How much of what he said could you believe? She couldn't picture him as ever having a job. She couldn't imagine anyone would want to hire him. He acted like he knew everything. How could anyone get along with him?

"If we don't get this thing wrapped up soon, I'm out of it," said Dunleavy. "The longer this drags on, the riskier it is for us—now that the cops are interrogating me."

"You don't need to get out," said Catton. "I'm gonna take care of everything in a New York minute."

"Fine," said Dunleavy with a slight shrug, as if this was the best, if not optimal, result he could hope for.

He made a beeline for the door.

"Watch your back," said Catton.

Dunleavy halted in his tracks, but he neither turned around nor said anything. After a moment, he resumed walking and let himself out without looking back.

Chapter 53

"That guy's nothing but trouble," said Catton when Dunleavy was gone.

"We need him," said Mina.

"Why?"

"Because he'll tell the cops about you if we don't cut him in."

"We should eighty-six him."

"We can't."

"Why not?" said Catton, challenging her for an answer.

Mina thought fast. She had to come up with a convincing response. With Dunleavy out of the picture, Catton would have no reluctance to kill her. Dunleavy was her only ally against him.

"If you do anything to him, the cops'll be suspicious," said Mina.

"Suspicious of what?"

"Of you. They asked him about you. If something happens to him, they'll figure you're still alive and were the one behind it."

Catton gazed at the carpet, brooding. "He's gonna be trouble. What if he starts blackmailing us?"

"Why would he if we're cutting him in?"

"I don't trust him." He jerked his head up and fixed his eyes on her. "I don't trust you either. You sound like you want him in with us."

"It's the safest way to handle it."

"You better not get any ideas."

"What? What are you talking about?"

"About running off with him."

"That's crazy. Why would I do that?"

"Maybe you two got something going."

"That's stupid talk. Have you been drinking?"

195

"You can't escape me. I made you. Without me you're nothing. You would've killed yourself if I hadn't met you at the pier. Don't forget that. I'm the only reason you're alive today."

There he was trying to intimidate her again, decided Mina, resentful but scared at the same time. She wanted to kill him herself without hiring a hit man. She had to break free from him. Killing him would make her feel good.

"You got nothing to say," he said. "Because you know I'm right."

He stared at her, daring her to argue with him.

She said nothing.

Mina thought she was heading for a nervous breakdown. She didn't know how much more of this she could take.

The phone on the motel-room desk rang, breaking the tension between them.

Catton snapped up the handset in irritation. "Hello."

"Don't try anything funny," said Dunleavy.

"What are you talking about?"

"Emergency measures are in place in case something happens to me. I've arranged for an e-mail to be sent every day to Lion Life telling them I've found you alive. If I don't block just one of those e-mails from being sent daily, the insurance company will know you're alive and defrauding them. Understand?"

"You're worried about nothing."

Dunleavy hung up.

Catton slammed the handset into its cradle. "He doesn't know who he's dealing with."

Mina wasn't sure who she was dealing with either. A psychopath? A sadomasochist? A greedy con man? A homicidal maniac? She had never heard of a homicidal maniac that had attended Princeton.

In the end, maybe it didn't matter who he was. What mattered was she felt he was a threat to her existence. She had to find a way to neutralize that threat. She couldn't let this go on any longer.

She couldn't hire a hit man because she couldn't afford one. And she wasn't having any success enlisting Dunleavy's aid to get rid of Catton, either.

Which meant she was on her own, she decided. So what else was new? The only way to get rid of Catton for good was to kill him. It wasn't good enough just to flee him. She had to exterminate him. Otherwise, he would haunt her for as long as he lived. Her mind was made up.

The word *murder* kept pounding over and over again like a pulse in her brain. *Murder, murder, murder—*

"I know what you're thinking," he said.

Mina felt invaded, even though she knew better. "You can't read minds. Nobody can. Our minds are sanctuaries."

"I can read yours like a book. Always remember: without me, you're dead. You have no life on your own."

Mina looked at him, trying to decide how she would kill him.

"We're gonna have to make Dunleavy disappear," he said. "He's the only one that knows I'm still alive. Other than you." He scratched his fake beard. "I hate wearing this thing. It makes my face hot and itchy. But before we can get rid of him we have to disable those e-mails he set up to be sent."

"What e-mails?"

"That was what his phone call was about. He's set up his computer to send e-mails to the life insurance company saying I'm still alive, if he doesn't deactivate each one every twenty-four hours."

"If you kill him, he can't deactivate them from being sent."

"You figured that out all by yourself, huh?"

"How can you stop him?"

"By destroying his computer."

"You don't even know where it is."

Catton started laughing. It sounded more like a giggle than a laugh to Mina.

"What are you laughing at?" she said.

"He thinks he can blackmail me," he said, laughing. "What an idiot."

Mina knew she could kill him. After all, she had stabbed his wife to death. Why shouldn't she be able to do the same to him? *Murder, murder, murder.* All she had to do was hold on and wait for her chance.

But then again, the cops said Rachel was still alive according to the news, in which case Mina hadn't killed her. She suspected it was fake news, however. Only a miracle could have saved Rachel's life after what Mina and Catton had put her through. If Rachel hadn't bled out, she must have drowned.

Catton's expression hardened. "We need to convince him to move in with me."

"What good will that do?"

"It'll give me access to his computer. Right now I don't know where he's staying so how can I get to his computer? And, anyway, I want to keep my eye on him. We can't have him welshing on our deal and ratting me out to the cops."

Maybe that was for the best, decided Mina. If those two lived in the same room, Dunleavy was bound to see Catton was dangerous and had to be eliminated.

"Why would he agree to move in with you?" she said.

"Don't worry. I have powers of persuasion. Do you have some way of contacting him?"

"No," she lied. She had Dunleavy's phone number but wasn't going to tell Catton about it. If he knew the truth, he might be able to figure out she was the one that told Dunleavy Catton was still alive.

"Then we have no choice but to wait for him to contact us. In the meantime, we gotta find that password. You need to go back to Rachel's condo and get it."

"What are *you* going to do?"

"Have you heard any updates on the news about Rachel's condition?"

"No."

Catton angled toward the TV set and flicked it on. A game show with noisy contestants waving their arms in glee came on. Catton turned the channel and searched for the news. While he was surfing the channels he found a local news station on cable.

A blow-dried newscaster with grizzled hair was reading the teleprompter as chyrons ran below him.

Catton waited impatiently for any news about Rachel.

At last the newscaster gave a report about her as the TV screen showed news footage of a hospital.

"Rachel Catton is being guarded 24/7 at St. Luke's Hospital as her condition improves," said the newscaster in a voice-over.

"Oh sure," said Catton, watching the screen.

"What?" said Mina, watching also.

"Don't you think that's convenient? I want to know where she's staying, and the fake news gives the name of the hospital."

"You can't be sure it's fake. It's not out of the ordinary that news reports say where a patient is being treated."

Catton shrugged. "There's only one way to find out."

"You're going to the hospital?"

"I'm gonna find out if Rachel's really still alive like the news says."

"And?"

Without missing a beat he said, "And then I'll kill her again." He paused. "Unless you want to do it."

She ignored his suggestion. "Maybe that's what they're hoping you'll try to do. That could be why they're announcing the hospital's name on TV. They figure the killer will try to finish her off in the hospital so she can't testify against him."

"*Of course* that's why they said she's still alive and where she's being treated."

"Then you're walking straight into a trap."

"I'm doing what has to be done."

Chapter 54

Catton drove his Mustang to a costume store and bought green surgical scrubs from a walleyed middle-aged lady with an attitude.

"Who do you think you'll scare with that doctor's getup?" she said, eying his purchase.

"I'm trying to impress my date," said Catton. "I want her to think I'm a doctor when we meet tonight."

"I've heard it all," she said, and slapped the counter next to her cash register. "I want to tell you."

"Why's it so expensive?" said Catton, counting out the cash to pay for it.

"Better than a punch in the nose," she said with a crooked smile.

Catton left the store carrying a plastic bag with the scrubs in it. Opening his car door he tossed the plastic bag in the front passenger seat, got in, donned his sunglasses, fired the engine, put the car in gear, and drove to St. Luke's Hospital.

He found a space in the massive parking lot, parked the Mustang, and cut across the lot, bag in hand. As soon as he entered the lobby he searched for a restroom, careful not to make eye contact with the receptionist, who was flipping through a magazine, or with any of the medical staff who were bustling through the hallway. He didn't want any of them to remember him.

He ducked into a restroom, removed his sunglasses, found an empty stall, and put the scrubs on over his clothes. He checked himself out in the long horizontal mirror that extended over the row of sinks. The image of a bearded surgeon stared back at him. Why not? he thought, convinced he looked like any other doctor at the hospital.

From his trouser pocket he removed a pair of nonprescription spectacles with thick black bows and donned

201

them to help mask his features. There was no way he could wear the shades he had been using for his disguise inside a hospital without attracting unwanted attention, hence the spectacles.

From his pocket he also removed a disposable surgical cap, which had come with the scrubs costume, and set it on his head, covering his hair and ears.

From his other trouser pocket he fished out a crumpled pair of latex surgical gloves, which also came with the costume, and slipped them onto his hands. He didn't want to leave his prints anywhere, in case he touched something.

Now all he had to do was find the room where Rachel was being treated, according to the news. If she *was* still alive, she had to be in a comatose state—or she would have identified him as her would-be killer and the cops would have put out a BOLO on him, which they would have told Dunleavy about when they interrogated him.

According to Dunleavy, the cops hadn't a clue that Catton was still alive, which meant Rachel hadn't ID'd him as the killer.

Catton emerged from the restroom and blended into the hallway pedestrian traffic that consisted of medical staff and patients.

It was all about adopting a pose. He strutted down the hall like any other surgeon, cocksure of himself and his abilities to save human life with his massive intellect and his dexterous hands. A god among mortals. A charlatan.

He liked this role. He was having fun. A smile flickered across his lips. Some roles he felt he was born to play.

All the while he was searching for Rachel's room.

Once in a while he would spot a uniformed cop standing in the hall, but not often, and the ones he did spot weren't guarding a specific room.

Rachel's room must be on another floor, Catton decided. He was sure she would have a guard standing sentry on her room.

He had no idea which floor she was on. He would have to search all of them until he located her.

There were colored lines on the floor that led in different directions like they were trails you were supposed to follow, but that was only if you knew where you wanted to go. They didn't do him any good so he ignored them. If he had any idea where he was going, they would be helpful, but he didn't.

Walking down the hall he surveyed the rooms. Whenever he noticed a CCTV camera mounted on the walls near the ceiling, he kept his face averted from the lens.

He wasn't going to look in every room to scope out each patient. That would take forever. He figured a cop would be posted at Rachel's room, especially if this was a ruse to trap the killer. Even if it wasn't a trap, she would probably have a cop posted at her door since she was the victim of an assault and was therefore the subject of an ongoing police investigation, which warranted police protection.

He drew blanks on the first floor. He saw a couple of surly hospital rent-a-cops standing in the hall, but he doubted the LAPD had hired them. The force would use its own officers for an assault case.

He took the elevator to the second floor and cast around for a cop. He saw another security guard, but no cop.

He rode to the next floor. Trying to look businesslike, an expression of haughty concentration on his face, he wended his way down the hall checking for a cop. He suppressed an urge to break into laughter. His role as the great surgeon amused him. He didn't think he could bridle the urge much longer.

At the end of the corridor he saw a uniformed cop sitting in front of a room on a cheap plastic orange contoured chair, talking on his cell phone.

Barely able to keep his countenance grave, Catton decided to further conceal his face in case he started giggling. He ducked into a supply room, where he found a cardboard box full of surgical masks on one of the wooden shelves. Alone in the room, he giggled as he removed his cap and attached a mask to his face, looping its elastic straps around his ears. He replaced his cap. Nobody would recognize him now.

Taking a deep breath and gathering himself he became somber once again, playing the role of a surgeon, a master of the universe, a man who wielded the power of life and death over his fellow mortals. A total fraud.

Emerging from the closet he made for the patient's room that the cop was guarding. As he approached within earshot of the thirtyish cop he could hear him chatting to his wife, it sounded like.

Though the cop remarked Catton's presence, he didn't pay attention to Catton in his surgical getup.

Catton stood in front of the translucent plastic container affixed to the wall and withdrew the patient's file from it. The manila folder had Rachel Catton's name on it. Flipping through the pages he cast a furtive glance inside the room, whose door was open.

There was a woman lying on her back underneath the sheets, her face turned toward the window on the other side of the room, the blinds drawn open. He couldn't believe Rachel was still alive. How could she possibly survive drowning and being stabbed multiple times? He couldn't leave her like this, he knew.

All he had to do was walk over to her bed, press a pillow over her face, and smother her to finish her off.

His heartbeat accelerating, he deposited her folder into the plastic container on the wall and slipped into her room, a doctor treating his patient. Who would say otherwise?

Nearing her bed he got a clear view of her face, which had been canted away from the door as she took a nap.

"Doctor," said a male voice behind him.

Shoulders hunched, Catton froze. He wheeled around.

"Yes," he said to the cop, who was standing now in the doorway, doorknob in hand.

"Should I close the door while you examine her?"

"That won't be necessary," said Catton, and barreled past the cop, who released the doorknob to let him pass into the hall.

Head erect, Catton strode down the hall, a doctor in a hurry to examine his next patient. A half grin formed on his mouth.

He had to get out of here on the double, he knew, remembering to keep his face averted from the hospital's security cameras mounted throughout the building.

The grin was still on his face as he tore down the stairwell and rocketed down the steps to the main floor, where he emerged and entered the corridor at a steady pace, his mask in place.

He was even grinning when he debouched onto the street and detached the mask from his ears.

He was grinning because he had just found out that the patient known as "Rachel Catton" at the hospital wasn't Rachel Catton at all. Whoever it was didn't look anything like Rachel. It might have been a female cop posing as her. Catton couldn't say.

All he could say for sure was, it was as he had suspected. The cops had set a trap for the killer by promulgating the fake news that she was alive.

One less thing to worry about, he decided, detouring into a neighboring café that had a blackboard with today's specials chalked on it propped up on its patio. He crossed the patio and entered the café proper, where he used the restroom and flushed the surgical mask, cap, and latex gloves down the high-pressure toilet.

He removed his scrubs, bundled them into an unrecognizable wad, wedged them under his left arm, took leave of the café, and returned to the sidewalk.

He wouldn't have to kill Rachel again, however much he would like to now that he knew she had been fooling around behind his back with Bendix. The two-timing double-crosser.

Chapter 55

Mina wasn't happy to see Catton storming into her motel room.

"The whole thing was a setup," he said. "It was fake news, just like I told you."

"What's the point?" said Mina, closing and locking the door behind him.

"To trick us into killing Rachel again," said Catton, pivoting around to watch what she was doing.

"Rachel wasn't in the hospital?" she said, leaning back against the door.

She didn't want to get too close to him. He looked worked up enough that he might take a swing at her, or worse, he might chain her to the bed again and burn her. On the other hand, he appeared to be in a good mood, despite his access of energy.

"Nope," he said.

"How can you be sure?"

"I went into her hospital room and got a good look at her face. It must've been a cop posing as her as part of the trap."

"Why didn't they stop you from entering her room?"

"I was disguised as a doctor."

"Then Rachel's really dead," said Mina as if to herself, becoming depressed because it confirmed she really was a murderer.

Murder, murder, murder—the word kept repeating in her head again like hammer blows.

She had held out hope until that moment that the TV news report was true that Rachel had miraculously survived the assault. Now Mina's hopes were dashed.

She hated herself for following Catton's orders to stab his wife to death. He had made her feel like she had to do it, though. At the time, she couldn't resist him. Her spirits had been low as she was suicidal. She had been at the nadir of a bout of manic depression, and then he had come along, reeking of death, dragging a dying woman with him. Mina had had no energy left to resist him.

Now that she was guilty of murder, she saw no way she could go to the cops and tell them Gage Catton was alive and had defrauded Lion Life Insurance without his implicating her in retaliation. She had to deal with him herself before he killed her.

Catton poured himself a scotch and stalked around the room, his expression arrogant, drink in hand, the liquor sloshing fitfully out onto the carpet.

"They thought they could fool me with their stupid hoax," he said, holding his head high.

"How can you be sure nobody recognized you at the hospital?"

"No way. I looked just like any other doctor there in my scrubs."

"Maybe they have security cameras that photographed you."

"They did. I saw them mounted in the hallways. But so what? All the cameras recorded were pictures of a surgeon in scrubs making his rounds. Why would the cops even bother to watch the security video? They would have no reason. I didn't do anything to the fake Rachel. Nothing untoward happened while I was there."

"I don't know what you're so happy about. If Rachel's really dead, it means we're murderers."

"It means she can't testify against us. That was the only thing that could've put us in the slam." He took a pull on his scotch and put down the glass on the sideboard.

"What if it was a trick?"

"It *was* a trick. Haven't you been listening?"

Mina paced around the room. "What if the cops put Rachel in another room to protect her from the killer when he showed up at the hospital, and they planted a cop to impersonate her in the room supposedly assigned to her? That explains why it was so easy for you to enter her room."

"Wishful thinking on your part," Catton scoffed. "You're overcomplicating this. Cops aren't that bright. You desperately want Rachel to still be alive, but she isn't. Get over it. You killed her."

Of course, Rachel was dead, decided Mina, and *she* would be, too, soon, at the hands of a homicidal maniac.

"Maybe we should turn ourselves in," she said. "We might get a lighter sentence."

"Life imprisonment, instead of the death sentence? How comforting."

Mina gave him a look.

There was a knock on the door.

Bryan Cassiday

Chapter 56

"Who's that?" Catton asked her. "Are you making friends around this place?"

"No," said Mina, eying the door with uncertainty.

She approached it and peered through the peephole.

Seeing who it was, she unlocked the door and opened it.

Clad in Bermudas and espadrilles, Dunleavy walked in.

Mina smelled liquor on his breath. She shut the door behind him, wondering what he wanted.

"Am I interrupting something?" he said, picking up on the glare Catton was favoring him with.

"Why do you always show up whenever I come to Mina's room?" said Catton.

"I happened to see your car pull into the parking lot. I need to talk to you."

"Have you been tailing me?" said Catton, miffed, his mind clouded with suspicion.

"Not at all. I was pulling into the parking lot when I saw you leave your car."

Mina hoped Dunleavy was keeping watch of the motel so he could keep an eye on Catton and come to her aid if necessary. Somehow she doubted such was the case. But that didn't mean she couldn't hope for it. Then what was Dunleavy really up to?

"Hmm. I wonder." Catton changed the subject. "Why did you come here?"

"I want a down payment."

"What?" said Catton, screwing up his face.

Mina knew Dunleavy's request would rile Catton.

"I need some money," said Dunleavy, his expression set. "I want a down payment or I'm walking away from this and right into a police station."

"What makes you think I have any money?"

210

"Then you better get some. I have bills to pay."

"You'll get your money when I get mine from Rachel's bank account. We already agreed that was how our plan would work."

"I didn't plan on it taking this long, though. You're not making any progress getting the money that I can see."

"Just what am I supposed to pay you with?"

"That's up to you."

"You're skating on thin ice as it is, and you come here making demands?" said Catton. "You're a Johnny-come-lately to this deal."

"I have power."

Catton snickered. "You must be joking."

"Nobody but me knows you're alive. Me and Mina, I mean," said Dunleavy, glancing at Mina.

"This is still my operation," said Catton, angling over to the sofa. "You're not taking it over."

"All I want is a down payment. I don't want to take over anything."

Lost in thought, Catton walked to the wet bar and halted, his back to it. "For the sake of argument, how much to you want?"

Dunleavy didn't take long to answer. "Five grand would tide me over for now."

"Out of the question."

Dunleavy sighed. "If I walk out on this deal, I'll have to report seeing you to the cops. I know you don't want that."

Catton coughed and did a slow burn. "Are you blackmailing me?"

"No way. All I'm asking for is a down payment on the deal we cut."

"That's all, huh?"

"Otherwise, I'm outta here."

Mina wondered if Catton might try to kill Dunleavy on the spot. She could tell Catton was steaming, though he was

211

masking it to some degree. The guy didn't like taking orders from anyone, she had learned from her short but intense relationship with him.

"All right," said Catton, regaining his equanimity. "We certainly don't want you to leave our operation. If I *do* give you a down payment, I'll have to subtract the amount from your cut of our take."

Used to being with him, Mina wasn't surprised by his change in demeanor. She knew his moods were mercurial. She never knew what to expect from him at any given moment. She figured he was capable of anything, no matter what the occasion. He was, in a word, unpredictable. One minute he looked like he was going to tear your head off, the next he was all sweetness and light.

"No problem," said Dunleavy, closing his eyes and nodding his approval.

"Give me till tomorrow," said Catton.

Dunleavy mulled over Catton's counteroffer. "Are you sure you can get it?"

"Of course."

"Tomorrow's the soonest you can get it?"

"Yeah."

Dunleavy shrugged, not eager about the idea of waiting another day, but he figured it was the best offer Catton would come up with.

"I wouldn't try any funny business if I was you," said Catton.

Dunleavy shook his head like he didn't understand what Catton was talking about.

"You can't kill a dead man," said Catton with a lopsided grin.

Dunleavy didn't look any wiser.

Catton's answer gave Mina food for thought. Since everyone believed Catton was dead, how could she or anyone be convicted of killing him? She could kill him with impunity. How could you go on trial for killing a man that was already dead? If she could only bring herself to actually commit the act of murder—or get Dunleavy to do it.

But it would still have to wait till they got their hands on the money. The question was, did they really need Catton alive to get ahold of the money if she could find the password? Why couldn't she transfer the money from Rachel's account to one she set up, if she had the password? Why did *Catton* have to make the online transfer? Anyone with the password could do it, it seemed to her. Or was she missing something?

Dunleavy left without saying anything, unsure what Catton meant.

"Do you have five thousand dollars?" said Mina.

"No," said Catton.

"Then how can you pay him tomorrow?"

"He won't be around tomorrow."

Chapter 57

Lieutenant Philippe Duquesne visited St. Luke's Hospital.

The guard he had posted in front of Catton's door was sitting on a chair blowing a pink bubble with his bubblegum. Though in his thirties he had a youthful face and looked like he would blend right in to the college crowd.

When he spotted Duquesne, the guard flew out of his seat in front of Catton's room and came to attention. The bubble burst and coated his face with a pink film. He tried to wipe it off his mouth with his hand but was only partially successful.

There wasn't a large amount of foot traffic in the hall at this time of the day, Duquesne noticed.

"What have you got, Pirelli?" said Duquesne.

"Nothing, sir."

Pirelli looked silly with that pink gunk all over his mouth like a cobweb, decided Duquesne.

"How long have you been on guard here?" he said.

"The whole day," said Pirelli.

"Just you? Nobody else."

"Right, sir."

"And you didn't see anybody try to get into Rachel Catton's room?"

"No. Uh, I mean, no, other than the doctor."

Pirelli's breath smelled sweet like bubblegum, Duquesne noticed.

"Why did a doctor go into the room?" said Duquesne.

"I dunno. He didn't stay very long."

"How do you know he was a doctor? Did you ask for ID?"

"He was wearing one of those green smocks that doctors wear."

"Surgeons, you mean?"

"Yeah. Come to think of it, he was wearing a surgical mask, too." Grimacing, Pirelli brushed more bubblegum off his mouth.

"The problem is, the woman lying in bed in that room isn't a real patient. She's one of us."

"I know that, sir."

"Then why would a doctor pay her a visit if she's not a real patient?"

Pirelli shrugged. "Maybe Carol knows."

"Is that the name of the policewoman?"

"Yep."

Duquesne entered the hospital room and greeted Carol, who was lying on her back, her face canted toward the door, watching him enter. She tried to get out of bed to stand at attention, but he held up his hand, gesturing for her to halt.

"Never mind," said Duquesne.

Carol lay back on the patient bed.

"What did the doctor want with you?" he said.

"What doctor?"

"Pirelli said a surgeon came in here to look at you."

"I didn't see any surgeon in here, sir."

"Pirelli," said Duquesne over his shoulder. "Come here."

Pirelli entered the room.

"She says she didn't see any surgeon in here," said Duquesne.

"I saw him come in here," said Pirelli.

Carol cleared her throat. "I may've nodded off for a while. Lying here in bed all day makes me sleepy."

"Nobody made an attempt on your life?" said Duquesne.

Carol chuckled. "Not even close. It's been all peace and quiet in here. That's what put me to sleep."

Duquesne turned to Pirelli. "How long was the surgeon in here?"

"A few seconds. I asked him if he wanted the door closed. He said no and left."

"Did he get a good look at Carol's face, did you notice?"

"I can't say for sure. I wasn't in here the whole time he was here."

"Did he give you his name?"

"I didn't ask for it. I saw his surgeon's smock. I didn't see any need to ask for ID."

"It's not a smock. Surgeons wear scrubs. Did he have a name tag on his scrubs?"

Pirelli shut his eyes, trying to recall. "I don't remember seeing one."

"Could you ID him if you saw him again?"

Pirelli picked at remnants of the bubblegum stuck on his face. "That would be tough. Like I said, he was wearing a mask that covered most of his face. He was also wearing glasses with thick black frames." Pirelli paused, remembering. "And he had a beard."

"What kind of beard? Like the three day's stubble that everybody wears nowadays ad nauseam?"

"It wasn't stubble. It was a full black beard."

"If the hospital showed you pictures of the doctors that work here, would you recognize him?"

"Maybe. I could try."

"Do you think that doctor was the killer, sir?" said Carol.

"I dunno. I don't understand why a surgeon would come in here, since you aren't really a patient."

"Maybe he came to the wrong room."

"That would explain why he left so quickly," said Pirelli.

"Possible," said Duquesne.

Creasing his brow Pirelli massaged his cheek. "But I could've sworn he checked the patient file near the door before he entered the room."

"Then we need to take a closer look at this guy," said Duquesne. "If he *was* the killer, he would've seen that Carol wasn't Rachel Catton and then beat it."

"Or he was a doctor that realized he was in the wrong room and left," said Carol.

"Then why didn't he leave when he read Rachel Catton's name on the patient file near your door?" said Pirelli.

"I'll get pictures of the medical staff for both of you to look at," said Duquesne, turning to leave. "And you keep guarding the door, Pirelli." He was on the point of leaving when he said, "If another doctor shows up here, be sure to get his name."

"What about the video feeds?" said Pirelli. "Maybe I can pick the guy out in one of the hospital security videos."

"I'm taking care of that. I'll send somebody else up here to take your place, then you go and watch the videos. But from what you said, we're not gonna be able to see his face because of that mask he was wearing. Facial recognition software won't work on a guy wearing a mask, as far as I know."

"I guess all we're gonna be able to figure out is whether he's a doctor here or not."

"If he *is* a doctor here, I doubt he's the killer, and we won't have to worry about him."

Invigorated at feeling he had uncovered a clue to the killer's identity, Duquesne stormed out of the room, bumping into a nurse as he burst into the hall.

"Excuse me," he said, flustered. "I'm—I'm in the way."

Regaining his composure he departed briskly.

Chapter 58

Dunleavy was driving Mina in his black Dodge Challenger along Wilshire Boulevard near the beach.

Mina didn't like riding in all-black cars. She found them depressing. Black everywhere. Black leather seats, black rugs, black dashboard, tinted black windshield, black hood in front of you . . . It might as well be a hearse. She could do without so much black surrounding her.

"You can't kill a dead man," she said.

"What?" said Dunleavy, one arm on the wheel, the other lying crosswise on the open window's metal sash, his elbow sticking outside.

"That's what Catton said. And it makes sense."

"If you say so," said Dunleavy, not getting it.

"Catton is officially dead. If you kill him, you'll never be convicted of murder."

"Wait a minute—"

"Just listen."

"When you kill him, his death won't be officially recorded anywhere. He's already considered dead, so the cops won't investigate. If the cops don't investigate, they'll never catch you."

"If the corpse was a victim of murder, the cops'll investigate. Take my word for it."

"Not if he was already reported dead. They'll take his fingerprints and find out Catton was ruled dead and his case has been closed for a year."

"It doesn't work like that. They always investigate murders, and they'll find out he died recently, not a year ago."

"Then hide the body so nobody can find it. He won't be reported missing because he's already been declared dead, so nobody'll investigate his disappearance."

"I told you before, I'm not a killer."

"Then you're dead."

Dunleavy snapped his head around to scrutinize her face. "You're not kidding."

"I'm afraid not. You're next on Catton's list."

"What list?"

"His hit list. He told me after you left us that you had to go."

Dunleavy heard a car's horn and whipped his head back toward the windshield to make sure he wasn't crashing into anyone.

"That can't be right," he said. "He just got through telling me he was gonna pay me."

"You can't believe anything he says."

"Does he know you're with me?"

"No. I told him I had to go out. He doesn't know I have your phone number. He doesn't want me to see you at all. Look, we're running out of time. You have to kill him, and you gotta do it fast."

They took a left on Ocean Avenue and headed toward Venice, past the Santa Monica Pier, which jutted out into the Pacific Ocean, a Ferris wheel and a roller coaster near its base.

"I gotta have money," said Dunleavy. "That's what I gotta have."

"And you'll get a lot of it by the time we're done. The life insurance policy was worth close to a million."

"Don't I know it? The insurers told me about it."

"I can't stay with you much longer. He wants me to go back with him to Rachel's condo and find her password."

"All right. I'll head back to your motel."

"You're missing the point of this visit," said Mina, becoming frustrated.

"What point?"

"You need to kill him today. You're gonna be gone by tomorrow."

"I'm not going anywhere till I get my cut."

"You're not going anywhere because you'll be dead."

Dunleavy turned on her. "Is that a threat?"

"*He's* the one that's gonna kill you. Not me. Can't you get that through your thick head? I'm on your side, and I want you to be on my side. That's why we're having this powwow."

"We hashed this out before." He turned back to the road in front of him. "I don't see that anything has changed."

"You don't believe he's gonna kill you?"

"No. He doesn't want a murder rap following him around. Committing fraud is one thing. Committing murder is a horse of a different color. They can give you the death penalty for it in California."

"He already killed Bendix. Why not kill you in the bargain?"

"I don't believe he did kill Bendix. He's a con man, not a murderer."

Mina smirked.

She felt tempted to tell him Catton had murdered Rachel, but she didn't want to get into that, and Dunleavy wouldn't believe her, anyway, since he didn't believe her about Bendix.

This guy was as stubborn as a mule, she decided. He had tunnel vision. He only believed what he wanted to believe. He refused to believe the truth even when she told it to him.

She was so put out by him she felt like punching him in the jaw. Grinding her teeth she didn't know what else she could say to convince him he had to take out Catton to save both himself and her.

It always came back to her. She was the one that would have to kill Catton. It was like that all her life. It was always her that had to get something done. Everything was up to *her* now. She had to eliminate Catton.

Murder, murder, murder . . . There it was again pounding in her head ad infinitum.

She wasn't a child anymore. She couldn't count on anybody to ever help her. She had to do everything herself. She had to find the courage to kill Catton with her own two hands.

Murder, murder, murder—

It had been a waste of time enlisting Dunleavy's aid in the scam. All Dunleavy wanted out of it was the money, and he was too pigheaded to see his life was in jeopardy. He couldn't care less about her life.

"Take me back to the motel," she said in resignation.

Bryan Cassiday

Chapter 59

Being dead was a trip, decided Catton, driving his
Mustang down Ocean Avenue. He found he could think better
while he was driving, and he needed to think.

Being dead, he didn't have to pay taxes to the IRS. He
didn't have to do anything. It was a great feeling. He could
float around, free as a bird, without anybody paying any
attention to him. Ironically, he felt liberated and powerful.

There was only one problem.

And it was a big one.

And it wasn't going away.

He needed money.

Even though he was presumed dead, he had to have
money. It was impossible to make money when you were
dead. He had to get his money back from his thieving wife
Rachel. Even though she was dead, she was still messing up
his life big time.

He had to create a phony bank account. He couldn't use
the joint bank account in his and her name because Rachel had
closed it after his presumed death.

He would have to open a new bank account under an
assumed name. Which meant he had to establish a false
identity and become one of the living once more. He would
have to rise like Lazarus from the grave, but unlike Lazarus he
would have to assume a new identity.

If only that woman, his partner in crime, hadn't swindled
him, the shekels would be his even now, decided Catton.

He knew the password to her bank account had to be
somewhere in her condo, since it hadn't been on her person
when he gutted her like a fish. He hadn't been thinking
clearly when he killed her, or he would have demanded her
bank account password from her before carving her up.
Blinded by his hatred of her for double-crossing him, all he

had managed to get from her before she passed out was her ATM PIN, which didn't give him access to her online bank account.

He was so furious with her for swindling him he had to kill her. She had to be punished for screwing him, after all the trouble he had taken to scam Lion Life Insurance. And then she had the gall to scam *him*. There was no way he could let her get away with that.

He glanced down at his speedometer in the dash and noticed he was speeding. He slowed down.

He had to avoid getting busted for a traffic violation. The traffic cop would demand to see his driver's license, and when the cop ran it, it would put Gage Catton's name back into play, dead no more and a suspect in Rachel Catton's murder and in an insurance scam.

Catton would have to lie low as the cops pursued their investigation of his wife's murder. He couldn't let them know he was still alive. Not only would he become a murder suspect, he would lose the life insurance policy his wife had collected on, since Lion Life would find out he wasn't really dead and revoke the policy's payout.

From his online research he knew the government could prosecute a scammer for filing a fake death claim to cash in on an insurance policy. You could get at least ten years for fraud, he had read. For murder you could get the death penalty, depending on which state you were tried in.

There was no way he could return to life as Gage Catton. Such a move would be an invitation to disaster. There were too many ways he could get nailed.

He would have to create a new identity with a phony birth certificate and a phony Social Security number in order to collect his stolen cash. He had no other alternative.

Or did he?

What if he transferred the money out of Rachel's account into Mina's? He didn't even know if Mina had her own bank account. He figured she did. Most people in their twenties had bank accounts. Didn't they? His father opened one for him when he went to college. He didn't know if Mina had gone to college. For that matter, he didn't know much of anything about her, except she was depressed over something when he had first met her.

He didn't think he could trust Mina with all that money. Why should he? It had turned out he couldn't even trust his own wife with that sum of money. *Money corrupts*, he thought. *And big money corrupts big time.*

He might be able to transfer the money to Mina's account only for the time being, then set up a phony account for himself later, maybe even an offshore account, and have it transferred there. An offshore account would be better, since the US authorities wouldn't be able to freeze it or access it if they happened to find out Gage Catton was still alive.

He hadn't gone to the trouble to set up an offshore account before he faked his death, because he hadn't expected Rachel to rob him, drain all the money out of their joint account, and transfer it to her own private account. Did she really think he could let her go on living if she pulled that stunt? And then it turned out she was cheating on him with another man to boot.

It just went to show you couldn't trust anyone, Catton decided. Then why should he trust Mina enough to store his money in her account? Because he wouldn't leave it there long. He would have it transferred to an offshore account as soon as he could set one up.

He wouldn't be able to eliminate Mina right away if he used her bank account to store his money. He had planned on getting rid of her soon, even though he was becoming very fond of her. She was eye candy and nice to have around. And she looked hot, her pink and white flesh writhing naked chained to a bed. An instant turn-on.

But he didn't trust her with his money. He would set up a bank account under a phony name. It wouldn't be difficult once he had a phony birth certificate.

Unlike Mina, Dunleavy had to go ASAP. He added nothing. He had invited himself where he wasn't wanted, had crashed the party, so to speak. His days were numbered.

The main snag remained.

Catton had to latch onto the password to Rachel's online bank account, or nothing else mattered. The scam was a bust.

Chapter 60

Duquesne was standing at the front of a police meeting room drawing up a whiteboard of the Rachel Catton murder investigation. With its rows of desks attached to chairs the meeting room looked like a schoolroom.

This must be how a professor felt, he decided. Except he wasn't going to lecture about higher learning. He was going to talk about murder.

He was alone save for Patrick, who watched him from a chair in the front row of the room as though his life depended on it. A Styrofoam cup of steaming coffee and a half-eaten tamale he had bought from a roach coach were sitting on his desktop.

"Rachel Catton was stabbed to death," said Duquesne, printing her name on the whiteboard in block letters with a black Sharpie. Beside her name he wrote Gage Catton's. "We also know that her husband disappeared under mysterious circumstances. What does that tell you, Patrick?" said Duquesne, turning around to face him.

"The same person had something to do with it?"

"Why?"

"Because the Cattons were husband and wife."

"Are you saying Gage Catton was murdered, too?"

"His disappearance looks suspicious since his wife was murdered."

"The official police report said Gage Catton drowned at sea by accident."

"But the corpse was never found."

Duquesne nodded. "I'm always suspicious of anyone that disappears without a trace. It happens so rarely. It's difficult to disappear from the face of the earth without deliberation behind it."

"The life insurance company still decided to pay out to his wife on his policy—even without the discovery of the corpse."

"Rachel Catton's lawyers applied pressure to them to pony up."

"Lawyers . . . ," said Patrick, picked up a white plastic fork from his desktop, and stuffed a bite-size portion of tamale into his mouth.

"It had all the appearances of a tragic accident at sea. Catton's boat was found adrift in the Pacific off the coast of Oahu with nobody aboard. The Coast Guard ruled he fell overboard and drowned during rough seas."

"But the corpse never washed up anywhere."

"No. For all we know, he could have been murdered at sea."

"I read the Coast Guard report. They didn't find any evidence of murder," said Patrick, and swallowed the morsel of tamale in his mouth.

"Any time a missing corpse and a life insurance policy are involved, I'm suspicious of foul play."

Rapt in thought, Duquesne marched back and forth in front of the whiteboard like a sentry on duty, only instead of a rifle he carried a Sharpie in his hand.

"And now Catton's wife ends up murdered," he said, "which makes me even more suspicious."

"You think we're looking at two murders?"

"I don't know why somebody would want to kill both of them."

Patrick pulled a face. "Maybe they had enemies."

Duquesne faced the whiteboard and used his Sharpie to print another name on it. Edward Bendix.

"You think the Bendix murder is connected to Rachel Catton's?" said Patrick.

Duquesne turned around to speak to Patrick. "The last call Bendix made before he was murdered was to Rachel

Catton. Her number was on his cell phone, which has a record of the calls he made."

"It could be a coincidence."

"I don't like coincidences when it comes to murder investigations. These two victims knew each other, and their murders occurred only days apart."

"But different MOs were used. Rachel was stabbed to death. Bendix was strangled."

"Garroted, to be exact," said Duquesne. "His head was practically severed from his body as the garrote sliced through his windpipe."

"If it's the same killer, wouldn't the MOs be the same?"

"Not necessarily. I don't believe we're dealing with a serial killer or a professional hit man, who would each use signature MOs."

"Why not a hit man? They've been known to use garrotes."

"Good point. But why didn't he use it on Rachel, too?"

"I dunno. What about fingerprints at the scene of the crime?"

"There are scores of fingerprints in restaurant bathrooms. How would we know which ones belonged to the killer?"

"We could narrow down the suspects to those that left prints."

"How do we know that the killer didn't wear gloves?"

Patrick conceded the point. "We don't. Still, we could try and see where it gets us."

"Agreed. See to it. But I'm not hopeful on that score."

"What else do we have to go on?"

"Ed Bendix was a garden-variety salesman. He sold car insurance. Who would want to hire a hit man to whack out a salesman?"

"Bendix doesn't have a hot sheet?"

"Nothing but a parking ticket six months ago. I don't believe we're dealing with a contract killer in these slayings."

"How did he meet Rachel?"

"They met on Tinder."

"Tinder?"

"An Internet dating site."

"Everything's on the Internet these days."

"Everything."

"A dating site?" said Patrick. "But Rachel was married. Why's she on a dating site?"

"You forget, her husband was declared dead. Why wouldn't she be on a dating site?"

Patrick nodded yes. "Further evidence her husband really is dead."

"Not really evidence. Just an interesting observation. By itself it proves nothing."

"If she knew her husband was alive, she wouldn't be fooling around with other guys. If he's still alive, she's not in on it. She must've believed he was dead," said Patrick with conviction, and sipped his coffee.

"I believe you're wrong on that count."

"How so?" said Patrick, looking up at him through the steam rising from his coffee cup.

"Sometimes I think you're not cynical enough to be a cop."

"Huh?"

"Knowing that her husband was alive wouldn't prevent Rachel from fooling around with other guys on Tinder."

Patrick digested Duquesne's opinion. "That would mean she was two-timing him."

"As a cop you should always believe the worst in people."

"Then we're back to square one."

"Not quite," said Duquesne, holding up his Sharpie. "We have two murders that are related somehow, I believe. And we have a suspicious disappearance at sea, which might also have been a homicide—though there's no evidence of it. And we also have the possibility, since there's no corpus delicti, that Gage Catton might still be alive."

"All we have are theories," said Patrick, his expression glum, gazing down at his desktop, which somebody had carved their initials into with a penknife.

"Ed Bendix knew Rachel Catton. His call to her right before he was murdered is proof of that. And we know they were both murdered. Those are facts, not theories." Duquesne paused. "Gage Catton is another story. His disappearance is a mystery."

Patrick looked up. "At the murder scene Bendix's murder looked like a robbery. His wallet was jacked. Maybe it is what it seems. Why couldn't a robber have clipped Bendix?"

"That's what the killer wants you to believe. Your scenario might make sense if it wasn't for the fact Bendix and Rachel knew each other—and knew each other very well, I'd say."

"It didn't do them any good."

"Now, what about the blank cell phone Bendix was carrying around with him?" said Duquesne, printing Blank Cell Phone on the whiteboard. "What do you make of it?"

"You got me."

"He was carrying a blank cell phone with no fingerprints on it. How did he put it into his pocket?"

"You asked me that before, and I still can't figure it out, since Bendix wasn't wearing gloves."

"I can think of only one explanation. Somebody else put it there. And that somebody was wearing gloves."

"The killer?"

Chapter 61

"I'm surprised the life insurance company paid out on Catton's policy, since nobody found his corpse," said Patrick.

"They were unable to find any evidence the guy's still alive," said Duquesne. "After he vanished at sea, nobody has heard from him since. And his wife was persistent. Her lawyers demanded the insurance company pay her. Eventually, Lion Life relented."

"So where's that leave us? Do we assume he's dead, too?"

"We never assume anything. We're cops. We dig until we find the truth."

"What happened to Gage Catton's bank account after he was declared dead?"

"Actually, he shared a joint account with his wife. He didn't have a personal account."

"And the life insurance payout went into the joint account?"

"That's right. And this is where it gets interesting," said Duquesne, holding up his forefinger near his face. "Rachel Catton closed that account and transferred all of the money to her own personal account after the insurance payout."

"Maybe it was easier to do it that way than remove her husband's name from their joint account."

"Maybe," said Duquesne, unconvinced. "There's one thing I don't understand."

"Only one? There's a lot here I don't get."

"Why did Rachel Catton's killer try to hide her body at sea?"

"So nobody would know she was murdered?"

"Why would that matter to him?"

"He didn't want to get caught. We wouldn't be searching for him as long as we didn't know the murder took place."

"Hmm. Maybe. Or maybe he didn't want anybody to know Rachel was dead."

"You're splitting hairs. What's the difference between *murdered* and *dead*?"

"There's a difference, but I'm not sure what it means. In any case, I do believe we spoiled his plans by finding the corpse."

"Yep." Patrick did a double take. "What plans?" he said, puzzled.

"That's what we need to find out."

"You think he's gonna whack out somebody else?"

"I do."

"Then he's a serial killer."

"Yeah, if we accept the FBI's definition of serial killing."

"Which is?"

Duquesne withdrew a three-by-five card from his blazer's inside breast pocket and read aloud the notes he had scribbled in ink on the card.

"'A serial killing is a series of two or more murders, committed as separate events, usually, but not always, by any offender acting alone.'"

"That description fits our guy," said Patrick.

"But he could also be considered a spree killer because he killed more than one person at multiple locations over a brief period of time."

"Then he's a spree killer."

"I don't think so. There was too big a time break between Rachel's murder and Bendix's. What the FBI calls a 'cooling-off period.'"

"But it *is* just one guy doing the killing. Right?"

"He or she could have a partner. We have two homicides that we know about here. Rachel Catton and Ed Bendix. Bendix called Rachel's number just before he died. There's gotta be a connection between their deaths."

A blonde policewoman pushing thirty, with good posture and her hair done up, entered the conference room carrying a report. "Lieutenant?"

"Yeah," said Duquesne.

"We traced the serial number of that blank iPhone that was found on Ed Bendix's corpse. The iPhone belonged to Rachel Catton."

Floored, Patrick stared at her. "That can't be right."

"There's no mistake," said the policewoman, waving the report in front of her. "The serial numbers match."

"Let me see that," said Duquesne.

She handed him the report and headed to the door.

"Want some of my coffee?" said Patrick with a grin, holding up his coffee cup.

"Not if you've been drinking it," she said, and stalked out.

"She loves me," said Patrick, smiling.

Duquesne couldn't help but notice her black trousers fit her curvy figure like a glove. After she swung out of the room, he redirected his attention to the report.

"But you said Bendix called Rachel's number just before he died," said Patrick, frowning in bemusement at Duquesne. "Why would he call himself?"

"There's only one answer," said Duquesne, looking up from his reading. "This is proof that the killer planted Rachel's wiped iPhone on him. He must have worn gloves so he wouldn't leave prints on it when he left it on Bendix's corpse. The killer must have had Rachel's phone, and he was the one that received Bendix's call, not Rachel."

"What's the point of planting Rachel's phone on Bendix's corpse?"

"Maybe the killer likes playing games. He could be toying with us."

"Then he's sick in the head, and he'll be easy to catch."

"Don't be so sure about the easy-to-catch part. Some of these head cases can be very clever."

"Nobody's too clever for you, Lieutenant," said Patrick, and sipped more coffee.

Duquesne didn't respond to the flattery. He turned toward the whiteboard, Sharpie in hand.

"To sum up," he said. "It looks like we have a romantic relationship between Rachel Catton and Ed Bendix, since they met on Tinder."

He drew a line between Rachel's name and Bendix's with an arrow's tip pointed at Rachel. Then he drew a heart impaled on the arrow between Rachel and Bendix.

"A lover's quarrel? Bendix killed Rachel and committed suicide?" said Patrick.

Duquesne faced Patrick. "It doesn't wash. How could Bendix have garroted himself in the restaurant bathroom?"

Patrick puzzled it out. "Maybe he hanged himself somehow with the garrote."

"Then why didn't we find the garrote at the scene of the crime?"

Patrick hiked his eyebrows. "Oh yeah. We didn't find the murder weapon there, did we?"

"And why was the corpse sitting on a toilet?"

"OK, I get your point. He didn't hang himself."

"Do you remember the scene of the crime?"

"Not as well as you, I guess."

"Why was the corpse sitting on a toilet? Doesn't that strike you as strange?"

"Maybe he was strangled there."

"That would mean the strangler was standing on the back of the toilet waiting for Bendix to enter the stall."

"Looks that way."

"How could the strangler possibly know which stall Bendix would use?"

"How many were there? I can't remember."

"There were four stalls in the restaurant restroom. The killer would have only a 25 percent chance of picking the right stall if he was lying in wait."

"Maybe he locked the other stalls so Bendix had to use the one the killer was waiting in."

"How did he lock the stalls from the outside?"

Patrick squinted in thought. "He locked them from the inside and crawled under the stall partitions to do the same to three of the four." He opened his eyes in triumph.

"Do you remember the crime scene? Picture it in your mind's eye."

"Yeah," said Patrick, shutting his eyes and picturing it.

"In this particular restroom there's not enough room under the stall partitions to allow someone to crawl underneath them, not even enough room for a child to do it."

Grimacing, Patrick scratched his scalp. "I can't recall that much detail."

"Well, I can."

"Then what's your explanation for the corpse sitting on a toilet?"

"The strangler dragged him there after he was dead for some reason."

"I don't get it."

"Perhaps the killer was interrupted during the murder and had to hide the corpse in the stall."

"But there was blood on the floor from Bendix's severed windpipe. The intruder would've seen that."

"Yeah." Duquesne paused. "Little things like that annoy me."

"Like what?"

"The victim propped on the toilet. The strangler didn't kill him there. He dragged him there."

"You may be overthinking this. Killers aren't as smart as you."

Duquesne wouldn't let it go. "There must be a reason."

"To make it look like Bendix was strangled as he was taking a dump? The killer did it as a joke? He's laughing at us now?"

"You may be onto something there. This whole thing could be a sick joke to him. He's taunting us."

Duquesne wrote on the bottom of the whiteboard Ha Ha Ha.

Patrick was startled Duquesne thought he was right.

Chapter 62

In his Mustang, Catton picked up Mina in their motel-room parking lot, where she was standing waiting, and drove her to Rachel's condo.

Neither of them spoke during the ride. Mina looked out the window the whole way watching the sidewalks, deserted for the most part save for vagrants.

"You gotta find her password," said Catton in the driver's seat as he parallel-parked on the side of the street.

"What if the cops are still at her condo?" said Mina.

"Why would they be?"

Some guy passing him in a pickup honked at him.

"What's wrong with that asshole?" said Catton, continuing to back up in order to park.

"Because it's a crime scene," said Mina.

"Her condo? No, it's not. The crime didn't happen there, and the cops know it didn't by now. I knifed her on the beach and covered up her blood with sand so nobody would ever see it."

This was not what Mina wanted to hear. Catton sounded like he was bragging about his knifing of Rachel. A murderer who enjoyed murder and saw it as sport. Like he was playing a game with the cops to prove he was smarter than them. Mina was more and more convinced she would end up dead by Catton's hand.

"Then why don't you come with me?" she said.

Catton shook his head no. "I can't be seen anywhere near her place. They've got CCTV in there."

"But you're in disguise."

"I don't care. I can't risk being seen in there again. The cops may have special facial recognition software that can ID pictures of people even when they're disguised."

Catton killed the Mustang's engine.

Mina climbed out of the car and stepped onto the sidewalk.

"If I see any cops heading toward the condo, I'll warn you on your burner," said Catton, leaning toward her over the empty passenger seat.

"OK," she said, and shut the car door.

She made her way to the condo and, walking up the steps to the lobby door, saw a middle-aged woman with orange hair in a perm leaving the building. Mina caught the plate-glass door before it closed all the way and scooted into the condo lobby, smiling at the lady and thanking her.

The woman glanced at her, thought nothing of it, and left, preoccupied with her own affairs.

Apprehensive that residents might see her, Mina hurried to Rachel's room and let herself in with the key Catton had given her, the one he had lifted from Rachel's corpse.

Where was she going to look this time? wondered Mina, entering the living room and looking around. She had searched all over the place the last time she was here.

She wandered into the bedroom, opened one of the closets, and searched it. She thought she might have searched this closet before, but wasn't sure. She couldn't reach the top shelf. She repaired into the kitchen, collected a wooden chair from it, and returned to the bedroom, lugging the chair with her.

Standing on the chair she was able to reach the top shelf. She saw a deal box, snagged it, and stepped off the chair to examine the contents on the bed. She laid the box on the counterpane and opened the box's lid.

Her burner chimed in her purse. She snapped open the purse, dug out the burner, and answered.

"Don't stay in there too long," said Catton. "I just saw a black-and-white cruise down the street outside the condo."

"Is there a cop outside?"

"Not right now. But get a move on it."

238

He terminated the call.

Wonderful, decided Mina. She had just got here. How was she supposed to find anything if she didn't have adequate time to conduct her search?

She rooted through the contents of the box, casting around for a set of numbers or letters or a combination of both that could serve as a password. She saw a card with numbers printed on it and realized it was Rachel Catton's Social Security number. She kept sorting through the miscellaneous items in the box: an outdated New York driver's license, a spare set of car keys, a spool of lavender thread, the pink slip for her car, a birth certificate, a lock of hair, an expired passport from 1990 . . .

This might be the place where Rachel would store a password number, Mina decided, continuing her rummaging. As thoroughly as she looked, she didn't see any scraps of papers nor pads nor notebook pages with numbers and letters printed on them.

Dismayed, she closed the box's lid. The password wasn't there.

She lifted the box and returned to the closet, planning to replace the box where she had found it.

A thought crossed her mind. Could Rachel have used her Social Security number as a password for her bank account? Or perhaps the first four digits, or the last four? If she forgot the numbers, she could always check her Social Security card to refresh her memory.

She was grasping at straws, she figured.

Deflated, she mounted the chair to replace the box on the closet's shelf. The box shelved, she dismounted the chair and hauled it back to the kitchen, where she had found it.

Having memorized Rachel's Social Security number Mina wrote it down on a pad in her purse. She wasn't optimistic it was the password, but it was worth a try in any case.

Striking out for the door, she wondered what Catton would think of her idea. Thinking, she came to a halt in the middle of the living room. What if she tried to access Rachel's online bank account with the Social Security number, or parts of it, without Catton's presence? She wondered if she would be successful.

Or did she need Catton to locate Rachel's online account? He had already told Mina the name of Rachel's bank. On the other hand, she didn't know Rachel's user name at the bank. Before you could supply the password, you had to supply the user name. She might be able to guess the user name, though. Most people used their own names as user names so they wouldn't forget them when going online.

There was only one way to find out if she needed to have Catton with her when she tried to break into Rachel's account online, decided Mina. She would go to an Internet café and try it.

She slipped out the door, down the hallway, and out the lobby onto the sidewalk, where she walked to Catton's Mustang.

"Did you find it?" he said, opening the door to let her in.

"No."

"Crap. We need that password."

"Then you find it," she said, getting in, annoyed at his chewing her out.

"It's gotta be in her condo somewhere. It's just a matter of finding it. You need to think like her to find it."

"I never even met her. How am I supposed to know how she thought?"

"It's in her condo, damn it."

Chapter 63

Sometimes Catton felt like he really *was* dead. It was like
feeling he didn't belong, like he shouldn't be here at this place
and time. It was a weird feeling, and he didn't enjoy it.
Nobody liked being the odd man out. It was a lonely place.

He was riled that Mina kept failing to find the password
in Rachel's condo. It shouldn't be this difficult. Rachel had
to have written it down somewhere. She didn't have a good
memory. Often she forgot to bring her car keys and her
sunglasses with her.

Catton searched Mina's face. "You're not lying to me,
are you?"

"Lying about what?"

"About finding the password."

"Why would I?"

"If you had the password, you might try to access
Rachel's account by yourself."

"I wouldn't know how to."

There was no way he could tell if she had the password or
not, he decided. He hadn't accompanied her to Rachel's
apartment. There was no telling what Mina found in there.
He was forced to trust her. He didn't like being in a position
where he was forced to trust anyone, especially after he had
trusted his own wife and she had swindled him.

"You'll never be able to access Rachel's account without
my help," he said, riveting his eyes on Mina's. "If you think
you can do it yourself, you're wrong."

"I didn't find any passwords in the condo," said Mina,
crossing her arms over her chest.

"None?"

"I saw nothing that looked like a password."

Frowning, Catton massaged his brow. "It doesn't make sense. The password wasn't on her person, so it must be in her condo."

"Maybe she had a safe deposit box where she keeps the password."

"We didn't have a box for our joint account."

"She wouldn't put it in a box she shared with you."

"True," he said, face glum. "Not if she had this double-cross in mind from the get-go of our scam. Then where the hell is it?"

"Maybe the password is something simple. Like her name, or birth date."

"That would be stupid of her. She wouldn't make it that simple. She knew I'd be coming for her after she pulled this fast one on me."

"Maybe she thought you really were dead."

"No way. She was in on it from day one. She wanted the money as much as me. More so, it appears. She wanted it all for herself."

Every time he thought about it, he got angry. The way she had played him. And he had fallen for it hook, line, and sinker. He hammered the steering wheel with his fist, cursing.

"Is it safe for us to be parked right outside her condo?" said Mina, craning her neck behind her apprehensively.

"If you're lying to me about finding that password, you know what I'll do to you. And it won't be pretty. I'll get it out of you one way or the other. You might as well give it to me now and spare yourself some pain."

"I told you, I didn't find any password."

"Fuck." Catton slammed the heel of his palm against the steering wheel. "Where is it? The money's right there in her account just waiting for me to take it, and I can't do a thing about it."

Catton listened to Mina's silence that followed, trying to interpret it.

Then Mina said, "What do we do now?"

"We have to whack out Dunleavy when it gets dark."

"Can't we put that off?"

"I haven't got anything to pay him with tomorrow. If he doesn't get paid, he'll rat us out."

Chapter 64

Mina thought maybe she could save Dunleavy's life tonight if she told Catton her idea about Rachel's Social Security number. She didn't want to be involved in any more murders, she decided, digging her fingernails into the back of her hand and gnashing her teeth. *Murder, murder, murder . . .* She had murdered her.

"You told me if anything happens to Dunleavy, he has his computer programmed to notify the insurance company that you're still alive," she said.

"He's a bigger risk to us alive than dead. He's never gonna stop blackmailing us. We're his cash cow, and he knows he can keep coming back to us for more."

"He said he wouldn't do that."

"When he runs out of money he will. I guarantee it."

"What if we get the money tonight? Then we can beat it and forget about Dunleavy."

"You're forgetting something. How are we supposed to get the money tonight without the password?"

Mina decided to tell him her idea. It was worth it if it would save Dunleavy's life.

"I've been thinking," she said. "What if Rachel used her Social Security number as her password for her bank account?"

Catton thought about it. "Possible. But what good does that do us? I don't know her Social Security number."

"But I do. I found it in her condo."

Catton sat up straight, eyes alert. "We could try it. Nothing ventured, nothing gained. The so-called experts say you shouldn't use your Social Security number as a password, but whoever listens to them?"

"What about her birth date?"

Catton shook his head no. "That was the first thing I tried. I didn't know her Social. Do you have the card with you?"

"I memorized the number."

"The thing about Rachel was, she didn't have a good memory. I doubt she could remember her Social Security number."

"She may've just used the first four digits or the last four."

"We have to get to a computer to try it," said Catton, and fired the Mustang's engine. "At least it's worth a try."

Mina felt relieved she had saved Dunleavy's life—at least for the time being. She had questions, though.

"What good is the password if you don't have anywhere to transfer the money out of Rachel's account?" she said.

"I'm way ahead of you. I already established a fake account at another bank."

"How did you do that?"

"I used a phony birth certificate and Social Security number when I set up the account at the bank."

"Is getting a phony birth certificate that easy?" said Mina in surprise.

"It is if you know where to look. I got it and a Social off the Dark Web using a Tor browser. They sell everything on the Dark Web, most of it illegal. You can buy legit Socials there and legit credit card numbers, whatever you want. Hackers steal this information from online accounts and then peddle it on the Dark Web."

"Do you have a computer with you?"

"It's in my motel room, and it has free Wi-Fi courtesy of the motel so I can get on the Internet. One thing worries me," he said, drumming his fingers on the steering wheel.

"What's that?"

"There's a limit on the amount of attempts I can make trying to access Rachel's bank account. Once I reach that limit, the bank will lock the account for the rest of the day. They might even lock it permanently."

Catton drove past a row of coral trees that were growing on the grassy ten-foot-wide median strip.

"Then what do we do?" said Mina.

"We can't let that happen, is all. Then . . ."

"Then what?"

"After I transfer the money, we have to whack out Dunleavy."

"I thought we didn't need to do that anymore," said Mina with alarm.

"Not right now. We'll do it later. As long as he's alive he's a threat to us. We can't trust him. Ever."

"You said we didn't have to kill him anymore."

"I never said that. Whatever happens, he's gotta go. I wish we had some way to contact him so we could arrange a meet. He can contact us because he knows where we're staying, but we can't contact him. I don't like it."

Mina knew how to contact Dunleavy, but she had no intention of telling Catton she had Dunleavy's phone number. She didn't want any part of luring Dunleavy into a trap set by Catton.

On the other hand, she wished she could come up with an idea how to lure Catton into a trap where she could kill *him*. The more she thought about it, the more she became convinced that maybe if they set up a meeting with Dunleavy, she could catch Catton off guard and kill him at that time.

But what would she use to kill him? she wondered. She didn't have a gun, and she didn't have money to buy one.

She was still tempted to try and flee, but she was convinced Catton would track her down and kill her. She knew she had to take him out before he did the same to her.

She was giving herself a headache thinking about it. She told herself to relax and think clearly. It was easier to give advice than to take it, she was learning. She was never very good at taking it.

She never should have run away from home, she decided with regret. On the other hand, she had to learn how to take care of herself at some point. She wasn't going to stay at home for the rest of her life and live in the basement. She had to make her own way.

But nothing in her life had prepared her for a psychopath named Catton.

Chapter 65

Duquesne was standing beside Pirelli in St. Luke's security office watching a CCTV tape of the bearded man in scrubs that had visited Rachel Catton's hospital room.

Wearing bifocals and a navy blue uniform a middle-aged hospital security guard with greying muttonchops was sitting in front of the console and working the controls of the tape. He had a dark complexion and looked of Indian or Pakistani descent to Duquesne.

Muttonchops froze the tape so Duquesne could get a better look at it.

"That's him," said Pirelli, chewing bubblegum, his jaw working, pointing his index finger at the videotape.

Muttonchops freeze-framed the tape of the bearded man walking down the hall.

"That's the guy that entered Rachel's hospital room?" said Duquesne.

"Yes, sir," said Pirelli.

"He's trying not to look at the CCTV camera. See how he's turned away from it?"

"Yeah, but I can still see his beard and those black-rimmed glasses he was wearing."

"You sure it's him," said Duquesne, eying Pirelli, eyebrow cocked.

Pirelli nodded yes. "I checked with the chief of staff here and described this guy to her. She couldn't understand it. She told me they don't have any surgeons with full beards working here."

"Could he be from another hospital?"

"She said it's very rare that surgeons have a lot of facial hair. Surgeons don't want their loose whiskers falling out and infecting a patient they're operating on."

"Don't surgeons wear masks when they operate?"

"That's what I asked her."

"Well?"

"She said those work for a short beard, but not for a heavy beard like our boy has. There's plenty of beard below his mask."

"Are you saying what I think you're saying?"

"I'm telling you what the chief of staff told me."

"Did she recognize this guy?" said Duquesne, nodding at the bearded man on the videotape.

"She never saw him before."

"Then this guy was either a surgeon from another hospital or he was impersonating a doctor. But why would a surgeon from another hospital be paying a visit to Rachel Catton's room? Did somebody at the hospital request him?"

Pirelli thought about blowing a bubble, but decided not to. "The chief of staff said she never heard of any surgeon with a full beard, and she's never seen one here."

"Then this guy's an impostor." Duquesne turned to Muttonchops. "Keep running the tape."

"I have repetitive motion disorder," said Muttonchops in a high-pitched voice, making no attempt to run the tape.

Duquesne gave him a look.

"Then take your time," said Duquesne, glancing wearily at Pirelli, who rolled his eyes.

Muttonchops complied, throwing in a grimace as he pressed a button on the machine.

The tape showed the bearded surgeon striding down the hall, never looking into the camera, face averted from the lens.

"What are you looking for, Lieutenant?" said Pirelli.

"I wanted to make sure. It's no accident he's looking away from the camera. He knows where it is. Another indication he's a fake."

"Do you think he has a background in security? He seems to know where all of the cameras are located."

"He may just be perceptive."

Bryan Cassiday

"Is this the perp that murdered Rachel Catton?"

"I believe so. Or he had something to do with it."

"Why did he come here? It's like asking to be caught."

"He came here to finish her off. He thought she was still alive and could testify against him because of the bogus news reports I gave out to the media about her being alive."

Pirelli cursed himself. "And I could've busted him right there. Piece of cake."

"Don't be too hard on yourself. No way you could know who he was in that getup."

Pirelli looked out of his depth. "Why didn't he finish her off like he planned?"

"He saw our impersonator's face and realized it wasn't Rachel Catton lying in bed in the hospital room. There was no point in his killing the impersonator."

"Ah," said Pirelli, realization dawning on him. "Then he must also know Rachel Catton really is dead."

"Which is bad for us. It doesn't give us any leverage over him."

"At least we know what he looks like now."

"Do we? This video recording isn't much good. At best, we can only see the side of his face, but most of it's obscured by the surgeon's cap he's wearing and the beard. And what color are his eyes? We can't tell from this."

"I got a good look at his eyes. They were hard to forget. They were amethyst."

Duquesne was skeptical. "They could've been contact lenses. How many people do you know with amethyst eyes?"

"None."

"Exactly. In any case, talk to our sketch artist and see what he can draw up for us. You're our best shot now at ID'ing the guy."

"I dunno," said Pirelli, studying the bearded surgeon's image on the freeze-framed video. "Ears are supposed to be unique to each person, but the cap covers his ears."

"We got a guy with a full beard and amethyst eyes that may or may not be contacts. Of average stature."

"That's better than nothing."

"Not much. Dollars to donuts, those amethyst eyes are part of his disguise, and that beard's fake, too," said Duquesne, scrutinizing the freeze-frame of the surgeon.

"It's hard to tell the shape of his face with that beard all over it."

"And that mask covers the shape of his mouth. Regardless, we can run his image through our facial recognition software at headquarters, but I doubt we'll get any hits. His features are all hidden."

"What about an iris scan?"

"Even if we could do one from this video, which I doubt—"

"No way," said Muttonchops, sounding grumpy, opening his hand and holding it like it was a lobster claw in front of his face.

"It wouldn't do us much good, anyway, unless he had his iris scanned before and there's a record of it in some database," Duquesne went on, looking askance at Muttonchops. "Not that many people have their irises scanned, I'm afraid."

"What about his fingerprints?" said Pirelli.

Duquesne studied the freeze-frame of the surgeon, leaning on the desktop as he got a closer look. "No dice. Check out his hands. He was wearing surgical gloves."

"Don't that beat all? And nobody paid any attention to him because he fit right in at a hospital."

"This is somebody that doesn't want any attention. He wants to remain anonymous."

"Does that mean he's somebody we know, somebody we've seen before?"

"We can't be certain of that." Duquesne turned to Muttonchops, who was sitting beside him continuing to hold his hand up in front of him like a claw. If the guy was looking for pity, he came to the wrong place, decided Duquesne. "Do you have any CCTV cameras outside the hospital?"

"They're all inside the hospital corridors."

"Too bad we don't have a picture of him leaving the hospital, or entering it, for that matter. He might not've had his costume on at that time."

"The hospital is always cutting back on their security budget. They'd rather shell out money on pricy doctors and lawyers. We're lucky to have as many cameras as we do."

"All right, all right."

"So who is this guy?" said Pirelli, eyes glued on the video of the bearded surgeon.

"Someone who went to great lengths not to be recognized," said Duquesne.

Chapter 66

Catton was sitting at his laptop that was opened on the desk in his motel room, tapping away at the keys, his expression fixed.

Mina stood next to him watching.

"Back away from me," he told her.

"Why?"

"I don't want you to see how to access her account."

"What's the difference? I can't get the money out of it."

"You could transfer it to your account, if you watch what I'm doing."

"What account? I don't have an account."

"Just step back," he said, sweeping his arm behind him toward her.

Grudgingly, Mina took several steps back from him. "You're paranoid."

"That's why I'm still alive," he said, continuing to tap laptop keys, not looking at her.

"I'm on your side."

"Only as long as I've got leverage on you. I witnessed your killing of Rachel. Don't you forget it. And—"

"And what?"

"And I'm your meal ticket. You can't live without me."

"Then why do you keep threatening me?"

"I'm in!" he said, eyes glowing as he watched the computer screen.

"I was right about the password."

"Shit."

"What? What's wrong?"

Catton slumped in his chair, arms hanging loose at his sides, eyes lackluster. "The account's been deactivated."

"You said they wouldn't deactivate it yet."

"I was still able to withdraw cash from her bank's ATM yesterday. The bank must've deactivated her account recently."

"Why would they?"

"Somebody must've told them she was dead. Otherwise, how would they know?"

"I dunno. The news said she was still alive."

"It doesn't matter. The bank can't close the account until they have a copy of the deceased's death certificate."

"Who would send them that?"

"The next of kin would receive a death certificate. But she didn't have any next of kin."

"Then who sent it to the bank?"

"Maybe the cops. They would have access to the coroner's report of her death. I didn't think they'd move this fast on it. These things usually take weeks."

"Does this mean the cops suspect you're still alive?"

"Not necessarily. They might freeze bank accounts as a matter of course when the owner of the account was a murder victim. Anyway, the cops can't freeze anything. The DA's office would've been the ones that told the bank what to do."

"This sucks."

"Or maybe the insurance company had something to do with deactivating the account. If they suspect fraud, they'll want their money back. Rachel's murder might have aroused their suspicions about me."

"Then how will we get her money?" said Mina, twisting the ends of her mahogany hair between her fingers.

"We'll have to think of another way. If only they hadn't found Rachel's corpse, we'd be home free by now. My plan was working to a T, until her stiff floated to the surface." He wheeled around irately to confront her. "Because you didn't knot the ropes around her."

"I-I-I didn't do it on purpose. I was upset. I couldn't think straight."

"You screwed up my plans."

Their meeting had been a miserable accident, Mina knew. She had never wanted to get mixed up in his homicidal plans in the first place.

"What good will blaming me do?" she said, fretting he'd attack her.

He turned away from her and faced his laptop screen. "We have to think of another way."

Chapter 67

Mina felt relieved Catton's rage had been defused before he lost control, because she knew she would've been the target of it had it persisted.

"It was all going like a well-oiled machine," he muttered. "Now . . ."

"If Dunleavy doesn't get his money, he's gonna be mad at us."

"Fuck Dunleavy. He's dead meat. He's the least of our worries."

Catton's answer chilled her. Talking about murder was so matter of fact with him. It was like he was discussing the weather. Sunny, fair, and mild today. Partly cloudy with the temperature in the seventies. *He's dead meat.*

She hoped their arrangement would end soon, now that the money was out of the picture. Then she could go her own way. Or was she living in cloud-cuckoo-land thinking like that? she wondered. Would he ever really let her go her own way? She doubted it, she decided in consternation.

"There has to be another way," he said, his face hovering over the computer.

Mina hoped he'd come up with an idea or he might decide to take out his frustration on her with leather straps and burning cigarette butts. Her body already had enough burn marks on it to last her a lifetime.

"You'll think of something," she said, giving him encouragement so he wouldn't dwell on harming her.

"There is a way, but the risk factor is maximum. I don't know if it would be worth taking the chance."

"What way?"

Anything to keep him from taking it out on her tonight, she decided. As long as she kept him talking he wasn't torturing her.

"I could show up at the bank and reveal my true identity as Rachel's husband. They'd have to give me the money, since I'm her husband."

"Wouldn't they tell the cops?"

"That's the problem. Then the cops could bust me for staging a fake death in order to defraud Lion Life. I wouldn't be able to collect the money, and I might end up in jail. They also might suspect me of murdering Rachel if I tried to claim her money."

"Maybe the bank wouldn't tell the cops about you. Why should they?"

"Because I'm supposed to be dead."

"But does the bank know that?"

"They might not know it at first, but, because of the amount of money involved, they'd look into it, checking to make sure I'm really who I say I am."

"Don't you still have your driver's license?"

"Yeah. I'd have to ditch the false beard and purple contacts, of course."

"A driver's license is valid ID. What more would they want?"

"I dunno. It might work. It's so brazen it might just work," he said, sitting back in his chair, head tilted up, eyes blazing. "But there could be a holdup because the owner of the account was murdered. Which could convince them to contact the cops."

"Why? Even if Rachel *was* murdered, why does that give the bank the right to withhold her money from her husband?"

"Good point. They might call the cops, though. The bank doesn't want to pay out that amount of money if they don't have to. They'll try anything in order to keep it."

"I don't see how they can stop you if you give them valid ID."

"What if they happen to find somewhere that I'm dead?"

"They won't even think to look for that if you're standing there in front of them in the flesh."

"And then there's the DA's office. If they're the ones that ordered the account frozen, the bank won't be able to release the money without a court order."

"But you're not sure it *was* the DA that deactivated the account."

"True. It could've been the bank after they heard of Rachel's death on the news. They may even have put a temporary hold on the account till they clear things up."

"Let's wait and see. Maybe you'll be able to access the account in the future."

Rapt in his own thoughts, he ignored her advice. "There are a hell of a lot of risks in my identifying myself to the bank. This would've been much easier if I'd accessed the account before they froze it, like I planned." He fetched a loud sigh. "Best laid plans, and all that crap."

"But you can still do it. You're the husband, and you have every right to get the money."

"That's right. I'm her only living relative, and I *am* her husband."

Mina was hoping he would identify himself at the bank, and they would have him arrested on the spot. She wanted to get out of this sick relationship. If getting him tossed into the joint was the only way out for her, so be it. But then he would snitch to the cops she had murdered his wife . . .

Mina wanted to tear out her hair. She wished this nightmare was over. No matter what happened, she would get screwed. Her only way out was to kill him. As much as she hated to admit it, her successful escape hinged on that one solution.

The air smelled noxious to her, and she felt her eyes watering.

"Do you smell that?" she said.

"Something burning?"

Mina repaired to the window and peered outside. Wisps of smoke wafted through the air, and a sallow haze screened the blue sky. The stench of smoke was more intense here. She saw the window was open and slid it shut, her throat burning.

"Must be a brush fire nearby," she said, coughing on the smoke, feeling nauseous. "The Santa Anas are blowing it here."

"It would take a huge set of balls to show up at the bank and tell them my real name," said Catton, talking to himself. "I'd be risking everything."

She angled across the carpet back to him. "Let's forget about it and get out of town. The air's sickening here anyway."

It smelled like burning pumpkins, she decided, grimacing.

"I'm not afraid of risk," he said. "If you don't take any risks, you'll never get anywhere in this world."

Mina didn't want him to kill any more people, including herself. Maybe if she and Catton forgot about the money and left town, she would be safe. On the other hand, he would have no more use for her so he might try to kill her. She didn't want to think about it, but she had to think about it—the truth was, he had no more use for her now. He had gotten the password from her and accessed Rachel's account, which turned out to be frozen, so why did he need her anymore?

"It would be stupid to tell the bank who you really are," she said.

"And what'll we live on if we blow town?" he said, craning his neck around to look at her.

"You could get a job."

"And kiss another boss's ass for the rest of my life? No thanks. Been there, done that. Why do you think I dreamed up this scam in the first place? Anyway, that money's mine, not Rachel's. It was never hers. She jacked it from me. It was *my* life insurance policy. I'm the one that bought it."

259

"Isn't there any other way to get her money?"

"I can't think of one. The longer we go without claiming the money, the less chance we'll have of getting it. My eyes hurt."

"It's all the smoke in the air."

Catton plucked out a small plastic container from his trouser pocket and set it on the desk before him. Applying his forefinger to the corner of his eye he flipped out an amethyst gas permeable contact lens and inserted it into the container. He proceeded to do the same with his other eye. He pulled out a drawer under the desk, removed a plastic bottle of soaking solution, twisted off its lid, and dripped solution onto the lenses before closing their container.

"That feels better," he said, blinking his eyes and looking at her.

She saw that the real color of his eyes was blue. "Do you need those to see?"

"No. They're part of my disguise. They're not prescription lenses. They're a hassle, but it's better than getting caught. If I'm gonna reveal my ID to the bank, I don't need to wear them anymore."

The motel-room phone rang, interrupting them.

Without thinking, Mina picked up. "Hello."

"Who is it?" said Catton, watching her.

Mina was tempted to hang up so Catton wouldn't know who called, but she figured he would call back.

"Dunleavy," she said.

"Perfect. Give me it."

She knew it was Dunleavy's death sentence, but she didn't know what she could do about it.

Chapter 68

Mina offered the handset to Catton.

"Yeah," said Catton into the transmitter, and put the call on speaker.

"It's me," said Dunleavy. "There's been a change of plans."

"Not that I know of."

Mina feared for Dunleavy's life. She knew he shouldn't have called here. The only thing keeping him alive was Catton's inability to contact him and set up a meet, which would end with Dunleavy's murder.

"I want the money now," said Dunleavy.

"Why the change? You were OK with getting it tomorrow before."

"I get the feeling your scam's going south."

"Why do you say that?"

"I got a snitch in the LAPD. He told me they're looking with interest into your so-called death."

"Why are they doing that?" said Catton, becoming more attentive, hunching over the handset, yet trying to sound unconcerned.

"They found out somebody's been accessing your wife's bank account via ATMs after she died, and they're wondering who would be able to do that."

"My wife's killer could have jacked her ATM card."

"And you might have a card, too."

"They need to do their homework. Rachel closed our joint account after my disappearance. Her new account is all hers. How would I access it?"

"I'm just telling you what my little birdie told me. You have become a person of interest in Rachel's murder investigation."

"Don't worry about it."

"I *am* worried about it, and you should be too. And I want to make sure I get something out of this before the shit hits the fan. So pony up tonight."

"No problem. I suggest we meet in an out-of-the-way place."

"Why?"

"Because I know the last thing you want is to be seen with me."

Dunleavy paused a beat. "OK. Where?"

Mina was aching to tell Dunleavy not to do it, but she didn't want to face Catton's wrath. She kept her own counsel, gritting her teeth instead of speaking.

"A nice secluded place like Latigo Canyon Road," said Catton.

"Off the Coast Highway?"

"Yeah. We'll park up there on one of the turnarounds at eight o'clock, and you meet us there."

"It's a long road. How do I know which turnaround you're at?"

"You'll have to look at all of them till you see us."

Dunleavy didn't answer right away. "I got a better idea. Why don't you meet me there? I'll park there at eight, and *you* find *me*."

"Whatever floats your boat."

"And you'll have the cash?"

"I will."

Catton hung up, reflecting.

"What kind of car does Dunleavy drive?" he asked Mina.

"A black Dodge Challenger."

"Ah," he said with a smile. "And I have a Ford Mustang. It'll be like a scene out of that movie *Bullitt*. No, wait a minute. They used a Dodge Charger in that movie."

"Do you have his money?"

"No."

"Then why are we meeting him?"

"Because tonight is his last night on earth."

Mina figured that was what Catton would say or something to that effect. She had to fish or cut bait. She couldn't postpone killing him any longer. And yet . . .

"I think we should forget about him and get on with our lives," she said, still trying to get out of killing him.

"We've been all through this before. We have no choice. Tonight we eliminate him. If we don't, he'll rat us out."

"What about that e-mail he has rigged on his computer to be sent to the cops if anything happens to him?"

"We'll go to his motel after we whack him, and we'll trash his computer. It won't be sending anything by the time I'm done with it."

Mina was having misgivings. She wished she had a firmer plan in mind, instead of having to ad-lib Catton's murder. But she had no choice. She still didn't know how she was going to kill him.

Bryan Cassiday

Chapter 69

Mina riding shotgun, Catton drove his Mustang north on PCH that night till he reached Latigo Canyon Road, where he hung a right and drove up the winding route, unlit by streetlamps. Part of a hazy moon lit the way.

"Keep your eyes peeled for the turnarounds," he said.

Mina nodded yes.

"How are you going to kill him?" she said.

"Piano wire. I'll garrote him. I like killing people close-up. It's a personal thing with me. Shooting somebody is so impersonal. There's no satisfaction in it. I like to feel my victim squirming in my hands trying in futility to escape." He smiled. "It's almost like making love to someone the way I do it, except it's always a one-night stand for the victim, I'm sorry to say."

He didn't look sorry about it, decided Mina, watching him sitting beside her with a broad smile on his face.

"What do you want me to do?" she said, trying to figure out how she would kill him.

"Sit in the car and wait for me. It won't take long."

Maybe she could steal his car and run him over when he got out, she decided. But she doubted he'd leave the key in the ignition.

"Any problem with that?" he said.

"No."

Steering wheel in one hand, he reached with the other in front of her and flipped open the glove compartment, revealing a pistol ensconced inside. "I could shoot him if I wanted. You see? I always come prepared. But I don't want to. Shooting someone isn't any fun."

Catton slammed the compartment shut with a flourish and a death's-head grin.

Maybe this was going to work out after all, she decided, the image of the pistol in her mind's eye.

"OK," she said. "I'll wait here."

"I have the piece just in case things don't go according to plan. I always have a backup plan. You've heard of Murphy's Law. Right?"

"Yeah," she said, but her mind was elsewhere.

She was trying to decide when she would shoot him. She had never shot a gun before, but she didn't think it could be that difficult. You aimed it and pulled the trigger. How difficult could that be?

"There's one thing that's been bugging me," he said, glancing at her as he drove up the winding road in the moonlit darkness.

Mina said nothing.

"Don't you want to know what it is?" he said.

"Yes," she said, face blank.

"You don't sound like you do."

"I do," she said without changing her expression.

"How did you know what kind of car Dunleavy drives? I've never seen it."

Frantic, Mina thought fast. She had to come up with a plausible answer. She couldn't very well tell him she had ridden in Dunleavy's car. Catton would go through the roof if he heard that from her. He would think she was plotting with Dunleavy against him.

"I saw him park at our motel," she said.

"I never saw him park."

"You were doing something else at the time."

"Like what?"

"I-I-I don't remember."

"Oh."

He scoped out the next turnaround for sign of a car. A yellow Fiat was parked there. He slowed down as he approached it, craning to inspect its interior.

265

"What?" said Mina.

"Teenagers necking," he said, and gathered speed. "It's lucky you saw what kind of car he drives or we could pick the wrong car."

"I'm very observant. It's a trait I have."

What moonlight there was illuminating the canyon was dimmed by the sulfurous haze of smoke from the wildfires burning out of control in the Valley that was billowing across the canyon. Ashes like flakes of snow started drifting down from the sky and whirling in the bone-dry gusts of wind that rushed down the canyon. It all looked surreal to Mina. A scene out of hell.

"Why didn't Dunleavy want us to park first with him meeting us, instead of the other way around?" she said.

"He suspects an ambush. He's not the trusting type. He thought we would be lying in wait with guns drawn. This way he's waiting for us."

"How do you know *he* won't ambush *us*?"

"If he did, he'd only get the down payment and not his full cut of the take. He knows he'll get more moola if he keeps us alive."

Both of their windows were down. Mina coughed on the smoky air.

The Mustang's V8 thundered up the tortuous canyon road in second gear, Catton shifting only occasionally into third. He didn't want to go too fast lest he miss seeing Dunleavy's car through the shifting haze.

"He'll be dead soon," said Catton.

"Yeah, he will," said Mina, staring straight ahead through the windshield.

Catton searched her face then turned his attention back to driving.

Flakes of ash swirled in front of him, trammeled in his halogen headlight beams.

"This is California's version of snow," he said.

"Where is he?"

"He must think he's safer the farther up he goes. I have news for him. He's wrong."

"I think that's him now," she said, squinting through the scrim of ashes and buttery moonlight at a dark-painted car parked in the upcoming turnaround, a hardpan apron that overlooked the canyon.

Catton slowed down as he approached the apron.

Mina could discern the Challenger now, blurred by the smoke, but she was pretty sure it was Dunleavy's car.

Bryan Cassiday

Chapter 70

Mina still wanted to talk Catton out of killing Dunleavy.

Overhead, the coppery moon cried tears of ash that showered down on the dark chaparral of the canyon, as windswept wildfires from the northeast ravaged the land. The eerie landscape of winter in hell gave her goose bumps.

She reeled back in amazement as a pack of three sorrel horses came galloping out of the billowing smoke and falling ash and down the road toward them, their hooves clopping on the tarmac.

"Horses," said Catton, sharing her surprise.

"Where did they come from?"

"They must be fleeing the wildfires."

Snorting, their nostrils flaring, their brown eyes wild with fear, they galloped toward the Mustang. Neighing, its mouth gaping, the lead horse reared up and kicked out its two front hooves at the car. Catton braked to avoid hitting the horse. The three horses charged down the road, the clopping of their hooves dying out in the distance.

"This is a bad sign," said Mina.

"I don't believe in signs. They're superstitious nonsense."

"There were three horses. And there are three of us. It's a sign."

Catton snickered. "A sign of what? Nothing."

"Let's get out of here," she said, shifting in her seat uncomfortably. "Forget about Dunleavy."

"Not gonna happen."

"Look, if you tell the bank who you are, there's no point in killing Dunleavy," she said. "Don't you see?"

"He won't want his money anymore? I don't follow," he said, gazing at her.

268

"He won't have a hold on you, if you turn yourself in and let everybody know you're alive. What can he do to you?"

"I haven't made up my mind to ID myself to the bank. Anyway, he's never gonna leave us alone. He'll always want money."

"How can he blackmail you if you turn yourself in and admit you're still alive?"

"He suspects I killed Rachel, which means he's still dangerous to us."

"He may suspect it, but he has no proof."

"He'll never leave us alone. He has to go."

Catton drove the Mustang to the apron, killed the ignition, set the stick shift in first, and jerked up on the emergency brake between the bucket seats. He left his headlights on to be able to see the Challenger in the wash of their beams, which also caught the ash drifting down from the night sky. The Challenger's tinted back window was facing him.

"Do you see him?" he said.

"No."

"He must be sitting in his car, but I can't make him out in the dark, especially with his tinted windows. Does he know what kind of car I drive?"

"I think so. I don't know for sure."

"He wouldn't have agreed to this arrangement if he didn't know." As if to himself, he added, "Then why isn't he getting out of his car?"

"Let's go. He can't do anything to us."

"He's not gonna like it when I don't pay him."

"Then don't meet him. Let's get out of here right now."

"I never ran away from anybody in my life, and I don't plan on doing it now."

Eyes glued on the Challenger, he opened his door.

"Besides . . . ," he said.

"What?"

"I *want* to kill him. He deserves to die. The scumbag never should've tried to blackmail me."

He opened his hand and showed her the piano wire coiled in his palm.

She realized it wouldn't do any good to argue with him any longer. How could you reason with a homicidal maniac?

Gripping the piano wire Catton slid out of the Mustang and stole toward Dunleavy's car, a silhouette stalking his prey through the falling flakes of ash.

It was hard to see in the dim, smoky light even with the Mustang's headlights on thanks to her distance from the Challenger, but she was able to make out the car's door on the driver's side opening and a leg spilling out. The driver straightened up, facing Catton, and took a few steps toward him.

They were two blurry figures nearing each other as far as Mina could tell.

At that moment, the wind set to fanning swirling clouds of smoke into the canyon, making it even more difficult for her to see, like trying to see through a blizzard.

It was time to make her move, she decided.

She flipped open the glove compartment and snagged the pistol. Gun in hand, she opened her door and clambered out of the Mustang, hoping Catton, and for that matter Dunleavy, couldn't hear her. She didn't want to be noticed as she stood there, the gun in her hand.

Her heartbeat ratcheting up, she watched the two figures approach each other in the gloom. As soon as they met, they were scuffling with each other, whirling around together like a two-headed dervish.

She had to shoot now, before Catton garroted Dunleavy.

She wished she had a better view of them and that they would stop moving around, grappling with each other in their danse macabre. If that wasn't bad enough, she felt her eyes stinging on account of the wildfire smoke. Her tearing eyes blurred her vision.

Gripping the pistol in her right hand, she brought it to bear on Catton.

She fired the pistol.

Or thought she did.

But the trigger didn't move. Was the gun out of ammo? she wondered. It couldn't be. She hadn't taken a single shot yet. Why would Catton load his pistol with an empty magazine?

She had to think clearly. What was the problem with the gun? Why wouldn't it fire?

She realized there must be a safety that she needed to release.

Inspecting the pistol she saw that it was a Ruger LC9, which meant nothing to her. She picked up on a small metal lever located below the slide and flicked it down. It had to be the safety, she decided.

She drew a bead again on Catton, trying to keep her arm steady as the two dark figures tussled on the hardpan apron near a guardrail that skirted its edge. Face sweaty, eyes weeping from the smoke, she steadied her shaky outstretched arm with her free hand, gripping her elbow like she had seen cops do on TV crime shows. She squeezed the trigger.

The deafening clap of a gunshot resounded through the canyon.

One of the figures slid to the ground.

She heard a groan that emanated from the depths of his bowels. Mina dropped her pistol at the gruesome sound, appalled by what she had done.

Murder, murder, murder, came the words in her brain.

The other figure stood over his bullet-felled opponent, leering at the fallen victim at his feet, holding his arms out at his sides as if about to pounce on the crumpled body.

Tentatively, Mina edged toward them. She couldn't distinguish the features of either man through the ballooning smoke.

When she got closer she saw that the man sprawled prostrate on the ground at the feet of the other man was wearing khaki Bermudas.

Jesus Christ, she wanted to scream.

Chapter 71

"Good shot," said Catton. He scoped out her empty hands for sign of the Ruger.

Mina was too overcome to speak. Tears were running down her cheeks.

"Or was it a lousy shot?" he said, scrutinizing her grief-stricken countenance.

"You said he had to die," she muttered, face ashen. She wiped the tears from her face.

"But I wanted to kill him myself." He approached her. "I thought you wanted me to let him go. Why'd you change your mind?"

Mina had to think on her feet.

"I could see you were right," she blurted.

"Isn't this kind of sudden?"

"I thought he was reaching for a gun," she said, her eyes wide.

"Was he?"

"I saw him."

Catton inspected the ground around Dunleavy's motionless body then crouched over the corpse and patted down its Burmadas' pockets. He stood up.

"No piece anywhere around here," he said. "And he wasn't carrying."

"I thought he was setting an ambush for you."

Mina saw a pair of headlights at the bottom of the canyon road heading toward them. Catton followed her gaze.

"We gotta beat it," he said, seizing her wrist and dashing toward the Mustang. "We don't want anyone to see us here."

Not knowing what to do, Mina ran after him. She was trying to come to grips with her killing Dunleavy by mistake. None of this seemed real. Ashes flurrying out of the sky under a lachrymose moon. The crack of her gunshot. Dunleavy lying dead. It had to be a nightmare, she decided.

"Get in the car," said Catton, releasing her wrist.

He jerked to a halt, spotting the Ruger lying on the hardpan. Squatting, he gathered up the piece, wedged it into his waistband, and bolted to the car.

She darted-stumbled toward the car's passenger side, yanked open the door, clambered into the seat, and buckled her seat belt.

Catton slid into the driver's seat, fired the engine, put the transmission into gear, pulled out of the turnaround, and executed a U turn on the narrow road, whose poor lighting helped cover their escape. He drove back to PCH, able to coast in neutral part of the way on account of the downslope.

They met up with the white sedan they had seen from the turnaround that was tooling up the road.

"Don't let them get a good look at you," said Catton, whipping his head in Mina's direction away from the oncoming vehicle.

Mina snapped her neck toward her window, even though she didn't think it was necessary. She doubted the other driver could see much of her or Catton on the unlit street. Dimmed by the smoke, the sad moon by itself didn't produce enough light to reveal more than ghostly adumbrations in the canyon landscape.

They drove past the car and resumed looking ahead through their windshield.

"Do you think they saw us?" said Mina.

"No."

"They may have seen our car in the turnaround up above, but they have no idea what happened up there."

"Maybe they heard the gunshot."

Catton scowled. "There wasn't even supposed to be a gunshot. I wanted this taken care of on the qt. That's why I brought the garrote."

Mina wanted to change the subject. She couldn't stand thinking about shooting Dunleavy. She liked him. This was a debacle, she knew, in more ways than one.

First, she had killed a guy she liked. Second, he was the only one that could help her in her fight against Catton, as she saw it. Now she was on her own against a psychopath.

She didn't want to dwell on the subject, but she had to.

"Won't the cops be suspicious when they find out he's been murdered?" she said.

"Suspicious of what?"

"That it has something to do with Rachel's money."

"Maybe. So what?"

"So they might think you had something to do with it. Dunleavy said he told the cops he was investigating your death."

"So? I'm dead. Remember? Dead man can't kill anyone."

"But you're going to reveal your identity to the bank, you said."

Catton paused in thought. "There still isn't any evidence that can connect me to Dunleavy's murder, especially since I didn't even do it. You were the one that did it."

Why did he have to keep bringing that up? she wondered, feeling abysmal enough as it was.

Chapter 72

Emerging from Latigo Canyon Road, Catton hung a left onto PCH and bore south.

Five minutes later, he pulled over onto a dirt shoulder on a bluff that overlooked the gleaming petroleum black ocean, his tires crunching on the gravel.

"Why are we stopping?" said Mina, fearing for her life, her heartbeat ramping up.

Was she going to end up like Dunleavy now? she wondered. What did Catton need her for anymore?

Saying nothing he got out of the car and strode to the guardrail. He looked out at the ocean below and was happy to see it was high tide, the churning surf breaking near the boulder-strewn foot of the bluff. He scoped out his surroundings to make sure nobody was watching him, jerked the Ruger out of his waistband, and hurled it with all his might into the sea.

He watched the gun sail through the moonlit night sky like a petrel and arc into the ocean, where it splashed briefly and disappeared into the murky liquid depths.

He returned to the car.

"Now we have to destroy Dunleavy's computer so it won't send an e-mail to alert the authorities about me," he said, at the wheel.

He was pulling onto the highway when he slammed on the brakes, hammered the steering wheel with his fist, and said, "Shit."

The abruptness of the braking car jerked Mina forward in her seat, tightening her shoulder harness.

"What?" she said.

"I don't know where he was staying. We got out of there so quick, I forgot to check his pockets for his motel key." He punched the steering wheel again. "I have to destroy his computer. I can't let that e-mail be sent. Damn it."

"Let's go back and get the key," she faltered as she realized what she was saying. She had no desire to see Dunleavy's corpse again.

"No way. We can't go back there now. Somebody may've found the stiff."

He got an idea and turned to her hopefully. "Do you know where he was staying? You knew the kind of car he drove."

"I do. I know his motel."

Catton breathed a sigh of relief. "We're good to go, then. Where is it?"

She told him.

He pulled out onto PCH and continued south.

His good mood didn't last long.

"How do you know where he was staying?" he said, his mind clouded with suspicion.

"Beats me. I guess he must have told me," she said, shaking it off like it was no big deal.

"Why did he tell you and not me?"

"I dunno."

"So all along you've known where he was?"

"I guess."

"And maybe you paid him a couple of visits?"

"No," she said, almost coughing out the word, realizing what he was driving at. "No."

"You didn't invite him in on our little deal?"

"Why would I do that?"

He bored his eyes into hers. "Then how did he know where to find me?"

"He said he saw you and followed you."

He returned his attention to the road ahead.

"I always had trouble with that explanation," he said. "He recognized me on the street, even with this beard on?" he said, stroking his beard.

"He was looking for you because he was working for the insurance company. That was his job. And he knew what you looked like."

"Not with this beard on, he didn't."

She shrugged. "I guess your disguise isn't that good."

"What else do you know about him that you haven't told me?"

"You're making a mountain out of a molehill."

"Does that mean you're not gonna tell me?"

"There's nothing to tell," said Mina, feeling a bead of sweat roll out of her armpit and trickle down her flank, chilling her. She wished he would stop giving her the third degree.

"Maybe you two were in cahoots."

"That's ridiculous."

"Maybe you two wanted to gang up on me and take over my operation."

"Then why did I shoot him?" said Mina, dreading to talk about the murder, but desperate to deflect Catton's grilling.

"Maybe you two had a falling-out."

"You have an overactive imagination."

"Oh yeah?"

Mina said nothing.

He was silent for a couple of beats.

"Or maybe you were aiming for me," he said, craning around to eyeball her.

"That's not what happened, and you know it," she said, hoping he would believe her, feeling the hot gaze of his eyes raking her face.

He faced forward again negotiating the inchoate bend in the road.

"I don't know it," he said. "That's the problem."

Mina hated thinking about Dunleavy's bullet-torn corpse sprawled on the ground. Why did she have to be such a lousy shot? She doubted she would get another chance to kill Catton, not with his suspicions about her aroused and the gun at the bottom of the ocean.

Chapter 73

Five minutes later, Catton's mood lightened up. Smiling at the wheel he glanced at Mina.

"Why the long face?" he said.

"Why do you think?" she said.

"You should be happy. You killed the blackmailing prick Dunleavy. We don't have to worry about him anymore."

Mina's expression didn't change.

"Come on," he said. "Cheer up."

Mina looked at the variegated lights on the driver's-side dashboard and kept her own counsel.

"Come on," said Catton. "Let's sing. It'll cheer you up."

Mina shook her head.

"*Row, row, row your boat gently down the stream. Merrily, merrily, merrily, merrily, life is but a dream,*" he sang, grinning and gyrating rhythmically in his seat.

Mouth downturned, Mina stared at the lighted dashboard.

Catton slammed the bottom of his fist down on the inside of her thigh.

"Ouch," she said, wincing. "That hurt."

"I can't hear you," he said, smiling.

"I said, that hurt."

"That's not what I'm talking about."

Mina massaged her throbbing thigh.

"*Row, row, row your boat,*" Catton sang, smiling, cupping his ear to listen to Mina join in. "I can't hear you sing. *Row, row, row your boat . . .*"

"I don't want to sing. I just shot someone," she said, and stopped massaging her sore thigh.

"Don't you know the lyrics? You must be the only person in the world that doesn't know the lyrics."

"I know the lyrics," she said, scowling and looking away from his grinning face.

"*Row, row, row your boat*," he sang and stopped. "I still can't hear you."

Mina shook her head, sick of his stupid games.

Catton pounded the bottom of his fist down on the inside of her thigh again, this time with all of his might.

"Ow," Mina screamed, doubling up in pain in her seat. "You're hurting me," she said, whipping her head around toward him, her face contorted with anguish.

Her thigh was killing her. She knew she was going to end up with an ugly bruise there.

Catton's face clouded. "Start singing or I'll do it again."

She didn't feel like singing. She felt like screaming.

He held his fist up in the air in a menacing gesture. "You don't think I won't?"

Cringing, teeth clenched, she didn't know what to do. Was he going to punch her to death? she wondered.

"What do you want from me?" she said.

"I want you to sing. Be happy. Singing will lighten you up."

"I don't want to sing."

Catton cut his eyes to the windshield and eased up on the gas so he wouldn't hit an eighteen-wheeler that was groaning and lumbering in front of him, belching diesel exhaust, its dirt-streaked black rubber mudguards flapping, sporting the profile of a white silhouette of a nude curvaceous woman sitting on her haunches, knees flexed beneath her, in the beams of the Mustang's headlights.

"Now sing," he told her. "We're free of the scumbag Dunleavy."

She didn't want to think about Dunleavy anymore. She kept seeing his crumpled corpse at her feet. She wanted to forget him, forget the whole night ever happened.

"*Row, row, row your boat*," Catton crooned, staring at her through the dim interior of the Mustang, lit fitfully by the wash of sodium vapor streetlights that they passed.

281

Mina was terrified of being hit again. She saw his fist rising and knew he was going to take another swing at her.

"*Row, row, row your boat,*" she sang meekly, her voice barely audible, her throat tight.

"I can't hear you," he teased.

"*Row, row, row your boat gently down the stream,*" she sang, her voice louder.

"That's better."

"*Merrily, merrily, merrily, merrily, life is but a dream.*"

"Don't you feel better now?" he said with a smile, lowering his fist.

She wanted to kill him. She had had her chance in the canyon, and she had blown it. She wanted to kill him so bad now she could taste it.

Chapter 74

It didn't take them long to reach Dunleavy's motel in Santa Monica.

Catton parked in the lot in front of the motel.

"Not a bad place," he said. "I guess he wasn't starving. He's got a nice view of the ocean and everything."

"He was charging it to the insurance company that hired him."

"Which room was he in?" he said, killing the engine, putting the stick shift in first, and setting the emergency handbrake.

She debated whether she should tell him the truth. What if she gave him the wrong number? Then he'd beat it out of her, or worse.

"Two twenty-two," she said. "How do you expect to get in?"

He withdrew something from his trouser pocket. "You ought to get one of these. They come in handy."

"What is it?" she said, glancing at what looked sort of like a gun.

"A lock-pick gun. I got it on the Internet the other day," he said, smiling.

"Why?"

"I thought something like this might happen," he said, climbing out of the car.

She sat in her bucket seat looking at him.

He stood there, door in hand, waiting. "Well?"

"What?"

"You're coming with me. I want to keep my eye on you. The last time I left you alone, I almost got a slug in the back."

She got out of the car and closed the door.

They cut through the parking lot, entered the lobby, and took the elevator to the second floor, where they located Dunleavy's room.

Mina was glad she had given Catton the correct room number. She hadn't expected to accompany him here.

Casting around to make sure the hallway was empty, Catton used the lock-pick gun on both the Schlage dead bolt and the standard lock in the doorknob.

He and Mina entered the room.

He eased the door shut behind them, holding the doorknob twisted in the open position so the latch strike didn't click when it met the jamb. He wanted to make as little noise as possible. He released the doorknob in degrees till the latch strike hit quietly home.

The room was dark.

He kept his voice low. "Where are the lights?"

Mina felt along the wall near the doorjamb and flicked on the light switch.

Dunleavy hadn't bothered to hide his laptop. It was lying open on the desk in front of the window that gave onto a balcony that overlooked the ocean.

Catton reached the desk in three strides, sat in front of the computer, and awoke it from Sleep mode. As he had expected, the computer screen demanded a password.

Mina followed him to the laptop.

"Now what?" she said, watching the screen.

"I'm not even gonna try to guess the password. This guy was a private dick. He's not gonna use a simple password. We have to destroy the hard drive, like I said before."

His lock-pick gun had a screwdriver appurtenance attached to it. He used the screwdriver to unfasten the screws on the bottom of the laptop.

"Why don't we just take the computer with us?" she said.

"Taking it with us won't prevent the e-mail from being sent. We need to destroy the hard drive."

"We could take the computer and take care of the hard drive later."

"Somebody in the motel might take note of us if we walk out of here with a laptop. I don't want the attention. The cops'll be all over this place in a matter of hours."

He removed the hard drive from the bottom of the laptop, stood up, and slid it into his waistband out of sight.

He scanned the rest of the room for anything of interest, but Dunleavy traveled light. Nothing attracted Catton's attention.

"Let's beat it," said Catton. "We can't dick around. We don't know when he scheduled the e-mail to be sent. It could be any time now."

They edged through the doorway as stealthily as they had entered. As they made for the elevator, a middle-aged guest wearing glasses with a silver lanyard attached to them backed out of his room, locked his door, and also approached the elevator. He was dressed in jeans and a brown blazer. Underneath the blazer he wore a khaki T-shirt with a silk screen of the late actor Steve McQueen's face on it.

Mina thought about taking the stairs, but that would mean reversing their direction, which would look odd and draw suspicion from the newcomer.

Catton must have agreed with her, because he made no attempt to change course.

Mina and Catton met the guest at the elevator and waited for its doors to slide open. She noticed the guy was wearing an earphone and was listening to it intently. Mina and Catton said nothing to him.

The elevator arrived.

The three of them stepped in and rode down. Mina and Catton stared at the floor the whole way. They let the other passenger exit first.

As soon as they left the lobby, Catton hustled across the parking lot to his car, Mina in tow.

"We have to destroy this thing before it sends the e-mail," he said, ducking into the driver's seat.

"How can the hard drive send anything if it's not in the computer?"

"It can't. But as soon as somebody inserts it into the computer, it'll trigger the sending of the e-mail."

They pulled out of the parking lot into traffic.

"Why don't we just chuck it into the ocean?" she said.

"Water won't destroy a hard drive. We have to smash it with a hammer or rock. We have to break the platter."

He drove back to the Coast Highway and pulled into a parking lot adjacent to the beach. He parked in the near-deserted lot. From here they could see the Santa Monica Pier jutting into the ocean, illuminated in the darkness by a neon-lit Ferris wheel at its base. The various-colored neon streaks of light on the Ferris wheel were flashing like spokes.

Catton got out of the Mustang, hard drive in hand, and darted to the trunk in the rear, which he opened with his car fob. He retrieved a hammer from his car's toolkit.

He tossed the hard drive onto the sand-dusted asphalt, crouched on his haunches, and hammered the hard drive, contorting it and filling it with dents. The clanging of the hammer's blows punctuated the whooshing of traffic on nearby PCH.

He replaced the hammer in the toolkit in the trunk and closed the lid.

At the passenger-side window he said, "Let's go for a walk."

Perplexed, Mina climbed out of the car and shut the door behind her.

They walked to a cement bench on the buckled asphalt walking path that skirted the parking lot.

Catton set the mangled hard drive beside him as he sat on the bench and proceeded to remove his shoes and socks and roll up his trouser legs. Mina followed his example.

The Payout

"I still don't know why you're worried about the e-mail being sent if you're going to ID yourself to the bank," she said. "The e-mail just says you're still alive."

"I don't like being pressured into anything. I haven't decided whether I'm revealing myself to the bank yet. I have to give it more thought."

Shoes and socks in hand, he strode to the sand and trudged through it toward the boiling surf. Blown by the Santa Ana winds, clouds of brush-fire smoke drifted over the water like offshore fog.

Mina followed him. The sand felt cool against the naked soles of her feet as she slogged through it.

When Catton reached the water's frothing edge, he stood still and hurled the hard drive as far as he could into the rippling indigo sea like he was trying to hit the moon with it, as a small wave broke a few feet before him and sluiced against his shins.

"For good measure," he said.

Chapter 75

Duquesne was sitting behind his desk in his glass-enclosed office nursing a Styrofoam cup of coffee and studying a report on his desk. He noticed the old wooden desktop was scarred from use and wondered how many other lieutenants had sat at this same desk poring over crime reports. He felt a morose camaraderie with their ghosts. Had they ever experienced moments when they felt sickened by all the crime and wanted to change jobs?

His mind wandering from his work, he spotted Patrick at his open door, an earnest expression on his face.

"This better be important," said Duquesne, wishing he could regain the enthusiasm of youth.

"We just got a report about a corpse found on Latigo Canyon Road," said Patrick. "They ID'd the victim as Randall Dunleavy."

"Victim?"

"He was murdered. Gunshot to the chest last night."

"The name rings a bell."

"It was that insurance investigator we talked to. He was working for Lion Life."

"Oh yeah. About the Rachel Catton murder. Hmm."

"Do you think there's a connection between their murders?"

"We need to look into it. He was here trying to find her husband, who had disappeared and was assumed dead."

"And now all three of them are dead."

Duquesne sipped his coffee. "I'd say there's a connection."

"Do you think the murderer's the same guy?"

"I don't know about that. You said Dunleavy was shot?"

"Yep. Through and through."

Frowning, Duquesne shook his head. "The MO for all of these killings is different. One was shot, one garroted, and one knifed but actually died from drowning. On the face of it, that would indicate different killers involved."

"And what about Gage Catton?"

"We don't know how he died. By accident or by design."

"We won't know anything till we find his corpse. And it's a big ocean out there for a corpse to stay hidden in a long time."

Revolving thoughts Duquesne stared straight ahead, not blinking. "He was the first of this group to die."

"Why would a murderer choose to kill him and all of the others?"

"Some kind of vendetta against the Catton family?" said Duquesne, not believing it. "Did you find the murder weapon?"

"No."

"Do you know the caliber of the bullet used?"

"A nine mil. And investigators found the spent cartridge at the scene of the crime."

"Which means the killer didn't clean up after he fired the fatal shot. What does that suggest to you?"

"He didn't care if we found it?"

"And what does that tell you?"

"He wasn't worried that we would find it?"

"Which suggests he wasn't a professional killer. A contract killer would always clean up after a hit."

"But a contract killer *would* use a garrote like the one in the Bendix murder."

"Right."

"So what does that mean?"

"It means," said Duquesne, leaning back in his chair and looking up at Patrick, "we're probably dealing with two different killers, maybe even more. Dunleavy's murder was too sloppy to be the work of the killer who did Bendix."

"But the shooter was a crack shot. He only needed one slug to ice Dunleavy."

"Maybe the shooter got lucky. It happens."

"Do you have any suspects?"

"I have one main suspect, except for one thing."

"Meaning?"

"The guy's dead."

"Gage Catton."

Duquesne nodded yes. "Or at least he was reported dead."

"Why is he your main suspect?"

"Motive. He had a motive to kill Dunleavy because he didn't want Dunleavy to find him. Catton's wife was fooling around with Bendix, which is a motive for Catton to kill both of them."

"But you just got through saying two different killers offed Dunleavy and Bendix."

"The MOs of the two murders would indicate that."

"You think Catton faked his death to collect on his life insurance policy, which is why nobody can find his corpse?"

"It would explain a lot of what's going on here. Let me run this by you. He fakes his death, comes back here to split the money with his wife, finds out she's cheating on him, and kills her in a fit of jealous rage."

"But how did he expect to collect on his insurance policy, if he's still alive? As soon as he tells everyone he's alive, we can bust him for faking his death and defrauding the insurance company."

"I don't get it either. It doesn't make sense. By killing his wife, he loses the insurance money."

"Then we can rule him out as a suspect?"

"We can't rule anyone out. The fact remains, he still has more motive to kill his wife and Bendix than anyone else does."

"Are you also saying this guy Catton is a professional killer because he doesn't leave evidence behind at the scenes of his crimes?"

"I'm saying, he cleaned up after his killings. Probably because he didn't want anybody to know he was still alive, not because he was a hired gun."

"What about the insurance investigator Dunleavy? Who capped him?"

"I dunno. It was a sloppy job. The killer of Rachel and Bendix wouldn't have left a spent cartridge at the scene of the crime."

"If Catton killed the others, don't you think he wants the money? He knows Rachel had it."

"He does, indeed."

"Then jealousy wasn't his only motive."

"Greed makes the world go 'round."

Patrick pulled a face. "But how can he collect his wife's money if he doesn't reveal himself to the bank? We'll bust him for insurance fraud if he does."

Duquesne shook his head in puzzlement. "If he really is alive, I don't see his plan. He painted himself into a corner, if you ask me. I don't see how he gets the insurance money."

He studied the marred desktop, wondering if he could find an answer in the illegible runes left behind by fellow lieutenants, long since gone, or dead, or both. He ran his forefinger along one of the etchings.

"Then maybe he's not the killer," said Patrick.

Duquesne looked up and sipped his coffee. "Unless . . ."

"Unless what?"

"Unless something didn't go according to his original plan, and now he has to ad-lib."

"So how does he get Rachel's money without getting busted?"

Duquesne slammed his almost-empty coffee cup down on the desktop in frustration. "I have no idea."

291

Bryan Cassiday

Chapter 76

Catton couldn't figure out why he was keeping Mina alive, since he didn't need her to search Rachel's condo anymore. The only reason he could think of was that he liked her. He liked screwing her when she was bound to a bed, and he liked burning her hot flesh, listening to her groan in pain— so much like the groan of sexual pleasure.

The thing was, he wasn't sure he could trust her. He couldn't understand why she had shot Dunleavy. She kept telling him not to kill Dunleavy, and then she went and blew him away herself. It didn't jibe, decided Catton.

She could have been trying to shoot him, but missed. He doubted she had any experience with firearms, and yet she had whacked Dunleavy with one shot. And in the smoky darkness, to boot. It bordered on a miraculous shot. Or was it a blunder? Had she been aiming for him and hit Dunleavy by mistake? wondered Catton.

He glanced at Mina sitting beside him as he drove his Mustang down Wilshire Boulevard. He couldn't be sure of her. Had she tried to blow him away last night in the canyon? Yet this was the same woman that had helped him kill Rachel. Rachel's murder and the money that would result from it bound him and Mina inextricably, the way he saw it. It made it hard for him to believe Mina had tried to shoot him.

Did she like being tortured by him? he wondered. He didn't know. And he didn't care. He was the one that liked it, and that was all that mattered to him. He was convinced she couldn't live without him. She wouldn't dare try to escape.

He, on the other hand, could live without her.

Since he didn't need her anymore, he could finish her off any time he wanted.

"Were you really shooting at Dunleavy?" he said.

"He's dead, isn't he?" she said in a monotone.

293

He couldn't read her face, which gave nothing away.

"Then you're a regular Annie Oakley," he said.

She didn't answer.

After a while, she said, "Where are we going?"

"To the bank."

"You made up your mind to reveal yourself to them?"

"Why do you think I'm not wearing the beard and the contacts anymore?"

"Then we should've left Dunleavy alive."

"He knew too much."

"We already passed a couple banks," she said, watching as they passed a branch.

"I've been to the ones around here in my disguise. I want to go to a new one as a new person. There's one in Beverly Hills on Little Santa Monica Boulevard. It's near North Canon Drive."

"Do you think the cops will be nicer to you in Beverly Hills when they arrest you?"

He gave her a sidelong glance. "Is that supposed to be funny?"

"You do know you're going to be arrested when you give the bank your name."

"Not necessarily."

"They'll just give you all of Rachel's money? No questions asked?" She stared at him in disbelief.

"They'll ask questions, and I'll answer them. So what?"

"Nothing," she said, smiling.

"You want the cops to bust me, don't you?" said Catton, driving onto Santa Monica Boulevard, planning to park in the Beverly Hills Civic Center parking garage on North Rexford Drive, where they could walk to the bank on Little Santa Monica.

"What makes you think that? I want the money as much as you do."

"That's what I wanna hear. And we're gonna get it."

294

He drove into the crowded multilevel parking garage. Tiny lights over each parking space indicated whether the spot was occupied. All Catton could see were red lights, meaning the spaces were full. He kept driving up the spiral road all the way onto the roof before he found a green light and an empty parking space, where he parked.

He and Mina rode the elevator down to the street and walked to the bank, which was two blocks away.

The bank's entrance had a large bulletproof glass door, a lobby, then another bulletproof glass door that opened into the bank itself where the cashiers worked.

In his twenties and clad in a black suit and red tie, a slender black clerk with a hatchet face and a smooth manner was greeting customers near the center of the bank. He reeked of cologne. Like he had taken a bath in it, decided Catton, wincing, not a big fan of perfumes.

Catton told him what he wanted.

The clerk told him to take a seat and the next available clerk would take care of him.

An armed surly Hispanic security guard with thick features and a unibrow was standing in the corner of the bank in a grey uniform, solid as a tank, his hands clasped behind his back.

Catton and Mina sat down on a couch in the waiting lounge, where a flat-panel TV was playing on a two-foot-high wooden table across from the couch.

"You don't mind being arrested?" she said under her breath.

"I mind not getting my money back more," said Catton out of the side of his mouth. "This is the only way I can get it."

A TV newscaster with a square jaw was announcing the news that Dunleavy's body had been discovered in Latigo Canyon, a murder victim.

Chapter 77

Watching the TV Mina had the eerie feeling the murder was following her around like a guilty conscience. The last thing she wanted to hear was some newscaster with perfect hair and a Dick Tracy jaw announcing her bloody handiwork to millions of TV viewers.

Listening to the news she was sickened by her actions last night. She wanted to forget it ever happened. But the guy on TV wouldn't let her forget. It was like he was rubbing salt into her wound.

Murder, murder, murder . . . The word hammered her head again like it was being inculcated on her for the rest of her life. Why couldn't she flush the word out of her mind?

She started fidgeting in her seat. She wanted to tell the talking head to shut up. She couldn't sit still with him prattling accusations at her.

Murder, murder, murder.

"Are you all right?" said Catton.

"Yeah," she said, face twitching.

"You don't look all right. Take it easy. Relax. They'll ask me a few questions. It's just a formality."

She sprang to her feet and approached the TV set, planning to turn it off. She inspected it, searching for the on/off button. She couldn't find it.

"What are you doing?" said Catton.

"Turning the TV off."

"Forget the TV. Have a seat."

"Would you like some water?" said the clerk, ghosting up to Mina from behind.

Mina startled. She whipped her head around to see the guy standing a couple inches behind her. She almost brushed against him as she turned around, he was so close. Hadn't the guy ever heard of breathing room? she wondered, backing away from him. Maybe he wanted her to get a whiff of his cologne.

"Uh, yes," she said, and sat down.

The clerk returned with a paper cup of water from a nearby water cooler.

"Thanks," she said, accepting the cup.

She took a sip of the water.

She couldn't block the newscaster out. He was still blatting away about the homicide victim, describing him as an insurance investigator who worked out of San Francisco.

She looked around making sure the clerk had retreated out of earshot.

"They ID'd Dunleavy," she said, leaning toward Catton, cup in hand.

"So? Why wouldn't they? We left his ID," said Catton, keeping his voice low.

Mina leaned back in her chair, telling herself to unwind.

Instead of listening to herself, she got more keyed up when she began wondering if Catton was carrying a gun with him. Was he going to try to force the clerk to give him the money in Rachel's account at gunpoint? If he was going to get arrested anyway, he might think a gun would be more effective than just giving the clerk his ID.

Catton was capable of anything, as far as she was concerned. Was he going to start a bloody shootout in the bank? She wished she could figure out his plan. If he told the bank he was Rachel's husband, the bank could find out he was dead, and then they would notify the cops that he had faked his death.

"I hope you know what you're doing," she said.

"I didn't get this far by being stupid."

Mina wondered how far he had actually gotten. He had no money and no job. He had gotten nowhere.

The clerk glided across the carpet to them, startling Mina out of her thoughts. Why didn't he make any noise when he

Bryan Cassiday

approached? She was getting tired of jumping out of her skin whenever he cropped up.

"Our representative will see you now," he told Catton, gesturing to a small room surrounded by plate-glass windows. Its door open, the room had a desk in it with a blonde fortysomething woman sitting behind it eying a computer screen on her desktop.

"Here goes," Catton told Mina, getting up from the couch.

Grinding her teeth Mina followed him to the room, wishing it was all over with and they could get out of there.

Chapter 78

Wearing a navy blue pin-striped suit, the fortyish bank rep smiled cordially at them as Mina and Catton entered her office.

"Please sit down," she said. "My name is Lillian."

As if to confirm her answer, a wooden block with a slat of black metal wedged in it displayed her name printed in white block letters, which faced the front of the desk.

Mina and Catton sat on two chairs opposite the desk and a foot away from it.

The hatchet-faced clerk, who had followed them, closed the door behind them and left.

"What is the nature of your business with us today?" said Lillian.

"I'm Rachel Catton's husband Gage, Lillian," said Catton, taking in her sign on the desktop. "I want to withdraw her money from her checking account and close the account."

Catton's answer gave her pause. "Does she know you're requesting this?"

"She doesn't know anything."

"Pardon?"

"She's dead."

Again his answer caught her off guard. "Oh. I see. What is her name again?"

"Rachel Catton. Spelled like it sounds."

She entered the name into her computer and studied the screen. She furrowed her Botox-smooth brow.

"According to our records, Rachel Catton's spouse Gage is dead," she said, looking at Catton. "How do you explain that?"

"Your records are wrong, as you can see. I'm healthy as an ox."

"Do you have some form of ID as proof?"

Catton dug his wallet out of his trouser pocket, plucked out his California driver's license, and handed it to Lillian.

"Thank you," she said, pored over it, and made sure the photo matched his face.

"Is there a problem?"

"I'll have to take this to my supervisor," she said, standing up behind her desk, the driver's license wedged between her fingers that had mauve polish on their nails. "I'll be right back."

"I don't understand."

She smiled, tightly it seemed to Catton.

"I'll be right back," she repeated.

She departed, shutting the door behind her, leaving a trace of subtle perfume in her wake.

"What's that all about?" said Mina.

"She doesn't want the bank to lose all the money Rachel had stashed here."

"Do you really think this is gonna work?"

"Why not? It's the truth."

Chapter 79

Five minutes later, a five-ten white-haired sixtyish man wearing a bespoke navy blue suit and a glossy pink silk tie opened the door and entered the office.

"Hello," he said. "I'm Eric Lombard the president of the bank."

"Hello, Eric," said Catton, an amiable smile on his face.

"We'll need more documentation to fulfill your request."

"No problem."

"Do you have a certified copy of Rachel's death certificate with the official state seal on it?"

"I don't. As I understand it, the bank already has a copy. Isn't that why you froze her checking account?"

"I'll have that checked out," said Eric. He walked behind the desk, a concerned expression on his face like that of a doctor interrogating an ailing patient. "According to our records, Rachel's husband Gage died at sea. Do you see what my problem is?"

"Your records are incorrect. I'm not dead, as you can see. And I would like my money now."

"According to our records, Rachel doesn't have a joint account with you."

"What difference does that make?"

"If you had a joint account, we could give you the money right now, but—"

"But I'm her husband. She has no other next of kin. That money belongs to me."

"You'll need to show us a will, and, since more than $150,000 is involved, Rachel's estate has to go through probate. Do you have a copy of Rachel's last will and testament?"

"No. But I'm her only heir. The money has to go to me. There's no one else it can go to."

"You'll have to tell that to the probate court."

"There aren't any other heirs. Nobody but me can claim her estate. We can take care of this right now. Just give me the papers I need to sign."

"We also have a flag on this account."

"What kind of flag?"

"The money in this account was collected from an insurance company who paid out on your life insurance policy with them."

"So?"

"So we can't authorize your withdrawal of Rachel's money."

"What business is it of the insurance company? It's not their money any more. They already paid it to Rachel."

"Our attorneys tell me if the payout was awarded as a result of a fake death report, it constitutes fraud, and the life insurance company can notify the courts and reclaim their money."

"Who filed a fake death report?"

"You did."

"I didn't file any report."

"But you falsely made it look like you had died at sea."

"No, I didn't."

"Then why didn't you report to the police that you were still alive when the life insurance company was trying to figure out whether to pay out on your policy?"

"I didn't know."

Eric cocked his head, an expression of curiosity on his broad face. "You didn't know what?"

"I didn't know they thought I was dead."

"You never read the papers or watched TV and heard the news about your death? Why didn't you ever go home and tell your wife you were still alive?"

"Why would I?"

Confused, Eric shook his head. "You survive a boating accident and you don't immediately report it to your wife? Don't you think she would want to know? Your actions make no sense. *She was your wife, Mr. Catton.*"

"I didn't know she thought I was dead."

Mina couldn't figure out what Catton was trying to pull.

"She was the one that reported you missing to the police," said Eric. "Obviously she was worried about you since you never returned home to her."

"I didn't know anything."

"How could you not know? The story was all over the news."

"I didn't know anything."

Eric scrunched up his face. "What?"

At that moment, the door opened, and two police officers appeared in the doorway.

"I didn't know who I was," said Catton.

"I'm not following," said Eric.

Mina, however, saw what Catton was getting at. She wondered if it was going to work.

"I lost my memory," said Catton. "I was wandering around in a daze for I don't know how long. I only just recovered it."

Eric crossed his arms over his chest and leaned his head backward. "You'll have to tell it to the judge, I'm afraid, Mr. Catton."

The two cops stomped into the office and braced Catton.

"Please come with us, sir," said the lead cop, a beefy guy pushing thirty with a buzz cut and thin lips, his pink face chapped by the SoCal sun.

"This is ridiculous. Are you arresting me?"

"Yes, sir. Stand up. We're going to the station."

"Why? What did I do?"

"You faked your death to collect on your life insurance policy."

Catton bolted to his feet, knocking the chair over behind him. "I didn't fake anything."

Buzz Cut latched onto Catton's arms and wrenched them behind his back, while the barrel-chested cop behind him approached, clutching a pair of cuffs.

"Put your hands behind your back, sir," said Buzz Cut.

"They're already there," said Catton, grimacing in discomfort in Buzz Cut's grasp.

Buzz Cut took this as resisting arrest, pinioned Catton's arms behind him, and rammed him face-first against the wall.

"Ow! Damn it," said Catton, his face pressed sideways against the drywall, as Buzz Cut leaned his full weight against Catton's back, driving a knee into the base of Catton's spine for good measure.

Catton felt warm blood rilling from the corner of his mouth that Buzz Cut had smashed against the wall.

Barrel Chest came up and handcuffed Catton's wrists behind his back.

"I want a lawyer," Catton managed to say through his mouth jammed against the wall.

In response Buzz Cut, stone-faced, read him his Miranda rights, knowing them verbatim.

"You have the right to remain silent—"

"What about the girl?" said Barrel Chest.

"Take her in as an accessory," said Buzz Cut.

He finished Mirandizing Catton and Mina.

Barrel Chest cuffed Mina's hands behind her back.

Buzz Cut and Barrel Chest shepherded Catton and Mina out of the bank and into the back of their squad car that was parked in front of the bank entrance, shoving their captives' heads down so they wouldn't strike the car's roof on their way to the backseat.

Barrel Chest shut the door behind them.

Buzz Cut took the wheel, and Barrel Chest rode shotgun.

They pulled onto Little Santa Monica Boulevard and headed west.

"Where are we going?" said Barrel Chest in surprise. "The station's a block away."

"I got orders," said Buzz Cut. "They want these two in LA."

"But they're in our jurisdiction in Beverly Hills."

"The way I hear it, they've got something to do with a murder in LA."

Discomfited, sitting with her hands bound behind her back, Mina wondered if Catton knew what he was doing. If he did, why were they headed to jail? The cop car smelled bad, like an unwashed vagrant had been sitting in it not long ago. She hoped she didn't end up with lice or fleas from sitting here.

What was this about murder? she wondered. She could understand if the cops were arresting them for insurance fraud after Catton had ID'd himself to the bank staff, but nobody had said anything about murder in the bank.

Chapter 80

A half hour later, Mina and Catton ended up in an interrogation room in an LA police station, presided over by Lieutenant Duquesne.

Mina and Catton sat at a rectangular deal table in an empty room. The four walls were empty, save one, which had a mirror large enough to be a picture window hanging on it.

In a brown blazer and white button-down shirt, Duquesne was standing in front of them, eyeballing them.

"I want a lawyer," said Catton.

"Why?" said Duquesne. "Do you have something to hide?"

"No. I want a lawyer because I'm under arrest."

"You're not under arrest."

"Then what am I doing here?"

"You're simply here for questioning."

"Then why am I in handcuffs?" said Catton, trying to pull his bound hands out from behind his back.

"It's just a precaution."

"The cops at the bank Mirandized us and told us we were under arrest."

"They made a mistake. We simply want to question you."

"I think I need a lawyer."

"Not yet. I simply want some information. There's no reason for you to be hostile."

Catton said nothing.

"Do you have anything to hide?" said Duquesne.

"No," said Catton.

"Then let's proceed. You went to the bank in Beverly Hills to withdraw money from your wife's checking account. Correct?"

"Yeah."

"Did you know that your wife is dead?"

"Yeah. I told them that at the bank."

Duquesne lifted his foot, placed it on the seat of the empty chair on his side of the table, and, clasping his hands together, rested his elbow on his knee. "Did you know she was murdered?"

"I heard about it on the news."

"Is that why you wanted to withdraw her money from the bank?"

"I'm her husband, so the money belongs to me."

"OK. Now let's go back a ways. It was reported, what was it? A year ago? About that, I think. That you died at sea. Is that right?"

"I dunno."

"You don't know what?"

"I don't know what you're talking about."

"You're supposed to be dead. You don't know anything about that?" said Duquesne, squinting his right eye in skepticism.

"I'm not dead, as you can see."

"So where have you been for the last year?"

"I dunno."

"I'm supposed to believe this?" said Duquesne, unclasped his hands, lifted his foot off the chair, and walked away from the table.

"What am I being charged with?"

Duquesne turned around to face Catton. "I told you, you're not being charged with anything. You're being held for questioning as a person of interest."

"Regarding what?"

"What do you know about your wife's murder?"

"Only what I saw on the news."

"You saw your wife's murder reported on the news, so you went to the bank to withdraw her money from her checking account. Is that right?"

"Yeah. Can I go now?"

"No."

"Why not?"

"Because you're gonna need a lawyer pretty soon."

"What kind of a game are you playing?"

Duquesne turned to Mina. "What do you know about this?"

"Nothing," said Mina.

"What's your name?"

"Mina."

"Mina what?"

"Mina Deerling."

"How are you two related?" said Duquesne, glancing from one to the other.

"We're friends."

"How long have you known him?"

"A couple of days."

"Friendship at first sight, huh?"

Mina looked blank.

"Why were you at the bank with him in Beverly Hills?" said Duquesne.

"He wanted me to go with him."

"You've been friends for only two days, and he wants you with him when he withdraws almost a million dollars from the bank?"

"Yep."

"Does that sound credible to you?"

"It is what it is."

"So you're just two friends?"

She nodded.

She felt tempted to tell the cops about her whole wretched ordeal suffered at Catton's hands, but she knew she was the one, not Catton, that had finished off Rachel, and the cops could bust her for murder as soon as Catton told them about it, which he would do if she started blabbing about what had really happened the last couple of days.

Mina hated this place. She would hate it even worse if she had to spend the rest of her life rotting away in the joint. As yet, neither Catton nor she was being charged with murder. She still didn't know what Duquesne was going to charge them with.

Maybe it wouldn't be a murder charge. She doubted the cops had any evidence that either she or Catton was involved in Rachel's murder.

"You've known him for a couple of days and then you go to the bank to collect all of his wife's money," said Duquesne. "Is that your story?"

"We want a lawyer," chimed in Catton.

"You're gonna need one," said Duquesne. "Go ahead and call him."

"I don't have one. You'll have to provide me with one."

"Does that mean you can't afford one?"

"Not unless I can get my money out of my wife's bank account."

"Well, that's not gonna happen."

"Then I need a public defender."

"You heard him," said Duquesne, addressing the mirror and gesturing toward it with a sweep of his hand. "Get Vitti."

A two-way mirror, decided Mina. She was being interviewed in a fishbowl. No telling how many others were watching her at this very moment.

"Can you at least tell us what we're being charged with?" said Catton.

"Of course. Defrauding your life insurance company by faking your death," said Duquesne. "Happy now?"

Chapter 81

Ten minutes later, a clean-cut guy pushing fifty and
dressed in a charcoal grey suit and a turquoise knit tie breezed
into the interrogation room, a black leather attaché case in his
hand.

Mina figured he must be the public defender, thanks to
the baleful glances Duquesne was shooting at him as he
entered.

"This is Michael Vitti, your lawyer," Duquesne told Mina
and Catton, barely disguising his contempt. He turned to Vitti.
"I'll give you time to talk to your clients."

"Not in this room," said Vitti. "We have attorney-client
privilege. You know that."

"You got it," said Duquesne, and headed to the door.

Vitti gave him a world-weary look. "This room is as
private as Grand Central Station. Come on, Lieutenant. We
both know it's wired in here and has an audience watching
us," he said, nodding at the two-way mirror.

"Suit yourself."

Duquesne opened the door and let two cops in, who
escorted Mina and Catton along with Vitti to another room,
where they showed them in and, leaving them alone, locked
the door behind the three of them.

"Do they really think we're gonna try to escape?" said
Catton in the room that looked similar to the one they had just
left except for the mirror on the wall.

The room was even furnished in the same manner with a
deal table and chairs in the middle of it.

"Have a seat," said Vitti.

Still handcuffed, Mina and Catton sat uncomfortably at
the table.

Vitti pulled up a chair across from them. He set his
attaché case on the tabletop, popped open the lid, and removed

a blank yellow legal pad. He produced a pen from his jacket's breast pocket.

"OK. So what's your story?" he said, his pen hovering over the legal pad.

"I thought you were the public defender, not the DA," said Catton.

"I am."

"Then why are you insinuating I'm telling a story?"

"It's a figure of speech. What I'm asking you is, what happened? You're charged with faking your death in order to defraud your insurance company."

"I didn't fake anything."

Vitti turned the ballpoint over in his hand. "Explain."

"I don't know what's going on. I went to my wife's bank and tried to withdraw her money because I'm her husband and she's dead, so the money's mine."

"Then why do the police say you faked your death to collect on your life insurance policy?"

"I dunno."

"OK. Let's try a different tack. Where have you been for the last year?"

"I dunno."

Vitti paused, assimilating Catton's info. "How can you not know?"

"My mind's a complete blank. I don't know what I've been doing for a year. The last thing I remember I was watching the news and I saw that my wife had died. So I decided to claim her money as her husband."

"Let me get this straight," said Vitti, head cocked to the side. "You're saying, you had amnesia?"

"I guess. If that's what you want to call it."

"When you lose your memory, it's called amnesia."

"Yeah. OK. I don't know medical lingo."

"Do you know how you got it?"

"The cops told me I died at sea in a boating accident. Maybe I got amnesia there."

"You had a boating accident and disappeared at sea. Is that right?"

"That's what the cops say."

Chapter 82

"All right. Let's get down to business. What's your occupation?" said Vitti, preparing to jot Catton's answer on his legal pad.

"I dunno," said Catton.

"You're not helping your case much."

"I went to Princeton and graduated summa cum laude. I can remember that."

"That's a start," said Vitti, scribbling notes on his pad. "When did you take out your life insurance policy?"

Catton shook his head in confusion. "I dunno."

"The cops say you disappeared about a week after you took our your policy."

Catton said nothing.

"Doing that looks suspicious," said Vitti. "It makes it look like you planned to fake your death all along so your wife could claim the insurance money."

"I can't help it if I lost my memory. Is losing your memory illegal?"

"No. Neither is faking your own death, also known as pseudocide."

"Then what are they charging me with?"

"You're being charged with fraud. The police say you defrauded Lion Life Insurance when you faked your death and collected on your insurance policy. Did you take out an insurance policy with them?"

Catton looked glassy-eyed. "I dunno."

"Did you collect any money from your insurance policy?"

"How could I? I was declared dead."

"Good point. But your wife collected on your policy." Vitti paused, then offhanded asked, "Were you two in cahoots?"

"No."

"Were you two going to link up and split the profits from the insurance company?"

"Wait a minute. I thought you were supposed to be *my* lawyer, representing *me*."

"Keep your shirt on," said Vitti, dropping his pen and holding his palms vertical in front of Catton like a mime pretending he's trapped in a box. "I'm on your side. I'm not asking you anything the DA won't ask you. You have to be prepared for his questions. I'm trying to understand exactly what happened."

Twisting in his seat Catton tried to pull his hands out of his handcuffs without success. "I'm not sure."

"Do you recall having a boating accident at sea?"

Catton frowned in thought. "Vaguely. There are huge gaps in my memory."

"OK. Let me recapitulate. You took out a life insurance policy. You had an accident at sea and developed amnesia. You saw on TV that your wife had died, which jogged your memory so you recalled who you were. Then you went to the bank to collect your wife's money from her checking account, since you're her husband." Vitti trained his brown eyes on Catton. "Is that about it?"

Catton gave a slight shrug. "More or less."

"We have a strong case, then, for your being innocent of committing fraud."

Catton sprang to his feet. "Then I want to collect my money."

"What money?"

"The money in my wife's account."

"There won't be any once Lion Life is through with this."

"What are you talking about?"

"They're claiming you defrauded them by faking your death."

"But I didn't."

314

"But they paid out on your policy, and now they find out you're alive. Therefore, they didn't have to pay out anything. The money's still theirs in the eyes of the law, and they want it back."

Catton fell back into his seat and slumped in dejection. "That can't be true."

"What are you worried about? You lost your memory, so you can't go to jail for faking your death and committing fraud. You'll be a free man after the trial. The DA'll never be able to prove his case against you."

"But it's my money. I want my money."

"It's not your money as long as you're still alive."

"So what do you want me to do? Commit suicide?"

"Of course not. You'll be a free man after your trial. Why would you want to commit suicide?"

"Free and broke."

Vitti pocketed his pen, deposited his legal pad into his attaché case, snapped the lid shut, fastened its clasps, got to his feet, and angled to the closed door.

"I want to get out of here," said Catton.

"Can you post bond?" said Vitti, standing at the door, the doorknob in his hand.

"How much is it?"

"Twenty thousand dollars."

"Not without my money in my wife's account."

Vitti left without comment.

"No wonder this guy's a public defender," Catton told Mina. "He has no idea what he's doing. He'd never cut it at an upscale law firm. He'd be chasing ambulances if he wasn't doing this."

"I can't stand going to jail."

Chapter 83

Mina would rather be anywhere than here in what amounted to a prison cell, since she was in handcuffs in a locked room.

"He said we can't collect the money as long as I'm alive," said Catton, dialing back his anger at Vitti and thinking up a scheme.

"I heard him."

"What about if I'm dead?"

"But you're not dead, and they know you're not dead because you're sitting here in the flesh."

"It's catch-22," he said, grim-faced.

"I don't know why they're holding me here. I didn't even do anything."

"Neither one of us did anything."

"You faked your death."

"The lawyer said that's not illegal. And, anyway, I didn't fake my death. I lost my memory for a year and didn't know everybody thought I was dead. That's no crime."

He was a good liar, decided Mina. She wondered if he was lying now or lying before when he told her he and his wife had colluded to defraud the insurance company. She couldn't tell when he was lying to her or telling the truth. Maybe even he didn't know—which was why he was so convincing.

"You cheated the insurance company out of their money, according to the cops," she said.

"What money? I don't have any money."

"Then why don't they let us go?"

Catton remained hangdog. "The government can do whatever they want."

"Then what good's that lawyer they sent us?"

Catton looked around the barren walls. "I wonder if they're listening to us," he said under his breath.

"This room isn't supposed to be bugged because of attorney-client privilege. You heard what Vitti said."

"I don't trust the government," said Catton, still taking stock of the walls.

Mina wondered if the cops were really holding them for fraud or for suspicion of Rachel's murder. If it was for murder, didn't they have to tell her or Catton about it? She wanted to ask Catton about it, but decided it would be best to bring up the subject elsewhere—since he suspected the room might be wired for sound.

Even if Catton didn't fake his death, as he now claimed, he had murdered his wife, so Mina knew he was guilty of a crime, as was she since she had helped him commit the murder. But only because he urged her to do it, Mina decided. She would never have done it on her own. Why would she? Rachel was a complete stranger to her. Why kill a complete stranger?

Murder, murder, murder. The word kept creeping back into her mind, hounding her. Why did she have to keep thinking about it? she wondered, trying to shut the word out of her brain. *Murder, murder, murder.*

She didn't know what to do. She considered calling her mother and asking her for advice.

Catton's sweeping gaze alighted on Mina. "You better not get any ideas."

"What?"

"You know."

She figured he was talking about their murdering Rachel. In other words, if she ratted him out, he would return the favor. Then how was she supposed to get out of jail? The very idea of jail gave her the willies. She could feel her skin crawling and the blood draining from her face at the thought.

Chapter 84

Tobias Winterkill, Esquire, was feeling bored sitting in his penthouse in affluent Boca Grande on Gasparilla Island in southwest Florida, bordered on its west coast by sea grapes and lulling gulf breezes. Even his breathtaking view of the turquoise waters of the Gulf of Mexico that he commanded from his living-room picture window didn't interest him. Winterkill at the age of fifty-six with a pronounced mane of white hair was a millionaire many times over.

Gasparilla Island, where he had made his home for the last ten years, was so exclusive it had only one gas station. Most residents drove around on golf carts on the island thanks to the paucity of roads. What few roads there were had just as few cars navigating them. It was an island of tranquility. Perhaps that was the problem, decided Winterkill. He needed excitement.

What he needed was a new case. Litigation was his lifeblood and got his adrenaline going. Without it, he had no raison d'être. Sitting on his plush sofa he idly picked up a newspaper on the glass-topped coffee table that squatted on metal ogee legs beside him and commenced flipping through the national news pages till he noticed an article about an LA man accused of defrauding a life insurance company by faking his death.

Winterkill came to attention, his large and arrogant patrician face becoming animated. He hated insurance companies, particularly ones in California. Ever since he had had a car accident in California while working on a libel trial there, he hated them. He hated seeing them win in court. Saying it was his fault, his car insurance company had refused to reimburse him when he crashed his prize fluorescent lime Lamborghini Huracan while driving on the San Diego Freeway. Winterkill had sued them and lost.

Their refusal infuriated him, and from that day on he swore he'd get even with insurance companies any way he could.

Over nine hundred thousand dollars was at stake in this current case in LA. Not bad. Normally he wouldn't handle a case for under a million, but he hated insurance companies so much he would never turn down a chance to stick it to them.

He read the newspaper article further and found out that the case involved a murder as well as insurance fraud. A good murder always ginned up excitement in a case, he decided. It would grab headlines, especially when he arrived as the attorney of record representing the accused.

Newspaper in hand, he bolted to his feet. He saw a cause. And he saw a case he knew he could win. It would launch his name into national prominence.

He swiped up his cell phone from the coffee table. The cell phone's facial ID recognized his face and opened. He punched a name on his list of contacts.

"Hey, Juan," he said. "Saddle up the Learjet for a trip to LA."

Chapter 85

Locked in the holding tank in LA, Catton and Mina were awaiting transfer to separate cells.

The tank smelled like Lysol, decided Mina, curling her lip in distaste. At least they washed the place, though. It could have smelled worse—like the vomit-reeking back of that squad car they had arrived in at the police station.

She was surprised they were the only two occupants in the cell. She thought it would be more crowded. Probably, it would get more crowded as the day wore on.

She wondered how long they would be stuck here. Then again, she didn't look forward to going to a regular cell, enduring a strip search and all that degrading stuff she saw in movies. At least, the cops had removed her and Catton's handcuffs while they were in here.

"Don't worry," said Catton. "They got nothing on us. We'll walk."

"Then why are we still behind bars?"

"Intimidation. They want us to confess we're guilty."

A burly wide-hipped thirtysomething guard strutted toward them with a slight limp, jaw set.

Mina figured he was going to tell them to shut up.

Instead, he opened the tank door.

"Where we going now?" said Catton.

"That's up to you," said the guard.

"Huh?"

"You're free to go. Your lawyer posted bail."

Mina followed Catton out of the cell.

"Vitti?" said Catton, finding it hard to believe. "Why would a public defender put up twenty thousand dollars of his own money to post my bail?"

"It wasn't Vitti," said the guard. "It was your new lawyer."

Mina turned to Catton. "When did you change lawyers?"

"I didn't know I did," said Catton. He faced the guard. "Don't I have any say in this?"

"Yeah. You can stay in the tank if you don't want to hire him."

"Ha ha," said Catton, not laughing. "What's his name?"

"How should I know? Do I look like I care? The only good lawyer's a dead lawyer," said the guard, locking the tank's door after releasing Catton and Mina.

"Where do I find him?"

"That's your problem."

As they walked out of the one-story brick police station, Mina and Catton stood on the landing of the cement steps that led down to the sidewalk and, hearing a deafening noise in the sky, looked up as a Learjet 40XR screamed overhead. Flying at a lower altitude and slower, trailing it, was a yellow prop plane that looked like a throwback to the Red Baron's Fokker D.VII he piloted during World War I. It was pulling a rippling sign behind it that said in huge block letters: Make a Legal Killing with Winterkill.

On the other side of the street, black-and-whites were parked along the curb.

At that moment, a white stretch limo screeched to a halt in front of the police station. The clean-cut thirtyish chauffeur, clad in black livery, bounded out of the driver's seat, circled the limo, and opened the back door for Catton and Mina, who stood on the landing wondering what was happening.

The chauffeur remained on the sidewalk holding the door for them.

"What's going on?" said Catton.

"Mr. Winterkill wants to discuss your case with you," said the chauffeur. "He'll be arriving at the airport soon and would like to meet with you at his hotel."

"This the guy that bailed us out?" Catton asked Mina, descending the cement steps with her toward the limo.

"It must be," she said.

When Catton reached the chauffeur, he said, "Who's this Winterkill you're talking about?"

"He told me you're his clients. Please get in," said the chauffeur, gesturing toward the backseat.

"Do you know this Winterkill?" Mina asked Catton.

"Never heard of him," said Catton, and climbed into the backseat.

Mina took his cue and slid in next to him.

The chauffeur closed the door behind them and scurried around to the driver's seat.

"This should be interesting," said Catton, taking in the limo's pricy leather upholstery and interior and stroking the seat covers next to his thighs with his palms with appreciation.

"How are we supposed to pay for this guy?" said Mina.

"I guess he wants a cut of the insurance money."

"Sit back and enjoy the trip," said the chauffeur, as he fired the ignition, put the transmission into drive, and pulled into sparse traffic.

Catton saw no reason to argue. It wasn't every day he got to ride in a stretch limo. It beat a jail cell by half.

Chapter 86

"We now have a viable suspect in Rachel Catton's murder," said Duquesne, sitting at his desk in his office, addressing Patrick, who was standing near the open door watching him.

"Who?" said Patrick.

"What about this guy Catton who turns up conveniently to claim all of her money?"

"The guy charged with insurance fraud?"

"Why not murder as well? He has strong motives. Both jealousy and greed."

"Greed for his wife's money?"

"Exactly."

"And jealousy of Ed Bendix, who was fooling around with her?"

Duquesne nodded yes. "Both strong motives for murder."

"But there's no evidence."

"We need to look at that hospital video of the bearded surgeon that visited what he thought was Rachel's hospital room."

Patrick pulled a face. "I dunno. That guy had purple eyes and a beard. This guy Catton has blue eyes and no beard."

"You've heard of phony beards and contacts, right?"

"Do you think our facial recognition software would help now that we have somebody we can compare the bearded surgeon to?"

"I do. Though I'm not sure the software can recognize a face that's as heavily disguised as the surgeon's was, to wit the beard, the cap, and the mask that covered most of his face. Let's give it a shot and see."

Patrick was turning on his heel to leave when he thought of something. "What about the insurance investigator Dunleavy?"

Duquesne stroked his chin in thought. "Maybe Dunleavy recognized Catton and was gonna report him to Lion Life, so Catton decided Dunleavy had to go. Again Catton had a motive to commit murder. All we have now is motive. We need more than that to go to court with." He looked up at Patrick. "Right now, check out that hospital video and see if you can get a match on the bearded surgeon's face with Catton's with the facial recognition software."

Patrick took off, his stride determined, footsteps firm.

Duquesne figured Catton was dirty, but the guy was also clever with all that hogwash he was spewing about losing his memory and being unable to tell anyone he was still alive because he had no idea who he was. Duquesne didn't buy it, though he admitted it was possible. Unlikely but possible. It was too pat, though, for his liking.

There was something about this Catton that rubbed him the wrong way. He couldn't put his finger on what. It was a feeling he had. Like maybe the guy thought he was smarter than everyone else? Not that that was a crime. But Duquesne wasn't sure if that was it. Something . . .

And why was Catton hanging around with that girl in her twenties? Duquesne wondered. Was there some attraction between the two? She met him only a little while ago, and now they were best buds. In fact, they were so close she accompanied him when he went to the bank to claim his wife's money. Love at first sight? Were they in love? Why would a guy want to share almost a million bucks with a girl he just met? Something else must be holding the two together, but he had no idea what it could be.

Chapter 87

Mina and Catton met Winterkill at a $3-thousand-a-night, thousand-square-foot two-story garden bungalow he was renting at the Fairmont Miramar Hotel that bordered the Palisades Park in Santa Monica and overlooked the monolithic Pacific Ocean, which lay beyond the park and unfurled to the horizon.

"Nice digs," said Catton, walking into the well-appointed living room, inhaling the fragrance of the garden flowers, which included roses and sage, borne on the ocean breeze that wafted through the bungalow's open casement windows.

A six-foot-high ivy-clad brick wall skirted the bungalow's northern side, while due west was the garden and a cozy patio furnished with a fountain, white metal tables, and cushioned chairs where you could sit and drink in the sea breeze that swept up the California Incline while you listened to the fountain babble.

She could get comfortable real easy here, decided Mina.

As much as she liked his hotel, Mina had her doubts about this guy Winterkill. She wondered what kind of game he was playing. Why should a multimillion-dollar lawyer take their case? They were the great unwashed compared to him. They didn't know him from Adam, and vice versa.

"Nice," she said, but her suspicions weren't alleviated by the splendors encompassing her.

Mina watched Winterkill strut into the room, bearing his large head crowned with a shock of white hair and perched on his broad shoulders like it was some kind of trophy he had won. Of average height, he stood a shade under five nine, but the size of his body was no match for that of his disproportionate head, which dominated it.

He was dressed in khaki Bermuda shorts and a mint linen guayabera shirt with French cuffs. On his feet he wore white

325

Rhyton Gucci leather sneakers with the Gucci logo immodestly visible.

"Was that your private jet we saw in the sky a little while ago?" said Catton.

"Damn right," said Winterkill. "A Learjet 40XR. Seats six passengers and still has room for my golf bag. I never fly anywhere without it. California has some nice links I'd like to try. Not anywhere near as nice as Florida's. But . . . ," he trailed off with a shrug.

"And you're the guy that posted our bail?"

"I am," said Winterkill. "Tobias Winterkill, Esquire."

"I don't get it."

"I want to represent you."

"I doubt we can afford you," said Catton, taking in the bungalow's pricy interior.

"No worries. You don't need to pay me anything unless we win. Then it'll cost you a million."

"That all, huh? I got news for you. Even if we win, we won't have that much."

"Rest assured, you shall by the time I get through filing suit against the police for false arrest and false imprisonment. LA County has deep pockets," said Winterkill with a wink.

"So what do you want from us?"

"Don't jump bail. That would make you look guilty."

"I'm not going anywhere. I want my money."

"Excellent. Have a seat," said Winterkill, gesturing to a sumptuous leather-upholstered sofa.

Catton and Mina sat down.

"Thanks," said Mina.

"Fill me in on a few things," said Winterkill. "You've had amnesia for a year?"

"I guess. I can't say for sure how long," said Catton. "They say I had an accident at sea. I don't remember."

"And you didn't see any newspapers that said you were dead?"

"Even if I did, I didn't know what my name was, so what difference would it make what I saw in the papers?"

"So you were wandering around for a year not knowing who you were?"

"That's right."

"Didn't you have ID in your wallet to let you know your name?"

"I guess I lost my wallet in the accident at sea."

Mina knew Catton was lying. She had seen his driver's license at the bank. If he really had amnesia, he could have checked his driver's license and found out his identity. She wondered how many other lies he had told her.

"How did you support yourself?" said Winterkill.

"I got odd jobs," said Catton. "Low-paying jobs where they didn't ask questions—like picking fruit and day-labor jobs."

"You don't know how you lost your memory?"

"Beats me."

"How did you get your memory back?"

"I saw a TV report that said my wife was killed, and they showed a photo of her. I recognized her as my wife."

"You didn't take out the life insurance policy with the intent to defraud the insurance company?"

"Of course not."

"Why did you decide to take out the policy when you did take it?"

"I don't remember taking it out."

"What about your wife?"

"What about her?"

"Why did she transfer all of the insurance payout out of your joint account to a new account that she opened in her name only?"

"I can only hazard a guess. Apparently, she thought I was dead, and she saw no need to share a joint account with a corpse."

His hands clasped behind his back, Winterkill ambled around the room in a semicircle, stopped, and gazed at Catton. "OK. The only way the insurance company can win this case is if they can prove you didn't have amnesia for a year, which they can't do. And even if they could prove it, that by itself wouldn't prove your guilt, though it *would* make you look awfully suspicious for not returning to your wife for a year. In that case, circumstantial evidence could well put you behind bars."

"Why?"

"Because it would look like you were waiting for the insurance company to pay out on your policy before you let everyone know you were still alive. But, like I said, there's no way they can prove you didn't have amnesia." Winterkill paused. "The way I see it, this case is yours to lose."

"And what about me?" said Mina.

"They're charging you as an accessory. Don't worry. If your friend Gage here walks, you walk with him."

"And then we sue the cops for false arrest," said Catton, relishing the idea.

"No question about it," said Winterkill. "That should be good for another couple of million."

"You sure?"

"They've got no evidence against you. Just because you're alive doesn't mean you're guilty of anything. All you did was identify yourself to the bank, and then the cops busted you. For what? What law does going to a bank break?"

"Right," said Catton, smiling.

"They crossed the line on this one. And we'll make them pay through the nose for it."

Catton and Mina stood up to leave.

As they departed through the bungalow door, he told her, "This is gonna work out even better than I thought. We could wind up being multimillionaires."

Chapter 88

Duquesne paid a visit to the Forensics Department, where he met Patrick who was gazing over the shoulder of an LAPD technician named Kopalov that was sitting at a desk in a blue blazer analyzing the St. Luke's security videotape of the bearded surgeon on his computer monitor.

An image of the surgeon strolling through the hospital hall was freeze-framed, and Kopalov was analyzing the bearded surgeon's obscured face with his facial recognition software.

"Is that the best picture of him you can get?" said Duquesne, joining Patrick and studying the photo of the bearded surgeon on the computer screen.

"It's better than any of the other shots, Lieutenant," said Patrick. "He was always trying to avert his face from the CCTV cameras. Plus he's wearing that surgeon's cap and mask. And the beard and the glasses."

"What about it? Is that our boy Catton?"

"Too much of his face is hidden for us to be a hundred percent sure," said the fortyish jug-eared Kopalov, who sported a shaving-brush mustache and was wearing a pair of horn-rimmed glasses whose bows sat on his ears that had lobes that hung well below the bottom of his chin.

"Is that your way of saying you don't know?"

"We're at about 60 percent," said Kopalov, scrutinizing the computer image of the surgeon.

"Meaning what?"

"We're 60 percent sure it's Catton. We can make out pretty clearly his forehead and his eyes and their position on his face—and even the basic shape of his head, although the mask, cap, and beard distort it to some degree."

"Would that kind of a match hold up in court?"

"No. Sixty percent wouldn't cut it. You would need more accuracy than that."

"What about you? Do *you* think it's Catton?"

Kopalov sat back in his chair, crossed his arms on his chest, and regarded the frozen image of the surgeon on the computer screen. "I believe it's him."

Patrick looked at Duquesne. "What does it mean if it's Catton?"

"It means he's the one that killed his wife."

"How do you figure?"

"We tricked him into thinking his wife was still alive and in the hospital, so he went to her room in disguise with the intent to kill her so she couldn't ID him as her attacker. I'm all but certain that bearded surgeon is her killer."

"Do we book him for his wife's murder?"

"Forget it. We'll need more than this to press murder charges. You heard him, the face ID isn't accurate enough for court. Even if it was, we'd need more than this to get a conviction. After all, this bearded surgeon never harmed anyone at the hospital, and we can't prove why he was there." Fixing his stare on the surgeon's face on the computer screen Duquesne pointed his finger at it. "But this is our killer. I'm sure of it."

"Too bad we had to release him."

Duquesne swung his hard gaze to Patrick. "What?"

"We had to."

"Who posted his bail?"

"That lawyer."

Duquesne shut his eyes and shook his head. "What lawyer? The public defender Vitti? He's not gonna post anybody's bail."

"Not him. What's his name? Uh—Winter something."

Duquesne's eyes widened in amazement. "Tell me you don't mean Tobias Winterkill."

"That's it."

"Not *him*. Get ready for a lawsuit."

Chapter 89

Alone, back in her motel room, Mina felt terrible. She couldn't get Dunleavy out of her mind. She had shot and killed the guy. She had also killed Rachel Catton. Mina felt like she was turning into a serial killer. It was a horrible feeling. Was she some kind of homicidal monster? Why did she keep killing people?

Murder, murder, murder—Shut up, she told herself.

Catton had killed Rachel and her lover Bendix, but he didn't look tormented about it. He seemed downright happy. Though it didn't have to do with the murders. It had to do with all the money he thought he was going to get after the trial. His committing of murders had no effect on him. She wondered how many others he had murdered.

She didn't want to end up like him. He was a homicidal sociopath who had no feelings for others.

On the other hand, she didn't want to feel horrible for the rest of her life, riddled with guilt for the killings she had committed. Why should she feel remorse for killing Dunleavy? It was an accident. She was trying to hit Catton, not Dunleavy.

Even if it *was* an accident, she had killed a man. There was no escaping that.

She had left home to escape her mother's domination and to make her way in the world, and she had ended up a serial killer. All because she had met Catton. He had turned her into a murderer. She hated him. What if he tried to get her to kill for him again?

Murder, murder, murder—

She told herself she had to resist him.

Everybody thought she liked him. Nothing could be further from the truth. He terrified her. She was even more terrified of leaving him, because he said he would hunt her down and kill her.

You're a murderer, said the voice in her brain that wouldn't leave her alone. She blotted it out, so she could think.

She didn't see any way of freeing herself from him, except by killing him. Which meant she would have to commit yet another murder. How could she cope with killing yet again? She couldn't even cope with the other murders she had already committed, let alone a third. How many people did she have to kill?

And, anyway, how could she kill him? she wondered. He had taken the gun from her.

Here she was thinking about committing another murder. What was happening to her? Why did everything come down to murder?

Was she going mad?

That was when Catton opened her door and walked into her room, smoking a cigarette.

The sight of him and his burning cigarette filled her with dread.

It was time for another session, she knew, sick with fear.

"I'm really happy," he said, exhaling smoke, approaching her, the smoking cigarette wedged between his fingers, tendrils of smoke lazily spiraling upward. "And I want you to be happy with me. Take off your clothes."

Why couldn't anyone understand what he was doing to her? she wondered in dismay, as she began to remove her blouse.

Chapter 90

Duquesne, in mufti, and Patrick, in his black uniform, made their way into the Pacific Dining Car.

In her late twenties, a brunette hostess with olive eyes greeted them.

She had a pink and yellow tattoo of a rose on each of her well-turned calf muscles, Duquesne couldn't help but notice.

"How many in your party?" she said.

Duquesne fished his badge out of his pocket and displayed it to her. "I want to talk to the manager."

"Oh. OK. I'll get him," she said, and disappeared into the back of the restaurant.

"Nice place," said Patrick, scoping out the dining room. "Let's stay and have a brew."

"Let's not," said Duquesne, face impassive.

"I was kidding."

A few minutes later, a balding roly-poly man with a double chin in his forties, dressed casually in short sleeves and dark slacks, approached them from the bowels of the restaurant. He had blue eyes and a florid complexion. A brown dachshund waddled after him, clicking its paws against the cement floor.

"Can I be of help?" he said courteously, coming to a halt in front of them, his dachshund stopping next to him and looking up at Duquesne with inquisitive brown eyes.

Patrick eyed the dachshund warily. "Does he bite?"

"Only mailmen," said the manager.

Patrick offered an uncomfortable smile.

Duquesne identified himself. "We're investigating the murder that took place in your restaurant the other day."

"I already talked to somebody in your department about that."

"But you didn't talk to me. I'm in charge of the investigation."

"I see. What do you want to know?"

Running his eyes along the restaurant's walls Duquesne said, "I see you have CCTV."

"We do." The manager shrugged. "And it costs me a fortune."

"Do you have the security videotape on the day of the murder?"

"It would be in the security guard's room where the monitors are located."

"Mind if we take a look?"

"Not at all. I have to warn you, though, that the cameras go to sleep sometimes."

"We're familiar with security cameras, Mr. . . ."

"Bronkowsky. Harvey Bronkowsky," said the manager, making a beeline for the security guard's office. "Follow me."

The dachshund waddled after him, claws clicking the floor. Duquesne and Patrick brought up the rear.

The guard's office door was open. Bronkowsky knocked on the door anyway, peering in at a twentysomething Hispanic woman dressed in a grey uniform sitting in front of the CCTV screens mounted on the wall.

"Lupe, the police want a word with you," said Bronkowsky.

Lupe had brunette, shoulder-length hair and a tawny complexion. She turned in her seat and eyed the three of them.

"Sure," she said.

"We want to see the videotape taken on the day of the murder."

"I already showed it to you guys when you were here the first time."

"You didn't show it to me."

"They didn't say there was anything on it they could use."

335

Bryan Cassiday

"They didn't know what they were looking for."

"Suit yourself."

She prepared the tape for viewing and ran it on one of the CCTV screens on the wall.

The video showed customers walking into the restaurant and making for tables or for the bar.

"Skip to the afternoon to about a half hour before the time of the murder, according to the ME," said Duquesne.

Lupe fast-forwarded the tape then slowed it back to regular speed.

After watching it and rewatching it for the better part of fifteen minutes, Duquesne said, "Stop it there."

She complied.

Duquesne craned forward and studied the image of a bearded man wearing glasses.

"The surgeon at St. Luke's, you think?" said Patrick, examining the image.

"Looks about the same height. Same type of beard and glasses," said Duquesne.

"Hard to be sure though, because he was wearing a cap and a mask at the hospital."

"Looks like this guy's got purple eyes like the surgeon, but the color isn't that great on this video. They could just as easily be blue." To Lupe Duquesne said, "Keep rolling the video. I want to see when this guy leaves."

The video showed him leaving some twenty minutes later.

"He wasn't here very long," said Patrick, consulting the white numbers on the bottom of the screen for the time of day the video was shot.

"And he left through the rear door, unlike the rest of the customers," said Duquesne.

"I guess he could've ordered just a drink and left."

"Or he could've garroted somebody and left."

"You think it's the killer?"

336

"I do. He's got the same type of beard as the phony surgeon *and* the same type of thick black-framed glasses."

"Can we build a case against him?"

"It's all circumstantial. And the facial recognition software didn't get a positive match on the surgeon's face with Catton's."

"We couldn't get a conviction?"

"Not at this point. We might have enough to haul him down to the station and sweat him. But that's gonna be difficult because he's lawyered up."

"How do we handle it?"

"We need to get more on this guy. All we have for sure is motive. The rest is probability and speculation."

Patrick nodded in agreement. "Videos of someone that may be him. We think they're him, but nothing concrete. They won't convince a jury beyond a reasonable doubt."

"I just hope he doesn't get it into his head to kill again."

"Do you think he did Dunleavy?"

"He has the motive if Dunleavy threatened to expose him to Lion Life, but the MO's different. Our boy likes to get up close and personal when he kills. He knifed Rachel and garroted Bendix. But Dunleavy was shot. I doubt it's the same perp."

"Will that be all?" said Lupe, twisting around in her seat to peer up at Duquesne.

"Could you e-mail a copy of that videotape to the LAPD?" Duquesne pulled a business card out of his jacket pocket and handed it to her.

Duquesne and Patrick were getting ready to leave when they heard the clatter of the dachshund's nails on the floor as it approached them from the dining room.

Agitated at the dog's presence, Patrick picked up on the location of the rear door and bolted for it. Seeing him take off, the dachshund whipped after him barking on its churning short legs, scrabbling at the floor with its claws.

Duquesne watched them with amusement.

"He shouldn't run," said Lupe. "Dogs chase you if you run away from them."

"I know."

Chapter 91

Kopalov was waiting for Duquesne in the forensics lab when Duquesne and Patrick arrived back at the station.

"What did you want to see me about?" said Duquesne.

Kopalov was propped in front of his computer running the security video that the Pacific Dining Car guard Lupe had e-mailed to the LAPD. As he studied the video he munched on a large soft pretzel with thick gobs of mustard smeared on it.

"Want a pretzel with that mustard?" said Duquesne.

Kopalov's face remained static.

"This match is over 90 percent certain, and it will stand up in court," he said, looking over his shoulder at Duquesne.

"A match with Catton's face?"

"That the name of the guy you showed me before?"

"Yeah."

"It's a match with him."

"Even though he's wearing the beard and sunglasses?"

Kopalov nodded yes. "Maybe he didn't spot all of the CCTV cameras in the restaurant in order to avoid them. He would've been better off if he had. In any case, this video here has a clear shot of his ear."

"His ear?" said Patrick, and chuckled.

Kopalov shot him a dirty look. "Don't laugh. Ears are unique to each individual, just as unique as fingerprints."

"I never knew that," said Patrick, scratching his hair and knitting his brow into wales.

"In the hospital video we never got a clear view of the surgeon's ears because of the cap he was wearing, which covered them. Therefore, that video is legally inconclusive and cannot be used to match Catton's face. However, this one is legally admissible in court as an identifier of Catton."

"Then we got him."

"No, we don't," said Duquesne.

"Why not?" said Patrick, caught off guard by Duquesne's rebuttal.

"All this video proves is that Catton was in the Pacific Dining Car at the time of the murder. So were scores of other customers."

"But he had motive to kill Bendix, and the other customers didn't."

"How can you be sure some of the other customers didn't have a motive?"

"What are the chances?"

"Still, a lawyer could make that case and block a conviction in court."

Patrick pulled at his earlobe in frustration. "Well, he's definitely a suspect because he was at the restaurant at the time of the murder."

"He's Bendix's killer."

"But you said—"

"I said we can't *prove* he is in a court of law. Not if we just have these security video feeds."

"Isn't this at least enough to bust him for suspicion of murder?"

"We could take it to the DA and try. I'm not optimistic about what he's gonna say, though."

Duquesne retreated into the hallway, dug his cell phone out of his trouser pocket, and put a call through to the DA at city hall. His name was Jeffery Bowdin, a hard-charging guy in his early forties, who had political designs and didn't like losing. As a consequence, he didn't take on cases unless he thought he had a lock on the case, which meant hordes of criminals remained at large, as Duquesne saw it with his jaundiced eye.

When Bowdin answered, Duquesne explained the evidence he had gathered against Catton regarding Rachel Catton's murder.

"You're holding him right now for insurance fraud?" said Bowdin.

"Yeah."

"And now you want to charge him with murder one?"

"Right."

Duquesne got the feeling Bowdin was reading him the riot act, and he didn't understand why.

"Try him one case at a time," said Bowdin.

"The murder charge takes precedence over fraud. We don't want a murderer running around loose."

"All you have is circumstantial evidence."

"You can get a conviction in California with only circumstantial evidence."

"Don't give me a lecture on the law, Lieutenant. Is Vitti representing Catton in the fraud case?"

Duquesne cleared his throat, anticipating Bowdin's next question. "Catton got another lawyer."

"Who?"

"Tobias Winterkill," said Duquesne, wincing like he was extracting a splinter from under his fingernail.

"Stop wasting my time. There's no way I'm going to file a murder charge if this Catton's got Winterkill representing him. Winterkill's a moneygrubbing snake. He'll sue the county for false arrest, false imprisonment, defamation, and God knows what else he's got up his sleeve if we don't have a murder case tighter than a rat's ass. What you've given me so far doesn't even come close to cutting it."

"We let Catton get away with murder?" said Duquesne in an even voice, which belied the anger he was holding in check.

"You're the one that's letting him get away with it because you're the one that hasn't built a strong-enough case against him. Don't put this on me. We need an airtight case. Get me a smoking gun."

Bowdin terminated the call.

"What did he say?" said Patrick, sidling up to Duquesne, who was giving his cell phone a smoldering look.

Duquesne jumped on him. "What do you think?"

Chapter 92

Catton was standing at the wet bar in his motel room, pouring himself a drink of Bordeaux. Mina was sitting on the sofa, her legs crossed in a defensive manner.

She wondered if he was going to get drunk. As bad as he was when sober, he was even worse when he was sloshed.

"I need more money," said Catton. "I have to pay the motel manager for our rooms."

"Can't you get more out of Rachel's bank account?"

Drink in hand, Catton shot her a reproachful look. "No. They froze it. You know that."

"Are they gonna kick us out of here?"

"I'll get the money."

"How?"

Catton thought about it. "I'll put the arm on Tobias."

"You're calling him Tobias. Now you and him are good buddies, huh?"

"You heard him. If we lose the case, we don't owe him a thing."

"That doesn't mean he'll pay our rent."

"Why not? He knows I'll be good for it after the trial."

Catton put down his drink, dredged his burner phone out of his trouser pocket, and called Winterkill.

"Hello, Tobias. This is Catton. I'm running low on money. I need to pay for my rent. Could you help out with a couple grand?"

"I never carry cash," said Winterkill.

"I'll pay you back after we win the case," said Catton, brimming with confidence.

"I never carry cash," repeated Winterkill, and hung up.

Catton stared at his cell phone in stupefaction. "How do you like that? The guy's filthy rich, rolling in bucks, and he can't spare us a measly couple grand."

"How do you think he got rich?" said Mina, knowingly.

"I said I'd pay him back."

"You don't get rich by giving all your money away."

"It's a loan, not a handout."

"Maybe he thinks he might lose the case."

"No way."

"So how are we gonna get the rent money?"

Catton took a pull on his Bordeaux. "We'll have to rob a bank." He paused and stared at her. "Or maybe you can turn some thousand-dollar tricks."

Mina detested him. First, he made her his killer. Now he wanted to make her his whore. She had to get out of this relationship before she went insane. It couldn't go on this way. She could endure only so much abuse then she would crack, she was sure of it. She was barely holding herself together as it was. And then what would happen to her? What came after insanity?

She didn't want to find out.

Maybe she was already nuts. With all she'd been through, it might explain a lot. How could you tell if you were nuts or not?

"Now we have to find johns for you," he said. "Any suggestions?"

Infuriated, she averted her gaze from him and directed it at the floor.

"Lemme snap some pictures of you in your lingerie with my cell phone, and we'll post them on the Internet with the phone number to your room."

"This is a bad idea," she said, not looking up at him.

"Face it, honey, a lot of men would like to fuck you, especially when they see you half-naked. You're a hot piece of tail."

"That's what you really think of me, huh?" she said, spitting out the words. "A piece of tail?"

"You're useful to me. The only reason I kept you alive before was because you were useful to me when I wanted Rachel's password to her bank account. I was getting ready to whack you after you got the password and had served your purpose. You see, you had no purpose anymore. Now you're useful to me again. You should be happy I don't want to waste you right away."

A side of meat, she decided in a brown study. A side of meat to be passed around and then killed. She wanted to throw up.

"Start stripping," he said, "so I can snap pics of you, and we can get this show on the road." Seeing she wasn't disrobing he paused. "Or do you want to be evicted?"

Chapter 93

"What do we know about Catton's accomplice?" said
Duquesne, sitting at his desk with his laptop open, a
Styrofoam cup of hot coffee steaming in front of him on his
desktop.

Patrick stood in front of him. "What's her name? Mina
something?"

"Mina Deerling."

"Nothing. We haven't been researching her. We've been
concentrating on Catton."

"Nobody grilled her?"

"We didn't see any point. Catton's the mastermind
behind this scam. He's the one that took out the insurance
policy before he faked his death."

"How does she fit into this?"

"Apparently, he met her recently. She must be his shack
job."

"Let's see what we come up with when we google her
name," said Duquesne, and commenced tapping on his laptop
keyboard. "We need to think outside the box. Let's attack
this case through her, instead of through Catton."

Patrick shrugged. "She's an innocent bystander who got
messed up with this creep. We need to concentrate on Catton,
pin one of these murders on him. It's gotta be him that did his
wife and Bendix."

Duquesne scrutinized the computer screen. "This is
interesting."

"What?"

"Phyllis Deerling was found dead in her apartment in
Ventura a week ago, according to this newspaper article."

"Any relation to Mina? Does it say?"

"Phyllis had a daughter named Mina."

"How old was this Phyllis?"

"Forty-six."

"Forty-six?" said Patrick in amazement. "That's pretty young to die. What did she die of? The Big C?"

"She was stabbed in the chest and abdomen multiple times with her kitchen steak knife."

"Murder. Did they catch the guy who did it?" said Patrick, his interest piqued.

"They don't know who did it."

"Why didn't we get any reports on this?"

"Ventura. It's out of our jurisdiction."

"But we could've helped them search for the suspect."

"They don't have a suspect," said Duquesne, scrolling down the screen and continuing to read.

"Maybe it was one of these homeless vagrants that are all over the place. They're all a bunch of speed freaks."

"The Ventura police haven't been able to locate the daughter to notify her of her mother's death."

"She doesn't know about it?"

"They don't know. They haven't been able to find her to talk to her." Duquesne pulled back from the screen. "I want you to pull her in."

"For what?"

"She's a person of interest in her mother's murder. Maybe she saw the guy that did it. Or maybe she could help us draw up a list of suspects."

"Why don't we just tell the Ventura department she's here?"

"Just do it. I want to ask her some other questions, and I don't want that lawyer Winterkill here when I do it. She'll never say anything with him here."

"I don't get it. What am I pulling her in for?"

"Tell her she's a person of interest in a homicide in Ventura. That way Winterkill's not involved. He has nothing to do with that case."

"Oh. I get it," said Patrick, nodding.

"What are you waiting for?"

Chapter 94

Catton was playing AC/DC's "Highway to Hell" on his laptop as he was snapping pictures with his smartphone of Mina, who was clad only in mauve lingerie as she sat on the bed in a provocative pose leaning forward, thrusting her firm young breasts in front of her, her tongue licking her lips, and her legs spread out, when he started at the rapping on his motel-room door.

Mina jumped to her feet and started yanking her jeans back on, all but falling in the attempt as she hopped around on one leg. She got the paranoid feeling that whoever was knocking was going to break the door down any second from the assertive way they were pounding on it. She didn't want to be seen naked.

Regaining her balance she finished putting on her jeans, buttoned them, and flung on her blouse.

"Why don't you answer it?" she said in a low voice so they couldn't hear her in the hall.

"Who would knock on my door?" said Catton. "I don't want any guests. Maybe they'll go away."

The rapping on the door increased in intensity.

"I guess not," he muttered.

"We know you're in there," said a man's voice in the hall.

"They can hear the music," said Catton, glancing at his laptop, as Bon Scott howled to the accompaniment of Angus Young's infamous wailing guitar riff.

"They're not gonna leave," whispered Mina.

Whoever they were Mina was glad they had interrupted the photo shoot. She didn't look forward to having her half-nude body splayed all over the Internet advertising tricks.

"Who is it?" Catton said through the door, raising his voice.

"LAPD. Open the door or we'll break it down."

"You can't do that. I'm calling my lawyer."

"We're here for Mina Deerling."

Bowled over, Mina gazed at the door with gaping eyes. She couldn't believe it when the cop said her name. What did they want with her?

Relaxing somewhat, Catton glanced at Mina then approached the door and opened it.

Two cops in uniform were standing in the corridor, their expressions stony.

"Mina Deerling, we want to question you down at the station," said Patrick, the one who had spoken through the door.

Mina was terrified. But then she thought maybe this was the best thing that could happen, since it would spare her having to turn tricks for Catton to pay their motel bill. And maybe spare her another one of Catton's sessions she felt certain would ensue.

"I'm calling my lawyer," said Catton, reaching for his cell phone.

"Why?" said Patrick. "We're not taking you in."

"You're not?"

"This has nothing to do with you or your lawyer."

Baffled, Catton didn't put his call through to Winterkill.

Mina couldn't get her head around it either, trying to figure it out as she made a beeline toward the awaiting cops.

"What's the charge?" said Catton.

"She's a person of interest. That's all," said Patrick.

"Regarding the insurance-fraud charge against me?"

"No. I told you, it has nothing to do with you."

"Are you busting her?"

"No. All we want to do is talk to her down at the station."

"What if she doesn't want to go?"

"That wouldn't look good for her."

"I'll go," said Mina. "I don't want any trouble."

She didn't know what she was getting into with the cops, but she knew she didn't want to stay here with Catton so he could pimp her on the Internet to pay for their motel rooms.

"You're supposed to read her her Miranda rights," said Catton.

"Not unless she's under arrest," said Patrick, "and, like I said, she isn't."

"There's something fishy about this."

"We don't want trouble," said Mina, entering the corridor, where the cops were standing. To Catton she said, "I'll just go and get this over with."

"I don't like this," he said.

"Are you interfering with officers of the law?" said Patrick, his eyes dark as he took Catton's measure.

"I'm just saying," said Catton, bridling his anger.

"OK, then," said Patrick, preparing to leave.

"This is invasion of privacy."

Patrick, his partner, and Mina set out for the elevator.

Catton slammed the door after them in a pet.

Chapter 95

Catton got on his burner to Winterkill the moment the door shut. "The cops are trying to pull a fast one."

"In regards to what?" said Winterkill.

"They came and took away Mina."

"They arrested her? On what grounds?"

"They said she's a person of interest."

"Regarding your insurance-fraud case?"

"They said it was for something else. But they're lying. This is some kind of scam they got going to nail me."

"Settle down. Did they say what they were arresting her for?"

"They said they *weren't* arresting her."

"Then she didn't have to go with them."

"She agreed to go because she didn't want to make trouble."

"She should have refused. They can't force her to go to the police station unless they're arresting her."

"I don't believe them."

"Why would they lie?"

"So I don't call a lawyer." Catton paused. "And they're out to frame me. This is a plan the cops hatched to frame me. They want to flip Mina against me."

"Do you have proof of this?"

"It's obvious what they're up to."

"I need more than your opinion to get involved."

"You need to get her away from them," said Catton, scoffing up a gold pillow from the sofa and hurling it down on the cushion.

"I don't see what I can do. They have every right to question her without legal representation if it doesn't have to do with some charge they're leveling against her. And she has the right to keep her mouth shut. Maybe they want her as a witness to something."

"A witness against me. That's what they want."

"Is that what they said?"

"No. I'm telling you they lied, said they were gonna question her about something else."

"I see."

"She was scared she'd get charged with resisting arrest. That's the only reason she agreed to go with them."

"They can't make that charge unless she's being arrested. According to you, they said they weren't arresting her."

"That's what they *said*. Saying it doesn't make it true. The cops are pulling a scam to screw me. I'm sure of it. It doesn't pass the smell test. They want her to throw me under the bus."

"We have to wait for our day in court. Good-bye."

"Wait a minute—"

All Catton could hear was the dial tone. He slung his burner on the sofa with frustration.

He hated lawyers.

What good were they, anyway? he wondered. All they did was take your money. Did anyone ever really benefit from hiring a lawyer? After they got through bleeding you white for legal fees, you weren't left with much—*if* they got you off, that is. If they lost the case, the result was even worse—a stint behind bars or a reserved seat for the electric chair.

He ran his hand through his hair in anguish. What were the cops trying to pull by taking Mina in? he wondered. He couldn't figure it out. Why did they take her, but not him? Because they were trying to flip her to testify against him. That had to be the answer. But what could she do to him?

Had he goofed somewhere along the line? Were the cops onto something that could lead to his conviction for fraud? He couldn't for the life of him think of what it could be. He had covered his tracks to a T. Nobody could know he didn't have amnesia. Nobody could read minds. The cops couldn't get him on anything. He had left no evidence for them to find. He had made no mistakes while implementing his scheme.

Then why was he worried? He might as well sit back and relax. He was invincible. He was smarter than any cop. His plan was foolproof.

All he had to do was wait till after his trial, and then the money Rachel had jacked from him would be his.

What could Mina possibly do to him? She knew nothing of his plans, which he had concocted before he even met her. His meeting her at the Malibu dock that night when he was eighty-sixing Rachel's body had triggered the law of unintended consequences. Things he hadn't prepared for in his well-concocted scam of the insurance company were set into motion by Mina's presence on the dock.

Still, he had leverage against her.

If she ratted him out for Rachel's murder, he would turn the tables on her and rat her out. After all, she was the one that had finished Rachel off. He would testify under oath to that. Mina could flip to the cops all she wanted. Let her go ahead and try. It would have as much effect against him as a spitball against a battleship.

Why worry? he thought.

Body limp, holding his arms out at his sides, he fell back on the sofa. Feeling on top of the world, he mimicked making a snow angel with his arms. He had it made.

Chapter 96

Mina was sitting alone at the deal rectangular desk in the barren LAPD interrogation room when Duquesne and Patrick walked into the room. Patrick shut the door behind them.

Duquesne had a Styrofoam cup of steaming coffee in his hand. He offered the coffee to Mina.

"Is it black?" she said.

"It is," said Duquesne. "Do you want cream and sugar? I can have some brought for you."

"No, that's OK. I like it black."

Sitting down, Duquesne slid the coffee cup across the tabletop to her.

She accepted the coffee and waited for it to cool down in front of her before she could drink it. She figured they were buttering her up with the coffee. But if this wasn't about the insurance fraud, what was it about? she wondered.

In the dark about their true motives, she felt edgy. Sweat dripped from her armpits as she stewed. She didn't want to be sitting here in a cop station, but this was a good deal compared with the alternative of remaining with Catton, who wanted to whore her out on the Internet like she was a strung-out junkie he had picked up in an alley.

"Unfortunately, we have some bad news for you," said Duquesne, his expression gloomy. "I'm sorry we're the ones that have to break it to you."

"What happened?" she said, her face blank, her pulse racing.

She didn't know how much worse it could be than what she was already suffering. Bad news was her constant companion of late. How much worse could it get?

"Make yourself comfortable," said Duquesne.

"I'm fine," she said, retaining her blank expression, wishing he'd get it over with and tell her what she was doing here.

"Your mother was found dead last week. She was murdered in her kitchen with a steak knife."

Mina blanched.

"I'm sorry," said Duquesne, searching her face, "but we need to know if you know anything about the murder that could help us find the killer."

Mina didn't answer right away.

Duquesne gave her a look of encouragement.

"No," she sat at last.

"Did your mother have any enemies?"

"Not that I know of."

"What about your father? Did the two of them get along?"

"They were divorced. My father's back east in New York. He's a broker on Wall Street. We haven't seen him in ten years."

"Did your mother seem distraught last week?"

"I didn't see her last week."

"Where were you?"

"I was here."

"Not in Ventura?"

"No. Why are you asking me these questions?"

"We're trying to find out who killed your mother. We're hoping maybe you could help us."

Mina shifted uncomfortably in her wooden chair that was uncomfortable to begin with. "Do I need a lawyer?"

"Why would you? You're a possible witness. After all, you lived with your mother. Witnesses don't need lawyers."

"I used to live with her. I left. We had a falling-out."

"Nothing serious?"

"I wanted to live my own life."

"Did you two have a fight?"

Patrick glanced at Duquesne.

"I wouldn't call it that," said Mina. "Just a disagreement. It was time for me to leave the nest. You know how that goes. It happens to everyone."

"Do you have any idea who might have murdered your mother?"

"No."

Mina was having problems with this conversation. She didn't want to talk about this. On the other hand, she didn't want to go back to Catton. At least here, she was safe from him.

"Why did you move away from your mother last week?" said Duquesne.

"It was over a week ago."

"Fine. Why did you move out over a week ago?"

"I told you, it was time to move on."

"But why not move three or four weeks before you chose to? You see what I mean? Did you have a fight?"

"I already told you. It was time to move on. That's all. It wasn't time to move on three weeks ago."

"Do you have anything you want to tell us?"

Mina sipped her coffee. She was thinking about telling them that Catton had murdered Rachel. If she told them that, she wouldn't have to go back to him. Maybe it was the only way out of her depraved relationship with him short of killing him. And she wasn't having any luck with killing him. Dunleavy could attest to that—if he was still alive. Was this the time to tell the cops that Catton had killed his wife?

"I'm having a bad day," she said.

"You don't sound very upset that your mother was murdered."

"What do you want me to do? Faint?"

"Of course not. It's just that . . ." His voice trailed off.

"Are you making an accusation?"

"What gave you that idea?" said Duquesne, widening his eyes and pulling back from her. "I'm simply asking you questions that may help us find your mother's killer. You don't have to answer them if they make you feel uncomfortable."

"Why would they make me feel uncomfortable?"

"I couldn't say. Do you want to leave now?"

"No. My mother was a saint. She was an RN, you know. She was very dedicated to her patients."

"A saint?"

"Ask anyone. They all said the same thing. She was a saint."

"But you didn't get along with her? How could you not get along with a saint?"

"I already told you. It was time for me to live my own life. That was why I left her."

"OK," said Duquesne, leaning back in his chair. "You're free to go."

She didn't want to leave. She didn't want to return to Catton. She decided it was time for her to act. This might be the last and best chance she would ever get to break free of him. She couldn't stand the idea of going through another session with him and ending up with more cigarette burns on her stomach. *Branding*, he called it. Her stomach would wind up with more craters on it than the moon. She felt just as strongly against turning tricks for him. It was time to seize her opportunity.

She took a deep breath.

"Gage Catton murdered his wife Rachel," she said.

You couldn't hear a pin drop.

Chapter 97

After the initial shock of hearing her words, Duquesne recovered his composure. He had suspected as much, but hearing it from her lips had nonetheless caught him off guard.

"Are you willing to testify to that effect in court?" he said.

"Yeah."

"How did he do it?"

"He stabbed her multiple times, then wrapped her in a blanket, and dumped her in the ocean with an anchor tied to her."

"How do you know this?"

"I was there. I saw him do it."

Duquesne digested this new information in silence. Now he had evidence in the form of eyewitness testimony to link Catton to his wife's murder. Catton had a surfeit of motives. Duquesne wondered which one it was. Husbands had been killing their wives since the beginning of time. As every cop knew, the spouse was always the prime suspect in a murder.

"Why did he kill her?" he said, wanting to hear it from an eyewitness's mouth.

"She stole the insurance money from him."

Duquesne pricked up his ears. "How did she do that?"

"They were supposed to split the insurance payout between them, but Rachel took all the money from their joint account and transferred it to a new private account that she opened in her name only."

"And Catton found out about it?"

"Right. That's why he killed her. With her dead, the money would all belong to him."

"I figured it was something like that," chimed in Patrick.

"But how did he expect to claim the money in Rachel's account without revealing that he was really alive?" said Duquesne.

359

"That wasn't part of the plan," said Mina. "Rachel wasn't supposed to close out their joint account and take off with all the money. Rachel messed up his plan."

"I see. So he had to ad-lib after she double-crossed him. He knew he couldn't collect the money if everybody thought he was dead and Rachel's account was frozen. The only way he could get the money was to go to her bank and collect it."

"Right."

"He says he didn't commit insurance fraud. He claims he had amnesia."

"He's lying. He didn't have any amnesia when I first met him. He knew exactly what he was doing, and he told me his plan to defraud the insurance company. He concocted the plan with Rachel."

"We got him for murder one," said Patrick.

"I don't wanna go back to him," said Mina, biting her lower lip. "He'll kill me."

"He's not gonna do anything. We'll give you around-the-clock police protection," said Duquesne. "There's one thing I don't understand. Why were you with him when he killed Rachel?"

"I just happened to be in the area when he did it."

Nodding, Duquesne stroked his chin.

"We got him," repeated Patrick.

"Round him up and book him for murder one," said Duquesne.

Patrick was at the door in two strides, hell-bent on nabbing Catton.

Chapter 98

Catton was in his motel room nursing a beer and watching a college basketball game between UCLA and Stanford when the cops came for him.

When he let them in, they stormed in without ceremony and seized him, all but knocking him over. Patrick handcuffed Catton's wrists behind his back, ignoring Catton's protests.

"You can't do this," said Catton, annoyed.

What was with these storm-trooper tactics they were using? he wondered. All he was charged with was insurance fraud and he had already posted bail.

"You're under arrest for the murder of Rachel Catton," said Patrick, as if reading Catton's mind.

"What?"

"You heard me."

"That's crazy. She was my wife. Why would I kill my own wife? I'm innocent."

"Save it for the judge," said Patrick, and read him his Miranda rights.

"You got no evidence. It's impossible, because I didn't do it."

"We have plenty."

"I want to call my lawyer," said Catton, bewildered.

"Go ahead."

"How can I with these handcuffs on?" said Catton, trying to pull his manacled hands from behind his back with a grimace.

Patrick ushered Catton over to the landline phone that rested on the bureau in the corner of the room.

"Call him," said Patrick, lifting up the handset. "What's his number?"

Catton gave him Winterkill's number.

Patrick punched the numbers on the phone and held the handset to Catton's ear.

"Tobias," said Catton into the transmitter, "the cops are busting me."

"For what?" said Winterkill. "You made bail. What's the charge?"

"Murder."

"Murder in the first degree," said Patrick for Winterkill's benefit.

"Who's that?" said Winterkill.

"The cop," said Catton.

"Isn't this Gage Catton?"

"Of course, it is. Are you gonna pretend you don't know me now?" said Catton, outraged, suspecting Winterkill was going to hang him out to dry.

There was a pause on the line.

"Tobias?"

Did the son of a bitch hang up on him again? wondered Catton, eyes snapping.

"Then explain," said Winterkill. "The charge against you was fraud. Where's this murder charge coming from?"

"They say I murdered my wife. It's a trumped-up charge. I didn't murder anyone. Tell them to release me."

"I can't do that. If they're arresting you, they must have evidence. I'll meet you at the police station."

"What am I supposed to do?"

"Do what they tell you. Let them book you. But don't say anything to them. Don't talk till I meet you at the station. And don't say anything over the phone."

"But I didn't do it."

"Chill out and go with them."

"They're trying to squeeze me on the fraud case with this phony bust—"

Winterkill hung up.

"Tobias?" said Catton. "Tobias?"

The ass wipe, decided Catton.

Patrick snagged the handset from Catton, listened to its receiver, and returned it to its cradle on the bureau.

"I can't believe this is happening," said Catton, like the cops had just read him his death sentence.

Patrick latched onto Catton's cuffed arms and frog-marched him to the door.

"Take it easy," said Catton.

"You're under arrest."

"I'll be out of there in five seconds as soon as my lawyer works you guys over. He's gonna hit you with the biggest lawsuit you've ever seen."

"Yeah, yeah."

Catton wished he could believe it. He wished he could trust Winterkill. Had Winterkill played him for a fool? Was the guy going to sell him out like Rachel had?

Chapter 99

Alone in the dreary police interrogation room, his legs shackled to ringbolts set in the floor, his hands cuffed behind his back, Catton waited over forty-five minutes for Winterkill to show up.

What was taking the guy so long? Catton wondered. Was he getting his hair done at a Beverly Hills salon? A do like his must cost plenty.

Catton remarked names such as Red Crab Lou and Scorpion Pete carved in the deal desktop with some kind of sharp instruments, such as pen nibs or something similar, as he sat in his wooden chair wondering how many murderers had sat in this same room before him as they waited for their lawyers. And then there was the ever-present graffiti. After all, this was the joint. *Fuck* was a popular word with the inscribers, Catton could see.

At last the door swung open, and Winterkill cocked in, sporting a grey three-piece linen suit with a flamboyant shocking pink silk tie looking like he had just stepped out of a Tom Ford ad.

"I found out what's going on," he said, pulling up the chair opposite Catton.

"A mistake's going on. That's what's going on. How soon before they let me outta here?"

"Keep your shirt on."

"They got nothing. I didn't do it."

"They have testimony from an eyewitness that says you stabbed your wife, rolled her in a blanket, tied an anchor to her, and tossed her into the ocean."

Thrown by Winterkill's response, Catton said nothing as he chewed over the guy's words, keeping his face expressionless.

At last, Catton said, "Bullshit. How can there be an eyewitness to something I didn't do?"

For the first time since arriving here, Catton was starting to feel apprehensive. An eyewitness. There was only one eyewitness, other than himself. But she wouldn't dare talk. If she did, she'd end up in the slam, and he would be the one that put her there.

"The police say your friend Mina implicated you in the murder," said Winterkill, laying his palms flat on the tabletop, like he was preparing to type, and studying Catton's reaction.

The bitch, thought Catton. Letting him take the fall.

"She's making it up," he said.

"Why would she?"

"She's building an alibi."

Winterkill rucked his brow in befuddlement. "I'm not following."

"She's saying I did it to cover for herself. *She's* the one that did it. I witnessed her stabbing my wife to death."

"Why would she want to kill your wife?"

"She was jealous."

"You said you just met Mina. How could you two become lovers so fast?"

"It was love at first sight with her. It doesn't take long to fall in love."

"*Whoever loved that loved not at first sight*," muttered Winterkill.

"What?"

"Shakespeare stole the quote from Marlowe."

Catton looked blank.

"Anyway," said Winterkill, "let me get this straight. She fell in love with you and murdered your wife out of jealousy."

"Damn straight."

"And you saw her do it?"

"I did."

365

Winterkill thought about it. "Why did she wait so long to make this charge against you?"

"The cops took her away by herself earlier today and must've put the screws to her. She cut a deal. She gave them me, so she could walk. I knew they were gonna pull something like this when they took her."

"OK," said Winterkill, and got up to leave, scraping his wooden chair legs against the cement floor as he straightened up.

"OK? What do you mean, 'OK'? Get me out of here."

"That's not going to happen. You'll have to stay here for a while."

"Is this a joke? You're my lawyer. What do you think I'm paying you for? Post my bail for murder and get me out of here."

"That's the rub."

"Rub? What rub?"

"Since it's a murder charge, the judge didn't set bail. You'll have to stay locked up while we head for trial."

"No bail?" said Catton, crestfallen. "How could there be no bail?"

"A judge doesn't have to set bail for a murder charge. In your case, he might think you're a flight risk or that you might harm the star witness."

Catton sat speechless, as Winterkill slipped out of the room.

Harm her? he decided. He would fucking *kill* her the next time he saw her. The snake. The dirty, slithering snake in the grass. He was home free and all set to get his hands on millions of dollars after Tobias was going to make a legal killing for him. *And now this*.

He leaned forward and slammed his forehead against the tabletop. He lost consciousness for a few seconds thanks to the impact. Then he felt pain in his forehead and warm fluid flowing into his eye.

The full-lipped thirty-five-year-old female Vietnamese bailiff, her brunette hair in a bun, rushed into the room in response to the banging sound, grabbed him by his shoulders, and straightened him up in his chair, as blood jetted from a gash in his forehead a half inch above his right eye, pouring into his eye and down his cheek.

"We need a medic in here on the double," she cried, watching Catton's blood drip onto the tabletop.

Chapter 100

In a brown blazer and a navy blue tie, Duquesne was standing in LA District Attorney Jeffrey Bowdin's office in city hall, as Bowdin sat behind his neat desk, poring over a document laid out on the desktop.

"Give it to me in a nutshell," he said, looking up at Duquesne, as if he had just become aware of Duquesne's presence.

The truth was, Duquesne had been standing in front of Bowdin's desk like he didn't exist for the better part of five minutes waiting to talk to the DA, whose secretary had let him in for just that purpose. Which was one reason Duquesne hated making an appearance in Bowdin's office. Duquesne didn't care for the self-important careerist bureaucrat and visited his office as seldom as possible.

While he had been standing there, Duquesne had cleared his throat a couple of times for Bowdin's benefit, but Bowdin had paid no heed, further irritating Duquesne.

"Is it my turn?" said Duquesne with annoyance.

"You're the only one here. Guess?"

"We have a witness who says Gage Catton murdered his wife," said Duquesne, making his response short and to the point the better to get out of Bowdin's orbit ASAP.

Bowdin cocked his head. "Will the witness testify to that effect in court?"

"She says she will."

"She?"

"Mina Deerling."

"Mina Deerling. Isn't she the one that's Catton's friend?"

"Yep."

"We *are* talking about the Catton who is being charged with insurance fraud?"

"You got that right. A murder charge is more serious so I wanted to bring it to your attention."

"Do you have any corroborating evidence?" asked Bowdin.

"No."

"It's her word against his?"

"Yeah."

"What's he say?"

"He denies it. There's plenty of circumstantial evidence, though. He had motive to kill his wife."

"Such as?"

"We believe the couple were going to split the payout on his life insurance policy, but she double-crossed him and took all of the money for herself."

"Yes," said Bowdin, his eyes staring into the distance like he was eying a faraway goal—a run for mayor, perhaps.

All Duquesne knew was that Bowdin was always thinking in advance, thinking about how any case would affect his career goals, which was why he cultivated no facial hair. Bowdin believed whiskers and mustaches, and even sideburns, detracted from a candidate's electability.

"We believe we have a stronger case in the murder charge than in the fraud charge because of the eyewitness testimony," said Duquesne.

"I don't have to remind you that it's the district attorney's office, not the police, that makes the final assessment of the strength of a case," said Bowdin, switching the object of his gaze to Duquesne's face.

"I'm telling you what we have."

"In your opinion, does this Mina Deerling come off as a reliable witness?"

"She does. She's terrified of Catton. She requested police protection because she thinks he'll kill her."

Bowdin cut his gaze to his desktop. "In the fraud charge, it's going to be hard to prove Catton didn't have amnesia. It'll

369

depend on the believability of his testimony in court whether he comes off as guilty or not."

"Plus he's got Winterkill defending him."

"Do you have any other suspects in the Rachel Catton murder?" said Bowdin, looking up at Duquesne.

"Her husband is the only one we can find with a motive to kill her."

Bowdin nodded. "Because she swindled him out of the insurance policy."

"And—"

"And what?"

"Because his wife was fooling around with another man, we think."

"Think?"

"They met on an Internet dating site called Tinder and were seeing each other. That much we know."

"Will this other man testify that he was having an affair with Catton's wife?"

"No. He was murdered."

Bowdin stared at Duquesne. "By whom?"

"We suspect Catton, but have no proof."

"I see . . . Is Winterkill going to defend Catton on the murder charge?" said Bowdin.

"Yeah," said Duquesne with a sour expression.

"I know what he's going to do. He's going to crucify Mina in the courtroom and hope her testimony falls apart under his cross-examination."

"I know how the jackal works."

"You vouch for her, do you?"

"I *believe* her. I have no idea how she's gonna hold up under questioning. Winterkill may reduce her to a gibbering idiot by the time he's through dragging her name through the mud and discrediting her testimony."

"Dragging her name through the mud? Does she have a history I should know about?"

Duquesne shifted his stance. "Not that I know of. All we know is, her mother was murdered recently."

Bowdin pricked up his ears. "Do you know who did it?"

"Nobody's been charged. It happened up in Ventura, out of our jurisdiction."

"Her life is full of tragedy, it seems," mused Bowdin. "Poor girl."

Duquesne waited a minute before speaking. "Are you gonna prosecute Catton for murder?"

"We're going to prosecute him for murder in the first, and we're going to nail him. Be sure you keep Mina healthy. Don't let her out of your sight. Without her, we have no case."

"We have her in protective custody."

"And don't let Winterkill anywhere near her. I'm dropping the charge against her in the insurance-fraud case so he has no excuse to see her."

Duquesne nodded yes.

"Winning. It's all about winning," sad Bowdin, thrusting to his feet and pumping his fist.

"I thought it was about justice," said Duquesne on his way out, but didn't hang around to listen to Bowdin's response.

Chapter 101

Duquesne wasn't surprised when Winterkill showed up at his office at the station. Duquesne had been expecting him. Winterkill's Day-Glo lime silk tie was so bright Duquesne had to squint when looking at it. Even the guy's grey suit seemed to have a sheen to it. Maybe he had his clothes hooked up to a battery to make them shine.

"I want to see my client Mina Deerling," said Winterkill.

"You can't see Mina Deerling," said Duquesne, sitting behind his desk as Winterkill stood in front of him puffing out his chest.

"It's the law, Lieutenant. I have the right to see my client."

"You can't see her."

"No one is above the law. That includes you. You're not the law. You're an enforcer of the law. You act like you're Louis XIV. *L'etat c'est moi.* Except with you, instead of thinking you're the state, you think you're the law—and you're not."

"You're not the law either, Counselor." Duquesne had read somewhere that lawyers didn't like to be called "counselor," so he decided to use the term in front of the bumptious Winterkill. "You're a representative of the law."

"Can the LAPD afford another one of my lawsuits?"

Duquesne laid it on him. He had been waiting for this moment all day.

"Mina Deerling isn't your client anymore," he said. "All charges against her in the Catton insurance-fraud case have been dropped."

Duquesne's words left Winterkill speechless, a rare occasion for the glib lawyer, suspected Duquesne.

"On what grounds?" Winterkill said at length.

"The DA decided to drop the charges against her."

"Fine. I'll represent her when she files suit against the LAPD for false arrest."

"Not if she doesn't hire you."

"She already did hire me."

"This isn't a courtroom. I'm not arguing with you anymore. She hired you to represent her in the insurance-fraud trial. Those charges against her have been dropped. Therefore, she doesn't require your services. That's all I have to say about it."

"If the charges have been dropped against her, where is she?"

"It's none of your business."

"You can't hold her in jail if she's not accused of any crime."

"Who said we're holding her in jail?"

"Then where is she? I demand to see her," said Winterkill, fit to be tied.

"She's in protective police custody."

"Then let me see her."

"She doesn't want to see you. Good-bye."

"This is going to cost you."

"Good-bye, Counselor."

"You'll be hearing from me," said Winterkill, storming out of the office, eyes fiery.

Clasping his hands behind his head Duquesne leaned back in his chair, relishing the satisfaction he felt at having taken the wind out of the blowhard's sails.

Bryan Cassiday

Chapter 102

Catton, the accused perp in Rachel Catton's murder, sat at the defendant's table in one of the hundred courtrooms in the Stanley Mosk Courthouse on North Hill Street in downtown LA. His trial had attracted media attention thanks to the presence of Winterkill, one of the most celebrated lawyers in the country.

Catton knew the media weren't here on his account, nor were the other members in the audience. They had come to see the multimillion-dollar lawyer Winterkill in action. Even though they hadn't come to see him, Catton felt like a fish in a glass bowl as he sat near the front of the courtroom at his table that faced the judge, who was a middle-aged Japanese man that was bald, wore black-framed glasses on his small nose, and went by the name of Sakamoto.

Catton couldn't wait till he got on the stand. When they found out the truth, it would send shock waves throughout the courtroom.

Winterkill was prancing in front of the courtroom grilling Mina, who sat on the witness stand dressed demurely in a white pullover and a grey pleated skirt that reached below her knees.

Catton sat on the edge of his seat listening to Winterkill rip into Mina's testimony.

"You say you saw the defendant stab Rachel Catton to death," said Winterkill, standing in front of Mina.

"I did," said Mina.

"Where was this?"

"On a Malibu pier at night."

"At night? And you can see in the dark?"

"I was right next to him, and there was a bright moon that night."

"And he stabbed her to death?"

374

"He did."

"How can you be sure she wasn't still alive?"

"She wasn't moving."

"Did you take her pulse?"

"No."

"How many times did he stab her?"

"I dunno."

"Why don't you know?"

"I didn't count the times."

"Why not?"

"Why should I?" said Mina, flustered.

"Because you were an eyewitness."

"I was too scared to be counting stab wounds."

"So, even though you were an eyewitness, you don't know how many times he stabbed her?"

"That's right."

Winterkill gave her an incredulous look.

She didn't respond.

Winterkill turned and checked out the jurors' faces to see if they were siding with him.

"Why would he want to kill his own wife?" Winterkill asked Mina, facing her again.

"She betrayed him. She stole the money they were supposed to split as a result of their insurance-fraud scheme."

"The defendant claims he didn't defraud anybody. He was in a boating accident and suffered amnesia. While he had amnesia, his wife applied for his life insurance claim."

"He's lying."

Winterkill slewed around and searched the jurors' expressions, which, for the most part, were watching Mina intently.

"What kind of a knife did he use?" he asked Mina.

"Just a knife."

"What type of knife? A hunting knife? A pocketknife? Come on. You said you were an eyewitness."

"Objection," said Bowdin, leaping to his feet at the prosecutor's table. "Mr. Winterkill is badgering the witness."

"I'm merely trying to get at the truth," said Winterkill.

"Proceed, Mr. Winterkill," said Judge Sakamoto, "but without the histrionics."

Winterkill turned to Mina. "What type of knife did Gage Catton use to kill his wife?"

"Some type of butcher knife, it looked like," said Mina. "I don't know anything about knives."

"Where is the knife now?"

"He threw it in the ocean."

"You have testified that Rachel Catton's body was wrapped in a blanket."

"A powder blue blanket. He was dragging it to his boat, and then he was going to throw it into the sea, tied to an anchor."

"Didn't she resist?"

"No."

"Why not? How would you like being dragged wrapped in a blanket?"

"He had already stabbed her. She was too weak to resist."

"He had already stabbed her? But you said you *saw* him stab her."

"I saw him stab her after that," said Mina, becoming annoyed.

"Are you changing your story?"

"I am not."

"When did you see him stab her?"

"On the pier."

"Why did he have to stab her again if she was already dead?"

"She wasn't dead."

"Even though she had been stabbed already?" said Winterkill, looking puzzled and skeptical.

"That's right. She was still alive in the blanket."

"This is all very interesting. Except for one thing." Winterkill paused to build up the suspense. "You're not telling us the truth."

"I saw him kill her."

"That's not what he says. What does Gage Catton say, Mina?"

"I have no idea."

"You do know, because it's the truth about what really happened that night."

"I just told you what really happened."

"Then explain why Gage Catton says otherwise."

"He's lying."

"I'll tell you what he says, and you know in your heart that this is what really happened. He says *you're* the one that stabbed Rachel Catton to death that night in Malibu."

The audience in the courtroom murmured in surprise, punctuated by gasps here and there.

"*He* murdered her and forced me to help him dispose of the body," said Mina, bursting into tears. "He tortured me and held me captive."

She yanked her pullover off over her head and stood up to expose the quincunx of cigarette-burn marks all over her stomach and display them to the jury.

"Ms. Deerling, please," said Judge Sakamoto, gesturing and reaching toward her in his black robe. "Please put on your blouse and sit down."

"He tortured me with burning cigarettes and raped me," she said, sobbing. "He said he'd kill me if I tried to leave him."

"Please put your blouse back on."

Overcome, Mina collapsed in her seat, covering her eyes with her hands and sobbing.

Catton trained a baleful glance on Mina. He bolted to his feet, kicking his chair back behind him.

"She's lying," he yelled.

377

"Bailiff, restrain the defendant," said Judge Sakamoto.

"She's the one that stabbed my wife to death. Not me. She was jealous of Rachel," said Catton, jabbing his forefinger in Mina's direction.

The muscle-bound black bailiff who stood six five and had a keloid on the right side of his neck seized Catton and held him, pinning Catton's arms behind his back in order to apply handcuffs.

"Order in the court," said Judge Sakamoto, sensing pandemonium was on the verge of erupting as spectators in the audience were rising to their feet watching with concern Catton wrestle the bailiff and debating whether they should flee the premises to escape harm. "Order in the court."

"Put your blouse back on," Winterkill told Mina like he was pronouncing judgment on a tart. "Have you no shame?"

Mina sobbed uncontrollably.

DA Bowdin sprang to his feet. "Objection, Your Honor. Counselor is making false insinuations and bullying the witness to sully her reputation."

"I demand a retrial, Your Honor," said Winterkill.

"On what grounds?" said Judge Sakamoto.

"On the grounds that the witness's shameful and obscene performance has irrevocably prejudiced the jury against my client."

"I object, Your Honor," said Bowdin.

"I'm declaring a mistrial. Court adjourned," said Judge Sakamoto above the hubbub, slamming his gavel and rising from his seat. "Clear the courtroom."

The din grew louder as the spectators piled out of the courtroom, struggling to come to grips with the revelations elicited before their very eyes.

Dumbfounded by Sakamoto's ruling, Bowdin pelted over to Mina and helped her on with her blouse, trying to comfort her as she continued to weep.

The bailiff handcuffed Catton and frog-marched him out of the courtroom, as Catton struggled to free himself.

"She did it," he cried over his shoulder into the courtroom as the bailiff bulled him through the doorway. "She's the one that killed Rachel."

Chapter 103

Pleased that Bowdin was pursuing a first-degree murder charge against Catton after Judge Sakamoto had declared a mistrial, a smile radiating from his face, Duquesne sat in his office with the *Times* spread on his desktop, the headline blaring the news: Long-lost Husband to Be Retried for Murder.

The jury had believed Mina, as had Duquesne, and would have convicted Catton if not for the mistrial, decided Duquesne. Mina had been an innocent bystander at the murder of Rachel Catton and she had been enslaved by the murderer Gage Catton who coerced her to do his bidding under the threat of death.

Duquesne also figured Catton had murdered Bendix and the insurance investigator Dunleavy—Bendix because Catton found out that Bendix was having an affair with Rachel, and Dunleavy because he was investigating Catton's unexplained disappearance and was coming too close to discovering the truth about Catton's scheme to defraud Lion Life.

Duquesne didn't know if he could ever prove that Catton had taken out Bendix and Dunleavy, but maybe in the end it didn't matter, because Catton was going to do time for his wife's murder. Duquesne was sure Mina's testimony would put Catton away for life.

Duquesne would like to hit Catton with two more murder charges, but both cases would be difficult to prove with neither hard evidence nor eyewitnesses.

All Duquesne had as evidence for the Bendix murder was the Pacific Dining Car security videotape that had recorded Catton's presence in the restaurant at the time of Bendix's murder. Duquesne didn't think that was enough to motivate Bowdin to prosecute Catton for the Bendix murder.

Duquesne knew Bowdin would want a lock on a win if he was to file murder charges against Catton for Bendix's murder. In the case of the Bendix murder, there was no guarantee of a conviction, as Duquesne saw it, and he was sure Bowdin thought the same. It was never easy to get twelve jurors to agree on anything, especially in a murder trial, where the stakes of a conviction were high with a death sentence in the balance.

The bottom line was, Catton was going to serve time for murder, decided Duquesne. The killer would be punished. Justice was going to be meted out.

"Lieutenant?"

Catton looked up from his newspaper to see Patrick hovering uncomfortably in the office doorway with a young woman about Mina's age, maybe a little younger by a year or so. A blonde, she was wearing a pink scrunchie around her forehead, a pink blouse, and faded blue jeans with fashionable holes torn in both thighs. A slender gold ring hung from a pierced nostril in her retroussé nose.

"What is it, Patrick?"

"I think you should talk to Lana here."

"Why?"

"You should hear what she has to say."

"Same question."

"She says she's Mina's sister."

Duquesne came to attention. "I didn't know she had a sister."

"The Ventura station confirmed it. I already talked to them."

"Why is she here?"

"Why don't you ask her?"

"OK," said Duquesne, and gazed at Lana expectantly.

"I saw the news about the Catton trial and decided it was time for me to come in," said Lana.

"Come in?"

"The Ventura station has been unable to locate her since her mother's murder," said Patrick.

"Why is that?" Duquesne asked Lana.

"I didn't want to be found," she answered, and shifted nervously in her white track shoes.

"Go on. You don't have to be worried here."

"I saw who killed my mother and I was afraid the murderer would come for me if I told the police what I had seen. And because the murderer is—" Overcome, Lana couldn't finish her sentence.

"The murderer is what?"

Lana couldn't proceed.

"No problem," said Duquesne, trying to soothe her. "Take it easy. We're here to help." He decided to change the subject. "Have you told the Ventura station this?"

"She already did," inserted Patrick. "That's why they told her to come down here and talk to you in person."

"I don't see the connection. Am I missing something?"

"You will," said Patrick. He turned to Lana. "Go ahead and tell him what you saw."

Lana gathered herself.

"It's OK," Duquesne told her. "Please go on."

"You're not gonna like what she has to say," said Patrick.

Duquesne's face registered surprise.

"I saw my sister Mina murder my mother with a steak knife in our kitchen," said Lana, her wide blue eyes welling with tears.

The room fell silent, as Duquesne took in her words without speaking.

"No," was all he said, grasping the full impact of what she was saying.

Nonplussed, he cast a blank stare ahead of him, as though he had been shot in the gut by a .45 hollow point and the pain was just now spreading through his body.

Chapter 104

Sitting on the bunk in his jail cell in LA County Men's Central Jail on Bauchet Street, Catton stewed.

He never told anyone a thing. After all, he was innocent.

He never told anyone how he faked his death.

The reason he could disappear from his motorboat out of Oahu without any witnesses seeing him leave it was because he had never been on the boat in the first place when it sailed out to sea. He had used a radio transmitter to control his boat, which was equipped with GPS, as he watched it from a sequestered boulder-strewn area along the Oahu shore.

Catton didn't want to take the chance of a witness seeing him dive off his boat at sea and swim away. Such a witness would jeopardize Catton's wife's claim on his life insurance policy.

Going to ground in Oahu after his staged drowning was easy. He paid for everything in cash, leaving no paper trail for the cops to pick up.

He didn't risk returning to the mainland till after the news reports of the Honolulu Police Department's search for his body died down and disappeared from the 24/7 news cycle.

Soon afterward, he boarded a jet with a phony ID he had bought from the Honolulu criminal underground that peddled in narcotics. He flew back to California, where he continued to stay off the grid by paying for everything with the cash he made from doing odd jobs like picking fruit where his employers didn't ask him too many questions lest they find out he was an illegal alien and then they would have to report him to the feds and lose him as a laborer that worked for below minimum wage.

He didn't mind picking fruit and doing other hard labor, because he knew it would be only temporary till he and Rachel fled the country with the payout on his insurance policy.

But then he found out Rachel had other ideas—and she had to pay for those ideas with her life.

And now, now what kept him going wasn't his hatred for Rachel but for Mina, yet another woman that had double-crossed him because he had let her get too close to him. Women—you couldn't live with them and you couldn't live without them. He should have let Mina drown in the ocean that night he first met her. *Shoulda, woulda, coulda . . .*

What was done was done.

But he wasn't going to give up. He wasn't going to allow himself to be convicted. Winterkill would see to that. The truth would come out—that he, Catton, was not guilty of murdering Rachel. And then he was going to hunt down Mina Deerling, and she would pay just like Rachel had with her life.

He saw an inch-long cockroach scuttle to a stop on the cement floor in front of him. He watched the cockroach for the better part of a minute. It stood motionless, playing dead, hoping not to attract the attention of any predators. It was a good ploy by the bug, but he had already seen it move and knew it was alive.

He wondered if the insect knew he was there.

Stealthily, he raised his foot, hoping not to stir the air, whose movement would impact the roach's antennae and alert it to impending danger. He held his foot frozen above the roach, as still as the bug.

The roach didn't move. Neither did Catton's foot.

Watching the roach he held his foot motionless in the air for twenty seconds.

Then he brought his shoe's heel down on the roach and smashed it to smithereens. He didn't lift his foot to inspect the mess.

Instead, he lay back and relaxed on his bunk. He had nothing but time on his hands to figure out how he would torture Mina and let her die a slow, agonizing death.

"Wake up, Catton," said the prison guard, running his baton along Catton's cell bars, ginning up a racket.

Chapter 105

Catton sat up on his bunk.

The prison guard Saenz was standing in front of Catton's cell under the fluorescent strip light, a shit-eating grin on his face, a foot-long cube-shaped pasteboard box in one hand, his billy club in the other.

The five-nine, thirtysomething Saenz wore his black hair in a flattop with the sides and back of his head shaved. A large crescent-shaped mole protruded from the left side of his head above his ear. His nose bent to the right courtesy of a football teammate who had broken it in a fistfight in high school.

"What do you want?" said Catton.

"You got a package," said Saenz.

"From who?" said Catton, puzzled.

Saenz inspected the address label. "Amazon."

"I didn't order anything."

Catton could see that the package had been opened and crudely taped shut. Whoever had opened it could care less if Catton knew about it since they had made no attempt to conceal their violation of his property.

"What's in it?" he said.

"You think I'm Superman with X-ray eyes?"

"You already opened it."

"Not me. Security had a look. House rules."

"Did they leave anything for me?"

Saenz put away his baton, got out his key, and opened the cell door.

"Come over here and take it," he said, holding out the package with one hand, his other hand hovering near the Glock in the holster on his waist.

As Catton approached and reached out for the package, Saenz dropped it on purpose on the floor.

"Excuse me," said Saenz, face blank.

Standing in the hall he slammed the cell door shut with a clang and locked it.

Catton gazed at the package at his feet.

He had no idea what was inside it. He couldn't understand why Amazon would send him a package. He didn't know of anyone that would send him a gift.

"Are you sure this is for me?" he asked Saenz.

"It has your name on it."

Curious but circumspect at the same time, Catton crouched beside the box, double-checked the name on the address label, saw that it was his, and peeled off the grey duct tape to open the box. It was easy to open since the guards had inspected its contents and had done a cursory job of repackaging.

He reached into the box, sorted through the white Styrofoam packing peanuts, and withdrew the contents.

It was a folded powder blue blanket—just like the one he had used to wrap Rachel's dying body in before he dumped her in the ocean.

Stunned, wordless, he let the blanket fall to the floor.

Mina, he decided. The bitch. She had sent it to him to rub his nose in it, knowing he was locked up for Rachel's murder. She must be having a good laugh at his expense even now—wherever she was. *The murdering bitch.*

In white heat he kicked the box, which skittered across the length of the floor and crashed against the wall on the other side of his cell, spilling packing peanuts onto the floor.

Saenz laughed. "You were expecting a hacksaw?"

Roaring, Catton leapt onto the blanket in a rage and jumped up and down on it wishing it was Mina's body lying under him and he was stamping her into pulp.

"You're gonna pay for this, Mina," he said.

Saenz guffawed.

Chapter 106

Wearing outsized sunglasses, the woman was lying on her back in a one-piece white bathing suit on a chaise longue on the beach at the Playa Blanca resort in Tangier, Morocco, basking in the sun under a cloud-blotched sky, a tall, sweating glass of mint-flavored iced tea at her side. A thatched umbrella canted above her to her right, which did little to screen out the sun thanks to its position in relation to the direction of the sun's rays.

She didn't need the umbrella. The white sun hat with a wide curvy brim she was wearing shielded her face from the bright rays that bore down on her and the sand around her.

She was reading a thriller novel she had propped on her stomach.

She looked up from her book and gazed out over the North Atlantic, the word *murder, murder, murder* threshing her mind.

She couldn't figure out why her sister Lana had accused her of killing their mother. Her mother wasn't dead. She couldn't be. Who would want to murder her? It was some kind of dreadful trick. *Murder, murder, murder.* Mina hadn't wanted to kill any of them. Not Rachel Catton. Not Randall Dunleavy. Not her mother. But it was either them or her. They lost their lives—except her mother, of course—and Mina won hers, along with her freedom. Her mother with a blood-soaked knife sticking out of her stomach. Mother screaming in pain, blood sluicing out of her mouth instead of words, blood gushing out of her stomach and splashing the linoleum tiles in a thick stream in the kitchen and—Mina's hands covered with blood—Mina backing away with bloody outstretched hands dripping on the floor—plink, plink, plink. A nightmare, that was all. It was Lana's fault. Lana planted the nightmare in Mina's mind with her trumped-up accusation of matricide.

Mina didn't want to think about it. You couldn't let people's lies ruin your life, she decided, even if it was your own sister's lies.

She missed her mother. But not Rachel and Dunleavy. She barely knew the latter, though she did like him with his funny shorts. Rachel Catton she didn't know at all. Unfortunately for Dunleavy, he was a fool who was standing in the wrong place at the wrong time in Latigo Canyon. If he had killed Catton like she wanted him to, Dunleavy would still be alive.

Mina felt safe here in Tangier. Morocco had no extradition treaty with the United States. In Morocco, she knew Lana's testimony wasn't going to put her behind bars. Eventually, her mother would come forward to the LAPD and give the lie to Lana's murder accusation. But Mina would have to wait here in Tangier for that day to arrive.

When the *National Enquirer* had offered Mina a cool million dollars to publish her life story, she had accepted and had no problem paying for her flight to Morocco. For maybe the first time in her life she wasn't worried.

She couldn't call herself happy, but happiness wasn't everything.

She sipped her iced tea and went back to reading her book.

ABOUT THE AUTHOR

Bryan Cassiday writes thrillers and horror fiction. This is his fourteenth published novel. He wrote *Zombie Apocalypse: The Chad Halverson Series*. He also wrote the Ethan Carr Thriller Series. His short stories have appeared in anthologies, such as *Shadows and Teeth Volume Two*, which won the International Book Award for best adult horror anthology series 2017. He lives in Southern California.